THROUGH FIRE AND RUIN

First Paperback Edition, May 2022
First Hardback Edition, May 2022
First eBook Edition, May 2022

ISBN: 978-3-9505180-1-6 (Paperback)
ISBN: 978-3-9505180-2-3 (Hardback)
ISBN: 978-3-9505180-0-9 (eBook)

www.authorsjbandak.com

THROUGH FIRE AND RUIN

JENNIFER BECKER, ALICE
KARPIEL

ALLAM

AMRYNE

SAPHAROS

LAKE OF NUBILAE

LAZULI

PARAE

KENSYN

CHRYSA

THE BORDER

CINNITE

EMERLANE

JAZDEL

RUBIEN

LIRAEN
THE FAE LAND

THE CLEAR SEA

OPALIA

THE STRAIT OF TENAE

QUARNIAN

THE SILVER SEA

OBLIVERYN

SARNYX

TUROSIAN

THE CURSED WOODS

PYRIA

CARNYLEN

LIRAEN – THE FAE WORLD
The Seven Kingdoms

Kingdom of Turosian
Capital: Parae
Ruler: King Karwyn Adelway
Royal Stone: Turquoise
Patron: Falea, Goddess of Fortune

Kingdom of Carnylen
Capital: Pyria
Ruler: King Tarnan Ellevarn
Royal Stone: Carnelian
Patron: Hamadrae, God of Wisdom

Kingdom of Obliveryn
Capital: Sarnyx
Ruler: King Quintin Nylwood
Royal Stone: Obsidian
Patron: Kalvaeros, God of Courage

Kingdom of Emerlane
Capital: Jazdel
Ruler: King Mayrick Palendro
Royal Stone: Emerald
Patron: Vilvosmae, Goddess of Vitality

Kingdom of Allamyst
Capital: Amryne
Ruler: King Wryen Rosston
Royal Stone: Amethyst
Patron: Bellrasae, God of Beauty

Kingdom of Sapharos
Capital: Lazuli
Ruler: Queen Kaede Garrock
Royal Stone: Sapphire
Patron: Saenrytas, God of Strategy

Kingdom of Quarnian
Capital: Opalia
Ruler: Queen Kaylanthea Zhengass
Royal Stone: Rose Quartz
Patron: Shinlea, Goddess of Loyalt

The Abandoned (Eighth) Kingdom
Kingdom of Rubien
Capital: Cinnite
Ruler: Variel Sartoya, deceased
Royal Stone: Ruby
Former Patron: Adeartas, God of Justice

Pronunciation Guide

Characters

Eyden: Ai-den
Karwyn: Kar-win
Wryen: Ry-an
Sahalie: Sa-ha-lee
Cirny: Sir-nee
Kaylanthea: Kay-lan-thea

Gods

Caelo: Ca-eh-lo
Falea: Fah-lea
Bellrasae: Bell-ras-ey
Hamadrae: Ha-madra-ey

Places

Liraen: Lee-ren
Chrysa: Cry-sa
Parae: Pah-ray
Allamyst: Allah-mist
Amryne: Em-rin
Cinnite: See-neet

THROUGH FIRE & RUIN

To you, the reader –
May all promises to you come true.

CHAPTER 1

LORA

Lora's eyes tracked the odd reflections on the sapphire waves as they glistened in the evening sun. It almost looked too lovely for such a dark time, but she knew the otherworldly magical border was responsible for the image before her. Even though her view was partly blocked by a high wire fence, the shimmer of the portal, stretching from the ocean until halfway into the town of Bournchester, was always hard to avoid from her vantage point above the beach.

Lora caught sight of a car pulling to a stop in front of her mother's restaurant. As she stepped off the sidewalk, she glanced back at the neon "Buffalo Diner" sign above the restaurant door. The light was turned off, as it was the majority of the time nowadays. What used to be a busy street above the beach was now almost deserted, and it had nothing to do with the cold September wind.

Music was blasting from the speakers of the car, distracting

Lora from her thoughts. She smiled at the girl behind the wheel as she got into the passenger seat.

"Slow day, huh?" Maja said over the chorus of the song, waiting for Lora to fasten her seatbelt.

Business was indeed slow these days. With the virus sweeping Earth, a dark cloud hung over the town—over a large part of the world, really—taking away people's incentive to leave their homes. Lora should have been home now too; she wasn't needed at the diner with barely any customers coming in.

But home felt suffocating. Everyone was trying their hardest to stay positive while waiting for the moment everything would shift to normal again. Lora, on the other hand, was waiting for things to take a turn for the worse.

"Earth to Lora. You okay?" her friend asked. Maja's hands lingered on the steering wheel. Her fingers tapped to the rhythm of the pop song filling the small car. If they had been living in another time, a better one, Maja would have been singing off-key in full force, and she would've made Lora join her. Lora desperately wished to get back to that place, but singing hardly felt right with everything going on in their world.

Lora quickly adjusted her seatbelt. "Yes, sorry. Thanks for picking me up." Her gaze involuntarily flew back to the water, to the magical portal lightening up the area. Fenced-in and surrounded by warning signs, the tear in their universe was almost like a divider of Bournchester, splitting the town into two parts. The light indigo shimmer, reaching about ten meters into the air, was their reminder that Earth wasn't the only world out there. It didn't give away what lurked on the other side, but everyone knew it led to the fae world of Liraen.

"Don't thank me yet," Maja said. Lora flashed her friend a confused look but Maja's gaze was fixated on the traffic as she hit the gas. "I have to make a short stop on the way. My dad asked me to deliver some stuff."

"Since when do you help with the black market?"

Maja sighed as she fumbled with the radio, turning up the volume even more. Her dark bangs fell into her face and she hastily swiped them back. "Don't get me wrong, I hate it, but it's not like there's a lot of work. There aren't any graphic design gigs for me and my mum was laid off this morning."

"She was?" Lora shifted in her seat, turning towards her friend. "I'm sorry, that's awful. Did they say why?"

"The usual—the company can't afford it. They already cut everyone's hours, but it wasn't enough." Maja shrugged. Her mother was an accountant. Very different from her father's risky trading work. Though Marcel, Maja's father, was quite successful, it was Maja's mother who provided the steady paycheck. "The only thing I can do is work on my *brilliant* portfolio and help my dad with his *oh-so-important* business endeavours," she said with forced enthusiasm.

Lora could tell Maja's cheery attitude didn't quite reach her smile. This was a tough time for everyone. It felt as if someone had pushed the pause button on normal everyday life.

Maja's grin slowly disappeared as she locked eyes with Lora for a brief second. She knew Maja was trying to decide whether she should ask about Lora's own job hunt, a reoccurring, depressing topic.

"The museum isn't hiring anymore," Lora said. "Maybe once this is all over, they'll need help adding this pandemic to their history archives." She gave her friend a sad smile before shifting her gaze to the window.

Down the street, close to the magical border shimmering in the distance, was the Museum of Human and Fae History. Lora had imagined her future there, working while surrounded by rich history and fascinating facts. She had finished her master's degree online even with the pandemic taking over the world, but now she didn't know what the future held for her.

The uncertainty nagged at her as if it was a virus itself, not letting her go. Incurable.

"Did your dad hear anything new about a cure? Is that what this delivery is about?" Lora asked, a hint of hope carried in her voice. The virus didn't only affect their everyday lives, it threatened humanity's very existence. So far, no medicine had worked. Some of the infected managed to recover, but far too many didn't. As soon as the first symptoms showed, they rarely made it longer than three weeks. Lora glanced at the empty streets through the passenger window. The atmosphere sent a chill through her.

Maja bit her lip. "Nope. There's still nothing that could help. But business is booming nonetheless. Fae items are hot right now. Of course, Dad keeps trying. I swear, if the virus doesn't get him, the black market will."

"I get why you worry about him." Lora almost leaned closer to comfort her friend, then remembered to keep her distance. She cursed the virus. It had been months, but they still didn't know how it spread so quickly. Even though it seemed as if the virus wasn't actually that contagious, the high death rate had everyone on edge. There were too many scary possibilities taking over Lora's mind at all times. A chill spread in the rhythm of the familiar panic settling in her heart and she forced her attention back on Maja. "If anyone can handle the black market, it's Marcel. He knows what he's doing. I just wish he, or anyone, would find some way to cure this bloody virus."

Maja didn't look convinced but quickly continued, "Yeah, me too. If only the virus gave people scraped knees, then we'd be in business."

A smile almost made its way to Lora's lips but the steady panic overrode it. "Can't your dad talk to whoever he works with on the fae side? There has to be something."

Lora's gaze found the portal again in the distance. She wouldn't be able to see the illegal black market from here as it was below surface level, but it wasn't the first time she'd wondered where the secret entrance was. Years ago, when she was still a teenager, someone had dared her to enter the underground tunnel that supposedly led to the black market. Ignoring her mother's strict rules about never going near the market or going beyond the fence surrounding the border, Lora had taken the dare only to find herself at a dead end soon after. It had been for the best. She would rather research and read about such things than take unnecessary risks anyway.

"I wish there was. He told me that the few fae traders he knows aren't healers. And they aren't putting in an ounce of effort to save humanity. Those arseholes are lacking the right motivation." Maja huffed in frustration.

"I guess they couldn't care less about humans dying." Lora felt a familiar anger building up. The fae had taken too much from humans already. In her opinion, they could at least try to make up for the horror they had put humans through. Even though the fae could never erase enslaving humans for over a hundred years after dark magic had ripped a tear in both worlds.

It wasn't until the fae had needed help that they had agreed to close the portal as much as possible. Witches of Liraen had been called to eradicate the portal but even with the help of magical artefacts, they hadn't been powerful enough to close it completely. Instead, they had settled on putting a spell on it, making it impossible for humans, fae, or witches to cross the border and survive. Both sides had tried and, as a result, the border had been lined with corpses on either side for some time; a haunting image that Lora had studied in detail during her history studies. It might be morbid at times, but the history between the humans and fae had always been a fascinating topic to her, much to her mother's dismay. She would have preferred Lora had stayed away from anything related to the fae world, but Lora couldn't help but be curious. Still, she was glad the border had been fenced off for decades now, preventing anyone else from trying and failing to cross over.

As Maja turned the car to the right, she said, "We're almost there." Her voice pulled Lora back to the present.

"What did they order?" Lora had never understood the appeal of fae items. Was it the fact that it was forbidden that made it so interesting? Her mother Karla would never allow anything fae in their house. It was the one thing Karla and Marcel always disagreed on. The two had been friends for most of Lora's life and, naturally, she and Maja had become best friends too.

"Just some herbs and indigo wine," Maja said, turning down the volume as she seemed to search for the correct house number.

Lora was about to speak when flashes of red and blue caught her attention. Three police cars were parked outside a suburban house toward the end of the street.

"Fuck." Maja stepped off the gas as they neared the residence.

Lora looked from the scene before them to her friend's shocked expression. "Please tell me that's not the house we were going to."

"Stay calm. I'll just drive by." The masked worry didn't slip by Lora. She nervously glanced around the car as if she could spot the fae items Maja had undoubtedly hidden in the car. "I said act normal!" Maja's high-pitched voice made Lora freeze. A wave of panic swept over her and it appeared her friend mirrored her feelings.

Lora turned to stare straight ahead. She instinctively reached for her rose gold necklace. "Right. Normal."

They drove by in a matter of seconds, but it felt like hours. Lora couldn't help but turn her head. She caught sight of a young man being escorted outside of his home by two policemen. Another officer was carrying a black box. They were clearly confiscating illegal items. As one of the officers looked up, Lora averted her gaze, looking at her heart-shaped pendant. Her heart threatened to jump out of her chest.

"Goddammit, do the police really have nothing better to do?" Maja said once they were out of sight. "Everything's so fucked up. Honestly, the government should send the fae a huge gift basket and beg them to reschedule their official treaty meeting instead of this shit. It should happen now. Who knows how many lives will be lost by December?"

"We shouldn't have to beg. But yes, those infected don't have three months," Lora agreed as she tugged a dark blonde strand of hair behind her ear. She wished her heart would stop beating so damn fast. She didn't think anyone was following them, but it took her heart a few minutes to catch up.

"If he could, my dad would go to Liraen himself, find a healer, and get a cure. But we all know he wouldn't even take one breath across the border."

Lora could only agree. There wasn't anything one single individual could do. Not for the first time that day, she wondered when the government would finally react. If there was ever a time to interact with the fae, it was now. Yet, the thought of fae magic taking a more prominent role in their lives and future history again didn't sit well with her either.

The sun was finally setting when Maja dropped Lora off in front of her family's home. Soft rain poured down on her as she ran up the steps to her front door. The weather wasn't unusual for the English seaside town she'd lived in her whole life.

Lora was already tired from yet another day with no change, no mention of a miraculous cure that would signal the end of this dark time for humanity. The only hope she had was an update from her father, who often brought home news from the hospital where he worked. Although his reports were rarely good, she appreciated being in the loop.

Lora reached around her Buffalo Diner apron in her bag to find her keys when the front door swung open. Startled, she took a step back and met her brother's intense gaze.

"God, you scared me," she screeched.

Oscar merely stared at her, his feet rooted to the ground, blocking the doorway. His dark brown eyes seemed to radiate both concern and anger. She wasn't sure what to make of it. Before Lora had left for university, she had found it easy to read him. He'd grown up since then. He was no longer the kid who followed Lora everywhere and told her everything, sometimes in painful detail.

"Hey, is Dad back from work yet?" she asked as she moved into the house, forcing Oscar to take a step back.

He closed the door behind her with more momentum than necessary. "He got back ten minutes ago. There's no news. No cure, no meds that work. Nothing." Oscar lowered his gaze. "There's something else you need to know..."

A wave of fear hit Lora immediately. It overshadowed everything else, immobilising her. She was surprised she stayed standing. Part of her wanted to cover her ears and run back outside. The worst-case scenario was already taking root in her mind. But she needed to know. Not knowing for sure would eat at her even more.

"What is it?" Her voice wavered slightly.

"It's Mum." Oscar tilted his head up and now Lora could see the intense sadness coming from him as a tear ran down his cheek. She expected his next words. They barely left his lips, as if they were too terrible to utter aloud. "She is sick," he said.

It was only three words, but they changed everything. Numbness took hold of Lora's body so quickly that it scared her. She wanted nothing more than to detach herself from this situation and pretend it wasn't happening. That her worst nightmare was still that—merely a nightmare she would wake up from any moment. Her mum couldn't be infected. This couldn't be real.

"Oscar, is your sister home yet?"

Her mother's voice brought her back into the moment. "Yes, I'm home," she said. Her voice was barely louder than a whisper. She was feeling lightheaded. How was one supposed to act in a life-altering moment such as this?

"Come on," Oscar said, leading the way to the living room. He used the end of his sleeve to wipe his eyes.

Lora forced her legs to move, to follow her brother's direction, a mute command. It felt like she was drifting in a state of frightening uncertainty, similar to when she would wake up from a nightmare and not yet know it wasn't real. As she rounded the corner to the living room, three different words kept repeating in her head: *This isn't real.*

Then she spotted her mum sitting on the end of the sofa in the spacious, colourful room. She almost looked the same as she had earlier that afternoon. Her tan skin had a new paleness to it, but that could easily be explained by lack of sunlight. Maybe they really were wrong. What if they were just paranoid?

This isn't real, her inner voice continued. Before Lora could convince herself fully, her eyes travelled from her mother's face to where her sleeve was rolled up, exposing her arm. Lora's gaze fixated on the prominent dark purple veins and her previous delusions vanished. She felt immense pressure building in her chest, crushing her spirit. She could see how this would end, the inevitable darkness that would soon come over her family. Her head began spinning with possible scenarios and all of them had the same tragic ending.

Her mum noticed Lora staring and pulled her sleeve down, hiding the first warning sign of the virus. "It's not that bad. I feel okay. Promise."

Her mother's words snapped the hold Lora had on her emotions. The last bit of the wall of numbness she had built earlier seemed to shatter. She looked up into the concerned faces of her mother and younger brother.

"How can you say that? None of this is okay!" Lora shook her head, locking eyes with her mother. "It might not be bad now, but we all know what comes next."

"They'll find the right medicine, a cure. I know it," her mum said, smiling gently.

"Oscar said there are no new developments. They'll never find a cure in time."

"You have to have some faith, Lora. No point in giving up hope yet." Her mother's grin looked forced, as if she was only putting on a brave face for her children.

Lora wanted to protest, to tell her to speak honestly, but when she glanced at her brother, she knew she couldn't take his hope away. Not yet. But she couldn't agree and pretend to be hopeful either. All the different scenarios that had gone through her mind were telling her the same thing: it was no use to hope. They'd been hoping the virus would run its course months ago and they still weren't any closer to a so-called *cure*.

The house suddenly felt stifling, as if the walls were already streaked with grief, threatening to cave in. All Lora could think of was the virus that had clearly chosen her mother as its next victim. The anxiousness that filled her felt like fire in her veins. It overwhelmed her senses. Lora reached for the pendant around her neck as she closed her eyes and tried to shut out the crushing fear.

She reopened her eyes when she heard footsteps drawing closer. Her father, Isaac, walked through the door, a medical kit in hand. His eyes quickly scanned the room and paused on Lora.

"Lora, honey, you're home," he said. "I'm so sorry I don't have any new developments to report on. But I'm not giving up. We're not giving up. Okay?"

The tears started falling. The dam was fully broken. Hearing her dad say it made it completely real. She pressed her lips together, trying to keep silent, to keep it contained. In her hazy state, her eyes flickered to her brother, who was crying silently into his hands. Her mother reached over, putting her hand on his leg.

Lora heard her dad drop his bag before she felt his arms surround her. She let herself be wrapped in a hug, but it only made her cry harder.

For a few seconds, Lora clung to the comfort of his embrace. Then she thought of her mother's brave attitude. She met her mum's dark eyes and quickly pulled away, forcing herself to calm down. Lora tilted her head up as if to keep the tears from falling. She wiped the fallen ones away with shaking hands, avoiding everyone's eyes. Isaac was reluctant to let her go but he must have realised Lora needed him to divert his attention elsewhere.

He turned to her mother as he picked up his bag again. "I'm going to take your blood and then I'm heading back to the hospital. I don't want us to assume anything before I've done some thorough testing. We can't be a hundred percent sure you have venousphilia."

It seemed pretty obvious to Lora that her mother had caught the virus and she wasn't the doctor in the family, but who was she to take away her family's remaining optimism? "Okay, that's a good plan. Text us when you get the results," she said.

As her father unpacked his medical equipment, Lora turned around and fled the room. If she had to pretend for another minute that this wasn't going to end tragically, she would lose her mind. As much as she craved to join them in their hopeful illusion, she couldn't.

Lora leaned her head back against the cold kitchen wall. The electric blue curtains and shiny white marble counter did nothing to brighten up the room. It was quiet here except for the low mumblings from her parents in the next room. She tried to envision a day where everything was perfect. Maybe last Easter. She had come home for a few days and had tried not to get sucked into her research projects. Back then, no one had an inkling of what would take over their lives not even a month later.

The sound of the door opening made Lora look up. Oscar walked into the kitchen. With his dark hair and eyes, he resembled their mother so much more than Lora did. But now his eyes were bloodshot, his cheeks tear-streaked. The sight broke her heart.

"Why did you storm out?" The accusation in his voice made her wince.

It was a difficult question. One that Lora didn't wish to go into detail to answer. "I didn't mean to storm out. I needed to clear my head."

"You should've stayed."

"I just walked out for a moment. I'm still here." She started towards him but he held up his hand.

"No, I mean you shouldn't have gone to the diner today. I was all alone with Mum." He leaned against the kitchen counter and moved his face away from Lora.

Guilt spread through her, settling in her heart like a heavy stone. She hadn't even thought of that. Lora reached out to comfort her brother but he quickly moved back again. "You haven't been around as much all year, really—which is fine, whatever. But now?"

"That's not fair. I was finishing my master's. That doesn't mean I don't care. I moved back when all of this started." The personal attack dwindled Lora's empathy. Anger was taking over her body, reigniting her spirit.

"You moved back because you graduated."

The comment stung more than Lora wanted to admit. She didn't know if he was mad at her in earnest or merely saddened and scared by today's events. The latter she could understand all too well. The former came as a surprise to her. Oscar had never made a comment like that about Lora leaving for university. She'd missed her younger brother, but since she had come back from London quite often, it had never felt as if she had truly left for good.

"Are you serious? Where is this coming from?" She could tell Oscar realised his mistake, the regret was written on his face. Lora was unsure if she was relieved because he didn't seem to mean his last comment or because she was finally able to grasp what he was feeling. Probably a combination of both.

"I can't deal with this alone," he admitted, almost choking on his words.

Lora pulled him into a hug. He gave in with no resistance this time, resting his head on Lora's shoulder.

"You don't have to. I meant what I said. I'm here. Promise." Even though Oscar was almost seventeen and taller than Lora, he was still her kid brother. If she could take his pain away and bear it herself, she'd do it in a heartbeat.

When Oscar pulled back, he quickly wiped the fresh tears from his eyes. "Brilliant. I'm a complete mess now," he said.

Lora laughed and handed him a tissue from the counter. "How about we watch some trash reality TV to take our minds off this for a bit?"

"Sure. Maybe Mum will join us." A faint smile appeared on his face. Lora realised she hadn't seen it in a while. She promised herself to make sure it would show up more often, even if things went the way she expected. The real possibility of losing her mum was too much to accept at this moment. She wasn't in denial, but she was incapable of fully thinking the thought. Lora couldn't picture a future without her. She prayed against her instincts that they never had to.

"I'll go check on her and ask if she's feeling up to it," Lora said, trying to banish her negative thoughts.

Oscar nodded and the smile grew, revealing the gap in his teeth.

Lora felt a little lighter after their conversation, but she had to admit that he was partly right. Her master's degree had kept her busy at the start of the year and she hadn't spent as much time home until she'd moved back a couple of months ago.

But she would be here now. She would make sure no one felt alone in this nightmare.

CHAPTER 2
LORA

Raised voices pulled Lora from her restless sleep. She reached for her phone on the antique, taupe nightstand that was covered in history books, notebooks, and one too many highlighters. Lora sat up as she unlocked her screen. It was only midnight. She must have unintentionally dozed off a little while ago. She was considering trying to go back to sleep when the events of the day hit her again, fear taking her breath away.

Her father hadn't been back when she'd gone to her room to rest, but she could make out his voice now, which meant he must have the results. Deep down, Lora knew it was futile, but she couldn't help but hope. Part of her wanted to imagine that today had never happened, that she'd find her parents and they wouldn't even know why she'd been so worried.

Her feet hit the ground fast and she took the steps two at a time as she headed to her parent's bedroom. She raised her arm to knock on their door when she heard her father's raised voice.

"I don't either! Do you really think I would even bring it up if I thought there was any other way?"

Lora lowered her fist and considered leaving them to hash it out, but her curiosity got the better of her. She stayed to listen.

"You don't know for sure what will happen in the next weeks," her mum answered.

"I know that you're going to die in three weeks *or less*. That's a fact. You're delusional if you think there's any other outcome." Lora flinched at the conviction in her father's voice. So much for hope. This *was* real. "Think about Oscar. He could be next. There's no progress on a cure—none. I hate to bring this up, but the only miracle we can hope for is fae magic."

"So what?" Her mother's voice sounded strained, she must have been crying. "You want to send our daughter on a suicide mission? If one of us is going to die, I choose *me*."

Lora almost gasped out loud. She didn't know what to make of this. Her heartbeat quickened, any leftover sleep was replaced by shock. Her sweaty hand clasped her pendant so tightly that the heart pricked her palm.

"This isn't about choosing. I would never even consider it. I didn't mean I'd send her off to walk around Liraen by herself, she just needs to talk to Marcel's fae trader, convince them to help, and come right back," Isaac said.

Her mum's answering dark, hysteric laugh rattled Lora's bones. It drove straight to her heart, stealing her breath and leaving a bitter taste in her mouth. "Now who's delusional? We don't know for sure that half-fae can survive crossing. And Liraen is the opposite of safe no matter how far into it you go.

What if someone discovered her secret? Did you think about that at all?"

There was a heavy silence. Lora considered making her presence known when she heard her father's voice again, this time quiet and crushed. "You're right. I don't know what I was thinking. We can't risk it. I would never forgive myself if anything happened to Lora." He sounded defeated, as if he had been putting his last hope in Lora and somehow she had failed him before she was even asked to try.

Lora didn't know what she was getting herself into. The only thing she was sure of was that if there was even a tiny chance she could save her mother, she needed to know more.

She swung open the door.

Her mum looked at her in pure shock. She nervously glanced at her husband, clearly at a loss for words, before refocusing on Lora.

"What do you mean half-fae can cross?" Lora asked. Of all the research she'd done, this fact had never come up. Not once.

Her mother gave Isaac a warning look but it wasn't enough to keep him quiet.

"Your mum overhead your...well, your biological father talk to someone about a half-fae boy who crossed the border and came back unharmed. He assumed half-fae must be some kind of loophole. Apparently, the border spell doesn't apply to them."

Lora met her mum's questioning, panicked eyes. All of this was more than overwhelming. She didn't know what to focus on first. She had never heard her step-father mention her fae father aloud. They didn't discuss it. And although she'd had conversations with her mum about her hidden fae side, she had kept this secret from her. Had her mum ever actually been afraid Lora could get hurt if she got too close to the border or was she scared she would feel compelled to walk through it? And who was this other half-fae? They'd always assumed Lora was the only one and for good reason.

If Lora had known this last year, it wouldn't have mattered. She wouldn't have felt the need to cross the border. She'd never felt any kind of pull—quite the opposite, actually. She wanted to understand the history between humans and fae, not take part in it. But now she had a reason, a motivation. And she was looking right at her.

"But that was almost 25 years ago," her mum said. "There's no way of knowing if he was correct in his assumptions. It's too risky, Lora."

Her mother's pleading words made Lora reconsider her options. She couldn't decide what to believe. But when she imagined the next few weeks, all she saw was grief. Could she believe her biological father's words? He was nothing more than a stranger. It was likely that he was wrong. They didn't have any proof beyond some whispered words.

But if she didn't take the risk, would she be giving up the only chance to find a cure? Or would she simply avoid death herself? Could she live with herself knowing she could have possibly prevented her mum's death? *Death.* The word had never sounded as scary, as final, as it did in this instant.

Her mother took a step towards her. "Do you understand?"

Lora tried to avoid her mother's searching glance. "Yes, it's too risky."

CHAPTER 3

AMIRA

Amira was suffocating in her dress yet her half-brother seemed unbothered by her laboured breathing. On the contrary, he seemed to be enjoying her suffering. Wryen's olive skin appeared brighter than usual, though his lilac eyes were not distracting enough for her to forget about their mischievous glint.

Amira shifted on the carriage bench, hoping to find a more comfortable position. She brought herself closer to Wryen unintentionally. As soon as the heavy embroidered material of her long dress brushed his feet, he pushed it as far away from him as possible and turned that sly gaze on her again.

He smirked and lit his hand on fire. "Careful, Amira. You wouldn't want your pretty dress to catch on fire."

Amira froze, her eyes wide in terror. Wryen pushed his hand closer to Amira's face. She sat completely still as he laughed. The flame was just close enough to heat her skin without burning her. She pulled back on instinct.

"Pathetic," he snarled.

Amira didn't say anything and closed her eyes. Soon she would be in Parae, free of her brother's shadow. She just needed her marriage to King Karwyn Adelway to go through. After all, it was probably her only chance at having a semi-happy life.

She had only seen Karwyn once and she remembered thinking he was not bad-looking, yet she had felt nothing when their eyes had met. Karwyn had wonderful, vibrant turquoise eyes, the shade mirroring the stone of his kingdom. Wryen had admired Karwyn's mesmerising eyes as a sign of his noble lineage and high powers. All Amira could see, though, was the emptiness hidden inside them. She truly hoped that after spending some actual time with him, they would grow to appreciate each other.

Amira's own eyes weren't as pure. The deep purple of her iris was lathered with dark brown speckles. Some had called it unique. Her half-brother, on the other hand, thought it was another sign of her bastard origins. Unlike Wryen, she was a level one fae—stronger and faster than an unblessed human, but still useless. If she hadn't been born into a royal family, she would have probably worked in one of the fabric factories in Amryne. It was one of the things her half-brother liked to remind her of. As if she could ever forget. Her lack of powers had haunted Amira her whole life. Not only had she not inherited the same fire powers as Wryen had, she had no special powers to speak of.

The carriage came to a halt and Amira looked through the glazed windows. The gates of Parae stood in front of them, their silver decor blinding her. The sounds of the bustling city overwhelmed her heightened senses. She wondered if she would be able to see more of the city and its surroundings in the days to come. Her restless mind had hated being confined to the four walls of her bedroom for the better part of the last six years.

She knew the border to the human world was not far from the capital, yet as she peered through the window, twisting her neck to see more of the landscape, she saw nothing. Not even the faint indigo glimmer her late father had described.

A barely audible sigh escaped her as she moved away from the window. Amira didn't know if it was from relief or disappointment. Back in Amryne, since the magical border was impossible to see from her city, she'd never thought much of it and the human world it kept at bay. Yet the thought of being so close to the border did frighten her a little. When she was a child, her brother had told her stories of fae who had felt irresistibly compelled to cross the border and had died a painful death as a result.

She felt her brother's burning gaze on her as if he was trying to read her mind. In order to avoid whatever twisted comment was lying on his tongue, Amira focused her eyes on the streets the carriage was passing through.

A natural look of boredom settled on her face. She was disappointed by the architecture of the houses they were driving by. Only two or three stories high with flat rooftops and muted walls, they were far from the wonderful and extravagant houses of her home kingdom, Allamyst. Turosian didn't place the same high value on beauty as Allamyst did, even though the latter was the less wealthy kingdom. Before the death of her father, Amira had taken a horse on a stroll through the streets of the capital, Amryne. She had marveled at the eccentric architecture and admired the nuance of colour; walking through Amryne felt like walking through the palette of the most brilliant painter. Here, she felt like she was passing through the thoughts of a very uninspired artist.

As she was reminiscing about her dear hometown and the freedom she used to have, Amira felt a kick on her leg. She opened her eyes to find Wryen staring at her impatiently.

"We have arrived at your new home, little sister," he said sharply.

Amira put her hand on the carriage handle, ready to open the door, but her half-brother grabbed her arm and dragged her towards him. "Remember what I told you: Play nice and do not embarrass me more than you already do. And do not mess up my alliance with Karwyn." He squeezed her arm so tightly that Amira let out an audible gasp. "Or else..."

He didn't need to complete his threat. Amira knew perfectly well what he was capable of. The scars of his twisted punishments were still ingrained in her head. He let go of her arm and Amira tried to look unbothered. She would not give him the satisfaction of seeing her in distress. She straightened her back, gently smoothed her long dark hair, and made sure the fabric of her dress did not show one wrinkle. Then she took a deep breath and opened the door.

Amira was immediately welcomed by a gentle breeze. Her eyes fluttered, blinded by the shining sun. She could feel its warmth spreading on her skin. She moved to exit the carriage before her eyes had adjusted to the daylight and her feet missed a step. Two hands grabbed her waist to prevent her from falling on her face. She was lifted for a brief second, a second of overwhelming freedom, and then her feet touched the ground and she came face to face with a strangely beautiful man. His pale, almost white hair was artfully painted with strokes of pastel pink. Smooth as enchanted glass, his dark bronze skin glistened in the warm sun. But the most special thing about him was that she did not feel the tiniest bit threatened by him. On the contrary, she felt like she could tell him all of her darkest secrets and he would just smile at her and make all her worries disappear. But she would never do that.

She smiled at him, not sure if the warmth she felt was from the bright sunshine or the man's reassuring presence.

He removed his hands from around her waist and bowed deeply. "It would have been terrible to break your nose on your first day here," the young man said with a cheeky smile.

Before she could thank him, a tall and serious man standing a few feet behind them walked up to her. "Enough chit-chat, Rhay. That is no proper way to welcome your future queen." The stern man bowed before her. He held a striking resemblance to the man who had helped her out of the carriage, Rhay. Amira was surprised that a stranger had been the one to rescue her. Where was her fiancé?

Behind her, she felt her brother's ever-present, torching gaze. The warmth of the sun seemed to vanish even though it still shone as brightly as before.

The serious man extended his hand and she forced herself to take it. "Princess Amira Rosston of Allamyst, it is my honour to welcome you to Parae in the name of the interim High King, Karwyn Adelway of Turosian."

Amira looked over Rhay's shoulder, but there was still no sign of her betrothed.

Her brother seemed to have the same thought. "Where is the interim high king?" he said. Amira could hear the tension in his voice.

"His Majesty has been held back by court matters. But he sent me, Nouis Messler, his royal advisor, and my son, Rhay, one of his other advisors, to make sure you were properly welcomed."

Wryen put an arm around Amira. She tensed up immediately but let a polite smile live on her lips. Playing along was always the best option with Wryen.

"So he sent his lackey. I thought my little sister meant more to him." His smile contradicted the coldness of his tone.

Amira felt embarrassment taking over. She saw Rhay open his mouth, clearly upset by Wryen's comment, but his father put a warning hand on his shoulder. Even if they were working for the King of Turosian, Wryen was also a king. He was above them.

Nouis offered his arm. She took it with a shaky hand, relieved to be taken away from her brother's hold. "Let us show you to your room. You will see His Majesty tonight at the welcome feast."

As Amira walked forward, she felt her brother's eyes on the back of her head. Just one more day and he would be gone. She would start a new life here in the court of Turosian, the most powerful kingdom in Liraen. Unless Karwyn's absence indicated some hesitation on his part...

As they walked towards the grand doors, Amira couldn't help but compare the Turosian palace to the one she used to live in. Even though the place didn't lack prestige, it certainly didn't feel welcoming. Barely paying attention to the fae walking alongside her, Amira noted that the palace was bigger and darker than the one in Amryne. Some parts appeared to be as old as the creation of Liraen itself. Amira guessed that the most recent renovations of the palace dated back to before the end of the Dark King's reign, over 75 years ago. She felt a shiver run down her spine as she walked inside the cold grey walls of the hallway. Everywhere she looked, she found herself wondering why they had not added any colours. The atmosphere was heavy and Amira could feel her breath turning cold. She looked back at the open doors, longing for the warm sun outside.

She followed Nouis and Rhay through numerous corridors, sometimes decorated with paintings of stone-faced kings and queens, sometimes left bare. Strangely, she wanted Rhay to hold her hand again so that the wonderful feeling would come back. Instead, she had to stop herself from screaming. It was like she could no longer breathe properly. This time it was not only the dress that made her feel that way.

Her brother was walking alongside her, closely monitoring her reactions. In the corner of her eye, she could see him smile, the same wicked grin he always sported when she was in pain.

They stopped in front of an intricate wooden door. Nouis knocked twice and the door opened to reveal the sweet, almond-shaped face of a motherly woman dressed in the uniform Amira had previously seen on other fae. The woman bowed deeply but didn't say anything.

Nouis looked at Amira. "This is Nalani, she will take care of you until your wedding. Once you are married, more servants will be assigned to you."

Amira smiled softly at the woman. Another welcoming face in this dark palace. Nalani moved away from the door to let

Amira in. Before she could enter the room, her brother grabbed her arm and pulled her into a hug. Amira let out a gasp of surprise. He tightened his grip and she immediately understood his intention.

"Don't forget what I told you earlier. Your engagement isn't completely official yet," he whispered in her ear, careful of his words with the advisors within hearing distance. He squeezed her so tightly that she felt the fabric of her dress cutting deep into her flesh.

"I'll always be there to protect you, little sister. Even against yourself," he said. Wryen kissed her on the cheek before letting go. She stopped herself from wiping at the spot on her face.

Nouis and Rhay looked almost moved by this show of brotherly love. Wryen was about to leave when Nouis discreetly hit Rhay. The young fae looked at his father, who gestured to his pocket.

Rhay hit his forehead with the palm of his hand. "Shit—I mean, right. I completely forgot about the gift." Amira was utterly confused.

Rhay took out a flat jewellery box from his jacket pocket and was about to give it to Amira when Wryen grabbed it and opened it himself. He let out an appreciative sound. Inside was a gorgeous turquoise and silver bracelet. The five polished stones were in the shape of stars.

"It's a gift for the princess. Karwyn picked it out himself. The turquoise is supposed to repel cursed beings." Rhay's sharp tone seemed to upset her brother.

"What a silly little superstition. At least it's worth something," Wryen replied, stone-faced as he slowly dropped the bracelet into Amira's waiting hand. She curled her fingers around the delicate chain.

Cursed beings, Rhay had said. Was he thinking of humans and witches? Amira couldn't imagine she would be seeing much of their kinds inside the palace and she was glad for it. She knew some royals liked to keep witches for their magic but they were kept far away from the living, locked away where no one had to bear their presence.

Wryen had often told Amira that he would never fall so low as to work with a witch. He was powerful enough on his own and didn't need any cursed spells.

She watched Wryen leave with the advisor, conspiring about something Amira would never know about.

Rhay bowed before her. "Your belongings will be delivered soon. You'll be expected at nine bells tonight. Your brother will escort you," he said. "In the meantime, if you need anything, ask Nalani or come looking for me. Begone in fortune, princess." Rhay kissed her hand softly, his eyes sparking with charm, before leaving her alone with her maid.

"I will draw you a bath, my lady, as you must be tired from your journey," Nalani said.

Amira nodded and closed the door behind her. It was true, she was exhausted. But not from the journey, however long it was. No, she was tired from years of faking happiness. Now, it was time to feel it for real.

CHAPTER 4

LORA

The lie bothered Lora more than she expected, keeping her awake until early morning. When her alarm had rung a few hours later, it was the first thing on her mind again.

She knew her mum well enough to know she would never be convinced to let her go. Her whole life, she'd wanted nothing more than for Lora to have a normal, danger-free life. Going to Liraen was neither of those things. Then again, one could argue that her life in the human world was currently far from peaceful too. In the end, it didn't seem like a choice at all. It made her skin crawl thinking about crossing over and fear laced her heart. She knew her survival wasn't guaranteed, but the image of her mum growing sicker and sicker while she stood by, aware that she might have been able to prevent it, was too painful to live through.

Maybe something good would finally come from her fae ancestry, even if the concept of her fae heritage bringing anything remotely positive to her life seemed unimaginable. The fae world had always been unattainable—a dark piece of history to dissect from a safe distance—and she'd been glad for it.

On silent feet, Lora crept to the kitchen where she waited for her father who always left early for work. She nervously clutched her pendant, moving it back and forth on the chain as she rehearsed in her mind the words she needed to say. She was looking forward to getting this over with, for the endless loop in her head to come to a stop.

Isaac stormed into the kitchen and immediately began shuffling around, throwing together a quick breakfast. He paused mid-movement as he spotted Lora sitting at the table.

"What are you doing up so early?" he said in a suspicious tone.

All her carefully planned words went out the window as she blurted, "I'm going to the diner to talk to Maja. I've decided I'm going to Liraen." Isaac moved forward but Lora held up her hand. "You can't change my mind. We both know it's our best shot. I have to try and you have to let me."

Saying the words out loud made it real. She was committing to going to the fae land; the last place in the universe she wanted to be. It was now also the only place that provided hope for her family. She took a deep breath, forcing herself not to panic.

Isaac glanced at a family picture hanging on the kitchen wall. He swallowed as if to control his rising emotions. "I shouldn't have brought it up, Lora. Don't do this just because you think you have to. I would never ask you to." A sob got stuck in his throat as he sought out her eyes.

Lora noted the guilt he showed—and a more carefully hidden feeling of relief. It told her that she was doing the right thing. If her father, a medical professional, didn't see another way out of this, then this really was their last hope.

"You don't have to ask. I'm doing this because it needs to be done. You know it as much as I do."

Isaac shook his head in defeat. He had to know that there was no changing Lora's mind. She could be just as stubborn as her mother. However, she'd rather go on this mission with her dad's blessing. At least one family member should hear her reasoning face-to-face.

"Promise me you'll come right back if you sense any danger—any danger at all," he insisted, his voice a mix of fear and guilt.

Lora nodded in quick agreement even though she wasn't sure at all if this was a promise she could keep. Considering the history she had studied, it seemed unlikely her plan would go smoothly. Still, she put on a comforting smile, a picture of perfect calmness, and said, "I'll be fine. I have a degree in history. This will be like a long overdue research trip."

"Promise, Lora." His brown-green eyes held her gaze.

She sighed as if he was overreacting. "Fine. I promise, I'll be careful. I need one thing from you." If she was taking the risk to cross, she wasn't going empty-handed. "Mum's blood sample."

For a few moments neither of them said anything else, yet their eyes spoke volumes. Lora could tell Isaac was considering taking it all back. Telling Lora that this was a horrible idea. That it would break her mother's heart and his too, should anything happen to Lora.

She silently screamed to let it be, to accept this was the only way. She tried to project her silent plea, radiating her desperation and need of support in this mission.

Her father broke their staring match, sighed, and turned to where he'd dropped his bag by the door. He fished out her mother's blood sample and held it out to Lora.

"I hope a fae healer will be able to make use of it. This needs to be worth the risk."

Lora took the half-full vial and observed the dark red blood that was once coursing through her mother's veins. The sleek glass felt cold against her skin. It was hard to imagine that she was holding a sample of what could very well be the downfall of her family should she be unable to succeed.

"When are you leaving?" Isaac closed his bag again and tried to catch Lora's gaze. "I want to go with you to the border." Unspoken words hung in the air. She knew he wanted to be there in case anything happened to her. But if it did, even the best doctor wouldn't be able to save her.

"I have to see if Maja can help me convince Marcel to show me the way first, so hopefully in the next few days. Whenever Marcel can take me." The truth was, she had no idea when she would go, but it didn't matter. She didn't want him to witness what could potentially happen and she wasn't going to say goodbye—that much she was sure of. She couldn't risk anyone holding her back or possibly changing her mind. Turning her face away, Lora hid her expression, already feeling guilty for telling yet another lie.

"Let me get this straight," Maja said as she adjusted her glasses. "You want me to ask my dad to help you get to the black market so you can cross the border in secret?"

"Correct," Lora said, leaning back against the faded brown leather booth in her mum's diner.

Maja shook her head in disbelief. Lora could only imagine what she was thinking. She'd basically asked her friend to help her with a suicide mission.

"You do know you've completely lost your mind, right?"

She might have lost it the second she'd heard about her mother's infection, yet she had never felt more certain in her life. Which might mean that she, indeed, had lost the part of her that could make reasonable decisions. Lora's gaze wandered around the familiar diner. She remembered sitting on the counter as a child, watching her mum set up the place. She was only ten years old when she'd watched her turn over the "Open" sign for the first time. Her mum's face had been the epitome of happiness.

Before her mum had started her own business, she'd struggled quite a lot. As a child, Lora hadn't been able to see it, but looking back she knew her mum had been afraid to leave Lora in the care of others for fear they would find out her true heritage. It had made it difficult for her mother to make ends meet. Protecting Lora had always been her mum's priority. Now it was Lora's turn to do the protecting.

Her skin heated as she wondered why she didn't feel more scared. Maybe at some point she'd run out of fear. It was all too much, forcing denial to take over.

Pushing her emotions aside she said, "My mum is sick, Maja. There's no other way to save her."

If her friend was shocked she didn't let it show. Maja's features softened as her chocolate brown eyes sought out Lora's lighter ones. "I'm so sorry. I really am. I can't even begin to imagine what you're feeling right now. But I know your mum wouldn't want you to throw your life away."

Lora turned her face to the side. They were sitting at their usual spot, next to the window overlooking the beautifully disturbing scenery the border at the beach provided. Next to the forgotten Ferris wheel by the pier, the portal glowed brightly, like a beacon of hope. A deadly one. Her friend wasn't wrong, yet she lacked some crucial details.

Maja continued her argument as she tried to catch Lora's gaze, "You're brilliant. You're the smartest cookie I know. Which is why I know that you know how absolutely, incredibly dumb this plan is."

Lora avoided Maja's gaze as she reached for her pendant, the familiarity of the sensation cooling her anguish.

"Unless there's something I don't know," Maja said as she read Lora's stoic face. She'd always been able to see through Lora's façade. "Spill it."

Could she tell her the secret she had kept her whole life? It wasn't that she had never wanted to share it with her best friend, but it was not only a risk, it would also open the floodgates to a million questions she'd not even let herself think about. But she did trust Maja and she needed her on her side.

"I know I can cross the border because there's a loophole. If you're half-human and half-fae, the border spell won't affect you." Lora took a deep breath as she gathered her words. She noted the expectant and baffled look in Maja's eyes encouraging her to continue. "I'm...I'm half-fae."

"What?" Maja's eyes widened in surprise. Her glasses slid

down her nose as she leaned forward, closer to Lora. She quickly pushed them back. "How?"

"My mother met my biological father when she worked catering at the treaty meeting 25 years ago," she said it as if it wasn't a big deal, trying to downplay the significance of her reveal.

Every quarter century, the fae and human leaders met in a sort of void, a place that neither belonged to Earth nor to Liraen, to renew the border treaty. Usually nothing came of it. The humans didn't want anything from the fae except to be left alone. Everyone knew the meeting was mostly for show. To maintain the peace and keep an eye on the fae. Her mother had only been there once for work, but it had been an honour for her. An exciting adventure. Up until the moment she got her heart broken.

Lora didn't want to go into more painful details so she simply added, "I think the rest is self-explanatory."

Maja's expression turned from confusion to pure excitement. "That's amazing!"

"Is it?"

"Yes. Totally. Half-fae—that's, like, unheard of. Maybe you're literally one of a kind." During the time of human slavery, pregnancies did happen, but none were viable. No matter if the mother was fae or human, half-fae had never been born. In most cases, history books stated that if the mothers didn't immediately miscarry, they would die before even reaching their second trimester. Of course, now Lora was hoping her mother wasn't the only one who had brought a half-fae into the world. If she was the only one, that meant her biological fae father had been wrongly informed about a half-fae crossing.

"Do you have any powers?" Maja asked.

Lora wanted nothing more than to fast-forward past these questions. "No, I don't. Look, I know you must have a thousand questions and I'm sorry to put it off, but I need to cross as soon as possible. As in, right this minute would be best."

Lora watched her friend's excited mood drop to cold worry. Maja seemed to consider how to respond and settled on, "You're sure you'll be absolutely fine crossing?"

"Yes, promise." At this point she was throwing out empty promises left and right. How much damage could one more do? She forced her practiced smile and added, "It'll be an adventure. You're always telling me to try more things. Get out of my comfort zone."

"As in go out, meet new people. If you want to be really wild, have a one-night stand. Not go on a heroic mission to save the world."

"Oh, please don't put the whole world on me. Saving my family is already enough pressure," Lora half-joked.

Maja searched Lora's gaze, seeming to sense the heaviness that threatened to pull Lora under. "You'll save them. With your determination, you can do anything you set your mind to."

Lora's aquamarine eyes brightened. She'd craved a little encouragement. "Thanks. Do you think your dad will agree to help me?"

"I'll convince him. He's so obsessed with the market anyway. Anything that might improve business is like music to his ears."

Lora didn't fail to notice the sarcastic undertone in Maja's words. "You can't tell him I'm half-fae," Lora said.

"I won't mention it. All you need to do is promise him a sample of the cure. He'll jump at the opportunity."

Lora nodded, feeling dazed at the possibility of being able to actually get her hands on a cure and the impact her mission could have on the world. It hadn't crossed her mind really until Maja had brought it up. She couldn't let her mind wander there. She couldn't let her focus shift one bit. Her family was her priority.

"I can call him now and see if he can meet us here," Maja said as she unlocked her phone, "but are you sure you want to leave today? Don't you want some time to prepare?"

"I have a bag in my car—some essentials. I shouldn't be gone long. I hope." She had grabbed some things before leaving the house. A change of clothes, a bottle of water, some food. Then she had contemplated what she could trade. The currency in Liraen was different. So she'd done the only plausible thing and snuck into her parent's bedroom to take any jewellery she could find after packing the few pieces she owned herself.

The hectic morning flashed before Lora's eyes, reminding her that she wasn't going back home. Not until she got her hands on their remedy. "I do have another favour to ask you," Lora said.

"Sure. Shoot."

"I can't say goodbye to my family. I think I would lose my nerve. Once I've crossed, could you give them these letters?" Lora opened her bag and pulled out three letters addressed to each family member. She handed them to Maja, who hesitantly accepted them.

"I can do that. I think my dad can hook you up with some

spelled tech. If you're able to send messages from Liraen, you'll let me know you're safe, right?"

"Of course."

"And keep me updated if you meet any hot fae." Maja's concerned expression vanished as she smirked.

Lora welcomed the attempt to lighten the mood and smiled genuinely. "I don't think this will be like one of your books where every fae is a charming, perfect gentleman," she teased.

"Oh, they're not all gentlemen. But definitely irresistible and sexy as hell." Maja sighed as she probably imagined stepping into the fictional world of her better-than-reality books.

"I promise I'll give you all the details when I'm back." Finally, a promise Lora was sure to keep—assuming she survived. Maybe no promises could be assured. Maybe some are meant to be broken from the start, the promised words accepted besides their inevitable emptiness.

"You better," Maja said with a wink before she added in a more serious tone, "Okay, let's call my dad."

Hours later, Lora found herself in a car driving towards the promise of hope or her ultimate demise. Two very different outcomes. She tried to focus on the first option, hoping the more she believed it would work, the more likely it would become reality. But if life worked that way, she would have never found herself in this position to begin with.

Her brother had texted her earlier asking when she'd be back home. She could almost hear his disappointed voice when she had read the message. He would soon be even more upset. The thought increased the heaviness that threatened to crush her. The only thing keeping her upright was knowing it would all be worth it if she got a cure. If not...well, she was still trying to erase that possibility from her mind.

She glanced at the driver next to her. Maja had been able to persuade Marcel quicker than she had expected. He had accepted her promise to share the cure with him and merely asked that they wait until evening when less suspicious minds would cross paths with them in the black market.

She had agreed and thus followed a day of obsessing over every possible outcome as she waited at the diner. Maja had tried to distract her but even she was at a loss for once. It wasn't every day that you found yourself in the middle of a pandemic, waiting to step into an even more deadly reality—assuming the journey there didn't kill you first. Lora had tried to divert the attention to Maja's family, asking about her mother, but their conversations always seemed to come back to the inevitable.

Marcel stared straight ahead, dark brown eyes focused on the road. Lora wondered what was going on inside his mind. She didn't know Maja's father that well but since he was also her mum's friend, she had seen him at her house many times over the years. Did he simply agree because of the potential business opportunity or did he desperately want to save Karla's life too? He must know her mum well enough to know she would never agree to Lora's plan, yet he hadn't questioned her. Lora was aware she should let it go, yet the curiosity wouldn't let her.

"Why did you agree to this?"

Marcel briefly glanced in her direction before shifting his eyes back to the road. "Does it matter?"

Avoiding the question made Lora think that there was indeed more to it. "I don't know, does it?" She didn't let her stare break as she waited for an answer.

Marcel gave her another quick glance, then shook his head as he said, "You're still as stubborn as ever." He kept one gloved hand on the wheel as he reached for his long sleeve and pushed it up.

Lora realised his motive before her eyes even focused on the swollen, dark purple veins sticking out beneath his sweater. Thinking back, she now realised he had kept his distance from them in the diner today.

"Don't tell Maja. She doesn't need to know yet. Maybe she never will," Marcel said as he pulled into an almost empty parking lot. "Look, Lora. I don't know exactly why you think you can cross, but I know there's something your mum has been keeping secret for a long time." He paused, catching her gaze. She traced her heart-shaped pendant with one finger. "And I'm sure you both have your reasons, which is why I won't push further."

Lora wanted him to say more but she sensed there would be no further discussion.

Marcel turned off the engine. "Pull your hood up and keep your head down, okay? And don't speak until we're at my work station."

Lora nodded, her anxiety increasing. She couldn't believe this was really going to happen. But she knew she couldn't escape it, not when she was the only one who could save them.

She pulled her cobalt blue hoodie over her head and reached for her bag on the back seat. Her legs felt shaky as she climbed out of the car and surveyed her surroundings. The parking lot belonged to what looked like an old factory, a fitting place for a secret entrance. Marcel headed in the opposite direction. He must have sensed Lora's confusion because he slowed down, looking over his shoulder at her.

"The entrance isn't here. We park here as a cover."

They crossed the street and walked until more buildings came into view. Lora could see the faint shimmer of the portal in the distance, beckoning her. Marcel stopped in front of an old, unsuspecting building and opened the door to a small corner shop. Lora's friends would have never guessed the entrance was here when they'd dared her to go to the black market.

Marcel held the door for Lora and looked at her expectantly. She quickly forced her legs to move again. Marcel didn't waste time as he led her to the back of the shop, walking past the shop owner who didn't look at them twice, to a locked door. After moving past several heavy doors that Marcel unlocked with ease, two flights of stairs, and a long darkly lit corridor, they seemed to have reached their destination.

Marcel stopped in front of a massive steel door with a keypad. He entered the code with no trouble and they were greeted by an aggressive-looking man who frowned at them. Lora didn't fail to notice the gun strapped to his waist. The man looked Lora over with wary eyes.

"This is my daughter. I'm showing her the ropes," Marcel said. He gave Lora a proud look and didn't wait for an answer as he led her further down the corridor.

They rounded a corner and entered what looked like a maze of more shiny, grey corridors, each one leading to yet another door. A few people were walking around, some sorting through piles of shiny onyx boxes while others pulled small wagons with packed items. Some rooms provided a look inside as the top half of the door was open, inviting buyers. Lora tried to read some of the many signs plastered around the walls, listing prices and advertising special deals, mostly for indigo wine, spelled tech, and other items that promised to make one's life easier. One of the signs advertised spelled jewellery that supposedly ensured good luck. Lora would never understand why humans bothered with these black market items.

Turning her head, her eyes landed on the bright indigo shimmer of the border at the end of the small spaces up ahead.

Marcel quickened his pace and led her to another locked door. Before she could take in all the details of the market, she found herself in an enclosed space, the portal a few steps ahead of her. A conveyor belt sat on one side of the concrete wall, stopping less than an inch before the portal. It wasn't running but Lora guessed this was how Marcel avoided getting too close to the portal when making deliveries to Liraen. There was a big container on the other side of the wall filled with a few shiny onyx boxes—trading parcels.

Lora had never been this close to the border. There was no fence, nothing to separate them. She took a step forward without even realising. The portal was different than before. Lora had never felt how alive it was, buzzing with energy, making her skin shiver in anticipation. She was about to take another step but a gloved hand made her stop in her tracks.

"Not so fast. We need to go over a few things." Marcel handed her a folded piece of paper. "As I said, a fae trader, Eyden, will be waiting for you on the other side. Give him this note." As soon as she took the letter, Marcel turned to one of the many shelves on the wall.

Lora didn't recognise most of the items displayed nor did she know the small, faintly glowing cube Marcel took off the shelf.

"This is one of our newest products. It's a WiFi cube. It connects to the network we have running here at the black market. You'll be able to go online in Liraen. Just connect it to your phone. But there's limited data, we haven't perfected it yet. We recently added a feature that automatically uploads a map of Liraen to your phone once connected. Fae don't seem to care for it but I imagine you might need it." He pulled out another, smaller item from his pocket. It looked like a normal phone battery. "This battery is spelled to last forever. You'll need it—no electricity in Liraen."

Lora already knew that much. Maja had one of these batteries. Spelled tech wasn't something that she would imagine finding in Liraen often. The fae had no interest in human technology. And humans supposedly had no interest in fae magic, yet here she was at the black market, the one place where humans and fae traded items illegally despite their animosity towards each other.

She took both items and stored them in her bag, zipping it shut tightly as she turned to the portal again. "Anything else?" she asked.

Marcel glanced around the small space. "Be careful, okay? Eyden seems decent but I've never met him in person and he hasn't been of any help so far with the virus. Don't trust anyone. Your mother needs you to stay safe." His voice had a new gravity to it. "Goodbye, Lora."

The way he said those last words made it sound like she was

on her deathbed. She supposed she could be. But she could feel the magic of the border calling her, her blood heating as her tan skin turned flush. Slowly, she walked up to the portal.

Her hand instinctively reached out. Before she could think twice about it, her fingertips traced the surface of the portal. It felt like charged air, electricity awakening all her senses. She could do this. The spell didn't seem to affect her. Relief flooded through her as she craned her neck, locking eyes with Marcel.

He looked at her in plain astonishment and a shimmer of hope seemed to take over his face. "Good luck," he said.

She could feel new fears taking over her mind. She might be able to touch the border, but there were still so many obstacles ahead of her. Before Lora could fall down another thought spiral, she quietly nodded and turned back to the border, to the unpredictable challenge awaiting her.

Without looking back, she took a final shaky, yet determined, breath and headed into the unknown.

CHAPTER 5

AMIRA

"A dress fit for a princess from Allamyst," her brother had said when he had picked her outfit. Amira looked at the garment laid out in front of her. The bodice was made of a silky, almost watery material. The tight waist spread out into a cascade of fabric, heavy and expensive. The bubbled sleeves were the most spectacular part; they looked like blown glass dyed with a bloodish colour. "Maybe you can fool Karwyn into thinking you are worth something when you wear it," Wryen had added.

Nalani stared at the dress, utterly confused by its extravagant design. "How the hell are you supposed to wear that?" she muttered under her breath. Amira let out a stressed giggle. She was going to look ridiculous.

The maid panicked, realising that she had made her comment aloud. "It's a wonderful dress, my lady," she eagerly said.

Amira sighed. "Let's try to put it on."

Nalani nodded and unfastened the myriad of pearl buttons set in the back of the dress. She then raised the heavy fabric above Amira's head. Very slowly, she lowered the fabric, letting it hug Amira's curves. The extravagant dress quickly became smothering. Amira tugged at the dress, trying to stretch the heavy material to allow her freedom, something she had been denied all too often.

"Do you want to wear this tonight, my lady?" Nalani asked, forcing Amira to stop obsessing over her dress. Her eyes drifted to the silver bracelet she'd been given earlier today.

"I suppose I should." She was sure Karwyn would appreciate Amira wearing the gift he had given her.

Nalani wrapped the cold, thin chain around her wrist. Even though the turquoise stones sparkled elegantly against Amira's olive skin, she couldn't help but think it was chaining her to a future she had not chosen herself. *It doesn't matter*, she told herself. As long as her future didn't involve Wryen, she would be fine. She would find happiness.

After fastening the clasp, Nalani patiently brushed and braided Amira's hair with fresh flowers. The gentle motion of the brush reminded Amira of a time when her mother would slowly comb through her long, dark brown locks, whispering sweet words in her ear.

She closed her eyes, not wanting to cry in front of a stranger. The scent of the flowers infiltrated Amira's nose and her head started to ache. She could feel copper bells ringing against her skull. Her mouth felt weirdly dry. Her hands twitched nervously. She held them close to her heart in an attempt to calm herself. Thousands of painful thoughts and memories ran through her head. She could feel all of them, every single time she had ever ached. She tried to breathe slowly but her tongue kept getting stuck on the roof of her mouth. A bright flash and a scream echoed through her mind before she forced herself to return to the present.

The pain subsided as she looked up and she managed to smile at her maid. Amira looked at herself in the mirror. She looked so perfect that the painters of Allamyst would have begged her to pose for them.

A knock on the door of the antechamber made Amira straighten her back. She had made a promise to herself and to her mother to do whatever it took to get away from her half-brother. And she intended to keep her promise.

She walked to the antechamber, almost tripping over her dress. Amira opened the door to face Wryen, who had chosen a rather plain outfit for himself compared to her eye-catching dress. But she wasn't fooled. Knowing Wryen, the simple but well-cut prussian blue jacket and trousers he was wearing was probably more in fashion in Turosian than Amira's outfit. He took her hand before she could dwell on it any longer and Amira let him take the lead.

The party would be her first in a couple of years, yet Amira didn't feel the tiniest bit of excitement as they walked up to the heavy silver doors. Dread was her companion for the night, a feeling her half-brother had instilled on the way there.

"Everyone will be staring at you, waiting for your first mistake. The court of Turosian is ruthless, as is Karwyn. Don't expect to make any friends." He stopped to stare at the fear spreading on her face. "The only person who you should care to be liked by is your fiancé." His glacial tone had made her want to vanish forever.

Waves of unknown voices and music were waiting for them on the other side of the doors, a new world that she had to call her own now. Wryen pulled on her arm, turning her attention to him. She could feel his gaze on her body, scrutinizing every little detail, every little imperfection. He grabbed her chin.

"Chin up, sister," he said with a wicked smile. "Try to make a good impression for once."

Amira's chin was burning from his touch. She felt his fire magic just underneath the surface, ready to claw its way out of Wryen's skin to burn her flesh. One little move from her brother and the fire could feed on her. But she knew he would never do it. As all fae, she would heal quickly, but ruining her beauty even for one instant would surely be noticed. No, Wryen preferred more invisible torments. Insidious ones that made Amira live in fear of making the wrong move. His fire was for the people that dared defy him and Amira had never had the strength to fight back.

She took a big breath when the door opened in front of her. She felt herself moving forward, almost dragged by her brother. He leaned in and whispered something in her ear. She didn't quite hear it.

"Smile, it's a party," he repeated. Amira forced her lips to showcase a shining smile. "Much better."

"His Majesty Wryen Rosston, King of Allamyst and his sister, Princess Amira Rosston," she heard a man say. She felt her brother's hand tighten on her arm.

The crowd parted in front of them. Looking at the other fae's clothes, Amira truly felt out of place. No one was wearing anything half as extravagant as her dress. She wasn't sure if she was imagining all the mocking whispers or if people were actually making fun of her. Or maybe it was Wryen's voice that was whispering such thoughts to her. She straightened her back, trying to convince herself of her own confidence.

On the other side of the room, she saw Karwyn waiting on his throne. His pale face was completely devoid of emotion. Pure boredom, that was his aura. Next to him were Nouis and Rhay. The colourful outfit Rhay was wearing made Amira feel more at ease. Her smile almost made its way to her eyes but a sense of decorum stopped her. Her attention should be focused on her fiancé, not on his advisor.

To avoid the staring faces of the crowd, she looked straight ahead, her eyes focusing on her future husband. Trying to channel some affection for the man she was promised to, she couldn't chase the sour taste in her mouth. On the contrary, she sensed her brother revelling in the attention they were given.

The final steps towards Karwyn seemed to last hours. And then suddenly, she was in front of him. He looked different than the boy she remembered from her childhood. His hair was still golden, swept away from his face to reveal sharp cheekbones, but she didn't think his eyes had always looked this haunted.

Her brother bowed deeply and she followed his example. When she stood straight again, she met Karwyn's gaze. Maybe haunted hadn't been the correct word. *Indifference* was more like it.

"Your Majesty, may I present to you my sister, Lady Amira Rosston." Wryen reluctantly added, "Princess of Allamyst. It is my honour to express in front of Your Majesty and your court my intention to give you her hand in marriage." Wryen placed

Amira's hand into Karwyn's open one. Her fingers laid there, flat and lifeless.

"I gladly accept Princess Amira as my fiancée," he said. His face was telling a different story. He didn't even glance at the bracelet around her wrist.

Amira stayed silent, staring at her small hand lost in Karwyn's. She knew what to expect when Wryen had told her that she was to be engaged to Karwyn in order to secure a powerful alliance for their kingdom. She had been raised to be a wife and a queen. But stupidly, Amira had dreamt that she would feel something when she'd look at the person she would be spending her whole life with. As she stared into Karwyn's eyes, she realised the thought was nothing more than a childish dream.

"I hope you had a pleasant journey to Parae, princess," Karwyn said.

Amira was pleasantly surprised by his question.

"I did, my king, thank you. I took great pleasure in seeing your lovely capital. I do hope I will get the chance to visit more soon. Maybe you could show me around?"

Karwyn looked quite annoyed by the proposition. "I will see if my duty allows me the freedom to answer your request." He turned his gaze to Wryen. "The contract has been prepared. If you want to read it beforehand, do so now."

Amira was taken aback by Karwyn not offering her the chance to read it too. After all, she was the one who was going to sign it, not her brother. Even if their engagement had already been decided months ago and she had never had a say in it, Amira had still entertained the thought that she would have at least a little agency in the matter.

"I trust Your Majesty," said Wryen in a falsely sweet tone.

"You should always read a blood contract. After all, this one concerns your precious sister."

Amira's blood turned cold. She felt Wryen's burning hand on the nape of her neck. A silent protest died in her mouth. She watched Karwyn gesture to Nouis, who took out a scroll from his coat's pocket and offered it to Wryen. With relief, Wryen's hand left her skin to accept the scroll.

He unrolled it and Amira tried to read some of it. There wasn't much written. The most important article was that Karwyn and Amira could only proceed with the wedding once Karwyn was selected for the High King Contest, which would take place at the end of the year. Three kings or queens would be given the opportunity to showcase their power in the contest. The winner would be the next high king or queen of Liraen, ruling over all seven kingdoms.

Amira would have expected the wedding to take place after the contest of power, not before. She thought Karwyn would be too busy preparing for the contest to plan a wedding. But maybe he didn't need much preparation. After all, he was already the interim high king, taking on the title after his father's passing until the contest decided who would rule moving forward.

A smaller written paragraph offered Karwyn the opportunity to renounce the wedding before that time if Amira was proven unfit to be his queen. Amira was expecting this clause, after all, Karwyn was the one with most of the negotiation power. But it still pained her to see that she wasn't also offered the opportunity to reject Karwyn.

Karwyn's face stayed emotionless. Rhay seemed bored, his

gaze longingly set on the empty dance floor. When he turned his head, his eyes met hers briefly before meeting the king's. Rhay's easy smile eased Karwyn's stern expression for a few seconds.

"This seems all right," Wryen said, nodding. "More favourable to you, but still all right."

"Then let us sign," Karwyn replied, his expression void of emotion again.

Nouis quickly brought him a fountain pen and Karwyn pricked his finger with the sharp nib. Droplets of blood coated the iron part of the pen. The interim high king signed with a flourish before giving the pen to Amira. With some hesitation, she pricked her finger. A drop of blood fell on the contract, staining it with a bright red dot. Amira felt the burning eyes of the crowd on her back. But the most pressing ones were her brother's.

She took a deep breath and signed with her still-childish handwriting. The two signatures glowed brightly as the magic bound them to their word. The crowd cheered and Karwyn took Amira's hand, making her face the court. With a fake smile plastered on her face, she waved at the ecstatic crowd.

Karwyn let go of her hand. "You must forgive me, princess, but I have important matters to discuss."

He didn't add "*with fae more important than you*," but Amira knew that was implied. But she intended on showing her commitment to her new position. "I would be happy to learn more about the court's predicaments."

Wryen's eyes burned into her skull. "Don't annoy the king with your questions, silly girl," she heard him say between his teeth.

All the men were now staring at her. Feeling the pressure,

Amira bowed deeply. The king gestured to Wryen and the two men left, accompanied by Nouis. Rhay stayed there and gave Amira an encouraging smile. As she was about to go talk to him, a gorgeous, dark-skinned woman swooped in and grabbed Rhay's arm, leading him to what had become a dancing hall.

Left alone in the middle of the crowd, surrounded by unknown faces, Amira felt strangely at home. In the last half-decade, Wryen had removed every familiar face from her life, firing people left and right. He wanted her to feel completely alone, with only a handful of people allowed to interact with her.

This time, her brother wasn't looking at her. With Wryen distracted, Amira decided she was going to make the most of the evening.

She took a good look around her. The large room was made of a pale blue marble speckled with silver. In the centre, men and women danced gracefully to the sound of a hidden orchestra. The turquoise velvet curtains were drawn open, letting Amira's gaze wander to the shimmering sky. All around the room, tables were filled with food and drinks. Small groups of fae conversed with glasses in their hands.

Amira walked away from the throne and made her way towards one of the tables. On her way, she noticed many fae staring at her, but they chose not to speak to her. She wondered if it was because of the impossibly obnoxious dress or because of the person who was inside of it. To avoid furthering her embarrassment by staring back, she looked up at the painted ceiling. In a dark blue sky lathered with tiny bright stars, stood the figure of the glorious goddess Falea, the protector of Turosian. She was the bringer of fortune and good luck.

Amira ran her finger over the smooth silver around her wrist. In Allamyst it would only be seen as a beautiful accessory, but she knew here in Turosian, good luck charms held importance. She wondered if it really could repel evil or if it was merely a superstition they chose to believe.

Her eyes travelled up to the ceiling again. Falea's amber skin was lightened by her extraordinary blue eyes and shining locks of brown hair. Amira's mother would have said that Amira looked like her. Her half-brother would have laughed in their faces.

Amira shook her head and turned her attention to the table nearby. It was filled to the brim with food and drinks to the point of obscenity.

She poured herself a glass of iridos and admired its pale colour. She could see all the nuances of a rainbow echoing in the crystal glass. It was the most marvellous drink. The sparkling liquid coated her tongue, revealing its lightly floral and spicy taste.

As she was finishing her glass, a hand lightly touched her arm. Her muscles tensed up, expecting the worst, but when she turned around, she only saw Rhay. His large welcoming smile eased her worries.

"Princess Amira, I hope you are enjoying your evening. I know how hard it must be for you to start a new life in a completely different kingdom. Well, I'm sure it won't be that different."

"Oh, I hope it is." She had been praying for a different life ever since her father had died.

"You're saying that now, but I'm sure you'll be sad when it's time to say goodbye to your only brother."

If only he knew how wrong he was. But Amira could never

say those things. Not even to friendly Rhay. "I will do my best not to cry too much," she said with an even tone.

"I remember leaving Sapharos. I think I cried on the whole way to Turosian. By the end, I was crying without tears."

Amira was surprised by this admission of weakness. "Have you ever gone back to Sapharos?"

Rhay's gaze lingered on the ceiling. "No, my father has always made sure we didn't have to."

She wanted to ask more, but it felt like prying. Instead, she decided to learn more about her new home. "How long have you been an advisor?" she said right as Rhay grabbed her hand.

"Come on, let's dance a bit. It would be a shame to waste this beautiful music."

Amira removed her hand from Rhay's grip. Would it be seen as improper for the future queen to be dancing with her fiancé's advisor? She desperately needed this wedding to happen; it was her only way out of Wryen's controlling hands. Instead of losing herself to mindless dancing, she should focus on building a relationship with Karwyn.

"I'm sorry, Rhay. I appreciate your offer, but I think I'd better go find my future husband." *Husband.* It sounded empty to her, yet she would have to grow accustomed to it.

Rhay bowed deeply. "Then I wish you the best of luck. Karwyn has never been fond of small talk but you might be the one to change that."

With a little twirl, Rhay joined the waltzing couples, quickly stealing a man's partner. Amira felt a sharp jab in her heart. How she envied his careless attitude.

Grabbing her long skirt, she went to the door. The last time she had seen Karwyn, he was exiting the room.

Darkness surrounded her as she walked away from the safe haven of the throne room. The joyous sounds of the ball disappeared into the background. Nighttime was not helping her poor first impression of the palace. A few torches illuminated the corridor she had taken, splashing dim light on the stone walls. Amira kept walking, hoping to encounter a welcoming face or at least a better lit area. But the more she walked, the more fear settled in her bones.

The eerie silence was broken by what sounded like whimpering. Amira froze; only her eyes moved to look for the source of the sound. She was still alone. On her left, she heard a doorknob rattling. Her head slowly turned. Time slowed as the door crept open.

Amira had never felt more relieved to see Karwyn's annoyed face. "What are you doing here?" he asked as he moved away from the door.

"Actually, I was looking for you," she said, her voice wavering.

A dark-haired man with piercing grey eyes appeared behind Karwyn. Disregarding Amira, he whispered something in the king's ear before swiftly walking away.

Amira wanted to ask who the mysterious man was but Karwyn interrupted her. "You should go back to the party."

She looked around, unsettled. "I'm afraid I'm lost."

Karwyn looked at her as if she was an annoying child. "Fine, I will walk you back." Without waiting for her, he started forward.

Amira had to run to match his fast steps. She almost tripped over her long dress.

Karwyn glanced over his shoulder. "By Caelo, you are as regal as a kitchen maid," he said.

Amira bit back her reply. "Did you enjoy your evening, my king?" Amira asked, trying to ignore Karwyn's insult. Some light conversation would help her forget about the dreary atmosphere of the palace.

"Do you really feel the need to do this?" Karwyn sighed.

Amira frowned. "Do what?"

"Fill the silence with pointless, empty conversation. I take no pleasure in the pretend politeness that strangers force themselves to have."

"Soon we won't be strangers." Amira tried to catch his gaze as she walked next to him. "If we are to be wedded, I think we should try to get to know each other."

Karwyn finally faced her. "Do not fool yourself. Our marriage will never be based on love. Its only purpose is to brighten up my image."

Amira couldn't help but feel offended by Karwyn's words. She could see his reasoning—the royals usually preferred married fae ruling over Liraen. She wasn't expecting true love, but she had hoped that Karwyn would see her as a companion, not just as a pawn in his game.

She held his gaze. "I can be more than just your wife. I want to be involved in politics. I want to be useful. I want to make things better for the people of Turosian."

Karwyn let out a cold laugh. "We are far better off than Allamyst. Insinuating my kingdom needs improvement only further shows your lack of knowledge. I only chose you because your lack of power presents no threat to mine during our union."

So that was it. She was his fiancée because in marrying a level one fae, he could be sure not to lose any power during the ceremony. In royal weddings, it was often customary to have a witch perform a blood ritual while they exchanged the sacred vows to connect their life force (and by extension, their powers) to one another. For the weaker of the two, it usually meant losing some power as the other, stronger one would absorb some of their strength.

"So that's it?" she asked. "You're not even going to try to get to know me?"

Karwyn looked her up and down. "I do not need to know you to make use of you. You will have a nice life here if you do as I say. You will be a queen, you will not lack for anything."

Anything but love, a voice whispered inside her head. But for a life away from her brother's influence, she'd do anything. Love had never worked out for her anyway.

The turquoise of Karwyn's eyes seemed to brighten before he looked straight ahead. "Play your part right and we will not have any issues. A loving marriage should not be a king or queen's priority." Karwyn halted and gestured to a door that led back towards the sounds of music and dancing. "Here you are. Do not get lost again. I have no patience for imbeciles."

He left her alone in the dark corridor with tears in her eyes and a heavy heart.

CHAPTER 6

LORA

For a moment, Lora felt as if she was floating, the electric air around her pushing her forward. She shut her eyes tightly against the intense glowing light of the portal. When her feet abruptly landed on solid ground again, she stumbled as she tried to find her footing. Squinting against the bright light, she looked up to shadows and blurry shapes and forced herself not to panic.

"What the fuck?" a voice said not far from her.

And there went her attempt to stay calm. Lora immediately shifted her head, alarmed, shielding her eyes with her hand as she tried to catch a glimpse of who that voice belonged to. Her heart was beating so fast she thought she'd pass out from sheer panic. She had done it. She'd managed to get to Liraen...and she had no idea what was awaiting her. Or *who*.

"By Caelo, how did you get here?" the voice said.

A blurry shape slowly walked towards her. Lora blinked and forced her eyes to focus. When she opened them again, she saw a tall man regarding her with curiosity. As he took another step, closing the distance between them, she found herself looking into intense, strikingly pale blue eyes. They were a stark contrast to his brown skin and dark hair.

He was undoubtedly fae. It wasn't just his unusual eye colour that gave him away, it was his whole presence. He gave off a foreign, almost inhuman, vibe.

"I asked you a question," the fae said, his voice stern and impatient. His eyes never left hers as he waited for an answer. His intense gaze was boring into her. Lora found it quite unsettling. Part of her wanted to turn around and flee. If she went now, she was sure she could still catch Marcel, leave the market, and forget this incident ever happened. Then she remembered Marcel's words.

"Are you Eyden?" Her voice shook slightly and she hated how insecure she sounded.

The fae looked taken aback, confusion colouring his features. "Yes. Who the hell are you?" He looked her up and down. "You're human?"

"Yes," she replied quickly. "Marcel sent me. He told you I was coming, didn't he?"

Eyden turned his head, finally breaking that unwavering stare, as he let out a short laugh. The movement let a black curl fall into his face, stopping right above his eye.

"He told me to wait here for a special delivery. And just how *special* are you?" Eyden asked as he turned that curious gaze on her once again.

Lora regained her composure, forcing her voice to come out even and decisive. "Marcel said you could help me. I came to get a cure. Might not be *your* top priority, but humans are dying right now from a nasty virus."

"So I've heard. But I don't have anything at the market here, I already told Marcel that."

His dismissive words invoked Lora's always-lingering anger. Of course, to a fae, this was nothing, least of all a pressing matter. Her first conversation with a fae was exactly as she'd always expected.

"Then I'm going somewhere else. Point me in the right direction, will you?" she asked sternly.

There was that laugh again, this time undeniably mocking her. "You want to go outside? Into Chrysa? Dressed like that, every fae will know you're human. You have no idea how to blend in. They'll try to kill you, or worse."

Her skin crawled as images flashed before her eyes. This was the history she had studied. A long history of mistreatment of humans—and mistreatment was putting it lightly. Yet Lora refused to dwell on the *or worse* Eyden had mentioned.

"Then help me," she replied. It took immense willpower to get out the words. Asking a fae for help, what had her life become? But this was the plan. She wasn't naïve enough to believe she could do this by herself. Marcel believed Eyden could help. She had to be careful in handling this, but she needed Eyden's knowledge of the fae land. She might have studied everything she could get her hands on about Liraen, but Lora knew she was lacking insider information. To succeed, she unfortunately needed a guide to this foreign world.

"And why would I do such a thing? What's in it for me? Sounds like more trouble than it's worth," Eyden said.

She reached into the front pocket of her black skinny jeans and pulled out a crumpled piece of paper. "Marcel thought you might say that."

Eyden took the letter without hesitation, taking in whatever Marcel had written to convince him to help. His nose crinkled as he seemed to wrestle with a decision.

Finally, he exhaled loudly and said, "I may be convinced to help with your...mission." Those piercing eyes locked on hers. "But I have conditions."

"Wouldn't expect anything else from a fae."

His dark eyebrows drew together as if he was irritated by her statement. It was simply the truth. Everyone knew the fae loved their agreements, binding others to keep their word.

"I didn't know that all humans are *oh so selfless*," he said. When Lora didn't reply, he added, "How did you cross?"

"I can't tell you that. I can trade you, though." Lora moved to take off her backpack. She could pay him, she was willing to bargain with him. "I have some jewellery. It's worth something."

"I have no need for that. Knowing how to cross on the other hand..."

"I already told you, I can't tell you that. Can't you just accept payment?" Lora swung her backpack over her shoulder again as she stared at him in annoyance. Her patience was wearing thin.

"If I remember correctly, you're the one who wants something. I'd take my offer if I were you. It's a scary world for humans out there."

Lora considered what was at stake. Telling him her secret could endanger her own life, yes, but he wouldn't be able to cross to Earth himself. Still, she'd rather not tell him. She was about to play a dangerous game, pretending she had a different kind of secret, a more valuable one, to share.

Lora couldn't allow him to suspect the deception she was planning, so she asked, "And what will you do if I tell you?"

Eyden shrugged. "This and that."

"Vague, much?"

"And you're so forthcoming? Then tell me, special one, why can't you tell me your little secret? You didn't sign a blood contract, did you?"

"I'd never." The mere thought was appalling to Lora. She continued her charade, "Isn't it obvious? I can't risk the fae invading my world again."

"I see. I wouldn't do that." A smug smile appeared on his face. "Sharing that secret would be bad for business, after all."

Her fury reached new limits. Who was he to make light of this situation? Lora swallowed her impulsive response. "And I'm supposed to take your word for it?"

Eyden pointed to the other side of the small, cave-like room. "There's the door if you'd rather try your luck on your own. If I find your corpse later, maybe I'll feel generous and send it back to Earth."

The snarky comment didn't discourage her. No, she welcomed it. It gave her incentive to agree with him. Lora bit her lip as she pretended to mull over his statement.

After a short pause, she purposely sought out his stare. "Fine. I'll tell you how I can cross after you help me get a cure. If something happens to me, you'll never know. And I'm not going to sign some fae blood contract, so you better get that out of your head."

Eyden seemed to consider her counteroffer as he shifted his feet. "I'll have to keep a close eye on you then." The words were meant as a warning, yet they had an undefined edge to them. Before she could dwell on them, Eyden said, "But we're getting the cure my way. You're in my territory. Don't go off seeking danger. Don't waste my time." His voice was back to a monotone, bored tone.

Lora waited a moment, this time truly considering what she had gotten herself into. Did she have any other choice but to agree? She couldn't picture another way forward, so she nodded.

"Then we have an agreement?" she asked.

"Sure, special one." The mocking tone was back, much to Lora's dismay.

"Lora. My name's Lora."

"We have a deal, *Lora*," Eyden said, emphasizing her name. It had a strange but not unpleasant ring to it. His Turosian accent made her name sound outlandish.

An uneasy feeling crept back in. A realisation that she was far from home, in a different world, talking to a different species than her own. She turned her head to the side to examine the room. Instead of smooth, painted grey walls, all she saw was stone surrounding her. The corners were littered with unknown artefacts and onyx boxes like the ones in Marcel's room piled on top of each other. There was no conveyor belt, only a big empty basket in front of the portal.

Lora grasped her pendant, wanting the comfort of something familiar.

When she turned her gaze back up, she noticed Eyden had moved to open a wooden box that was placed close to the door.

"What are you doing?" she asked, mistrust lacing her words.

Eyden didn't look up and continued going through the contents of the box. "You need a disguise."

"Right." Her suspicion of Eyden was like a nervous buzzing in her veins. "What level are you?" She wanted to be prepared for whatever powers he might demonstrate.

If he was a level one, that would make him the least dangerous. He would merely showcase advanced senses and strength. If he was above that, then he would exhibit an additional ability. Or as the fae would say, he would be *blessed* with a power. Power that allowed them to do terrible things. Power that convinced them they were superior. No one should possess such power. It was unnatural and frighteningly dangerous.

High-level fae had a more intense glow in their eyes than lower levels, their power seeping through. Although Eyden's eyes were unnaturally striking to the human eye, Lora didn't take note of any overwhelming power radiating off him.

"I don't need to define myself by any level. I built myself a reputation as a trader and that's all you need to know," he said.

The vague answer wasn't enough for Lora. She rephrased her question, demanding more. "Does that mean you don't have any special powers?"

"You're the only special one, I'm afraid."

Not quite an answer either, but she decided to let it go. For now.

Lora quickly put her new battery in her phone and connected her phone to the WiFi cube. With haste, she messaged Maja, telling her that she had crossed and was truly fine but couldn't talk much because of her limited data. She asked her friend to relay her message to her family before giving them her letters.

"Are we meeting a healer outside the market, then?" Lora asked, circling back to the mission at hand.

This time he did turn around, staring up at her from where he was kneeling on the floor. "Yes and no. I'll take you to a healer but not tonight. I'll have to—"

"What?" Lora immediately interrupted, irritation flowing over her. She had expected she might have to leave the underground market, but she had been naïve enough to hope she would be able to settle this immediately. "Why not tonight? Do I really have to explain how urgent this is? People are dying."

"Rushing it is a stupid way to go about it. Make no mistake, I may want to know your secret, but I'm in no mood to go on a fool's errand. You agreed to do this my way. Keep your word or walk away now. It's your funeral."

Lora glared at him. Not even five minutes passed and she was already regretting agreeing to this deal.

She took a deep breath and met his insistent stare. "So, what's your genius plan, then?"

A small smile appeared on Eyden's face but it was gone before Lora could even fully take it in. He grabbed a piece of black fabric and stood up, those ice blue eyes fixated on her.

"First, I'm going to sneak you out of here. And tomorrow...tomorrow we'll see about that cure."

The disguise Eyden had for her turned out to be a simple black cloak. It almost fell down to her shoes and Lora had pulled it closed tight around her, making sure her human clothes were hidden as much as possible. The hood blocked most of her view as she struggled to keep up with Eyden's quick pace. He led her through more stone corridors, walking close to her but far enough that they weren't touching.

Lora had been scared of encountering more fae but she was so focused on not tripping over her disguise that her mind had little time to take in the figures around her. There was more of a crowd here than in the human market. People—*fae*—rushing past them. She noticed others in similar cloaks. She supposed some buyers might prefer to remain anonymous. Whatever the reason, it worked to their advantage. They weren't stopped along the way and soon enough she could see a narrow staircase ahead of them.

Eyden opened a small, wooden cellar door and then they were outside, surrounded by trees. The cool but not unpleasant night air brushed her face. Behind them, she could make out the familiar indigo shimmer of the portal hidden in the woods.

Lora inspected the door. It was slightly raised from the ground and looked utterly simple, a far cry from the steel-reinforced security door in her world.

"Come on. Keep up," Eyden said as he started off towards faint lights in the opposite direction of the border.

Lora hurried after him, but she couldn't help but turn around one more time, thinking she should remember the location of the door. But when she looked back, all she saw was soil. No sign of a door. For a second Lora thought she had lost her mind before she remembered that it was most likely a spell. The possibility both intrigued and frightened her.

She quickly pulled up the map of Liraen on her phone, checking her current location before they walked too far away from the border. The last thing she wanted was to get lost in this terrible world.

Soon enough, they left the woods behind and walked on almost empty, narrow side streets. It was already dark out and the few street oil lamps provided little light. Lora wondered how well the fae could see in the dark. It was hard for her to adjust to the low light and make out details. Thankfully, they didn't run into any fae.

She did catch a glimpse of a horse strapped to a wooden post in front of a building. It was kicking up dirt as it shuffled around. Its glowing orange eyes were like two beacons in the night. According to her research, fae horses were stronger and more resilient than the ones she had encountered on Earth.

Eyden slowed down when they neared another building. He walked up the steep wooden stairs with no banister to the second floor and unlocked the mud brown door at the end of the short corridor. As he disappeared inside the flat, Lora had no choice but to follow.

The space reminded Lora of a studio apartment. To her left was a small kitchen with a table for four by one of the two windows. In the middle was a spacious black sofa opposite two comfy chairs and a tiny fireplace. And on the right side of the room was a large double bed partly hidden by a room divider, its design made out of black metal that didn't conceal the whole view. Eyden's flat had a minimalistic design with no bright colours in sight. It didn't show off anything personal and she couldn't glimpse any special fae artefacts either.

Eyden shut the door before taking off his coat. Lora felt stuck. She simply stood there, next to the door, still dressed in the large cloak. Was she really going to stay here? With this stranger—this fae? The thought was so absurd that she almost laughed, yet she knew this was her new reality. It had been too hopeful to think she could find a cure that same day.

She reached for the knot to open her coat but Eyden halted her. "Wait," he said as he walked towards the opposite side of the room and closed the curtains.

"Do a lot of people, I mean *fae*, peek into your window?" She meant it as a serious question yet it came out teasingly.

"No. I chose this place because it overlooks another building with no windows. And barely anyone walks the small path between them. Better not to risk it anyway."

Lora couldn't argue with that, even though his statement wasn't exactly comforting. She supposed the black market business here in Chrysa came with secrecy similar to the illegal trades in Bournchester. Nodding her agreement, she finally took off the cloak and her backpack, then continued looking around the room.

Eyden settled into the sofa, clearly not caring about Lora's discomfort. Was he not at all unsettled by the stranger in his flat?

"Do you think you can lose the British accent tomorrow? I have some clothes that should fit you but your voice will give you away. And I'm assuming you'll want to go with me, no?" he asked.

"Obviously. How would you explain the virus to a healer? Do you know anything about it?"

"Not really, that's why I didn't seriously suggest you stay

here," Eyden answered, arrogance radiating off him. "Now, the accent? Know anything about Turosian?"

Lora caught his gaze and held it. "I don't think it's all that difficult. I'll manage," she said, trying to imitate Eyden and channel what she had learned about the history of fae language, which was quite similar to her English. To her ears, the accent sounded like a mix of different human accents. Maybe how a well-travelled Brit might have adapted a blend of pronunciations from different cultures.

"Not quite there, but it'll do. We'll say you're not originally from here."

Lora gave him a questioning look. "As in, if anyone asks, you grew up in Quarnian. It's far enough that no one really travels there. At least, I've never met anyone from there, not even a trader."

Lora knew enough about the seven remaining kingdoms to understand his reasoning. Quarnian was farther north and sep-arated from Turosian—the kingdom she was currently in—and the other countries by the sea.

"So, should I say I'm from Opalia?" Lora asked, bringing up the kingdom's capital.

"I see you've done some research."

"I know a great deal of things."

"Not as much as you think, I'm sure." Eyden's eyes met hers as a small smile tugged at his lips.

"I know enough," she said, keeping her face blank.

"Let's hope you do." He studied her for a moment, maybe waiting for a reply that wouldn't come. "Okay then, let's try to get some rest. We'll have to get up early tomorrow to prepare and dress you up as fae."

Lora shuddered at the thought. He didn't know how close she was to being fae already. *Fae.* The word had always sounded dirty, shameful to her ears.

Suppressing the notion, she surveyed his flat again. "I don't suppose you have a guest room hidden somewhere?"

"I have this sofa." He gestured to the piece of furniture he was sitting on. "Is that not special enough for you?"

"I'd prefer a room with a lock." There was no way she'd be able to sleep in the same room as him.

"The bathroom locks if you'd rather sleep in the tub."

She actually considered the suggestion, but couldn't stand the idea of him mocking her for it. "Such a charming offer. I'll keep it in mind," she said, putting on an obviously fake smile.

"Speaking of, I'll take a quick shower. Feel free to make yourself at home. And by that I mean, don't touch *anything.*" Eyden didn't wait for a response as he got up and walked through the door next to the bedroom area.

Once he closed the door, Lora closed her eyes and exhaled slowly, trying to sort through the spiral of her thoughts. She sat down on the sofa and opened her backpack, unpacking some essential items. As she took a sip of her water, her phone vibrated. Lora could already guess what awaited her. It had been long enough for Maja to have gone to her house and make good on her promise.

Sure enough, when Lora checked her phone, she had a new message in her family group chat. It read, "Be safe. We love you.

Come back soon." It was her father who had written the message. Simple words that meant the world to her.

She wrote back, "Love you too. Be back as soon as I can."

Her brother replied, "I hope so."

Lora couldn't help but think his words had a double meaning. Did he solely hope she could come home soon? Or did he doubt she would come back as soon as she was able to?

She had decided to save her data when she received another message. This one wasn't in their group conversation, but in a private chat from her mother. "Don't tell anyone your secret. Stay yourself."

If only her whole deal with Eyden didn't rest on her secret. She hoped she'd be able to get away before he realised her deception. She didn't know what he would do if he found out. Leave her for dead? Leave her stranded in Liraen?

She supposed they were the same thing. After the fae and humans had come to an agreement, humans had been saved from enslavement, protected by the magical border. Yet she knew some humans had remained in Liraen when the border spell had separated their worlds again. No one ever spoke of the remaining humans who still lived in Liraen, if any had survived this long. Rumours were all she had. But those were enough to make her wish she would never be in their place.

Lora was entangled in a web of lies and she needed to adapt to Liraen to succeed. To escape this place with a cure, she needed to play along.

The thought of what she'd have to risk frightened her. She could already feel herself slipping away. In the last 24 hours, she had found out her mother was dying, decided to risk her own life, and crossed over into enemy territory. That had to change a person, for better or for worse.

CHAPTER 7

AMIRA

Amira opened her eyes to the sound of nearby bells ringing in her head. She didn't know by which miracle she had managed to sleep. Her exhausted body was probably the cause, although she was used to not sleeping much in Amryne.

Amira looked around the room. Meeting her gaze in the mirror facing her bed, she could see why nobody took her seriously. Physically, she was beautiful, but she lacked the interior flame that powerful fae had. Everyone who looked straight into her eyes would understand that she had no powers—nothing to defend herself, nothing to bring to the world.

Of course Wryen was a high-level fae. He often bragged he was a level five with his fire power even though their father had said he was most likely a level four. Without being officially tested, Wryen could pretend all he wanted. Royals were almost always high-level fae, either level fours or fives, so no one would dare question him.

She was lucky that royals didn't have to pass the Power Level

Identification test. It had saved her the humiliation of being forced to acknowledge her lack of power in front of everyone. Instead, she only had to deal with whispers and rumours. Most people attributed her lack of power to her bastard origins. *The bad seed is stronger than the good one*, she would hear them gossip.

For the High King Contest, the selected fae would have to prove their power level in front of all the courts. If they appeared weak, they would not only lose the contest, but would also be humiliated in front of the most important fae in Liraen.

Karwyn's power was well known amongst the courts. Amira had been told that with his air magic, there was no doubt he would follow in his father's footsteps and officially become high king.

Putting her feet on the ground, Amira stretched a bit before leaving her bed. She walked around the room aimlessly. The cobalt blue wallpaper made her feel like she was inside a jewellery box, a beautiful cage fit for a princess. Two large windows overlooked the palace's indoor garden. She glanced at the heavy foliage partly covering a large fountain before surveying her room.

The furniture was simple but of high quality: a large bed with a silver-ornamented frame, a wardrobe made of expensive carbon black wood, a small desk with a matching chair, a dressing table, and one empty bookcase. She looked at the bare shelves knowing that she didn't have anything to fill them with. Her brother had only allowed her to take clothes, claiming that her new role didn't call for much else.

The only personal things she had managed to hide inside one of her dresses were her mother's letters and a nacre comb her father had gifted her on her fifteenth birthday, a few days before his death. Both of these things were now displayed on her desk. She was relieved that Wryen hadn't taken them but she knew it was only a matter of time before somebody would want to steal the last objects she cared for. She had to find a place to hide them.

One of the silver squares on top of the pillars of her bed could be unscrewed. The pillar was hollow and the space was big enough to fit the rolled-up letters and the small comb. She screwed the square back on and immediately felt relieved. Knowing her most cherished belongings were close to her would make it easier to find sleep.

Still, she was all alone now, with no one in her corner to fight for her. Even her strong-willed mother had been kept far away. Amira closed her eyes. She didn't want to think of the last time she had seen her mother but she couldn't stop herself from picturing it.

Wryen had taken her to the minuscule house, tucked between much bigger villas. Amira knew that her mother didn't care about the size of the house or the lack of luxury it presented, she only cared about the distance between her house and the palace where Amira lived. That was the only complaint she had made when Wryen forced her to live there. Of course, Amira's half-brother hadn't listened. Amira's mother had merely been the king's mistress; once her lover was dead, she held no power.

When Amira had entered the house for what would be the last time, her mother's face had lit up before she quickly hid her smile as Wryen entered the house. She had made tea for the three of them and Wryen had complained about the sour taste caused by the public water. Amira's mother had offered to make him another one but he ignored her, focusing his attention on the pain he could read in his half-sister's eyes.

Wryen had announced the upcoming wedding and immediately added that only royal members of the family would be invited. Amira's mother's face had remained blank. But before she had closed the door behind Wryen and Amira, she had grabbed her daughter's hand and squeezed it so tight that Amira's eyes started to water. She had seen tears flooding her mother's cheeks. Silently, they had promised each other to keep in touch as much as possible. In the carriage, Amira had cried in front of Wryen. She had never felt smaller and she was sure he had never felt bigger.

Leaving that memory in the past, Amira decided to write a quick letter to her mother just to say she was okay. She wished Wryen would have allowed her to possess a runia back in Amryne. The spelled device let fae communicate with each other even when they were out of earshot. But Wryen swore they were just as cursed as the beings who spelled them. It was half true, she thought. Even if they had been blessed, he still wouldn't have let her have it. Now it wouldn't be of much use anyway, given the distance between the kingdom of Allamyst and the Turosian one. A letter would have to do.

Amira sighed and turned her gaze to the empty paper. She didn't feel guilty about lying to her mother, as she knew that she would only feel more hopeless if she found out her daughter was still truly unhappy.

Her pen glided easily on the thick paper. Just a few simple words, nothing too detailed so that her mother wouldn't be able to read between the lines. She would have to ask Nalani to send her letter.

As she thought of her, the maid opened the door behind her. "Good day, my lady."

"Good morning, Nalani."

"It is way past morning, princess. I brought you some late lunch. I figured you'd be hungry by now."

She carried a metallic tray to Amira and put it on the desk next to her. Amira wrinkled her nose at the purple stew.

"It's made with indioberries and deer meat," explained Nalani.

Amira took a spoonful of the sauce. When the hot liquid touched her tongue, she realised how famished she was.

Nalani watched her eat with a satisfied smile. "I was afraid you were going to let yourself waste away. I noticed your tearful eyes yesterday."

Most of the royals would have punished Nalani for speaking so freely, but Amira could sense the motherly concern in her voice. It almost made her feel like a little girl again, someone whose only worry was to make her parents proud. She wondered how her father would feel about her current situation. Most of the time, she avoided thinking about him too much. His death was painful, but the way he'd treated her mother was also difficult to forget.

Zain Rosston had never made his relationship with Amira's mother official and she couldn't help but suffer from the situation. She was still grateful to have been recognised by the king and raised at the palace, but she wished things would have been different for her mother, that she would have been treated with respect after her father's death.

"What are you going to do with the rest of your afternoon, princess?" asked Nalani once Amira pushed her plate away.

"Well, I don't know. What am I expected to do?"

"The king is usually very busy during the day. I don't think you'll be able to see him today."

She sought out Nalani's gaze with curiosity. "Is he having a meeting with his advisors?"

Nalani looked a bit lost. "It's possible. Truthfully, I am not familiar with His Majesty's schedule. I'm just the maid."

"Of course, I'm sorry, Nalani." She wondered if Wryen was with the king. It was the only explanation for why he hadn't bothered her yet today. Or maybe he had already left?

"Oh, it's all right, princess. I'm sure you'll soon be informed of all your future duties."

Amira hoped so. Now that she was away from her brother, she was planning to actually have an impact on her life—and even on Karwyn's, despite their conversation yesterday. She just needed to prove to him that she could be useful. Her father had often remarked that she shared his wits.

The silver and turquoise bracelet Karwyn had gifted her was displayed on her desk. Staring at it, Amira wondered if a present could be the way to Karwyn's heart. But what could she get him when she had no silver to her name? Ever since her father's death, Wryen had taken control of her finances.

Faced with the issue of money, Amira turned to her maid. "Nalani, if you wanted to give someone a present but you had no silver, what would you get?"

Nalani pondered. "Well, it depends, who is this gift for? A friend?"

"It's for my fiancé." Amira lowered her eyes, ashamed of her lack of means.

"I'm sure your brother will have your silver delivered soon," Nalani said, misreading her troubles. The maid picked up a brush and started smoothing Amira's dark locks. "My mother always told my sisters and I that what matters is the gesture, not the object itself. It should come from your heart." She put a gentle hand over Amira's heart.

Amira smiled, a flicker of hope flowing through her. "You're right, Nalani."

She let the maid finish brushing her hair, the motion soothing. Her eyes wandered to the window and she caught sight of the indoor garden again. An idea formed in her mind.

CHAPTER 8

ろ

LORA

"It could be worse," Eyden said as he took in Lora's appearance. She was wearing the clothes that he had given her. The wide-cut black trousers made from a rather flimsy material were a bit short on her and the simple olive shirt clung to her curves more than it was supposed to. Lora wondered who these clothes were meant for. Someone shorter, it seemed.

"It could be better. Don't you think people might be suspicious of why my own clothes don't fit me?" she asked.

"Not if they think you're poor. It's not unusual." Eyden made his way towards his walk-in closet as he continued talking, "Especially for level ones, which is what they'll assume you are."

This was news to Lora. From what she'd gathered, the fae had it quite good. But that was back when they had humans to exploit, humans they could force to do their labour. Her knowledge of fae history mostly stemmed from testimonies from enslaved humans who had returned to Earth right before the border spell was cast.

"Is poverty such a big issue here?" she asked as Eyden returned, carrying a beige jacket.

"That's an understatement."

He handed her the piece of clothing. "Here, it has inside pockets. If you're taking your phone device, make sure it stays silent."

Lora gratefully took the jacket. "Our research doesn't indicate it's that bad. Only for the humans who used to live here."

Eyden's eyes gleamed. "And here I thought you knew everything?"

Lora turned her head to hide her scowl instead of leaning into his taunt. She would learn more soon enough. The fatigue made her eyes feel heavy. She hadn't planned on sleeping at all, but exhaustion had taken over. She had fallen asleep on the couch, still fully dressed with her pocket knife clutched in her hand. When Lora had woken up a short while later, she had cursed herself for being so careless. But when she had scanned the flat for any danger, she'd sighed in relief at the sight of Eyden sound asleep on his bed. He clearly didn't regard her as a threat at all.

Lora slipped the jacket on and regarded herself in the mirror. Besides the new, or borrowed, clothes, she had braided a section of her straight, shoulder-length hair on her left side and had added dark grey eyeshadow that made her eyes appear brighter, more striking.

"You'll pass," Eyden said as their eyes met in the mirror. "It's lucky your eyes have a uniqueness about them. Not quite green nor blue." His eyes slid away from hers. "Just don't look anyone in the eyes for too long or they might suspect."

Eyes were the most telling physical attribute for fae. To

humans, their eyes were unnaturally coloured. Lora had gotten more than one remark about her bright aquamarine eyes in her lifetime, but they weren't unusual enough to raise real suspicion. It had made her uncomfortable, her mother even more so, but now it came in handy.

"Got it." Lora didn't want to attract any attention.

"And speak as little as possible."

He had already told her so earlier but she bit out, "Fine." She grabbed her backpack. "Is there anything I should know about this healer we're meeting? Will they take some of my jewellery as payment?"

He went to put on his own coat, a light black layer. "Leave that here. I've got it handled."

Before she could ask more, Eyden opened the front door and gestured for her to walk out. Familiar anxiety was building up inside her and she pushed it down to the best of her ability.

This would be different than yesterday. This would be walking in broad daylight. There was no hiding away anymore, only hiding in plain sight. If it worked.

The first thing Lora noticed was the pleasant weather. The sun was out but there were enough clouds that when she looked up towards the sky, it didn't blind her. She was warm enough in her jacket yet wouldn't be cold either if she were to take it off. September in England was much colder and windier, as Bournchester was a seaside town.

Then she took in the small buildings lining the street. The architecture was a stark contrast to what she was used to in her hometown. It was much simpler and almost unified here. The paths between buildings were rather narrow compared to the streets she grew up on. Since the fae weren't known for being travellers and didn't use cars but rather settled for horses, it made sense to her that they wouldn't put in as much work for road systems.

Her attention shifted to the few fae walking around, going about their day. Some were wearing similar clothes to hers. Some looked to be worse off, their clothes stained and worn out. Her eyes landed on a young girl, grime dirtying her face as she clutched a small bag to her chest and walked the streets by herself. She looked too young to be on her own.

Other fae looked more well-dressed. Lora assumed they had more silver to spare and were most likely higher level fae. None of them seemed to pay any attention to her and Eyden.

As they rounded a corner, she could make out a larger building in the distance. It was higher up, on a small mountain of sorts. Lora squinted as she tried to make out more details.

"Is that the palace?" she guessed.

Eyden followed her gaze and replied, "Yes."

"Chrysa must be a pretty small town." She hadn't expected to see the palace, as they weren't in the capital, Parae, but rather in a neighbouring town by the border. She had found an old photograph of the impressive building once during her research for a paper. Lora wondered how similar it would look from up close nowadays.

"Parae is the next town over. You can reach it on foot quite fast, including the palace," Eyden replied in a low voice. "It's why there are so many damn guards around."

And sure enough, Lora noticed two guards crossing the street ahead of them. Their black and turquoise uniforms shone in the sunlight. They each had swords sheathed at their sides.

The image made Lora uneasy but thankfully, they disappeared down the path.

Lora's fingers twitched. She wished she could write this all down, document the history she was experiencing firsthand. But it had to wait.

"We're here." Eyden pointed towards a small tavern to their right.

This wasn't exactly the meeting point she had imagined. It seemed too public for such a secretive case. Yet Eyden looked unbothered by the small fae crowd as they entered the building. Lora let her eyes wander, taking in the scene. It was around noon and many fae were enjoying their lunch or already drinking. They had gathered in small groups, sitting at round tables, eating some sort of vegetable dish.

Eyden ushered her towards the bar at the end of the room. Only two fae were seated on the high bar stools with a couple of spaces between them. Eyden approached a young woman. She was taking a sip of her steaming drink, sitting up straight, her sleek dark brown hair flowing down her back.

"Halie," Eyden said as he stopped close to her, leaning against the bar.

Lora stood awkwardly next to him, keeping her distance, letting Eyden take the lead as promised.

The fae turned her head lightly to the side, taking in Eyden. A pleasantly surprised smile formed on her lips. "Eyden, what brings you here?" She set down her mug, dark liquid shimmering inside.

Eyden returned the smile, more polite than genuine to Lora's observation. "I was looking for you, actually."

"Really? Miss me already?" Her smile turned teasing.

Eyden's smile brightened a bit. "I'm in need of a favour." He shifted, his smile fading as he looked at Lora before returning his attention to Halie.

Halie's vibrant emerald eyes travelled to Lora, irritation lingering in her gaze. "And who's this?"

"This is Lora. We're working on a trade deal together," Eyden replied matter-of-factly.

Lora took a tiny step towards her and almost extended her hand before she remembered it wasn't a fae tradition. "It's nice to meet you, Halie," she said, trying to muster up a polite smile. If Halie was the answer to her predicament, then she would suck it up and play nice.

"It's Sahalie to you," she replied, her warm tone gone.

Maybe it would be more difficult to act friendly than she had already anticipated.

Eyden either didn't notice the tension or decided to ignore it. He leaned in close to Sahalie. "How about we get a table?" he said, eyeing the small, isolated table in the back corner.

The implication was clear and Lora was itching to put some distance between her and the other customers. There were too many fae surrounding her. She felt like a fraud, as if at any moment, one of them would see right through her disguise.

"If you buy me another caftee," Sahalie said, seeking Eyden's eyes.

He nodded, already signalling the bartender. He got one for himself too and Lora ordered a water, not trusting any other substances in this enemy territory. Sahalie's caftee smelled like basic coffee with a hint of something sweet that Lora couldn't quite place.

As they moved to the table, Lora took in Sahalie's more elegant outfit. She wore similar trousers but they looked to be made out of a more comfortable, expensive material. They had a shiny dark grey stripe along the outer side of her legs that matched the colour of her thin-strapped top.

Sahalie chose the seat closest to Eyden, leaving Lora to sit opposite them. As she took in the two of them, sitting close together, their shoulders almost touching, Lora wondered what their history was. It wasn't any of her business but she couldn't help but try to assemble the pieces they had each revealed.

Eyden angled himself further away from Sahalie as if he wanted to be able to keep an eye on both women at the same time. His pale eyes shifted between them as he said, "Lora here has some information about the human virus that's plaguing Earth. You've heard about it, right?"

"Some rumours, yes. Why does it matter?" Sahalie replied. She seemed more bored than surprised by his question. It was exactly as Lora had imagined. She didn't feel an ounce of sympathy coming from Sahalie. Anger was starting to rise inside her, boiling her blood, yet she remained composed, tuning out her enraged thoughts.

Eyden kept his face indifferent. "I have a buyer who'll pay handsomely for a cure. I was hoping you'd help us out."

She seemed to consider his words. "How did you even know I'd be here?"

Eyden put on a smile again. This time, it looked genuine and softened his features. "It's Saturday. You always come here to sober up after a night out."

At that, Sahalie's teasing smile returned in full force. "You should've joined me. We could've had some fun."

Eyden broke their eye contact. "Another time, maybe."

"How about tonight?" Sahalie shifted her gaze towards Lora, taking in her full appearance, blatantly unimpressed. "Or are you otherwise occupied?" she asked, but it sounded as if she was joking.

"I'm afraid I have to take care of this trading deal first. If you can help us with this, it'd speed up the process."

Sahalie took a sip of her drink, making them wait for her reply. "All right, tell me more, then. What is this mysterious virus, exactly? How does it kill these fragile humans?"

Eyden turned to Lora, silently signalling that it was time to leap into her explanation. She hesitantly said, "The virus leads to blood clots that eventually multiply so rapidly, doctors—healers—can't stop them from reaching their patients' lungs and ultimately killing them."

"What an inconvenience that must be." Sahalie's words were utterly emotionless. "I can try to mix something up but I'm not sure how much help I can be without a test subject."

Lora had prepared herself for this moment, yet she still had to force out the words. "You'll keep this conversation secret?" she asked.

"For Eyden? Yes."

"I can't give you a test subject but I have the next best thing." She took out the vial filled with her mother's blood from her jacket pocket. She could feel Eyden's eyes on her. Lora remained focused on Sahalie as she held up the vial. "Infected blood. You can try it out with this, right?"

Lora sneaked a glance at Eyden. She could tell he was trying to hide his shock. He put on a mask of disinterest but she had seen that flicker of surprise.

Sahalie examined the blood and reached for the vial to get a closer look. Lora handed it over reluctantly, never letting it out of her sight.

"This will help, yes." Sahalie opened the vial and let a drop fall on the palm of her hand. Lora was taken aback by Sahalie's actions but quickly returned her expression to neutral. In her world, no one would dare touch infected blood like this. But Sahalie wasn't human, she had no reason to be afraid of being infected. Lora supposed she didn't have to be either. She had never even gotten the flu.

Sahalie closed her eyes in concentration. "I can feel it's a persistent virus. My magic isn't strong enough to separate the virus from the blood and heal it. It seems to me that this virus is infecting the blood much like a poison. It's fascinating, actually." She opened her eyes, meeting Lora's expectant ones, but then shifted her gaze to Eyden as she said, "I've worked on poisons before with the help of a healing crystal that channels power. It's called green aventurine. It's quite rare, but not impossible to get."

"The name sounds familiar," Eyden said.

"Ilario gave me the one I used last time. I don't have it anymore."

Eyden seemed to ponder Sahalie's words as a sense of realisation came over him. "I must have seen it at the market, then."

"If I had that and some arentae, it might be sufficient to mix a cure. Assuming you'll cut me in on the reward?"

"I'll make it worth your while, don't worry," Eyden replied, a lazy grin taking over his face.

Sahalie smiled in answer, her bright emerald eyes blazing. But the smile faded quickly as she focused on Lora again. She must have felt Lora's stare. "How did you get this blood anyway?" Sahalie asked, light suspicion reflecting in her eyes.

"I have my sources," Lora replied, masking the nervous feeling settling over her.

"Mhm, interesting." This was the longest Sahalie had looked at her and although Lora hated to break first, she lowered her gaze and pretended to be unbothered.

"Well, we better go. The sooner this deal is done, the better," Eyden said, giving Sahalie a wink before downing the last of his caftee.

Lora held out her hand, palm up. "I'll take that back now." She pointed her chin up as she gestured to the vial in Sahalie's grip.

Sahalie made no move. "I could study it more in the meantime. While you're off getting my supplies."

"No, thank you." When Sahalie remained still, her slender fingers wrapped around the vial, Lora added, "It's not yours to keep."

Sahalie looked as if she was about to argue but then Eyden

said, "Halie, give her the vial. We'll meet again once we have everything, okay?"

"All right. You know how to reach me," she replied, grinning at him before giving Lora one last sceptical look as she handed over the vial.

Eyden returned the smile and that was the extent of his goodbye. The two of them stood up and made for the door in a quick exit.

Lora followed Eyden's hurried steps, ignoring the fae they walked past, every step determined as she hoped it would bring them closer to the cure, closer to the end of this undesired trip.

Back to the place where she belonged.

CHAPTER 9

LORA

They walked in unexpected silence. Lora had more than one question churning in her head but she waited, unsure if anyone on the streets would overhear them since Eyden had chosen not to speak and they were still walking in broad daylight. As usual, he barely glanced in her direction as he led the way. *Usual.* No, this was not to become her new normal. She was going to be gone from this land soon enough.

"You never mentioned the vial," Eyden said, breaking their silence. They were now nearing the woods on the outskirts of the town, leaving the wandering fae folk behind.

Lora looked around and when she was satisfied she didn't see anyone who could spy on their conversation, she replied, "I know." She didn't owe him an explanation. She'd reveal her cards when it was necessary.

Before Eyden had a chance to react, all the questions she'd collected over the past hour spilled out. "Arentae is a healing herb, right? Do you think we'll get both of the items Sahalie wanted?"

Eyden looked over his shoulder. His face didn't give away any emotions besides his calculating stare. "That's a lot of questions for someone who hasn't answered mine yet."

"You didn't ask me anything. You made an observation."

Eyden glared at her, emotions seeping into his expression, that heavy gaze challenging her. "Okay, then. Why didn't you bring it up? Would've been good to know."

Lora didn't break his stare. "It must've slipped my mind," she said innocently.

Eyden shifted his bright eyes to the small path leading into the woods. "I don't think there's much that escapes you."

"Are you already admitting that I'm smarter than you? I thought it'd at least take you a day. Maybe I underestimated you, after all."

Eyden slowed down again as he half turned to her and let out a rich laugh. The sound echoed in Lora's bones, filling her with a pleasant warmth. She hadn't heard him laugh like this before. Free. Genuine. So *human.* She immediately scowled at her own thoughts. Eyden noticed and his laughter died abruptly. The joy in the air was sucked away as he picked up his pace again.

"I admitted no such thing," he replied a bit later, his back to her. "And to answer your question, I know who to ask, so we should be able to get both the crystal and the herb. Just let me do the talking. And if you have any more secrets that could help us, you'd better tell me now."

"There's nothing else to tell." Nothing she was willing to share, at least.

Eyden looked sceptical but didn't push it as they broke into the small clearing Lora vaguely recognised from the night before. In the daylight, it was easier for Lora to take in the details. Tiny midnight-blue flowers grew next to the massive oak tree in front them. There was no proof in sight that this was, indeed, the right spot, but as Eyden stopped, she knew it must be.

He kneeled on the ground and started to whisper. Lora's ears strained to make out his mumbling but she couldn't decipher the foreign words.

Eyden rose as the familiar entrance to the market appeared out of thin mist.

"How exactly does this work?" Lora gestured to the slim wooden door.

"That's not for you to know."

"Why? Because I'm human?"

"Yes, and I'd be a fool to trust you." Of course, he wouldn't share the fae's secrets. She wouldn't give away her own either. Yet it still drove her mad, not knowing and having to depend on Eyden instead of figuring it out herself.

Though she could feel her frustration rising up, enhancing her temper, she said as calmly as she could muster, "The feeling's mutual."

"Now that we've established the obvious, shall we go in?" Eyden pointedly looked at the door before addressing Lora again. "Keep the vial close to you and keep your distance from anyone else."

Lora was about to agree when a rush of nerves hit her. "Are there going to be more fae than last night?"

"Yes." Eyden's eyes drifted to the side of her jacket where her hand rested over her pocket. "It might be better if you give me the vial for the time being. Actually, it'll most definitely be safer with me."

Stunned, Lora moved her hand to cover the vial in a secure grip. "Didn't we just agree that neither one of us trusts the other?"

"Everyone with the code can go in. There's no other security. The market is technically illegal, so if something gets stolen, you either accept it or get it back yourself." He sought out her eyes. "I'm pretty sure you'd rather not lose the only thing that can get you what you want."

Lora returned his steely glare with one of her own. "Do I have to repeat myself? I'm not foolish enough to trust you with this."

He shook his head, his dark hair shifting with the movement, reflecting the soft sunlight filtering through the trees. "It's not about trust. It's about increasing your chances of not losing it. If there's one thing you can count on, it's that I'm no easy target to pickpocket."

"What makes you the expert?"

"Years of being a skilled thief." The proud smirk on his face was both irritating and amusing.

Lora furrowed her eyebrows. So, she was supposed to put her trust in someone who was not only a fae, but also a common thief? He could call it whatever he wanted to, agreeing with him still required a certain amount of trust that Lora didn't have in her to give. Especially not to him—a *fae*.

"What will it be, special one?" Eyden asked.

"I'll take my chances." She thought she saw disappointment dart over his face, just for a second. Maybe he did want to steal it from her. She swiftly suppressed the thought and shifted her focus to the next step. The black market. "Will I be fine without the cloak?"

"There are a lot of fae wandering around the market around this time. They'll assume you're a buyer." He looked her up and down, the smirk gone. "Or someone in desperate need of some silver, trying to sell something to a trader."

Lora glowered. "Let's get this over with."

Eyden opened the door, a glint in his eyes. "After you."

Lora immediately noted the shift in the air as they stepped into the stone corridor. Gone was the quiet, peaceful atmosphere from the woods; in its place grew the hustling noises of a busy market. When they rounded the corner, a mass of people came into view. Fae were hurrying along, walking in all directions. Some looked satisfied, clutching various items that Lora couldn't all identify. Others were arguing with fae traders, silver coins and notes catching the light.

If only she had her cloak from last night to hide behind. Too many eyes were on her. Never for long, merely passing glances as she walked beside Eyden into the heart of the chaos, but it was enough to leave her on edge. She was all too aware of the vial lying heavy in her pocket. Lora was paranoid of anyone she crossed paths with, Eyden's words echoing like a steady warning.

She noticed several fae nodding at Eyden as they walked past trading booths. Eyden returned the gesture without breaking his stride, fitting in seamlessly with the crowd. Lora wondered if he'd ever stolen from any of the fae he had greeted. If he had, he was probably proud of it.

Lora followed Eyden's gaze to a dark-haired fae standing behind one of the wooden booths.

As they got closer, she could see he was finishing up a deal, handing an onyx box to a young female fae who eagerly accepted it as she put a pouch of silver on the table.

"Begone in fortune, my dear," the trader said. The girl nodded and all but sprinted past them.

The fae took the silver and stored it somewhere Lora couldn't see. When he looked back up, he noticed Eyden approaching his booth. A friendly smile stretched across his face.

"Good day for trade, isn't it? I love busy weekends." He shifted his easy smile to Lora, who kept close to Eyden, the side pocket with the vial next to him. Protected from other thieves, she hoped.

"I'm hoping you can make this a good one for us too," Eyden said, one corner of his mouth lifting up in a half smile. "Ilario, meet special Lora." He looked at her for a brief moment, but she was taking in Ilario's lively dark emerald eyes as they widened in surprise.

"It's just Lora," she clarified, smiling politely, hoping for a different result than their last meeting with one of Eyden's acquaintances.

Ilario's smile never faltered as he said, "Well, just Lora, it's a pleasure to meet you. Dare I ask how you two know each other? Eyden has never introduced me to anyone. I was beginning to think I'm his only friend."

She fought a laugh, but felt the urge to correct his assumption right away. "We're not friends." Ilario raised his eyebrows, his eyes questioning. "Or anything else," she added immediately. He didn't look convinced.

Eyden seemed amused at their interaction, now fighting his own grin. He leaned against the booth and simply said, "It's strictly business. Lora and I are working on procuring a special kind of remedy."

"Let me guess, you need some arentae?" Ilario asked, assuming correctly. Lora figured the trader must be familiar with healing magic and she wondered if he was a healer himself. She was under the impression that healers were quite rare, at least in Turosian. What were the chances Eyden knew two of them?

"A small amount should suffice," Eyden replied.

"I'm currently out of stock, but I was going to get more next week, after all the commotion from Falea Night is over. I'll set some aside for you. No problem."

Lora didn't think before she said, "I need it now." The eagerness in her voice caught Ilario's attention, his curious eyes searched her aquamarine ones. "I mean, *we* need it."

"The buyer put a time restraint on his offer," Eyden said, the lie running smoothly from his lips. Lora knew she needed to keep her surging panic under control, sealed shut.

"I can't make the trip before then. I'm sorry. But I'll drop it off at Eyden's or here as soon as I have it," Ilario said, looking at Lora apologetically. She pressed her lips together in a tight line, telling herself she needed to let Eyden handle it, as much as it pained her.

Eyden seemed to sense Lora's breaking restraint and took over again. "What if we got it ourselves?"

"You, who barely tells me anything, are asking me to share

my hidden sources?" Ilario asked. There was a lightness to his voice that made Lora think he wasn't all that bothered by the question.

"You know more about me than most people, Ilario."

"Well, I like to think so, but you're still a man of many mysteries." Interesting. Or not. It didn't make any difference to her, she assured herself.

Eyden tensed slightly, a subtle change that Lora almost didn't notice. "Are you really refusing to help us?"

"Of course not. I'll help, I'm just enjoying making you sweat." Ilario's grin widened. Eyden's mouth twitched at his friend's good-natured teasing, the tension leaving him as if it was never there to begin with. "Although you're always the one telling me I'm too trusting. No offense to you, just Lora." He turned to her for a short moment. "But tell me, Eyden, how can I trust that she won't take more than needed? Or go back again?"

Lora considered his phrasing. He was only concerned about her, a stranger, not Eyden. Was Eyden truly his friend or was Eyden playing Ilario, taking advantage of his apparent trusting nature? Lora wasn't sure what bothered her more, being unable to figure out Eyden's intentions or the fact that she was even thinking about this at all.

"I'll make sure of it. You have my word," Eyden said.

Ilario barely waited a second before he agreed. "All right. You remember where my parents' house is?"

"Yeah."

"We'll meet there, then I can give you directions more easily. I'm going there soon to help prepare for the feast."

Another mention of Falea Night. Lora had read about it but

it was never explained in great detail. Humans hadn't exactly been invited to take part in the festivities, but she knew Falea was the Goddess of Fortune and sort of the patron of Turosian. Lora tried to remember what else she had learned, but Ilario's next question disrupted her stream of thoughts.

"You're still doing your shift?" he asked.

"Of course," Eyden said quickly.

"All right." Ilario looked to Lora, who was mostly confused about what exactly they had agreed on. Ilario gave her an encouraging grin. "It'll all work out, don't worry. You'll get your hands on some arentae before you know it."

She was about to speak up but Eyden beat her to it. "There's one last thing. We need a crystal. Green aventurine."

Ilario's face fell. "Oh, that's going to be tricky, seeing as I sold my last one earlier today and I won't have more until spring."

Lora tried to channel some of Eyden's calmness and kept quiet again. "Do you know if anyone else sells them?" Eyden said, eyes fixed on Ilario.

Ilario considered the question and said, "Not that I know of, no. I'm sure there's someone, but if you don't know either, then it'll probably take some time to find out."

"Who bought the last one?"

"One of my regulars. Has a thing for expensive crystals. I don't think he'd sell it to you. Looks like the type that has more silver than either one of us will ever earn."

"We can at least try to make him an offer. I can be convincing." Eyden flashed him a quick grin. "Do you know where he went?"

"No," Ilario answered. Lora's heart fell, her pretend calmness threatening to shatter at any moment as her skin turned hot from panic. "But I know where he'll be." The feeling retracted enough to keep her still.

Eyden didn't pay her any attention as he continued the conversation. "And where's that?"

"He mentioned he's going to Caligo. There's a theme tonight. He seemed really excited about it. Honestly, even I was almost convinced to go. But I have my shift."

Eyden's displeasure was written clearly on his face. He let out a low breath and said, "Not exactly where I'd want to be tonight, but so be it." He shifted his head in Lora's direction. "We'll have to find this guy and come to an agreement. Another trade deal."

Something told her this wasn't going to be a regular trade meeting. "How will we find him?" Lora asked.

"He's pretty easy to find. His hair is dyed a mix of faint pink and white blond. He has incredible deep blue eyes—really pretty, by the way—and every time I've seen him he was wearing some sort of extravagant outfit. He has an expensive yet unusual sense of style. Very unique. Sticks out from any crowd," Ilario assured her.

"So we're looking for a handsome fellow with a love for edgy fashion?" Lora caught Eyden's quick glance, a flash of warning, and she realised her comment might have come off more British than she'd intended it to.

Ilario hesitated only for a few seconds, hopefully oblivious to her slight slip up. "That sums it up, yes." She wouldn't look his way as she pretended to study his booth. She had to remind herself to avoid eye contact as much as possible. "But even if you get the crystal, you won't be able to wield it yourself."

Eyden replied, "I already talked to Halie. She agreed to help us."

"Oh, you two are talking again?"

"We never stopped talking."

"You stopped"—he looked to Lora, who was still avoiding his gaze—"hanging out." Lora had a feeling she knew what he was implying. She had suspected all along and this confirmed her presumption. She only hoped their relationship wouldn't cause any unnecessary distractions to their mission.

"Doesn't mean she isn't up to earning some silver."

"Right. Strictly business again?" Ilario teased, a friendly laugh escaping him.

Eyden kept his calm. "Yes, business comes first."

"Well, since we're talking about silver, if you take a handful of arentae, that'll be around forty silver." That sounded quite expensive. Lora attempted to guess how much silver they'd have to spend in total. They'd need to pay for the crystal and compensate Sahalie for her work. Would she have enough with the jewellery she had taken to Liraen?

Eyden didn't seem to share her concerns. "Do you want it now?"

"No, it's all right. You can bring it to the house."

"I'll see you at the house, then." Eyden took a step back and faced the path they'd taken to get here. Lora guessed he wasn't much for goodbyes. She threw a quick smile in Ilario's direction then turned to follow Eyden.

Before they went any farther, Ilario added, "My parents will be glad to see you again."

Eyden looked over his shoulder, his voice taking on an

affectionate, mocking tone. "I think your parents are excited about any visitors."

Then he walked off, Lora following quickly after briefly glancing at Ilario's cheerful expression. "There might be some truth to that," he called after them.

Lora focused on the crowd ahead of them, the sound of Ilario's laugh fading behind them as the chatter took over.

CHAPTER 10

AMIRA

It had only been a minute since she had left her room and Amira was already lost. Most of the corridors looked the same and every time she encountered a door, they were either guarded by mean-looking guards or locked.

Amira wandered around the stone hallway, not knowing which path to take. At one point, she thought she'd recognised Karwyn's voice on the other side of the wall, but as she'd tried to find a door, she'd only encountered more dark walls.

Amira chose another path that seemed to lead outside. Dusk was already falling when she reached the beautiful indoor garden. The peaceful sound of the fountain made her feel at ease. She could smell sweet blossoms, different from the headier scents of Allamyst's flowers. Strolling around the garden, Amira found herself admiring the pastel colours. Everything seemed so soft, too soft for what she had seen of the palace. Hiking up her skirt, she started picking flowers to create a small bouquet.

As most fae from Allamyst, Amira had an eye for beauty.

Her hand reached for the prettiest flowers, the ones that shone brighter than the rest. She walked around the garden, picking flowers as she went, enjoying their ravishing colours and their subtle scent.

When Amira stopped in front of a large bush covered in tiny pink flowers, she sensed a presence behind her. Her heart raced in her chest and she nervously pulled at a strand of her hair. What if she wasn't allowed to pick the flowers? Slowly, she turned around, hiding the bouquet behind her back.

"Good afternoon, princess. I hope I didn't scare you. I wouldn't want to ruin your perfect complexion," Rhay said as he bowed his head.

The tension in Amira's shoulders vanished. "Not at all. I was just surprised to not be alone in this garden. It feels like no one ever comes here."

"Well, that's mostly true. Karwyn and the rest of the court barely visit this place. But I personally enjoy taking a break here from my father." Rhay searched her gaze. "And his constant reminder that I'm an utter failure," he added in a playful tone.

Amira was pleasantly surprised by his openness. "I'm sure your father is very proud of you."

"I can assure you he's not. But it doesn't stop me from enjoying myself. What about you, princess, are you enjoying yourself in Parae?"

Amira wondered if she should be honest. But Rhay was one of Karwyn's advisors and she wouldn't want to offend him—or for him to repeat anything to Karwyn.

"It's all brand new, so..." she started.

"So you're completely bored," Rhay said with an excitement

she hadn't expected. "I can understand that. I love Karwyn, but he can be very cold to most people. Plus, he absolutely doesn't know how to treat a lady. To be frank, life in the palace is very much focused on politics."

Amira stopped him. "Speaking of, shouldn't you be with Karwyn in the council room?"

Rhay looked surprised by her question and he lifted a perfectly shaped eyebrow as he replied, "Why would I be with him?"

"Aren't you one of his advisors?"

Rhay let out a scoff. "Only in name, love. To my father's despair, I enjoy throwing parties more than negotiating with neighbouring kingdoms. My parties are quite legendary, though, and invitation only." He gestured for her to come closer. Amira found herself leaning in before she even noticed she had moved. "Would you like to go to one of them?"

She thought about it for a minute. Maybe it would help her make important connections at court. Her eyes widened. "Is Karwyn going to be there?"

"Well, I wouldn't be able to have my parties if Karwyn wasn't invited. Yet he doesn't come very often. It's not really his style. He's more of a loner, you know?"

Amira had also been quite a loner, but it wasn't by choice. "I see."

A bell rang six times in the distance. Rhay looked behind him, obviously late to something.

"It's settled, then. You're invited to the one I'm throwing tomorrow." He looked her up and down with a disapproving look. "Your dresses are lovely, but I'll send you something a bit less...formal."

"You don't have to." Amira blushed.

"Nonsense, I'll give you some options. Plus, as everyone here knows, I have an extraordinary flair for fashion." His eyes glowed with pride. "Before I go, I have one question."

Amira froze. "Yes?"

"Who's the bouquet for?" he said with a wink.

Amira let out a relieved laugh and moved her hand from behind her back. "It's for Karwyn."

Rhay bit his lip. "Sorry to break it to you, love, but that's a shit idea. Karwyn hates flowers. They're too colourful for his moody self. Plus, they remind him of his mother."

Amira's face dropped as she looked at her beautiful bouquet. It was a stupid idea. What had she been thinking, that a bouquet would impress the interim high king who seemed to have no interest in a companion?

"You should keep it for yourself. It fits your beauty." He gently touched her arm, sending some comforting warmth to her heart. "Apologies, princess, but I have to go now. I'm conducting a very important experiment tonight in Chrysa."

Amira's interest peaked. "Where's Chrysa?" The town sounded familiar.

"The town is right at the border. It's quite small, but definitely full of surprises. I should take you there some day."

Amira was definitely intrigued. Maybe her time in the Turosian kingdom would be better than expected.

"I'll let you enjoy the garden in peace," Rhay said as he brushed invisible dust off his shiny magenta jacket. "See you at nine bells tomorrow night."

Amira bowed her head and when she looked up again, Rhay was already gone.

CHAPTER 11

LORA

Lora had been waiting at Eyden's flat for hours now. He had left pretty quickly after they got back from the market around noon, mumbling something about some business he needed to take care of. He hadn't left her much time to question him as he grabbed a bag from his closet and dashed out the door, only looking at her long enough to tell her to stay put.

To say she didn't appreciate his behaviour would be an understatement. At the very least, it gave her some time to explore his place. She wasn't above snooping around.

So that's how she had spent the time, looking at drawer after drawer and coming up empty. There was nothing that gave an inkling of who Eyden really was and what his life looked like beyond the glimpses Lora had seen so far. If this flat represented his life, it was a reflection of a pretty empty one, decorated with a chic, soulless design.

There was no second mystery bag anywhere and she had

turned over the walk-in closet. She might have seen more of his wardrobe than she'd intended to.

All in all, her search didn't satisfy her curiosity of Eyden or the fae lifestyle in general. Still, she had taken it upon herself to write down in her phone every observation she had made these last few days.

The only interesting thing in the flat she took note of was that, as her research had indicated, the fae didn't have electricity. The lights in the flat were powered by magic, she assumed, as they weren't plugged into anything or battery-powered. There were also a couple of old-fashioned lanterns next to the fireplace that could be lit to add more warm light.

The fae did, thankfully, have a plumbing system. Lora was staring at the bathtub that doubled as a shower now, yearning to use it but hesitating, as she strongly disliked the idea of putting herself in a more vulnerable position. But she would probably not get a better opportunity anytime soon. Eyden wasn't here and the bathroom did have a lock. Walking around underground had left her with a feeling of dust and dirt on her skin.

Ignoring the opposing arguments swirling in her mind, Lora grabbed her change of clothes from her backpack and took all her crucial belongings with her to the bathroom. The small pocket knife that she had been keeping close to her had been placed next to her phone in her pocket. She decided to take it with her into the shower. Carrying it around gave her a sense of security. Lora was aware that it was only an illusion, as it would do little damage, if any, to a fae. Only weapons forged from the gemstone almandine could mortally wound them. But the fantasy of safety was enough to keep her from freaking out every minute and that was a win in Lora's opinion.

The water felt refreshing as she scrubbed at the dirt on her, worries going through her head. She wished she could clean her mind too.

She wanted to wash off all the scenarios she was imagining about how this could turn really bad, really quickly. Feeling anxious, she hurriedly exited the shower.

Dressed in her usual attire, skinny jeans and a comfy light blue sweater, Lora went on a search for food. Since crossing over, she had barely eaten anything. She was wary of any food Eyden had offered and had settled for only eating the plain bread he had given her.

When she opened the fridge, she didn't see many options. She had already opened every drawer in the kitchen so she knew there wasn't much food there either except for more bread and some items she didn't recognise.

Her stomach rumbled loudly and that was all the motivation she needed to get to it. She found a pan and took out the eggs from the fridge. Lora hadn't inherited her mum's cooking skills, but even she could make an omelette if need be.

Placing the pan on the gas stove, she took a look at the dials and noticed it didn't seem the same as she was used to. She turned it up anyway and a small flame appeared. Satisfied, Lora cracked open an egg and watched it sizzle in the pan, her stomach turning in anticipation.

The sound of jingling keys made her turn to the door just as Eyden walked in. His gaze landed on her but quickly shifted to the stove behind her.

"Fuck!" he shouted as he rushed towards her.

Lora turned back around in confusion and her fingers almost grazed the now burning pan. She let out a surprised gasp and took a step back on instinct and bumped into Eyden, who pushed her to the side. He switched off the stove and grabbed the pan, dumping it into the sink as he let cold water extinguish the flames.

"I leave you alone for a few hours and you decide to burn down my apartment?" He looked furious, but was that amusement she could hear underneath the anger?

"I was making an omelette." Said omelette was now a black blob of nothing, drowning in water.

Eyden gave her a look as if to say *please elaborate.*

"I didn't even turn up the heat that much. I think you should check your stove. It's clearly malfunctioning."

"Did you press the confirm button?" Eyden asked, eyes roaming over the kitchen.

"The what?"

"The stove is spelled to quickly increase heat until you confirm the temperature."

Lora didn't understand why he felt the need to spell a stove. The concept was utterly foreign to her. And how had he managed it? It must be the work of a witch. The word *witch* made her pause. As far as she knew, witches were all but extinct. The fae saw them as unnatural. While humans were simply unblessed by the fae's gods, witches were cursed beings who were either used by fae to do their bidding and create spells or killed off. Lora wondered if Eyden acquired spelled items through the black market.

"Well, that's...stupid," she concluded.

"How exactly is it stupid? It's much faster and practical than whatever stoves you use."

"It's a fire hazard."

"Only if you don't know how to use it."

Why would she? It's not like history books talked about such insignificant things as stoves. "If you're waiting for an apology, you'll get none. I was hungry. Did you want me to starve?"

Eyden grabbed a bar of soap and began washing his hands. There was soot all over him. Only now did Lora realise he had grabbed the pan with no hesitation. It hadn't left a wound behind. If it had burned him, he didn't show it and it must already be healed.

"I know humans are pretty fragile, but as far as I know, dying of starvation takes more time than that."

"Still need to eat," she replied dryly. For once, she was in no mood to argue.

"That's your great comeback?" Eyden turned off the tap and dried his hands. "Disappointing, but you'll be happy to know that I've actually considered that."

He walked back to the door. Lora noticed that his duffle bag from earlier was lying forgotten on the floor. Eyden moved his bag to the kitchen table. Lora regarded it with curiosity as he unknotted the top. He pulled out two small bowls, the tops covered with paper.

"Here you go," he said.

The smell of food invaded Lora's senses as Eyden removed the covers and revealed some sort of rice and vegetable dish. Eyden handed her a wooden spoon. She made no move to eat.

"I thought you were starving." Eyden looked at her expectantly, then lightly shook his head in frustration. He grabbed a spoon full of food from her bowl, ate it quickly, and caught her surprised glare. "See, no poison or whatever you're thinking of."

"It doesn't prove anything. What if it doesn't affect you because you're fae?"

Eyden stared at her. "You're impossible, you know that, right? Starve if you want to, but can you do it after our deal is done?"

On cue, Lora's stomach rumbled again. "Right. Once we're done, I'll be just another insignificant human." She swallowed her anger as she focused on the food in front of her. What did he have to gain by poisoning her? Not much. Not until he knew her secret. Besides, her unfortunate fae side would most likely hinder any poisoning attempts.

Reluctantly, Lora picked up her spoon and took a small bite. The taste was intense, not bad, but a bit overwhelming.

Before she knew it, she had eaten more than half of it. She looked up to find Eyden watching her, a small smile playing on his lips. She wasn't entirely sure if that was a good thing.

"What are you smiling at?" she asked, taking a break from eating.

"I'm glad I'm getting no more arguments." He took a big bite and seemed to savour the taste.

"Oh, I'm only taking a dinner break. Don't get used to it."

Eyden's smile increased a smidge. "I wouldn't expect anything else."

Lora couldn't help herself as the corners of her mouth tipped up. A quiet moment of short-lived peace. Then it was gone as they both dug back into their food, ignoring each other.

When both of them were done, Eyden stood up and opened his bag further. "I got you some options to wear for tonight. Well, two. Dresses aren't cheap."

Lora looked up at the mention of money. "That reminds me, should I pay Ilario with my jewellery?"

"I'll take care of it. Give me the jewellery and I'll eventually trade it and get back the silver I'm spending on you." He met her eyes, steel gaze blazing. "And more once our deal is done."

She ignored that last part and was about to ask how much silver he would get for the jewellery when Eyden pulled out a shiny emerald dress. She immediately noticed that there wasn't much fabric to it. It was tiny, strapless, and had multiple cut-outs on the sides. Lora rarely even wore dresses or skirts and if she did, they weren't considered bold. This dress was a whole other level. She would never have chosen it for herself.

Eyden hung it over the chair next to him and took out the second dress. This one was steel grey and would probably flow to her knees. It had long sleeves that were cuffed at the wrists and made of a more sheer material. The piece of clothing sparkled in the light and Lora noticed that this dress would also expose some skin, but it was modest compared to the first option.

She pointed at the dress. "This one."

He laid the dress across the back of another chair. "A safe choice."

Lora eyed the green dress. "The other one is barely even a dress. A towel covers more."

Eyden shrugged. "It's fashion, so I'm told."

"I don't care about fashion as long as I'm blending in. What kind of theme does this event have anyway?"

"No idea."

How were they supposed to blend in when he didn't know the specifics? Irritated, she asked, "What have you been doing, then?"

He flashed her another steely look. "I had business to do. Someone has to provide the silver, right?"

She hated feeling dependent, needing his help at every turn. He must have known she wouldn't have a good argument for this, so Lora decided not to give him the satisfaction of answering. She picked up the dress and her backpack and locked herself in the bathroom.

After applying a new layer of dark eyeshadow and eyeliner and styling her hair in a similar fashion to this morning, Lora stared at herself in the bathroom mirror. A thin braid was half-hidden in her shoulder-length, dark blonde hair that was a bit wavy from leaving it to air dry. The dark makeup accentuated her vibrant eyes. Her lips looked fuller with the dark red lipstick she had chosen from the small makeup collection she had taken with her. Lora was grateful she'd remembered to bring it.

Blending in was essential, even though she hated pretending to be fae. Half of her might technically be fae, but she'd done a fine job of ignoring that part of her for most of her life, keeping it hidden so deep within her, she could almost forget it was real.

The dress fit her pretty well. Her naturally tan skin peeked out on her sides, the cut-outs placed in a flattering matter.

She felt pretty yet somehow distant from herself. The eyes

staring back at her looked fae for the first time in her life, as if she could physically see the power burning behind her eyes, threatening to take over her human side. Lora grasped her heart-shaped pendant, closing her eyes as she focused on the memory of home. The cold chain settled her racing mind, grounding her.

A knock pulled her out of her search for inner peace. She wouldn't find it anyway.

"We have to go, special one," Eyden's voice was muffled by the door separating them.

"Just a minute." Lora met her own eyes again, taking a calming breath as she reminded herself that she was still the same human who left Bournchester yesterday.

She hastily pulled the vial from her jacket which was lying on the edge of the bathtub and glanced around the small room, looking for a hiding spot. The space was pretty sparse and she couldn't find a good place to hide the vial safely.

"I can always go without you," Eyden said, raising his voice.

Lora swung open the door, the vial still in her hand. "Don't even think about it."

He looked her over briefly, then quickly averted his eyes.

"Will I blend in?" Lora asked.

He didn't look at her again. "Yeah, should be fine."

She tightened her hold on the glass vial for a second before holding out her palm. "This dress doesn't have pockets." Really, why did most dresses not have pockets? It was such an inconvenience, apparently in both worlds.

Eyden finally focused on her and extended his arm, opening his hand. "I'll hide it."

"Where?"

"In the closet." His eyes shifted to the clock on the wall. "Just give it to me."

That would require trust. Something she didn't have. "No, show me exactly where to put it."

Eyden moved closer, his eyes tracking the vial in Lora's hand. "We don't have time to argue. Hand it over and I'll give it back later."

"Show me where I can hide it." She crossed her arms, the vial almost fully hidden in her palm.

Eyden dropped his gaze and seemed to try to compose himself. "I already said you're impossible, right?"

"Yes." *And so are you*, she almost added.

"I meant it," he said, looking at her for a short moment before moving away.

Eyden opened the closet door and gestured for her to follow him. The space wasn't big, her arm grazed his as she stood next to him, waiting to discover his secret hiding spot. He pushed back some clothes that hung on a rack, revealing the white wall.

There was a short pause as he seemed to rethink his decision. "If you try to steal anything, our deal is off," he said to her. "And don't think I won't notice, because I *will*."

Lora crossed her arms, tapping her fingers on her upper arm. "I thought we were in a hurry?"

Eyden opened his mouth then closed it as he turned back to the white wall. Then he whispered, "Nahla."

A door handle appeared. Another spell. Lora was aware of small spelled items from Maja and her father's business, but this was bigger. Was it more common here in Liraen than she'd expected or was Eyden personally connected with a witch?

Eyden gave her a brief glance, hesitating before moving to open the door. It revealed a small space taken up by a narrow shelf filled with multiple notebooks, pieces of paper, and locked boxes that Lora was yearning to take a peek inside.

"Go ahead, put the vial and anything else of value in here," he said.

Lora was the one hesitating this time. "Who spelled your closet? Are there many witches working at the black market?"

Serious steel eyes met hers. "I've shared more than enough with you, special one. Put your stuff in there before I change my mind. And don't breathe the password to anyone. Don't even say it unless I ask you to. Do you understand?"

She considered making a joke, but the intensity of his words had a vulnerability to it. It made him seem unsure for once.

"I won't repeat it to anyone," she replied, meaning it even though she knew promises meant nothing anymore.

The first thing Lora noticed when she entered the club was the music. She immediately recognised "Don't Start Now" playing on full volume and looked to Eyden in confusion only to find him looking just as baffled.

As they walked deeper into the club, they were greeted by colourful flashing lights and artificial fog, making it difficult for Lora to discover all the playful decorations. Besides the shiny streamers and balloons hanging from the ceiling, Lora noticed several walls were covered in artfully displayed records and CDs.

Eyden seemed to be taking it all in as well. He stood close to her and leaned in. "I'm not sure what the theme is supposed to be. Experimental music?"

Lora laughed but the sound was drowned out by a group of fae stumbling past them, cheering loudly. "It's from Earth—the music. I suppose the theme is human pop music."

As Lora watched a group of fae dancing ecstatically, she couldn't help but think of Maja. She would have loved this, the set-up, the atmosphere, the music. Maja would have grabbed her hand and dragged her onto the dancefloor in a flash, all the while on the lookout for any hot guys.

Lora wished she had her phone with her. If only she could text her friend and give her the run-down of what was going on and laugh at her friend's encouragement. She would have to describe everything in vivid detail once she was home. In the meantime, Lora had to stick to short update messages like the ones she had sent earlier while she was getting ready.

"Why would anybody choose this?" Eyden asked as he looked around, his attention shifting from one thing to another.

"You tell me, it's your town."

"This isn't exactly my scene."

She definitely couldn't imagine Eyden enjoying this, dancing to catchy pop songs that Lora knew all too well. But no matter how good the music was, Lora wasn't in the mood to dance either. Her goal was lying heavy on her spirit. The cheery scene around her that only minutes ago had made her laugh, now made her resentful. She didn't have the privilege to indulge in fun, to forget what she had come here to do.

Her eyes scanned the room. Pretty much everyone was wearing clothes in similar designs to her dress and Eyden's rather plain attire. Some of the men were wearing more interesting pieces than Eyden's button-down, midnight blue shirt, but nothing compared to the sparkling golden piece of clothing that caught Lora's eye.

The fae wore it half-unbuttoned and when the light swept over him, she noticed the shiny material was more copper than pure gold. He wore tight black leather trousers, something she hadn't seen anyone wear. Skin tight trousers apparently weren't a trend in Liraen, but he didn't seem to care one bit. He looked utterly comfortable, laughing with a group of fae next to one of the bars, his drink almost spilling over his multiple gold chain bracelets as they sparkled in the light.

"That's our target," Eyden said, following her line of sight as he moved closer to her so she could understand him over the noise of the club.

Lora took in the tousled yet styled pale hair, a hint of pink visible in the dark light. "Yes, it must be him." Although the word *target* wasn't one she would have used. The way Eyden said it made it seem like they were about to attack him. That didn't sound like a sensible plan, seeing as they were surrounded by fae and who knew what abilities they possessed.

"He sure looks rich." Eyden turned to her. Standing this close, his eyes looked even more striking as a beam of light swept over them. "We should keep an eye on him and follow him home."

Lora thought she might have misheard him over the noise around them. "You want to stalk him?"

"Desperate times call for desperate measures. Ilario was right. That guy"—Eyden briefly glanced in the fae's direction—"he's not going to sell us the crystal. Better to take it from his home while he doesn't suspect a thing."

That sounded like too long of a process for Lora. "What if he's not keeping it at home? Or what if he hid it well? We need to talk to him and see if we can narrow it down, at least."

"And how exactly do you casually bring up a healing crystal? He'll be suspicious and our window will be gone." Eyden took a small step back and half turned, pointing to an empty round booth to his left. "Come on. Let's sit down and *casually* observe what he does."

The group surrounding their target walked off, leaving the fashionable fae by himself as he ordered another drink.

Eyden walked towards the booth, fully turning away from her. She thought he might still be talking to her but his words got washed away by the music. It must have taken him a moment to realise she wasn't following him, but by then it was too late.

Lora was already across the floor, stopping right next to their target.

CHAPTER 12

LORA

"Hi," Lora said as she leaned one arm against the bar's sticky counter and locked eyes with the fae. In her peripheral vision, she could have sworn she saw Eyden's eyes blazing in anger.

"Well, hello there," the boldly dressed fae replied, smirking, clearly already buzzed. He thanked the bartender and took a sip of his indigo drink.

Up close, Lora noticed his half-open shirt revealed more than his athletic build. There was glitter smeared across his bronze chest and she could see two-thirds of a butterfly tattoo. She wondered if it was real. It was funny, she could definitely imagine a famous singer in her world sporting an outfit like this on stage. If that was his intention, he had nailed it.

"Like what you see?" The fae gave her a sexy grin.

Lora realised she had been openly staring at him, looking him up and down. Embarrassment washed over her, but she pushed the feeling aside.

"Maybe. You're not bad to look at," she said, shrugging, trying to sound as flirtatious as she could muster given she would much rather exit this conversation. Exit the club. No, exit the fae world altogether.

"Not the word I was looking for, but I'll take it."

Lora forced a smile as she went along with his game. "How would you describe yourself, then?"

The fae didn't need to think twice as he quickly answered in a somehow both light and serious tone, "Devilishly handsome, sexy as hell, ravishing. Any one of those will do."

"Someone has a high opinion of himself."

"Possibly."

Lora laughed despite herself. "Well, your outfit is definitely eye-catching."

His grin grew. "Glad you think so. Tonight, I'm a human pop star, here to melt the hearts of my fans."

"And who are those fans?" Lora asked even though she could predict his answer.

He leaned in closer. "I'm hoping you'll be my number one."

"We'll see about that." She risked a glance in Eyden's direction. He looked up in time to meet her eyes and Lora quickly turned back to the fae whose name she didn't know. "So, you enjoy this music?"

"Oh, I love it. The human world provides such great entertainment. Have you ever watched their films?"

She had to suppress a laugh. "Not really."

"What a shame. You most definitely should. I could show you some things." His smirk really did make him devilishly handsome, even though she hated to admit it. "What's your name, love?" he asked.

She considered lying, but no one knew her here anyway. "Lora. And you are?"

"I have many names. You can call me...Blue."

"Why Blue?"

He shrugged. "It's my favourite colour."

Lora nodded, pretending that that explained everything. "Mine too, actually." Finally, a truth she could tell without having to consider possible disastrous consequences.

"We already have so much in common," Blue said, finishing his drink in one gulp. "What's your poison?"

An alcoholic fae drink? That most definitely sounded disastrous to Lora's ears. "Oh, I'm good. But thanks." She put on another smile.

He seemed to consider offering again, then turned to the bar and ordered a single vodka indio. As soon as he got his drink, Blue downed the whole glass and signalled the bartender for another one.

He took a few sips before he asked, "What do you like to do for fun, love?"

Be anywhere but here, she thought. "Oh, you know, go to parties. That kind of thing." Then she quickly added, "When I get the chance. I'm quite busy helping out my father. He's a trader."

"I appreciate a good trader."

"Do you trade things yourself?" Lora asked attentively.

"Not exactly, but I buy things. Lots of things. It's quite hard work to put together breathtaking outfits like this." He gestured at himself.

She actually could imagine it would be, except he was obviously very wealthy so who was he kidding. He probably had servants who could fetch him anything he wanted. "What's the most interesting thing you've bought?" Lora asked.

He seemed to ponder the question, maybe going through a long list of purchases. He took a sip of his drink that turned into finishing the whole glass. "Choosing between my outstanding outfits is like choosing a favourite child. Harder, actually. Clothes don't act out," he joked.

Lora forced a smile. It wasn't the answer she was looking for. "Do you ever trade anything else besides clothes?"

"Sure, but what's more important than fashion? Well, maybe good alcohol..." he trailed off as he stared into his empty glass.

"Have you done any trades for crystals? My father sometimes does. I find it fascinating how many there are and each one is useful for something else." Crystals were a conundrum of sorts. Fae used them, especially healers. But so did witches, which— according to history books—gave crystals a bad reputation. Fae still used them, but they were hypocrites, after all.

Blue traced the rim of his glass. "Mhmm, I did get a gem today. A rare crystal. It's pretty amazing."

Now things were getting interesting. Lora forced herself to push down her excitement. "How so?" she asked, trying not to sound too eager.

"It has healing properties."

"Do you need to heal something?" He'd probably only bought it because he could.

"I do. There's something that's been plaguing me for quite some time now. On and off. It's horrendous, really."

Lora stared at him, puzzled. What could a fae possibly be suffering from?

Blue met her confused eyes, a slow grin taking over his face. "Hangovers. Terrible payment for getting drunk. But now I've got my remedy."

He bought the one stone that could help her...to cure a hangover. She suddenly felt sick to her stomach.

"That's...amazing," she said, her voice slightly uneven.

Maybe he picked up on her tone, because he suddenly seemed to regard her with new interest, as if he wanted to figure her out. He tried to hold eye contact but Lora quickly dropped her gaze, hoping the low light stopped him from suspecting anything was off about her. He would probably assume she was a level one, as Eyden had implied. She looked fae enough, she had to remind herself as boiling anxiety flowed through her. Funny how life worked out sometimes. Just a couple of days ago, she would have never wished to pass as fae.

Blue shifted his attention towards the dancefloor. A silence stretched between them. He couldn't leave yet, not before she found out more about the crystal's whereabouts.

Lora cursed herself for what she said next, but she needed to keep their conversation going. "On second thought, maybe I will have that drink." She gave him what she hoped was a genuine smile.

His face lit up again. "Sure thing, love. Vodka indio?"

Lora agreed and, less than a minute later, he handed her a glass filled with the same indigo, lightly shimmery liquid she'd seen earlier. One drink wouldn't hurt her, she hoped. She couldn't help but look to Eyden. Even from a distance, she could feel his disapproval, but there was no going back now.

Blue raised his glass and caught her gaze, smiling as he cheered, "To the sky!"

Lora clinked her glass with his and echoed his words.

The first sip tasted bittersweet. Blue kept drinking, so she hesitantly took a few more gulps, now savouring the taste. It reminded her a bit of her standard drink back home, vodka cranberry, but this one was better, more flavourful. Lora took another sip, a bigger one this time.

"I think I could probably use that crystal myself tomorrow morning," she joked.

Blue chuckled. "I only have the one, I'm afraid. I can show you, though, if you want?" His words sounded slurred to her.

Was he inviting her to his place?

"I wasn't, but that's a tempting idea. The crystal is with me."

Had she said that out loud or could he read her mind? No, she was being paranoid. Were the lights brighter than before? She squinted as she turned to the dancefloor and watched the colourful stream of lights move across the room. Fascinating.

"Apparently, it works best if you carry it around while you're drinking. I love a good experiment," Blue said.

Wait, did he say he had the crystal on him? Lora sought out his eyes. They really were such an incredibly deep blue, like nothing she'd ever seen before. Although she preferred Eyden's ice blue eyes. They had a fierceness about them. Why was she thinking about this now? *Focus*, she told herself.

"I'd love to see it," she finally managed to reply, grinning at him, probably like an idiot.

Blue moved closer to her and pulled out a small stone from the waistband of his leather trousers. "What do you think?" he asked as he held the crystal in front of her face. "It's quite pretty, isn't it?"

It looked so small, so insignificant. She reached out to touch it, but he retracted his hand.

"Sorry, love. Don't wanna risk messing up my experiment."

At that moment, the bartender asked if they wanted another round. Blue looked to Lora and she was about to say she still had some, but when she looked at her glass, she found it empty.

"I'll take another," she heard herself say.

Blue slipped the crystal into his pocket and moved to clink glasses with her again. Lora cheered with him and loudly shouted, "To the sky!" She almost spilled her drink and she giggled, unbothered, as she met Blue's amused eyes.

Her eyes drifted downwards. "I have an important question," she said as her gaze travelled up to his face again.

"Go ahead. I'm an open book." A sexy grin spread across his face.

Lora leaned in closer as if they shared a secret. "Is your tattoo real?"

Blue laughed and seemed to be unable to stop. "Can you keep a secret?" Lora nodded eagerly, eyes wide. "It's fake. It's part of my costume. Scandalous, right?"

Indeed, everything about him screamed scandalous. She didn't know if it was the alcohol or his smile that heated her skin and made her feel light-headed. She tilted her head back and looked at the ceiling, tracking the lights as they swept over her one by one. Bright, hopeful, bold, just as she wished to be. She reached out to try and catch the light, to bottle it up inside her. The movement made her feel dizzy and she swayed.

Blue was looking at her in amusement. "Are you all right, love?"

"Sure," she replied seriously. Or at least that was her attempt. She took a step forward as she asked, "So about that crystal—"

Lora stumbled over her own feet and ungracefully steadied herself. When she looked up, she first noticed Blue's amusement had vanished. Then she saw that the remainder of her drink was now all over Blue's copper shirt.

"Shit, I'm so sorry." She took in the stained shirt and its now weird-looking colour pattern. Lora couldn't restrain the laugh that came out of her.

Blue looked like he was at a loss for words, but then he joined her laughter. "Well, I guess every star gets something thrown at them every once in a while. Although a drink wouldn't be my first choice." Then he surprised her by pouring the rest of his own drink on himself. Blue raised his empty cup and said, "To the sky," as he met Lora's eyes. "Wouldn't want you to suffer from bad luck for a month."

That made absolutely no sense to Lora, but it was ridiculous enough to make her chuckle. "Maybe we should go somewhere more private and you can tell me more about your crystal." She tried to lean against the bar and almost missed the counter, fumbling as she tried to keep her cool.

Blue looked her over then shook his head. "Not this time, love. I think you had a little too much to drink. Until next time." He gave her a little bow and turned to leave.

She grabbed his arm. "Come on...don't leave yet."

He gently removed her fingers from his arm. "You should go sleep it off. You're pretty drunk."

"And you aren't?" How dare he judge her? From what she had seen tonight, he was the definition of a party boy.

"I am, but I can handle it. Take care of yourself and—"

"Sorry that I don't have...some fancy crystal keeping me in the perfect drunken state...or whatever." Anger fuelled her veins and the already warm room turned scorching hot.

"Lower your voice, love," Blue whispered under his breath.

Something snapped inside her, the little hold she had on her temper ran free. "Oh, now you're telling me how loud I can and cannot speak. The almighty Blue—what ridiculous name is that, by the way?—has spoken." The laugh she let out wasn't pretty but she didn't care. She was on a roll. "What are you gonna do if I refuse? Throw money at me? You're just—"

"I think it's time to go," Eyden said, suddenly appearing next to her. Lora was too surprised to say anything.

Blue looked taken aback too. "And you are?" he asked.

"A friend. We came here together, didn't we, Lora?" Eyden's eyes told her to agree.

"Yes, but I can't leave yet. I—"

Eyden cut her off again. "Excuse my friend's drunkenness. And if your shirt was caught in the crossfire, then sorry about that too. That's a great outfit. Kinda looks like what that guy on this cover is wearing." He pointed to the record wall.

Blue turned around. "Which one?"

"The one on the left." Eyden put an arm around Lora, who was heavily leaning against the bar. "By Caelo, I think she's going to throw up. We should go."

Lora gave him a death stare. "Am not! I need to stay, I'm not done."

"Yes, you are."

"No, I'm not." She kept arguing with him as he steered her away from Blue, who looked both entertained and puzzled.

"Hope I see you again when you're sober, Lora," he shouted after them.

Lora wanted to protest more, to get out of Eyden's grip and run back to Blue, to the crystal, but the room felt so blurry. Her eyes couldn't focus on Blue anymore—on anything. All she saw was a mix of colours and mist.

The night air cleared Lora's vision enough to ban the dancing lights shadowing her eyes. They were now in an alley around the corner, the noise of the club fading out like a song. Lora couldn't remember the whole walk out of the club. She had a distant thought that she should care about her state of mind, but something else took precedence.

"You fucked it all up, Eyden. I was so close," she yelled. Lora hit him on the shoulder and she finally got out of his hold on her. The bastard had stopped her from her mission. The crystal was still in the club. She had been so, so close.

Eyden stared at her, eyes blazing with frustration. "I did? Fuck, Lora, you were seconds away from telling that fae—everyone at the club, actually—that you wanted to take it from him. If I hadn't intervened, you might have spilled all your secrets."

"You wish. I had him right where I wanted!"

"Walking away from you?"

"Piss off." He was an insufferable liar. He only pulled her away from Blue because he didn't trust her to handle it. "God, you're such an arse."

He let out a short laugh before he said, "We have to keep going." He tried to take her arm to lead her farther away, but she moved back, out of his reach.

"What? Is this funny to you? Ruining our chance at getting that..." Bloody hell, what was the word again? "Stone thingie," she added angrily.

He laughed harder this time, the sound setting her skin on fire as her veins filled with anger and maybe something else too. Something she couldn't make sense of at the moment.

"Screw you, Eyden. I'm going back in." She turned and almost fell but steadied herself as she put a hand against the wall closest to them.

"Lora."

"What?" She turned back and saw Eyden holding out the crystal before he quickly hid it in his pocket. Was she hallucinating? "How in the hell?"

The corner of his mouth turned up into a smirk. "I told you, I'm an expert at pickpocketing."

In two steps, she was in front of him, throwing her arms around him. It threw him off so much that he almost tripped. Lora stumbled a bit too but Eyden steadied them. His hands were on her back, pressing against the thin material of her dress. She wasn't sure if he was returning the hug or simply trying not to let himself or her fall over.

"We really do have to keep going. He's going to realise it's gone sooner or later," Eyden mumbled as he broke their embrace. It sounded far away even though he was close enough that she could easily reach out and brush back the loose curl falling into his face.

His eyes shined bright against the backdrop of the haunting night. Beautiful pale blue was the last thing Lora saw before everything around her spun and her eyes closed slowly as she fell.

CHAPTER 13

LORA

Lora felt disoriented when she woke up. Her head was pounding. She could barely open her eyes, the room was too bright for her. At least her bed was comfortable. She drew the cover closer and snuggled in then slowly opened her eyes again only to realise these weren't her bed sheets. This wasn't her bed. She sat up so quickly it felt like a hammer was thrown against her skull and she called out in pain.

"You're awake. About time," Eyden said. He was walking over to her from the kitchen, a cup in his hand.

Lora's memories were a mess. Bits and pieces were flashing through her mind. She barely remembered getting here. The last thing she could picture was the blurry image of Eyden showing her the crystal he had stolen. Had she actually thrown herself at him? She shut down the thought and tried to concentrate on the present. The leftover taste of alcohol in her mouth almost made her gag. She was still wearing the grey dress. Her hair felt like a mess. And somehow, she'd ended up in Eyden's bed.

"How did I get here?" she asked. She couldn't help the accusing tone in her voice.

Eyden took a sip of his drink as he stopped next to the room divider in front of the bed. "Should I have left you in the alley? I'll remember that for next time."

"There won't be a next time." She glared at him.

"If that's what you have to tell yourself." The amusement in his voice made Lora's blood boil. "You completely blacked out. I had to carry you here and when you came to, you threw yourself on my bed, so I figured it was best to let you sleep it off."

If she could have died from embarrassment, she would've ceased to exist. Lora hid her face in her hands and gave herself a moment to process last night. She had made a complete fool of herself. But they had the crystal, so it was worth it. Nothing else mattered.

"How gracious of you." Lora threw the cover back and got up on shaky legs, her head screaming in protest. "I only had two drinks. I think. How did I get this drunk?"

Eyden smiled mockingly. "Fae don't get drunk as easily as humans. Our drinks are a lot stronger. I'm surprised you didn't blackout sooner, actually. Or die of alcohol poisoning. That would've been inconvenient."

She looked back at the bed and noticed her phone peeking out under one of the pillows. "Why is my phone not in the closet?"

"You insisted I get it." Eyden seemed to think for a moment. "To message someone named Maja?"

Lora hoped she hadn't wasted any unnecessary data as she reached for the device and checked her most recent messages.

Reading the short conversation, she bit her lip to hide the smile that was sneaking up on her. Even with everything going on, Maja was still Maja and if she was home, this would have been a purely fun exchange.

A sort of radio noise broke the silence hanging over the flat. Then someone said, "Hello. Eyden, you there?" The voice sounded familiar but it was a bit distorted. Lora followed Eyden's movements as he picked up what looked to be a walkie-talkie from the kitchen table.

Lora wondered if it was a runia. She'd read about such devices. They worked in a similar way to walkie-talkies but were powered by spells. Besides traditional letters, it was the only form of communication the fae used. Lora had always thought it was rather stupid of the fae to not take advantage of human technology. Phones were more convenient than runias. But with the exception of a few who might buy spelled tech at the black market, the fae were too proud to admit humans held any sort of advantage. The fae had magic and in their minds, that put them above anyone else. But technology was much safer than magic.

Eyden pressed a button and spoke into the device. "I'm here. What's the status?"

"He'll be at River's Point in about an hour," the voice on the other end said.

"Got it. I'll be there."

"Great. See you tomorrow. And say hi to just Lora."

Eyden looked at her briefly then said, "Bye, Ilario." The noise cut out as he dropped the runia on the table.

Once again, there were several questions going off in her

throbbing head. The loudest one screamed: *What the hell is he planning?*

Lora walked towards Eyden as she asked, "What was Ilario talking about? We're going to get the herbs today, aren't we?" She suspected she was going to hate his answer.

Eyden sighed. His face showed a twinge of regret, then it was replaced by indifference. "It's already late afternoon, Lora. Ilario won't be at his parents' house until tomorrow and I have things to take care of."

She stared at him quietly. Her emotions were building up, threatening to blow wide open.

"It will take time to get to the house and we should walk in daylight. Getting the herbs won't be a one-day mission," Eyden continued. Lora had stopped walking, remaining silent. "You're suspiciously quiet."

"You knew from the start that we wouldn't be going today, didn't you? You decided not to tell me," she said, her voice oddly calm.

"I thought it might take us longer to get the crystal anyway."

She held his gaze, projecting her anger through her eyes. "You thought wrong. There's no time to waste, Eyden."

"It's one day. I have a life, Lora. Ilario has a life. Tomorrow will have to do. My way, remember?"

The restraint in her broke free so violently that Lora couldn't process her feelings right away. "You know who else has a life?" she shouted. "My mum." A tear slid down her cheek. "She has a life and every day brings her one step closer to her end if we don't get that cure."

Now Eyden was silent. He turned away as he quietly asked, "When did she get sick?"

"A few days ago."

Eyden looked back at her. "Then she should have a few weeks, right? There's time."

Lora turned her face away as more tears escaped her. "Right. Why would I be worried? Of course, *you* wouldn't understand." She didn't look at him as she grabbed her belongings and disappeared inside the bathroom.

When Lora emerged after taking a quick shower to wall in her emotions, she found a new reason to be mad. Eyden was about to leave, stepping to the front door.

Lora halted in her steps and called out, "What, no goodbye?"

Eyden looked over his shoulder and took her in. He could probably still read the resentment on her face. She wasn't exactly trying to hide it.

He turned back to the door, not meeting her eyes. "I left you a note on the table. I figured you'd rather not talk to me now." Eyden pushed down the door handle.

"You're right," she said. But he wasn't leaving with no explanation again. In quick steps, she was next to him. She put a hand against the door, closing it shut again. "But if I'm stuck waiting for tomorrow, then at least tell me what you're up to that's so important. You owe me that much."

"I don't owe you anything." Lora's eyes must have been burning with fury. Eyden averted his gaze and added, "I gave you my word that I'd help you. And we're leaving tomorrow morning, I can promise you that. But right now, I have to go." He forced her hand back as he pulled the door open.

"Fine. Then I'm going too."

"Absolutely not." She opened her mouth to protest, but he continued, "I don't have time to look after you. Unfortunately, you dying doesn't help me." Eyden gave her one final glance and then disappeared through the door, pulling it shut behind him.

Lora almost screamed after him. She had given a piece of herself by telling Eyden about her mum's condition and all he said was that there was enough time. But time was a slippery thing. You never quite knew how much you had left.

She couldn't sit and wait for his return. Eyden was an infuriating mystery and she couldn't take it anymore.

Lora opened the door again and scanned the outside for his whereabouts. Eyden was walking down the street as if he had no care in the world. The sun had started to set, cloaking him in shadows as he disappeared.

Hastily, she checked her pocket. Her phone and pocket knife were still there. Lora might've blamed her unrelenting headache for the impulsive decision she was about to make, but she did it anyway. Good thing she had chosen to wear the new fae clothes Eyden had gotten her with the dresses.

Pulling the hood of her jacket over her head, Lora ran after Eyden. The door fell shut behind her, locking automatically.

She tried to move quietly but fast. It was a struggle to keep up with Eyden while also taking note of the route she was taking. She had saved Eyden's flat as a location on the map on her phone, but she couldn't be running around with it in plain sight. She needed to be able to find her way back on her own if she had to. The last thing Lora wanted was to get lost in the fae world.

Eyden turned left and, after waiting a few breaths, Lora sneaked into the same small alley. But there was no one in sight. The path wasn't short enough for Eyden to have disappeared this fast at his pace. Had he run? She almost started sprinting down the alley when a voice halted her in her tracks.

"You really thought you could spy on me, didn't you? And here I was beginning to believe you were smarter than that."

She turned around and, as expected, found Eyden standing there, a smug look on his face. How did he get behind her so fast? She must have underestimated the speed of the fae.

"You have an unfair advantage," she said.

"Intelligence? Yes, I'd say so."

She couldn't stop herself from rolling her eyes as she bit out, "Basic fae abilities. How long have you known I was following you?"

Eyden walked closer to where she was standing. "I knew as soon as you caught up with me. I could hear your steps trailing me."

"How did you know it was me?"

"A feeling. Also, your scent."

Now she smelled? Was this what their arguments had come to? "Your insults are getting lame. I just showered."

Eyden chuckled quietly, the sound deep yet restrained to their ears only. "You mostly smell like my soap."

Great, that wasn't weird at all. How did they get to this conversation? "Moving on, where are we going?" Lora asked.

Eyden dropped his head in defeat. "Since I don't have time to walk you back, we're going to a bar. And we're being stealthy." He gave her a serious look. "No more talking."

The last couple of hours had been pretty dull, but at least Lora's headache had subsided enough to let her think with more clarity. She had been contemplating what Eyden's motivations could be as they sneaked around Chrysa.

From what Lora could tell, Eyden's mission was to follow a guard from one bar to the next. To what end, she didn't know. She did realise it was far from safe, being this close to a guard and basically stalking him, but she wouldn't admit that now. They had stayed outside in the shadows, Eyden keeping an eye on the guard through windows, never getting too close to him.

It seemed like the guard had a pretty uneventful day, yet Eyden would sometimes pull out a small notebook, identical to the ones he had stored in the secret closet space. He would hastily scribble down notes with a shiny black pen that was decorated with delicate silver flowers and had a small ornament hanging from one end. Not exactly what she would have imagined Eyden to be writing with, but she had already established he was a mystery in many ways. The ballpoint pen probably came from the market, as it was a mundane thing to own. The fae usually wrote with fountain pens, according to her research.

As they waited outside a bar, Eyden seemed restless too. He was tapping his pen against his notebook impatiently. She guessed he wasn't getting whatever information he was looking for.

When he stopped his repetitive movement abruptly, Lora followed Eyden's eyes as a younger guard exited the bar they were currently surveilling. Eyden inclined his head with a new-found interest. He shoved his belongings into his pocket and off they went.

They walked far behind the guard and through a crowd of fae. Darkness had fallen over Chrysa, making it even more difficult to keep the guard in her sight. Lora couldn't keep track of their new target. Eyden seemed to have no such trouble. He led her forward with no hesitation then slowed down as they neared the busy nightlife district.

Lora recognised Caligo, the club they had gone to yesterday, a few buildings ahead of them. For a second, she was afraid they'd have to go back there and run into Blue, but Eyden wasn't looking in that direction. His eyes were trained on the club opposite Caligo. A club with blacked-out windows and lightly dressed fae waiting outside. Some disappeared inside the club as they linked arms with other fae, having a blast, it seemed. Lora had never been to a strip club or anything similar but she was certain she was looking at that kind of establishment.

"We'll have to go in there," Eyden said.

Her shocked eyes met his calm ones. "What? No," she hissed.

Eyden turned his eyes on the club. "Do you see the windows? I can't see him from here." He looked back at her, steel eyes unrelenting. "You can wait outside if you want but there are a lot of other guards and drunk fae wandering about. Your choice."

The way he put it made it sound like no choice at all. Lora surveyed the fae entering the building. They were all either dressed up, barely dressed at all, or both.

"Will they even let us in?" she asked.

"They let anyone in who can pay the entry fee. I've been there before." Seeing Lora's facial expression, he explained, "For surveillance."

What kind of surveillance was the question, but she didn't ask. Instead she said, "If I go in with you, you'll have to tell me why you're doing this. Something truthful."

"Are we making more bargains now?" He seemed to contemplate the possibilities, then said, "Okay, how about this? If you make it through this evening without asking me to leave at any point, I'll share one secret with you. Deal?" There was an excited glint in his eyes that she hadn't seen before. It made him look younger, playful.

She wondered how old he was. Grown fae, appearance-wise, usually stayed in their mid- to late-twenties for far longer than humans. He could be decades older than he looked.

Lora glanced back at the strip club. Eyden was underestimating her again. Lora was convinced she could deal with whatever she might see in this club. She wasn't a prude. She had Maja as a friend, after all, and that girl didn't shy away from anything. All she had to do was channel her inner Maja.

"Deal," she said, returning his smile with a devious, determined one of her own.

CHAPTER 14

AMIRA

Amira was excited to see one of the servants deliver a large package to her door. The attached note read, "*So you can dazzle me tonight –Rhay*"

She had been wondering all day if Rhay would keep to his word. Amira took a good look at the dress before laying it on the bed. The top part of the dress was artfully cut on the sides and the skirt was made of a textured material that looked like crystals. Amira was surprised by its design. Given her status in the court, she would have expected something more conventional, or at least less...provocative. Wryen would surely not approve.

Nalani helped her put on the garment. As the fabric slowly grasped her body, she felt a shudder run down her spine. Her excitement chased her fears away.

Even though the dress hugged her curves, she could still move freely in it. For once, she was actually going to wear comfortable clothes to an event. And she was invited to a party on her own, an informal one. If Karwyn was there, this could be a good opportunity for them to get to know each other. To break through his cold exterior.

Reassured, she let Nalani braid her hair on both sides, revealing the nape of her neck. She wasn't used to this type of hairstyle. In Amryne, she would keep her hair framing her face, but Nalani had assured her that this was the height of fashion in the Turosian kingdom.

She stared at her exposed skin in the mirror. The memory of a shadowy figure gently kissing her neck flickered in her mind. She closed her eyes, trying to remember if it had actually happened. All she could see were vibrant burning flames and blonde hair going up in smoke. The smell of burnt flesh stung her nose and brought tears to her eyes.

She suddenly felt a light hand on her cheek. When she opened her eyes, she saw Nalani's concerned eyes. "Are you all right, my lady?" the maid asked.

Amira took a deep breath and quickly wiped her tears away. "I'm okay. I just miss my family," she lied.

"Oh dear, of course. I hope your brother is staying for a bit longer, maybe until Falea Night. You seem to have such a close bond."

Amira almost let out an audible laugh, but she knew it would be wiser to pretend to care for Wryen, so she smiled and nodded. A practiced move.

Nalani opened one of the drawers of the dressing table and took out some small pots and tins. "Anyway, it's better to cry before I put on your makeup. I wouldn't want your pretty face to be covered with black smears."

Nalani started to apply the makeup she had selected and

Amira watched her face being moulded into a different woman. The amethyst colour of her eyes shined brighter and her olive skin became soft and dewy. She looked like a high-level fae, radiating confidence and power.

Smiling at her reflection, she kept herself from hugging Nalani for creating such a miracle. With her new look, no one would think that she didn't belong.

Along with the dress, Rhay had sent her an invitation and a map to find the location of the party, but the piece of paper was so full of details and intricate drawings that Amira was utterly confused about where to go. She walked around the darkly lit palace, moonlight streaming in through the big windows. She was very aware of her scandalous outfit every time she passed someone in the corridors and they stared at her. Suddenly, all the confidence that Nalani had brought out with the makeover vanished.

Amira stared at her reflection in the window. Her hand automatically grabbed the end of her braid and she started pulling it, first lightly and then with more strength. The familiar pain brought her much-needed comfort.

The sound of strong steps echoed through the corridor and Amira let go of her hair. She followed the sound on quick feet. Just as she turned around the corner, she saw Karwyn enter a dark passage to their left. She wondered if she should call out his name. Full of nerves, she glanced at her braided hair, her fingers grasping the ends of it as if by their own will. As she forced her gaze up, she realised her hesitation had made her lose sight of Karwyn.

Almost running, she aimed for a new corridor and found herself in a large hallway with multiple doors on each side.

"Dammit," she said before putting her hand over her mouth. Her brother would have told her to watch her language and pinched her hand hard enough to bruise for a few seconds.

A group of young fae dressed in a similar fashion to Amira came out of one of the rooms, laughing; they didn't even seem to notice her as they moved past her.

Now was her chance. Without saying anything, she followed them. She heard them laugh about the latest gossip. Amira was relieved to hear that it wasn't about her. A woman named Varsha had, according to the loud fae in front of her, gone to Rhay's last party with only paint on her body. Amira's cheeks turned red when she heard another one of the gossipy fae describe the situation in vivid detail.

Eventually, they led her to a flight of steep stairs hidden in a dark room. As the obscurity settled around her, Amira wondered if following them was the right decision. Would she be able to find her way back to her room?

Yet, she still followed them up the stairs. At first, she counted the steps, a childish reflex she never grew out of. But when she reached a hundred, she stopped. They kept climbing and climbing until they reached a plain cedar door. One of the fae swung open the door and Amira almost let out a gasp.

The room was set in what looked like a former observatory. A dark and silky tapestry covered the walls and all the furniture was black and smooth. The tables were filled with elegant delicacies and shiny bottles of indigo wine. All the guests were dressed in expensive clothes, perfectly tailored to their bodies.

The ceiling surprised her the most—or rather the absence of one. A dark sky spotted with stars overlooked the partygoers, the moonlight coating their perfect skin. Looking up at the night, Amira almost let out another gasp, but she didn't want to show people her profound inexperience with this type of party.

The fae she had followed disappeared from her view and she was left alone on the threshold. She took a step in and the door closed behind her. Amira turned around and was surprised to find that the once solid wood frame seemed to be disappearing into darkness. She rushed to it but when her hand reached the handle, she could only feel the cold stones of the wall. She was trapped. A sense of panic overwhelmed her for a second but then she felt a gentle, oddly calming hand on her arm.

"Leaving so soon, princess?" Rhay smiled at her and she was able to return it when she looked at him.

"No, it's just that I'm not—I didn't expect..."

He let out a delicate laugh. "You're more sheltered than I expected."

Amira frowned, ready to respond with a witty comment.

"Don't worry, no one will be judging you here. What happens at my parties, stays at my parties." He locked Amira's fingers in his. "I'll be your depraved guide this evening. First order of business, let's get a drink."

She followed him as he made his way through the partygoers. Everyone seemed to know Rhay. They tried to strike up a conversation, so their walk towards the bar took longer than Amira expected. A man with tousled dark hair and striking deep emerald eyes stared at them for longer than was comfortable before disappearing into the crowd.

After Rhay had greeted what appeared to be an unlimited number of guests, he poured a glass of indigo wine and gave it to Amira.

"To the sky," he cheered. But Amira's eyes were too focused on the shiny liquid. She gazed at the luscious indigo colour. Slightly tilting the glass, she saw sprinkles of rich violet appear. Rhay's eyes followed hers. "I guess you were raised to see beauty everywhere."

"My father used to say that, in order to honour Bellrasae, you should always find one beautiful thing in everything you encounter." She closed her eyes for a second just to catch a glimpse of her father and her in the royal temple, admiring the astonishingly divine murals of the creation of Allamyst. The legend said that Bellrasae himself, the God of Beauty and the patron of Allamyst, had painted those murals as a gift to his worshippers. Amira wasn't sure if it was true, but she knew that she would never be able to witness anything more ravishing.

Feeling the burning gaze of Rhay on her skin, she opened her eyes.

"So what's beautiful about me, princess?" he asked with a wicked grin.

Her cheeks burned. As Rhay had said, she'd lived a pretty sheltered life; being praised for your beauty was common but she, as a princess, was never expected to do the same. She tried to escape Rhay's intense gaze, but no matter where she looked, she could still feel it imprinted on her skin. She had to get over herself.

Raising her eyes, she held Rhay's gaze. "I'm sure you're already aware of how beautiful you are. You don't need me to tell you."

He drew his face closer to Amira's. She could feel his breath caressing her face. His eyes were not completely focused and she figured that he had been drinking for quite some time now.

"Maybe I want to hear *you* say it, princess," Rhay said.

Amira stopped breathing. What game was he playing? She felt like everyone was watching them. Completely frozen, she waited for Rhay to break the tension.

He let out a laugh and pulled away, raising his glass. "To the sky!" he cheered, joined by other voices around him.

Rhay took a big sip of wine, tinting his tongue blue. Amira did the same, trying to keep her hand from shaking. She could feel the beverage slowly coating her throat, making its way to her blood and raising her heartbeat.

A floating sensation took over her body. It was quite pleasant. She looked at Rhay and her vision blurred. For a second, she thought someone else was standing before her.

Banishing the thought, Amira downed her drink and immediately requested another one. The stars above her seemed to encourage her to let loose.

Rhay introduced her to so many different fae that she lost track of the names. But she didn't care, she babbled with everyone, exchanging laughs and witty banter. She danced too, on her own and with groups of fae. Moving along to the strange music, she smiled at Rhay. His appreciative look made her feel powerful.

She knew that if she had any powers, she would have shown everyone her magic. Some fae were actually showcasing their abilities and the room was filled with elemental figures. Roses made of purple fire and droplets of water shining like diamonds caressed the air while flower petals cascaded from the sky. Amira twirled underneath the explosion of magic, her lips stretched into a wide smile.

Once or twice, a sense of realisation would overcome her festive mood. She would wonder about Karwyn. After seeing him in the corridor, she had imagined that he would have arrived at the party before her. But now she had been at the party for what seemed like hours and she had never seen him. Where had he gone? She was about to ask Rhay when he grabbed her hand and brought her into another lively dance.

At one point, she did turn to Rhay, remembering their conversation from the previous day. "How did your experiment go yesterday?"

Her new friend let out a sad sigh. "I got my hands on an incredible crystal that prevents hangovers. So I went out to test it. I was having a grand time until this beautiful but strange woman distracted me and stole it. I can't tell you the hangover I had this morning. I'm never drinking again."

Amira stared at the glass filled with indigo wine Rhay was holding. She raised her eyebrows but Rhay was completely oblivious to the irony. She let out a sparkling laugh and went back to dancing.

Amira was resting on a soft sofa in one of the tiny alcoves surrounding the room. She could feel her head spinning and her breathing was uneven and loud. She tried to calm it but no matter how much she tried, she couldn't help but zero in on the sound.

When she turned her head to the left, she finally understood why. A couple on the sofa next to hers was heavily making out. Amira stood up so quickly that she almost fainted.

As Amira entered the main space, she realised that the mood had shifted from carefree, almost childish fun to a more intimate atmosphere. The music was slower, coating the guest in its voluptuous notes. Everywhere Amira looked, she could see couples engaged in affectionate conversations. Everyone seemed to have found a partner for the night. Even Rhay was busy flirting with a beautiful fae woman and what appeared to be her male companion. She avoided staring at the hands moving swiftly over exposed flesh.

In her home kingdom, it was uncommon to see such blatant displays of affection from same-sex couples. Although it wasn't forbidden, many fae from Allamyst believed the true picture of beauty was that of a man and woman sharing their life together. From her studies, Amira knew Turosian was more open about such things. It was one thing she had always admired about the kingdom. Same-sex marriages were only frowned upon when it concerned royals, since they needed an heir of royal blood.

Suddenly, she felt like the room was closing in on her. Her line of sight clouded, almost as if to protect her from seeing too much of the scandalous turn of events. She felt like she was being burned alive by an intense blaze. Panicked, Amira fled to the nearby terrace.

Overlooking the city of Parae, she felt completely alone but safe. The fire was gone and the peaceful night wind almost made her feel cold. Now that she thought of the situation with a clearer head, she wanted to punish herself for reacting in such a childish way. She was twenty-three, old enough to know about the instinctive desire to find a companion for life—or at least for the night.

But she wasn't able to stop herself from feeling uncomfortable. Maybe it was because of her lack of experience. But how could she change that?

With Karwyn, a tiny voice whispered in her ear, poisoning her brain with the dreadful expectation. In her heart, she knew that the two of them would never enjoy the intimate time they would have to spend together to produce heirs to the throne. Her eyes watered at the thought of having to share a bed with her future husband. How could she ever grow accustomed to a loveless marriage?

A sharp noise distracted her. She listened carefully. Two fae were whispering and then the noise broke through the silence again. It was a muffled scream, Amira realised, coming right from underneath her. She took a deep breath and looked over the railing.

At first, she wasn't sure she understood what she was seeing. But as the moonlight hit the scene, she almost shrieked.

CHAPTER 15

LORA

All it took was handing over a few silver notes and they were ushered in through a thick black curtain that veiled the events happening inside. As they walked into the main room of the club, Lora surveyed her surroundings in the dark red light.

There were several stages with performers. Some fae were watching them with eager eyes, sitting on the black chairs close to the action. Some were getting drunk by the bar. And others, occupying velvet couches, were too engrossed in their company and shared activities to pay their surroundings any attention. These lounging areas were partly hidden by blood-red, sheer curtains.

Not hidden enough, Lora thought. She got an eye full and quickly lowered her gaze, but it seemed like no matter where she looked, there was always something she'd rather avoid.

"How badly do you want to leave?" Eyden asked, watching her reaction closely as he grinned.

This would be so much more tolerable with alcohol running through her, but Lora had learned her lesson last night.

She kept her face expressionless. "Not at all. I have no problem being here."

When she looked away from Eyden, she noticed a shirtless fae who was sitting close to them trying to catch her eye. He nodded at her suggestively, his hand drifting down, and Lora turned a full 180 degrees.

Eyden chuckled softly. "Right. Doesn't bother you at all." He scanned the room again. "I don't see him. Let's look upstairs."

"What's upstairs?" she asked, hoping it would be less crowded. She already felt so uneasy being surrounded by fae—adding this atmosphere was not helping the least bit.

"Private rooms." Eyden moved closer to her side. "I'm going to take your hand." Lora stared at him. She was still processing the private room comment. "Better to pretend we're together than have others try to chat us up, isn't it?" Eyden asked.

Lora thought of the shirtless fae from earlier who was now getting more than enough attention from two other fae. "Right. Yes."

Eyden didn't look at her as he took her hand and led her towards the dark staircases that formed a half-circle. Both staircases led to an interior balcony overlooking the ground floor. Lora didn't have time to sneak a glance over the railing as Eyden whisked her away.

He led her into the nearest corridor. It was almost like a hotel, a long stretch lined with doors, painted in crimson light. No windows were in sight. They walked by door after door and avoided running into drunken fae who stumbled into rooms.

Lora trained her eyes to look straight ahead to avoid catching a peek of the fae who didn't bother closing the door before getting right to it.

When they turned onto another similar corridor, Lora caught a flash of turquoise—a guard's uniform—as he disappeared behind one of the doors. Eyden must have seen it too. He picked up his pace and encouraged Lora to do the same. His grip on her hand tightened, sending an unexpected jolt through her.

He stopped next to the door and put a finger to his lips as he let go of her hand. Lora stayed quiet and copied Eyden's movements, flattening herself against the wall next to him. She could tell he was trying to listen to whatever was going on inside. The distant sound of music drifting up from the ground floor didn't make it easy for Lora to hear anything. She was also distracted by the chatter and noises coming from the other rooms in their vicinity. Some of them made her cheeks flush.

But Eyden was focused, clinging to whatever he was listening to. Lora's curiosity increased and she was compelled to focus her hearing. She shifted slightly to bring her ear closer to the wall.

"All your suspects turned out negative?" a muffled, deep voice said.

"I would say so, yes. But I'm scheduled to do another round tomorrow to confirm."

Someone walked around the room, the floorboards creaked loudly and then the same deep voice asked, "Where's Layken?"

She felt Eyden move next to her in reaction to the guard's words. Were they talking about the brown-haired guard they'd started trailing, the one Eyden seemed so intrigued about?

"He gave us a brief update before you walked in. He has a

possible L5. We'll be getting in position now, sir, if you don't have any further questions," another voice said.

Lora looked to Eyden and saw his eyes widen. She'd never seen him caught off-guard like this. She wasn't sure what it meant but it was definitely related to their target.

"I'll expect a full briefing at the palace."

"Of course, sir," came the reply, and then there was the noise of movement.

Lora was still trying to interpret the guard's talk when she heard the fae's creaky steps quickly growing louder as they moved towards her. She realised the door was about to open and hastily looked for the nearest turn in the corridor to hide. Maybe if they ran, they could hide in time.

Lora turned to make a run for it when Eyden suddenly spun her around and trapped her against the wall just as the door handle rattled.

For a second her brain didn't catch on. All she could feel was how close Eyden was. His body leaning in, lining up with hers, his breath tickling her cheek and then her ear as he whispered, "Play along."

The door opened and Lora let her eyes drift shut as she put one hand on Eyden's shoulder and the other on the back of his head, drawing him closer. The movement made his lips graze her neck and she shivered instinctively. They were merely painting the picture of an intimate moment, she reminded herself, cursing her body's traitorous reaction.

"By Caelo, I hate this club," the fae with the deep voice said.

She could feel Eyden's hands tighten on her waist, his head moving as if he was caressing her neck. His warm breath felt like kisses made out of air trailing from her jaw to her collarbone, turning her skin flush. Lora let her fingers run through his hair, dishevelling his curls.

"Get a room, you two. Or a corner. There's no shortage here," another fae said, his laughter sounding farther away. Lora vaguely picked up on their steps disappearing in the distance.

For a moment, they were trapped in time. Holding each other, frozen in place. Lora was all too aware of Eyden's hands heating her skin through her clothes and his breath scorching her neck.

Eyden lifted his head. "I think we're okay."

Lora opened her eyes and found Eyden staring at her. She tried to read his face but couldn't make sense of it. She expected her own expression might mirror Eyden's confused state.

Lora quickly dropped her arms and Eyden followed her example. The distance between them felt like cool air washing over her.

Eyden cursed under his breath. "We need to find the guard." Even as he said it, he started running. Lora had no choice but to follow.

Her mind flashed back to the conversation she'd overheard. "You mean Layken?" she asked as she followed a few steps behind Eyden.

Eyden didn't slow down but he did risk a glance over his shoulder. "You heard that?"

"Bits and pieces, yes. What's L5? Did I hear that right?"

"I'll explain later." There was a sort of panicked determination behind his voice. Lora was still utterly confused about what Eyden was trying to achieve but it seemed urgent enough that she swallowed her questions. They could wait, but she would get answers later.

They took a few turns and then the mood in the room shifted drastically as they entered another hallway. Some doors were open and some fae, who had very obviously dressed in haste, were standing outside their rooms.

Confusion, anger, disgust, annoyance—a mix of emotions took over the fae's features. Some stood around anxiously, deciding what to do next. Others looked scared as they walked away quickly.

At the end of the corridor, one door was thrown wide open and Lora could see a chair that had fallen over and a few blood-stains leading out into the hall. She had the sense they'd walked into a crime scene. The red light filling the hall made the scene even more eerie.

Eyden swore again but didn't stop moving as he took Lora's hand, probably so he didn't have to check if she was still trailing him. They made their way through the gathered fae. Eyden only slowed down when they arrived at the balcony by the staircase. He looked over the railing, demanding a spot in between other curious fae.

Taking in the scene, Lora noted that the atmosphere had changed here too. Fae were hurrying around, scattered, either trying to get away from something or trying to catch a glimpse of what was going on near the entrance. That's when she spotted the guards. Three of them. They were pushing someone towards the exit.

Eyden dragged her down the stairs so fast, she almost tripped. They pushed through the crowd, fae shouting around them, trying to move in all directions. The music didn't fit the setting anymore and Lora tuned it out between the yells and panic around them.

The sound faded as they exited the club and joined a small crowd that had formed there. They stood by the side of the building, taking in the guards as they dragged a half-conscious fae towards a waiting carriage. His auburn hair hid his face as his head hung almost lifeless. The battered fae's shirt was half open, untucked from his trousers, revealing a gash on his stomach that had already stopped bleeding. He could barely stand upright as two guards hauled him forward.

Lora recognised the guard from earlier, Layken, their second target of the day. He opened the carriage door and gestured to the others to bring their captive closer. When they turned him to the side and Layken bound the fae's hands behind his back, the captured fae lifted his head just a smidge and a frightened face looked towards the crowd.

He looked quite young—younger than matured fae. This fae couldn't have been older than twenty, Lora decided. She wondered what he had done to deserve this treatment.

Eyden dropped her hand and she glanced over at him. He looked furious as he took a step forward. Lora instinctively grabbed his arm. "What are you doing?" Whatever was going on, Lora figured provoking the guard's attention was the last thing they should do.

"This wasn't supposed to happen," he answered, more to himself than her, eyes never leaving the young fae as Layken pushed him into the carriage.

Eyden moved again and Lora drew him back. "What are

you going to do against three guards?" She examined the scene and noticed two more guards with their own swords sheathed at their sides, standing on the other end of the street, ready to intervene if necessary. "Against five of them?"

Eyden's eyes radiated both anger and a hint of sadness that she hadn't noticed before. He stood rooted to the ground as the guards drove off in the carriage. The horse's bright orange eyes flashed when they passed a street light. It had a haunting aura to it, as if it was transporting the young fae to a worse fate than she could imagine.

Eyden didn't say a word as he walked away from the scene. When they had lost the crowd, he stopped and leaned his head against a wall, closing his eyes as if reality was too much for him.

Lora didn't know what to say. She wanted to know everything but sensed she was on thin ice here. For whatever reason, what happened tonight was affecting Eyden differently than most other fae who witnessed the arrest. He wasn't scared and he wasn't merely upset. He was outraged. Even though he was quiet, she could feel his anger. Somehow, she could relate to it. Life wasn't always fair. The cards you were handed were like empty promises, no guarantees for happy endings.

"Did you know him?" she asked carefully.

Eyden tilted his head up, opening his eyes to the night sky. "I briefly met him before. I warned him, told him not to trust anyone. To stay hidden and not seek out strangers. But he insisted he made good money there. That he would be all right." Eyden moved and looked straight at her. "He was wrong."

"Why did they take him? What did he do?"

"Exist?" Eyden let out a sad laugh. "He didn't do anything but try and survive. He's a level five. A high-level fae. He managed to avoid getting his PLI at sixteen, which means they had no idea. Until Layken found out, I suppose. He must have watched him, pretending to be a customer or even a friend. Something must have given him away."

Eyden's explanation confused Lora even more. Why would level fives have to be afraid? She had assumed they were regarded with respect. Only powerful fae could be guards or take on other esteemed and well-rewarded positions. And the more power a fae had, the more blessed they were by their main god, Caelo, the One who watches over the Sky, according to their religion.

"What's PLI?" she asked, settling for an easier question to answer.

"Power Level Identification. Every fae needs to have their powers tested at sixteen to determine their level."

Lora's mind was spinning, trying to piece everything together. "So they took him because he broke the law? He didn't take the test?"

"That's part of the reason, yes." Eyden turned towards what she assumed was the way back to his flat, but she wasn't done getting her promised answer.

"Why didn't he just do it? Why break the law to avoid a test?" Lora asked.

"Because fae get taken all the time. This isn't a one-time occurrence. If your level is high, chances are the guards will show up one day and take you." He exhaled loudly and leaned back against the wall. "Some of them even want to be taken. They want to become guards or healers at the palace, to be recruited and recognised in a high position. But the fae who are taken—freely or with force—a lot of them are never heard from again. It's as if they never existed. They don't become guards, they don't become anything. They're gone with no explanation."

"That's why you were following that guard? To see who he would take?" Eyden's voice echoed in her mind. Earlier, he had said that this wasn't supposed to happen. Could he have intended to intervene? "You wanted to prevent him from taking someone?" she asked.

He held her gaze as he said, "I'm following guards to see who they are targeting, to warn whoever could be next. And to find out who could potentially become an ally. Who can be turned to our side."

Lora wondered who his side included. She knew Ilario must be involved, he had given him the other guard's location. But were there others? Was there an uprising building in Liraen that the human world had no idea about?

"I'm guessing Layken can't," Lora said.

Eyden nodded, disappointment reflecting in his light eyes. "I wasn't sure before. I've been trying to find out more about him, but he's a hard one to pin down." His face turned serious, a deep pain surfacing behind his gaze. "Liraen, specifically Turosian, is more dangerous than you know, Lora. Not just for humans and witches, but for fae too. The king, he can do anything he wants."

"Why is the king ordering the guards to take level fives?"

"That's what I'm trying to find out. I had hoped with the new king taking over, things might change. But they haven't. By Caelo, Karwyn is just as bad, as far as I can tell. Another soon-to-be high king, ruling over everything with no regard, no answers for his people."

She had heard that name before. *Karwyn*. He was the son of Harten Adelway, who had made the agreement to end human slavery and had ordered the creation of the border spell. The history she had studied depicted Harten as a hero. He'd ended the darkness hanging over Liraen and allowed humans to go back to their home. But of course, only after they had helped him take over Liraen from the Dark King, and with no regard for the humans who hadn't made it back to Earth before the border spell was cast.

This summer, Lora's government had announced that their official treaty meeting in December would be with the new king, as Harten had reportedly died of old age recently after living almost two centuries, making Karwyn the King of Turosian and the interim High King of Liraen, until the contest would decide his fate. The Adelways had a long history of winning the crown and the people had no say in that. It was all about exerting power and who the royals preferred on the throne.

Lora hadn't known about high-level fae being taken, but she did know their system was flawed. The way Eyden was talking, it seemed like hope was escaping him and he feared an even darker future.

"Would you ever cross to the human world? To live there?" Lora had spoken without thinking and she didn't quite know what prompted the question. Even if he said yes, she knew he would never be able to cross. Eyden looked surprised. Before he could speak, Lora explained, "Since your world is so dangerous."

"I heard your world isn't all that safe everywhere either," he said.

"That's true, unfortunately. But Britain doesn't have a king who kidnaps his people." Eyden cut her a look. Lora ignored it and continued on, "And I saw how much it pained you, watching that fae get captured. You wouldn't want to get away from that?"

He shifted his head to the peaceful sky again. "I'd love to escape this," he whispered like a hushed confession. "But I couldn't if it was only me. Detaching myself from...my people, it's impossible. And pretending to be something you're not, pretending to be human, I imagine that must be tiresome."

Lora thought back on her childhood. On her mother's shocked expression when she first caught a glimpse of Lora's fae side. Her mum had wanted her to push it all down, bury that part of her for her own safety. Never let anyone see who she truly was. Seal it away forever.

"It must be, yes," Lora said as she followed Eyden's example and beheld the stars in the sky, lighting up the darkness of the fae world. It looked so similar to her world, but it wasn't hers. It never had been and she'd been thankful for it. Who would want to come from a world as dangerous and twisted as this one? Yet, she knew as much as she denied it, part of her had come from here. Could she really say this wasn't her world when there was something hidden within her that craved to be here, to let out her fae side?

The question died quickly as Lora pushed it away, locking it into a box that erased her treacherous thoughts.

CHAPTER 16

§

AMIRA

From the balcony, Amira could see two guards holding a fae tightly by his arms. His hands were bound behind his back and a black bag covered his face. By the strength the guards had to use to restrain him, Amira figured that he must be a high-level fae, either a four or a five. She wondered if he was from a powerful family. High-level fae tended to have high-level parents. But Amira knew that didn't guarantee strength and special abilities —she was the living proof.

The prisoner made an abrupt move to try to escape. He freed one of his hands, but the guard pulled out a longsword coated in a red tint and pressed it against the flesh of his neck without drawing blood. The struggling fae went limp.

"Almandine," Amira whispered to herself. His body now looked like a ragdoll in the arms of the guard. The prisoner's head flopped to the side and the bag fell off, revealing a younger face than Amira had expected. His eyes were closed and a strand of his wavy red hair covered his forehead. He looked almost peaceful, like a child fast asleep. On his stomach, she saw a recently closed wound. The almandine was slowing the healing process, leaving the gash an angry red.

Amira suddenly felt the urge to help, to scream, to do something. Even if he was a criminal, and he must be, did he deserve this treatment? Amira couldn't bear the sight of such gratuitous violence, but she forced herself to observe it anyway.

Pressing her body against the railing, she leaned in, trying to grasp details. Should she try to intervene? She turned around to the door leading back to the party but quickly realised she didn't even know how to get to the passage the guards were taking.

When she looked back over the balcony, the three men had disappeared. She closed her eyes, fighting back her exhausted tears.

The sound of the party startled her. Someone had opened the door to the balcony. Amira turned around and was surprised to find Rhay staring at her. He had seemed to be enjoying the company he was in when she had left the party, so she hadn't expected him to abandon his good time. But no, instead of kissing some random fae, he was studying her with a concerned look. She realised that she was shaking and that her braids were completely undone.

In two big steps, he was next to her. "Amira, are you okay?" he asked as he grabbed her hands.

She could feel the warmth coming from his skin slowly calming her. A sense of wellness and peacefulness overcame her. She realised that, for the first time, Rhay had called her by her first name. It made her smile.

"I'm fine, don't worry," she said, trying to sound reassuring.

She didn't think it wise to bring up the incident she'd witnessed, accusing Turosian guards of something she wasn't even sure she understood.

Rhay didn't seem to believe her. "Well, I was worried, I couldn't find you at the party. I thought..."

"You thought someone grabbed me, pulling me into one of the dark corners?"

"Oh, no, no one would dare do that to Karwyn," he said, avoiding her gaze.

Amira's happiness disappeared as she was reminded once again of her new fate, of the new wielder of her chains. Rhay must have noticed the change in her eyes but he didn't say anything, he just put his arm around her shoulder and led her to the door. "Come on, princess, let's get you to bed."

They walked in silence across the room. All the while, Amira avoided looking at the couples around her. Instead, she opted to look at the sky. The moon was already fading in the morning light. She hadn't realised that much time had passed.

They stopped at the exit and Amira lowered her chin to face the stone wall. Out of thin air, the door reappeared in front of them.

"How did you do that?" she asked.

One corner of Rhay's lips pulled up into a half-smile. "It's always there. You just can't see it until you really want to leave."

As they exited through the door, Amira looked back one last time. Some guests were still dancing, but their movements were slower and more languorous. Amira felt like she was seeing something that wasn't made for her. She turned her head and got swallowed by the darkness of the staircase.

They didn't say anything for a couple of minutes. Rhay appeared deep in his thoughts when Amira decided to finally ask him something that had been on her mind since their first encounter. "You're an empath, right?"

Rhay didn't seem surprised by the question. "I am. Like my father and his father before him."

She hesitated. Maybe her next question was too intimate. But Rhay seemed to understand what she wanted to ask next.

"I'm a level four," he said. "Level fives are very rare. The Queen of Sapharos, Kaede Garrock, is one of them."

The kingdom of Sapharos was known for their excellent strategists and advisors. Their patron was the God of Strategy, after all. Amira wasn't surprised the former King of Turosian, Karwyn's father, had employed Nouis and his son since Rhay had mentioned they were originally from there.

"How does it work, being an empath? Do you just have to be in the same room as the person whose emotion you want to read?" Amira asked.

"Reading emotions like that can be very confusing. I can sense some of it but it gets tangled with other passing emotions. Lust especially tends to take over when I enter the room." Rhay winked.

Amira didn't dignify his pretentious joke with a reply. "And when you touch the person, you can sense the nuances in their emotions?"

"Most of the time, yes. But some fae are better at hiding their emotions."

His answer made Amira wonder for a second. "Can you learn to block an empath's power?"

Rhay looked a bit uneasy. "It can take a lot of practice, but yes. Karwyn and I trained each other. But even without the training, we promised to never look into each other's thoughts or emotions. It would be a betrayal of our friendship."

Amira was surprised to hear Karwyn and Rhay were apparently close friends. The two were polar opposites.

Rhay gave her an appreciative look, as if he was seeing right through her. "You, on the other hand, are really easy to read."

Out of reflex, Amira crossed her arms against her chest. Her move made Rhay laugh and he kept walking.

"Are you saying Karwyn can read minds?" Amira asked, surprised again. No one had ever mentioned to her that Karwyn had a second power.

If Karwyn already possessed two powers, why would he care about gaining more through his marriage to her? Royal fae were usually blessed with one power at the highest level. But if Karwyn was a level five both in a mental and an elemental power, he was pretty much guaranteed to win the contest.

Rhay looked back at her. "He has been blessed twice, yes."

"How come I haven't seen him use any of his powers?" Amira thought of Wryen and how much he enjoyed showing his fire to the world. The smell of burnt flesh infiltrated her nostrils, almost causing her to gag.

Rhay ran his hand through his hair, trying to focus on Amira with his glassy eyes. He shrugged. "Consider yourself lucky you haven't seen his powers yet. He uses them only when necessary."

Amira wanted to push him with more questions, but Rhay put his hand right in front of her face to ask for a minute. His bronze skin looked a bit sickly in the candlelight. He held his stomach with his other hand and let out a few quick breaths. "Damn that wretched girl who stole my crystal. I could really use it now."

Amira put a concerned hand on his back. "You only have yourself to blame for downing all those drinks. I don't think a crystal could have saved you."

Rhay stood straight and let out a roaring laugh. "You're absolutely right, but it's always better to find an excuse." He gave her a half-smile. "Come on, I want you back in your room before sunrise, or Nalani is going to tell me off."

"Well, she should. You didn't tell me your parties were that scandalous."

Rhay shrugged, provoking a giggle from Amira. "You'll get used to it, princess."

They were laughing when they reached her door. Amira felt completely exhausted by the night but Rhay now looked like he could party on for days.

Gently, he took her hand and kissed it. "I'll see you tomorrow. Sleep well, princess."

He was about to leave when Amira turned to him. "Wait. Can I ask you a question?"

Rhay stared right at her with his ocean eyes. The colour reminded her of the natural pool in Amryne. "You can ask me anything, princess, but I'm not sure I'll have all the answers you're searching for."

"Do you think I'll be happy here?" she asked in one deep breath.

She could see the surprise painted on his face. He took some time to answer. "I think it depends on what you want out of life."

"The truth is, I don't know." She lowered her face, almost ashamed by her lack of ambition. Rhay gently grabbed her chin and raised her head.

"You're still very young—we both are. Us fae are gifted with a longer lifespan than most creatures. You'll figure it out, don't worry. And if you stick with me, I'll promise you'll have fun here."

She wanted to believe him but she was not able to imagine such things in her freedom-less life. If she was not going to get stuck as Karwyn's wife, she would end up as someone else's betrothed—or worse, she'd spend the rest of her fae life under the heel of her half-brother. As her older sibling and the King of Allamyst, Wryen had full control of her life until she was married. Amira had often dreamt of running away, fleeing to the neighbouring kingdom of Sapharos or Turosian. But she knew that even if she escaped, she had no means to support herself. And Wryen wasn't above punishing anyone who might have helped her. Her mother would certainly pay the price.

"Don't get stuck in your thoughts. It doesn't help," Rhay said before lowering his voice, "and it makes Karwyn's power easier for him to use."

As he spoke, Amira saw something move out of the corner of her eye. Just before it left her field of vision, she caught a glimpse of a shadowy figure that looked strangely familiar. Yet she wasn't able to remember when she had seen the dark-haired man who vanished into the darkness. Was it one of Karwyn's spies? Or worse, someone her brother had sent to watch her?

"You should get some sleep now," said Rhay as he opened her door.

Amira smiled at him even as fear took over her emotions. She quickly entered her room, trying to convince herself that she wasn't being watched.

A wave of tiredness hit her and she let herself fall on the bed. She closed her eyes, letting sleep gently coat her thoughts. The night had been eventful and her mind was trying to process all of it. Her heartbeat slowed down and her breathing evened out, but rest was still escaping her.

Behind closed eyes, she saw Rhay's face. But his eyes were different. Instead of his deep ocean eyes, his irises were as black as burned wood. Amira wanted to call out to him, but her voice stayed stuck in her throat. Slowly, everything turned to ashes.

CHAPTER 17

🔥 LORA

When Lora woke up the next day, she found Eyden's bed empty. She sat up quickly on the sofa, her head turning every direction in the dimly lit room, the curtains blocking the morning sun, until she spied the open closet door. Fighting sleep, Lora got up, smoothing down her plain white shirt and messy hair before looking for Eyden.

As suspected, she found him in the closet. Lora stood in the doorframe, taking him in as he sat next to his open secret shelf, writing in one of his many notebooks, still with the silver flower pen. The image made Lora smile.

Without looking up he said, "Sleep well?" The question was so normal and friendly that it actually took her by surprise.

"Or were you too scandalised by last night's events?" And there was the teasing that was missing before. Many things could fall under that question, though. He could even mean the fae getting taken, but judging from his voice, he didn't mean the tragic part of last night. He meant the strip club itself...or possibly their moment of close contact—which was merely pretend, of course.

She felt compelled to avoid his gaze. "I slept just fine."

And she realised it was true. Since getting here, this was the most she had slept. Before, it had been difficult for her to let herself be vulnerable and close her eyes, letting her guard down. But after last night, she realised Eyden could've hurt her multiple times or left her stranded somewhere, but he never did. And she had seen that there was some good in him, deep down.

It didn't mean that she had any illusions that he truly cared about her well-being. She wasn't really part of the fae world, part of the world he wished was different. When it came to Lora, it was all about the reward, getting her secret. Everything was always about money and power. But it didn't matter what Eyden's motivations were as long as it worked to Lora's advantage. She had her own people to save. She and Eyden might be on different sides, but they had similar goals for now.

When she looked back at him, Eyden had returned to moving his pen across the paper. "What are you doing?" she asked.

He didn't lift his head. "Finishing up some work."

Lora recalled last night, going through everything he'd said. She had gotten answers but she suspected there was much more. "You never told me why you're doing this. You promised me something real."

Eyden paused, his pen stilling on the paper. "I did. I told you all about why I followed that guard."

"Yes, but you never said what your motivations are. *Why* are you really doing this?" She wanted to understand what drove Eyden to almost confront the guards. She saw the determined anger in him when she'd held him back. He had known very well the young fae was doomed but something in him still wanted to try and save him.

He focused on his notebook again as he said, "I told you more than enough. And since our trip was cut short, the bargain wasn't fulfilled anyway."

"We never said we'd have to be in the club for a specific time. I didn't ask to leave, so I won."

He was quiet as the minutes passed. "I don't want to talk about the why of things. It is what it is." Eyden lifted his gaze, catching her eagerness for answers. "If I tell you what's in my notebooks, will you stop being insufferable?"

She wouldn't let it go forever, but for now she'd take any information. The fae world was a bigger mystery than she had imagined. Humans didn't know everything. The history books were lacking and she wanted to fill those gaps. Lora had always insisted that knowing about fae was important. Studying the fae and human history was like knowing your enemy. They might have an agreement now and a magical border keeping them apart, but you never knew what the future could hold. She was here now, after all, against all odds.

"Fine. Show me." She would have to add everything she learned to her notes in her phone later.

Eyden stood up and removed a notebook from a messy pile. "This one is filled with the names of fae who work at the palace. Each one has a number and an entry in another notebook with whatever we could find out about them."

Lora took the book and opened it at a random page. The names had a brief description next to them with their job title.

Some had an "X" written to their left, others were marked with an "A" but there were few of those.

"'A' for 'ally'?" Lora asked.

"Yes, but most of them are more *possible* allies. It's hard to determine. We can't risk exposing ourselves until we know for sure," Eyden answered, leaning against the secret door.

Lora flipped through the sheets of paper until she reached empty ones. On the last page, she found Layken's name that now had an "X" next to it. She also found the current king's name. It was the only other name Lora recognised. As she scanned the list, Eyden took the book from her hands before she could finish reading the last name "Varsha M—."

She pointed to a different pile of notebooks on another shelf. "Are these the same?" Without waiting for a reply, she picked the bottom one up and opened the first page. There was another list of names but this one was different. It didn't list positions. It listed powers and dates. Some were left blank, such as the first name on the top of the page "Adelio Kelstrel."

"These are all fae who got taken. We don't know everyone's powers, but I'm sure they were all level fives or level fours." Eyden snatched the book from her hands again and went to put it back in its spot. The movement made a piece of paper escape its folds. It fell to the floor and Lora took it before Eyden could react.

She unfolded the paper. It was a flyer with a sketch of someone's face. Dark violet eyes stared back at her. The pictured fae had short light brown hair, and she noticed a scar drawn through his left eyebrow. Under his face, the name "Damir" was written. It said he was missing, taken by guards at River's Point, the bar they'd been to yesterday on their stakeout.

"Who is he?" she asked.

Eyden shrugged. "One of the many fae I saw get taken."

"Were you trying to get information about his whereabouts?"

"I knew nothing would come of it but I want people to know when someone goes missing. To be aware this is happening. I make these flyers and I put them all over Chrysa and Parae. It's not enough, but it's something." Eyden picked up the notebook he'd been writing in earlier. He turned the open page towards her. Lora realised he hadn't been scribbling down notes, after all. He'd been drawing the young red-haired fae from last night.

"The guards don't stop you?" she asked.

He smirked, eyes gleaming with mischief. "Oh, they absolutely hate it. But they can't catch me."

She wondered if one day they would. It seemed inevitable. He was playing with fire and it would consume him soon enough. Lora found that the thought bothered her more than she wanted to admit. He couldn't get caught until she was home with the cure. That was it.

"We should go now. We have a long walk ahead of us." Eyden took the paper and stored it on the shelf before locking it shut.

Lora watched as the door disappeared in front of her eyes. The perfect hiding spot for all her valuables. Her phone was under her pillow and she planned to take it with her so she could write the same message she wrote every day. Something along the lines of, "Everything is fine. I'll be back soon." The more she wrote it, the less she believed it. Time was passing and the cure was still this blurry image she couldn't quite grasp.

One last adventure and she would get a clear picture. Everything was going to be fine, she promised herself.

Lora was unsure if she was lying to herself or truly believed it.

Besides the obvious things, what Lora missed the most now were cars—or any other form of transportation from the human world. They had been walking for a long time and her feet hurt. The shoes Eyden had gotten her were giving her blisters.

"Why couldn't we have taken a horse?" Lora said while trying to catch her breath.

Eyden, who walked a few paces ahead of her, glanced back at her. "I don't have a horse. They're expensive and I don't need one." He took in her exhausted appearance. "We should take a break. There's a diner coming up."

Before Lora could refuse, he said, "The path is going uphill soon. You'll need your strength. A short break won't change anything. I highly doubt we'll make it before dusk either way."

Lora spied the diner up ahead and gave in. Even ten minutes of sitting would be glorious.

Eyden opened the door for her and they entered a charming little place. It was a small restaurant but quite crowded. It was early afternoon, everyone was probably getting lunch.

"Why don't you grab us a table? I'll head to the bathroom quickly," Eyden said, and disappeared before she could agree.

Lora looked around and found a few empty tables but she decided to order a drink first. Eyden had given her a few silver coins before they left, just in case they were separated.

She walked up to the counter and ordered a caftee. A fae appeared next to her and said, "Make that two." The waiter nodded and took out two cups.

Lora had tried caffee before, having taken up Eyden's offer when he'd made some for himself earlier. She usually wasn't a big fan of coffee, but caffee tasted much sweeter. A dash of energy was what she needed now.

The waiter put the steaming cups in front of them and both Lora and the other fae paid for their drinks. The fae looked at her, so she gave him a polite smile as she picked up her drink and turned to take a seat at one of the tables.

Lora didn't make it two steps before the fae put a hand on her arm in a forceful manner, stopping her movement. Alarm bells rang in her head and she turned back slowly, meeting the repulsed gaze of the fae.

"You were just going to walk away? I've never seen such disrespect." The fury and disgust in his eyes made Lora more than uneasy.

"I was going to sit down. I meant no offense." She tried to walk away but the fae wouldn't let go of her arm. His grip started to hurt.

"You think playing innocent is going to work on me? You really have the audacity to give me that shameless smile as if you aren't completely revolting," he sneered, his voice raised. They were starting to attract attention.

Lora was panicking now. Did he suspect she was human? The fear was building up inside of her, burning out every other emotion. She moved her free hand to her pocket, flipping through scenarios of how she could best use her pocket knife to escape this situation.

"You don't have anything to say, bitch?" the fae demanded,

drawing her closer. She could feel his breath on her face. It smelled like alcohol.

"What's going on here?" Eyden asked as he showed up next to them. Lora gave him a confused, probably crazed look. She really had no idea what that fae's problem was. If he'd thought she was human, he would have already killed her, wouldn't he?

"This bitch was about to leave me in bad luck. Can you believe it? I think I'll have to give her a good beating to teach her some respect." His eyes glinted with sick joy. They now had an audience, but no one moved to intervene.

"I don't think that's necessary. You see, my friend here, she's not from Turosian. She's not used to our traditions. I'm sure she meant no offense, right?" Eyden shifted his attention to Lora.

"Of course not," she agreed swiftly. This man was exactly how she'd pictured fae. Violent. Repulsive. No empathy or care for others.

The fae didn't look satisfied. "It doesn't change what she did. She should learn her lesson." He started to pull her away. Her caftee was still in her hand and she almost spilled it. "You'll get her back later. Probably."

Eyden instantly stepped in front of him. "I'm afraid I can't let you take her."

A twisted grin took over the fae's face and a group of four fae got up from a table near them. They stared at Eyden, daring him to fight. "You think you can stop us? If I say I want to punish her, then I very well will do just that, boy," the fae said.

Lora regarded the five fae and decided right then that this was it. She didn't want to know what he had in mind for her.

Judging from the disgusting joy written on his face, if it didn't lead to her death, she would probably wish it had.

She could tell Eyden was trying to find a way out of this. His eyes settled on the table their opponents had previously occupied. Poker chips were swept to one side.

Eyden sought out the eyes of the fae who was still gripping her arm, probably bruising it. "You seem to be a man of reason. How about we play for her? If I win, you let us both leave with no issue. If you win, I won't give you any trouble. And trust me, even if I can't stop you, I'd get in a good fight and take out at least half of you."

The group of fae laughed and suddenly a knife found its way into the arm of Lora's captor. Cursing, he dropped his arm.

Eyden had taken a few steps back, another small knife in his hand, the dark blade gleaming red as it caught the light. "There's more where that came from," he said, his voice oozing with self-confidence.

The fae removed the knife from his flesh. Blood dripped on the floor as he moved to their table, putting the blood-streaked blade on the surface. "Let's see what you got, then." He seemed convinced he wouldn't lose. The fae pushed a tangled strand of light blonde hair from his face before taking a seat. "Lucky for you, boy, I'm always up for an interesting game. The higher the stakes, the better."

This was a bad idea, she thought. Gambling for her life? Who would come up with such a risky solution? He should have thrown his knives and then they could have made a run for it. He'd just given away his element of surprise.

Eyden sat down opposite the fae. The others kept close to

Lora, making sure she wouldn't run. Lora kept her caftee in her hand, thinking now that no one was holding her, she could always throw it in someone's face.

Their game of heads-up lasted about fifteen minutes. Fifteen excruciating minutes. Lora knew enough of the game to realise it was a close call. Eyden frowned in concentration, a worried look on his face. The other fae grinned as he put his cards on the table, satisfied by his impending win.

But then Eyden revealed his final cards and an arrogant smile replaced his concerned expression. His opponent looked pissed, as if he was about to attack Eyden, but the former said, "A deal is a deal."

The angry fae signalled the others and they moved away from Lora. "I'll respect our deal." He gave Lora a disgusted look. "But I'm a firm believer that you always meet twice in life. I'll have my justice. You better watch your back."

The threat made her shiver. She had to remind herself that she would be gone from this world soon enough and he could never reach her on Earth.

"Begone in fortune," Eyden said in a mocking manner. He took her hand, surprising her. Lora put her cup on the nearest surface and they left the diner as fast as they could.

Once they were out of sight, Lora dropped his hand and asked the question that had been nagging at her since all of this started, "Why the hell was he so offended?"

Eyden kept close to her side and watched her from the corner of his eye. "You didn't clink glasses with him. If you order the same drink at the same time and you don't do that, you're wishing the other person bad luck. Some fae find it extremely disrespectful, as you've just experienced."

"You're telling me he was about to fight us because I unknowingly wished him bad luck? Seriously?" Lora asked, outraged disbelief marking her words.

She knew the Turosian kingdom was supposedly created by the Goddess of Fortune, Falea, but she had never heard of this tradition.

"We put a lot of faith in the concept of luck. It might be a silly superstition to you but for some fae, it's their truth."

It seemed like a dangerous truth to Lora, taking it so literally that they would fight over it. Or maybe it had been an excuse for the fae to play out his twisted fantasies. It was likely a combination of both. "Do you believe it?" she asked.

"I like to follow along with most superstitions. You never know if there's something to it." Eyden glanced at her and he must have seen the judgment in her eyes. "But I would never beat someone over it. I'm not a complete ass."

"I'm not so sure about that last part. What the hell were you thinking, gambling for my life?"

"I was thinking I should probably save you."

He seemed to be very skilled with his knives. Lora recalled the red glint of the blade. It might have been almandine, forged from the stone that could physically harm the fae. "Your little knives seemed more reliable than letting fate decide," she said.

"I only had the two. One, now," Eyden answered, patting his pocket.

Realisation dawned over her. It had all been a game, a pretence. He couldn't have taken out half of them with just one knife. She shuddered and it wasn't from the breeze that ruffled her hair, loosening her braid. "What if he had won?"

Eyden scanned her face. "I would have saved you either way, special one. But it doesn't matter."

"Why?"

His smile was somehow both pure and devilish. "Because I never lose."

CHAPTER 18

AMIRA

Her night had been agitated by terrible nightmares, the kind that Amira couldn't remember when she woke up but that left her feeling deeply disturbed for the rest of the day. Yet when she wrote to her mother, she didn't mention the nightmares. How could she confess her unhappiness? Her infinite sadness? She refused to inflict any more pain and worries on her mother. Amira knew that it would only reinforce the feeling of helplessness her mother had felt since Zain Rosston's death eight years ago.

Once she had written her lies, Amira noticed a note had been left on her desk. Signed by Nouis, it said that her presence was requested for an important training session this morning at ten bells. Amira looked outside her window. The sun was already high in the sky—she was running late. Gathering her long skirt, she hurried out of her room.

Amira was out of breath when she finally reached the charming study. Nouis was sitting at the mahogany table, a large book open in front of him. He raised an eyebrow but didn't comment on Amira's lateness or the redness of her cheeks. She was grateful for it.

Joining him at the table, she noticed that the page he had stopped at showed a portrait of Harten Adelway, Karwyn's late father.

"His Majesty has requested that you be instructed on the ways of his kingdom," Nouis said. "I'm certain you've already gained much knowledge, growing up as a princess, but your education as the future Queen of the Turosian Kingdom is vital."

Amira was aware that her knowledge of her future kingdom was definitely lacking. Her father had provided her with the best education, but she wasn't the one he had been grooming for the throne. And as for Wryen, he had purposefully kept her in the dark about her fiancé's kingdom. About everything.

"I'm grateful to be able to learn," she said. Amira had longed to be taken seriously. In Amryne, she had felt her brain waste away as Wryen cut every little thing she enjoyed out of her life. It had been a long time since she had been able to learn something new.

Nouis gestured to Harten's portrait. "As you must know, this is His Majesty Harten Adelway, the last high king and the late King of Turosian. He liberated us from the Dark King and his reign as high king has allowed us to bring peace to our world and the human world. Karwyn is set to follow in his footsteps as the new high king."

Everyone knew Harten Adelway had been leading the Seven

Kingdoms after vanquishing the Dark King over seventy-five years ago. Who else could replace him but his son? Yet it was still undecided.

"Assuming he wins the contest," Amira said, looking at Nouis.

Nouis seemed annoyed by her interruption. "It's only a formality. His Majesty has been blessed by Falea, the Goddess of Fortune, and he comes from a long line of high kings. As his fiancée, you really shouldn't be questioning his chance at victory."

Amira lowered her head, hurt by Nouis' sharp tone.

Nouis flipped the page. "This portrait of the Adelway line was done during the Dark King's reign before Variel Sartoya was overthrown by King Harten," he said in a sombre voice.

Amira lifted her gaze, taking in the Adelway family. She recognised Harten right away. He was joined by a beautiful woman, a man who resembled Harten who had an arm around a smiling young woman, and two children.

"The late king's first wife was killed in the war. As was his brother's, Lozlan Adelway's, family," Nouis explained. "Being queen is no easy fate, Princess Amira. There will always be enemies. Even with the Dark King long gone, we always have to be one step ahead of any brewing conflicts."

Amira took in the smiling faces of a family who had been torn apart by needless violence. Any princess would have been happy to get married to the fae who was almost certain to be high king, yet in this moment, it had never scared her more. So much death.

It must have been a hard choice for Harten Adelway to banish his only brother. She didn't know the specifics but she remembered it had been a huge scandal when Amira was younger.

"What will my role be as his wife? Will I join His Majesty at the council?" she asked, hopeful despite all odds. She wanted to be involved. To make sure nothing like the last war ever happened again.

Nouis turned the page, revealing another portrait of Harten Adelway. This time he was joined by a different young woman. Amira only had time to see her haunted eyes before Nouis quickly turned the page again. He stopped on a map of Parae, the capital of Karwyn's kingdom.

"As the Queen of Turosian, you will be expected to attend all official court events and showcase your faith in Caelo and Falea." Amira had expected as much. Of course, everyone in Liraen was supposed to worship Caelo, the God of the Sky, the creator of their world. Falea, on the other hand, was new to her. She'd grown up attending ceremonies in the name of Allamyst's patron, Bellrasae.

"Of course, your most important role will be to provide an heir when the time has come. But His Majesty has requested that you be kept out of all political decisions," Nouis continued.

"He did? Why?" So Karwyn had really meant what he'd said that day.

Nouis sighed. "His Majesty insisted it's of no interest to you. After all, your brother has told us that you never had any interest in participating in Allamyst's politics."

Amira felt the air taken out of her lungs. Her brother's control was still present. As always, Wryen was desperate to stay her puppeteer, moving her strings as he pleased. Well, she wasn't going to wait until the strings got loose to cut them. If she could get Karwyn on her side, then maybe she'd be free of her brother's reach.

"I'm grown now and ready to participate in Turosian politics," Amira insisted.

Nouis looked doubtful but he still gave her a polite smile. "I will inform His Majesty."

A knock on the door disturbed the fake politeness. "Come in," Nouis answered.

Rhay's friendly face peered into the room. "Father, Karwyn has requested your presence in the council room."

Rhay's presence made the stuffy study more bearable. He leaned against the frame of the door, the picture of perfect nonchalance.

Nouis stood up. "I'll go to His Majesty. In my absence, I am putting you in charge of Princess Amira's training. See that she finishes going through this book on Turosian history." He pointed at the book in front of Amira.

"I will make sure that the princess knows *everything* that there is to know about Turosian," Rhay said with a devilish smile.

Nouis joined his son at the door and grabbed his shoulder. "Do not distract her, Rhay. I am trusting you with this, I expect to be pleased with you for once."

"Of course, you can trust me." Rhay put on a brave smile but Amira saw in his eyes that his father's mistrust pained him.

Nouis faced Amira and bowed. "I'll return to you soon, princess. In the meantime, focus on your studies if you wish to participate in the king's council."

When Nouis left the room, Rhay's eyes turned mischievous. He joined Amira at the table and closed the book.

"What are you doing?" Amira protested.

Rhay lounged on the chair next to Amira. "All you need to know about Turosian is right here," he said as he pointed to his head.

Amira scoffed and opened the book again. She started turning the pages quickly, searching for the portrait of Harten Adelway and the mysterious woman.

"I'm offended that you chose to write off my wisdom so quickly," Rhay said.

Amira stopped to stare at him with a teasing smile. "You can't be more than a few years older than me. I don't expect you to know centuries of history."

Rhay grabbed a strand of his pale pink hair and twisted it between his fingers. "I do know the juiciest stories, and that's all you need to know."

He had piqued her interest. "What kind of stories?"

"Oh, you know, who's in love with who, who betrayed who, who's jealous of me... The answer to the last one is everyone. Obviously."

Amira couldn't help but laugh. "Come on, Rhay. I actually want to make an impact as queen. Let me focus on this book if that's the way to prove to Karwyn how committed I am." She started turning the pages again, still thinking about the portrait.

"But it's no fun. It's just boring, old history. You don't need to learn the names of all the past Turosian kings to make history yourself." Rhay grabbed her hand. "Come on, I'll show you around the palace. I'm sure you haven't seen anything yet."

She really hadn't. "I'd love to, but I can't disappoint Nouis.

It'll get back to Karwyn and then back to..." *Wryen*. He was an ever-present shadow looming over her, making her shiver.

Rhay's hand squeezed hers gently and warmth spread through her, banishing the darkness. When he let go, Amira tried desperately to hold on to the feeling. But she couldn't give in to Rhay's friendliness completely. She knew what was at stake. Her role was to be Karwyn's fiancée.

She turned the page and found the portrait she was looking for. In Harten Adelway's regal face, Amira could see some of Karwyn's traits, yet the two men looked very different. No one could deny that Harten Adelway exuded power and strength. The painter seemed to have trouble containing Harten's aura into such a small representation. Every time Amira had seen Karwyn, she had sensed a sort of shyness, as if Karwyn was afraid to truly let his powers shine. As Amira's gaze turned to the woman sitting by Harten Adelway, she understood why.

The beautiful young woman was crushed by Harten's shadow. Her haunted eyes were the opposite of her male companion's.

"Who is she?" Amira asked Rhay. His smile slipped.

"It's the late queen." Rhay closed the book. "Don't speak of her to anyone here, especially not Karwyn."

Amira knew that the last queen, King Harten Adelway's second wife, had lived quite a reclusive life and died when Karwyn was still a child. She had heard rumours that the queen was a commoner and a level one like her. The high king had supposedly never revealed his wife's origin. But Harten Adelway was a highly respected high king and no one had dared to oppose him. The Queen of Turosian was also well known for her melancholia and quietness. Rare were the ones to have even heard her speak. It seemed that after the queen's death, her name fell into oblivion. Amira wondered if she would receive a similar fate.

Even as a non-empath, Amira felt that something had shifted in Rhay. His defensive reply made Amira very uncomfortable. Rhay was keeping something from her and she realised how unpleasant it was to see Rhay so serious.

"I'm sorry, I just..." she started.

"Let's move on," he interrupted her. "Come on, let's visit the palace. I'll show you the best rooms to hide in order to avoid your responsibilities." He extended his hand.

Amira was relieved that his playful tone had returned, but should she give in to his offer? She debated staying here to study alone. That would be the responsible thing to do. But she longed for something *more*. She longed for friendship, for warmth, for fun. Living in Wryen's world, she was never allowed to choose anything herself. But she could choose now.

Closing the book, she stood up, crushing the vague feeling of guilt in her head. She avoided taking Rhay's extended hand, fearing that the familiarity would be frowned upon by the court, yet a smile graced her lips.

"Show me," she said.

CHAPTER 19

AMIRA

The last room Rhay showed her was a vast kitchen. The soot coming from the large chimney had darkened the high ceiling. In it, there was enough room to roast a whole pig.

It was after lunchtime and the cooks were busy putting away the scraps left from the meal. In the air, the smells of juicy cooked meat, a flavourful vegetable broth, and luscious peaches mixed together perfectly.

No one seemed to be paying them any attention and Amira almost got hit by a young kitchen porter carrying a large burnt pan. "Sorry, m'lady," he quickly said before hurrying away to wash the pan.

Amira turned around to face Rhay. As she was about to speak, her belly rumbled, causing a chuckle from Rhay.

"I see I picked the right time to bring you here," Rhay stated.

"Do you think they have some leftovers from lunch? I haven't had breakfast," Amira said, a bit embarrassed.

Rhay looked around, an excited spark in his eyes. He went

to the pantry, gesturing for Amira to follow. He opened it and a wave of cold air brushed Amira's skin. The pantry had been spelled to keep food cold at all times. Rhay took out some plates and put them on a rustic table next to him. Amira's mouth salivated when she saw the leg of a roasted chicken.

She was about to seize it when Rhay gently tapped her hand away. "Wait, I'm going to cook you something." Amira must have looked shocked because he added proudly, "I've been told I'm a great cook."

She was really hungry but she didn't want to upset Rhay so she let him do his cooking. He seemed to be taking the most random things and combining them: shredded chicken, a thick chocolate ganache, and a stinky piece of melted cheese.

Amira had to repress her instinct to throw up when Rhay put the plate in front of her. Instead, she offered a fake smile. "That smells interesting."

"Come on, dig in. It's one of my specialties." Rhay was beaming, looking proudly at the meal he had created.

She carefully took a bite of the weirdly mushy meat covered in a yucky-coloured sauce. It was worse than she expected. The mix of textures and taste made her feel like she was eating raw meat left in the sunlight for days. She didn't know it was possible to cook something that disgusting. Amira was far from a great cook, she had only baked a few times back home with her mother, but she knew that she could have done ten times better than this...meal, if one could call it that.

"Are you practicing hiding your emotions?" Rhay asked, looking up from her barely touched food. Amira furrowed her brows, not understanding the question. "I can sense disgust, so

I thought you were trying to trick my power by leaning into an opposite emotion."

He looked so hopeful, like a young puppy waiting for praise. Amira debated lying to him, but she couldn't stop herself from gagging. She saw the joy disappearing from his eyes.

"It's not good?" he said, disappointed.

Amira swallowed with difficulty before speaking. "I'm sorry, it's awful."

"That bad? Karwyn told me it was delicious."

"Karwyn must be an excellent friend. Or a good liar."

Looking at Rhay's face, Amira was worried that she had gone too far. But he let out a loud laugh, throwing his head back. She joined him and quickly they couldn't stop laughing. Amira's eyes began to water and Rhay was out of breath.

"I can't believe I introduced myself as a professional chef to multiple people," Rhay said, glancing at his food creation.

Amira couldn't help her answering laugh. "I can believe it. You have such an inflated ego."

"But I have every reason to. Everyone loves me," he said with a cheeky smile.

They kept laughing while everyone else in the kitchen worked like nothing was happening. Amira couldn't remember the last time she'd laughed this much. She'd missed this, having a friend to joke around with.

Suddenly, Rhay's laugh died in his throat. He straightened his back and stood almost in a soldier's salute. Concerned by this sudden change of mood, Amira turned around. Her laugh was cut short and a sense of dread overcame her. Facing them were Nouis and Wryen. And both of them were looking very angry.

"We've been looking for you everywhere. But thankfully you indicated your presence well with that obnoxious laugh of yours, Rhay," Nouis said in a harsh tone.

"I'm sorry, Father, we were just taking a break to get some lunch. The princess was hungry."

"We're aware of that. Her brother was expecting her in the dining room. That's why we came looking for you," Nouis replied.

Amira had kept her head low to avoid Wryen's gaze, but she could feel his piercing eyes burning her skin. "Come with me, sister. We have to talk." His voice was as cold as a winter river and she felt like every word squeezed tighter around her neck.

Without saying anything, she followed him. Behind her, she could hear Nouis admonishing Rhay. "I trusted you, Rhay, and once again you have failed me. What were you thinking?"

She must have slowed down because her brother violently grabbed her arm and dragged her out of the kitchen.

Wryen stayed silent the whole way to her room, but Amira could feel the anger boiling inside him. When he closed the bedroom door behind them, she wished she could have just evaporated into thin mist. He stayed with his back to her for one excruciating minute. The heat coming from his body was suffocating.

When Wryen turned around, a large smile took over his face. "What do you think you're doing?" he asked in a voice as cutting as broken glass.

Amira opened her mouth but he immediately shushed her with a flaming finger. She forced herself to keep her fear at bay by pretending that everything was fine. It worked but it only seemed to anger her half-brother more.

He moved forward quickly, forcing her to back up until she was stuck against the window. He lightly caressed her face with his scalding finger. The pain only lasted for a few seconds before he removed his finger. Amira felt sick to her stomach but she knew the only way to survive her brother's wrath was to let him do whatever he wanted.

"You know I could just push you out of this window. The pain you'd be in would be unbearable, but you'd survive," he whispered in her ear.

She closed her eyes, imagining the long fall. The wind caressing her skin, her lungs gasping for air, and then the impact. Quick, brutal, painful.

"Why do I find you spending time with Karwyn's lackey instead of the interim high king himself? By Caelo, is it too hard for your stupid brain to understand who you're here for?"

"I'm trying, but Karwyn has no interest in spending time with me," she dared reply.

"That's not my problem. Make him like you. Beauty will always be your only advantage. So use it!" He looked at her with such disgust in his eyes that Amira wanted to burst into tears. "Do you understand?" Amira nodded. "Good. You wouldn't want me to get angry, would you? Remember what happened to your little friend the last time you upset me."

It was like a dagger hit her right in the heart. She couldn't breathe. A thin veil fell in front of her eyes as if ashes coated her vision. His words cut so deep into her mind that Amira almost didn't even notice that her brother was stroking her hair.

"Don't cry, dear sister. It only makes you hideous. Now, I'm going to leave and you're going to be a good girl. If you ruin my alliance with Karwyn, I will know no sleep until I've broken you into the tiniest pieces." He squeezed her throat lightly with his fiery hand. Amira went limp, focusing the last of her strength on staying conscious. Satisfied with her obedience, Wryen removed his hand.

Swaying on her feet, Amira tried to clear her head. Something Nalani mentioned came to her mind. "You're not staying for Falea Night?"

He scoffed. "I have no care for luck, sister. I just seize what I want without waiting for chance to smile at me."

The tension in her body eased up a little. At least he was finally leaving.

A wicked smile spread his lips. "Don't be sad. I'll be back the day after for the official contest dinner."

Her freedom would be short lived yet again.

"I will take my leave now," Wryen said. But he didn't leave. Instead, he stared right into her eyes, expecting something. He cleared his throat but Amira was too distressed to think straight. He grabbed her by the head and forced her into a bow, hurting the nape of her neck. Satisfied, he walked out.

Once again, she thought about what would've happened if she had escaped somehow. But where could she have gone? She had spent her whole life in Amryne's palace. And she knew that if her half-brother even suspected she might run, he would have unleashed hell on her and her mother. He had already demonstrated a million times how chilling his wrath could be.

No, her best shot at a better future was to marry Karwyn. To become a queen herself. Once her marriage was secured, she would never have to answer to Wryen ever again. His influence on her life would stop there.

Maybe with a bit of convincing, Karwyn would let her mother live in the Turosian palace too. Amira sighed. Giving her current relationship with Karwyn, she'd need *a lot* of convincing. But it wasn't impossible.

The door to her bedroom opened on a cheery Nalani carrying fresh bed sheets. She looked puzzled. Following her gaze, Amira realised that she had been forcefully pulling on her hair, making a complete mess of her once perfectly smooth braids. She immediately let go of her hair.

The maid furrowed her brows but said nothing. She put the fresh bed sheets on a chair and went up to the vanity table to grab a hairbrush. In silence, she slowly brushed Amira's hair. She made it look as if nothing had happened. Amira knew she should feel embarrassed, but in this moment, she was only glad not to be alone.

Nalani softly stroked Amira's cheek. "I noticed your brother leaving. I know how hard it is to be away from your family."

Amira had to change the subject if she wanted to avoid spiraling into terrifying thoughts. "Are you married, Nalani?"

Nalani's honey-coloured eyes became melancholic. "No, my parents were blessed with lots of children but not a lot of money. I've had to work since I was sixteen. Blessed be Falea, I found good work in the palace. But it takes too much of my time for me to be looking for a husband. It's all right, though. I'd rather send the money to my sisters."

How Amira wished she could have had sisters. Or even another brother. Just someone to side with her against Wryen, to protect her. "You must really care about them."

"They're my little sisters, I have to protect them. Like your brother does for you."

If the kind of "protecting" her brother provided should suddenly disappear, Amira would not miss it in the slightest. She tried to change the subject. "What will happen tomorrow during Falea Night?"

Nalani opened her mouth and then closed it. She stared at Amira in the mirror. "Did you learn anything about it during your studies in Allamyst?"

"Not much. For our god, Bellrasae the God of Beauty, we do a celebration at the temple and then all the artists of the kingdom present their most magnificent masterpiece in honour of the god."

A bright smile spread on Nalani's lips. "We do have a ceremony at the temple with the high priestess in honour of Falea. And then the king and you will go to the town centre to give out food." Nalani saw Amira's concerned face. "Don't worry, everything will be very easy. And you will get to see more of the city."

Amira was relieved to know more about the upcoming day. Tomorrow would be her chance to impress Karwyn with her first public appearance to the people of Parae. Amira couldn't mess things up tomorrow. She'd have to follow Karwyn's lead and be the picture of polite happiness. A perfect future queen.

Lucky for her, the time spent with her brother had taught her how to fake it.

CHAPTER 20

LORA

"We're here," Eyden said as a one-storey farmhouse came into view. The sun was setting, bathing the surrounding fields and spacious garden in a glowing orange light. They had passed a few other buildings but none had their own farm attached.

The village they were currently in was a tiny speck in the kingdom. Eyden had called it Kensyn.

Lora was glad that, after passing through a handful of villages, they had finally reached their destination and could rest. They hadn't stopped for long after the debacle at the diner.

Eyden went up the few steps onto the well-kept porch that was decorated with blooming flowers. Through the nearest window, Lora could see two fae moving about in the kitchen. She'd barely eaten today and the idea of food made her stomach contract in answer.

Before she could think much about whether Ilario's family would be welcoming, Eyden knocked on the wooden door. She could hear footsteps getting closer and then the door opened swiftly, revealing a woman with dark emerald eyes who Lora would describe as East Asian on Earth. She could see the resemblance to Ilario.

"Eyden, so good to see you again. I almost didn't believe Ilario when he said you'd be coming over. It's been too long since you showed your face." The fae smiled at them warmly as she held the door and gestured for them to come in.

"I'm sorry, Mrs Marsyn. Business has been taking up all my time," Eyden replied as they entered the hallway.

"I'm sure that's it." The fae turned to Lora. "And you must be Lora. My son mentioned Eyden would be bringing someone."

Mrs Marsyn looked barely over thirty yet she must be Ilario's mother. The fae's aging process was a confusing concept to Lora. She really couldn't tell how old anyone was. For the second time, she wondered about Eyden's age.

"Yes, thank you so much for having us," Lora said, smiling, surprisingly not finding it hard to do. The fae had a welcoming presence about her. The realisation almost made her frown. After witnessing the violent behaviour of fae at the diner earlier, Lora should focus more on keeping her guard up.

"It's no trouble, darling," Mrs Marsyn replied. "I hope you two are hungry. We were just setting the table."

She led them to the dining room where a man was placing a steaming bowl in the middle of the table. His head veered in their direction. "Oh, hello, Eyden. Nice of you to join us again." His tone was warm but there was a layer of teasing to it as well.

Eyden ignored it, his expression almost blank, but she noted the subtle lift of his lips and knew he felt at ease. "Nice to be back." His eyes slid over to her. "This is Lora."

"Good to meet you, Lora. Please have a seat. Hope you like cheese and vegetable brew."

Lora was about to reply when the back door opened and a familiar face came into view.

"You made it," Ilario exclaimed excitedly, walking up to Eyden and giving him a quick hug before he had a chance to react. Eyden hugged him back a second later. When they broke apart, Ilario's eyes shifted to Lora. "Welcome to my childhood home, special Lora."

She wanted to correct him again but he pulled her into an unexpected hug and the words died on her lips. Lora awkwardly returned the gesture.

Once they were all seated and food was passed around the table, Ilario picked up the conversation. "How was the walk here? I keep telling Eyden to get a horse, it makes things much easier."

Lora gave him a quick sideways glance. Eyden chose not to look at her and said, "You know horses eat up too much money." He took a bite of the food and Lora decided to give it a try as well, her hunger encouraging her. The brew was better than she expected and not that far off from human food.

"If I can afford it, so should you," Ilario said as he picked apart a slice of bread, dunking it into his brew. "Unless you're spending it all on *other* things?" He met Eyden's stare and she could tell they were having a silent conversation about something she wouldn't guess even if she tried. And she did try.

Eyden broke their eye contact and said, "Anyway, the walk here was fine." Sure, if you ignored the part where she almost got killed. Absolutely fine. "How are the preparations for Falea Night going?" he asked.

Mrs Marsyn's face lit up. "It's going well. I'm excited to have more company tomorrow." She looked at Lora. "We are throwing the feast on our farm every year, since we don't have a town square in our little village. I hope you'll both attend after your trip."

Eyden answered for them both. "I'm not sure—"

Ilario interrupted him, pointing his fork at his friend. "Come on, Eyden, you've never taken me up on the offer and you'll be here anyway."

"I suppose we might," Eyden said, darting a peek at Lora, who was too lost to really agree or disagree. She knew Falea was their Goddess of Fortune and they celebrated her but she didn't know what tomorrow's feast would include. It sounded like it was more than solely enjoying a meal together. Did Eyden not want to join the festivities or was he trying to decline for Lora's sake?

"It'll be good to have some young folk around," Mr Marsyn added. "I still can't believe Halie is turning down our gathering for the big feast in Chrysa. You kids and Chrysa, always hunting down something bigger."

Lora turned to Eyden, a silent question on her face. Did Eyden bring Halie here? Maybe they were more serious than she had assumed. Ilario must have noticed Lora's quiet confusion. "Halie is my cousin. You've met, right?" he asked.

"Oh, yes, only once. She seems...friendly."

Ilario laughed and she noticed his mother and Eyden tried to hide their grins. "I'm sorry, I love Halie dearly, but friendly is not the first word I'd use to describe her."

"Our Halie is quite the spirit. She always says what's on her mind," Mrs Marsyn added, a smile on her lips. "But I want to know more about you, Lora. How did you meet Eyden?"

Lora didn't hesitate as a half-truth formed in her mind. "Through the market. We're working on a deal together."

"Did you grow up in Chrysa?" Ilario's father chimed in.

The full-blown lie ran over her tongue instantly. "No, I'm from Opalia."

His eyes reflected surprise. "Really. What drew you here?"

"My father grew up here. He left when he met my mother on a trading deal in Opalia. After his passing, I decided to expand my trades outside of Quarnian and go back to my roots." Lora almost tripped over her last words.

Ilario frowned. Before he could ask a question, Eyden intercepted, "This meal is delicious."

Mrs Marsyn beamed and Ilario's face relaxed as he asked, "Remember that time you gambled for that turkey brew?" He didn't pause for Eyden to reply. "The guy was so mad he lost, he threw the dish in your face."

"If I remembered correctly, you told him he was a fool for having taken me up on the challenge." Eyden cracked a smile and the same happy expression was mirrored on Ilario's face.

Ilario threw his hands up. "I was innocent in all of this. I only stated the obvious."

"Well, the few bites I actually managed to eat were worth it," Eyden said.

Their infectious laughter made Lora smile at their recollection.

"Lora, did you know Eyden here has a habit of getting himself into these situations? He has a real knack for provoking people," Ilario said.

Lora bit her lip, trying to pull back the grin that wanted to spill out. "Really, I would've never guessed." She shifted her eyes to Eyden and raised her dark-blonde eyebrows. She thought she saw a spark in his eyes and it made it difficult for her to look away.

Mrs Marsyn's voice broke the spell. "Well, I'm going to bed. I have an early morning. But your room is ready. Ilario can show you later," she said as she got up. "Good night."

They said their thanks and when she left the room, Eyden took in their empty plates. "On that note, I think we should go rest too."

"It's still early," Ilario said, leaning back in his chair, up for more conversation, apparently.

"Lora?" Eyden said in a commanding tone as he stood up.

She eyed Eyden and then Ilario before turning her gaze to the window. It wasn't completely dark outside yet and she saw an opportunity here. Lora met Ilario's welcoming deep emerald eyes. "I'd love to hear another story."

"I really think you should rest up for tomorrow," Eyden insisted.

She turned her eyes on him and was met with unrelenting blue. "I'm fine, Eyden."

The mood shifted. Suddenly there was tension building up accompanied by an awkward silence.

Mr Marsyn cleared his throat and announced he would get more firewood. Before he reached the back door, Eyden sighed and said, "I'll help."

Mr Marsyn halted at the door. "Are you sure? I wouldn't want to pull you away from your girlfriend."

"She's not—" Eyden said at the same time Lora explained, "We're not together." She tried to stifle a nervous laugh.

Eyden turned away before Lora could gauge his reaction. He gestured to Mr Marsyn to lead the way. Right before he followed the fae outside, Eyden looked back at her. His eyes resembled a cloudy storm, warning her not to mess things up.

What could go wrong?

As soon as the door closed Ilario asked, "You're not from Quarnian, are you?"

Well, that went south very fast, Lora thought. She was scrambling for the perfect reply and nearly stuttered when she asked, "Why would you say that?"

"It doesn't make sense." He seemed to notice the nervous expression she couldn't shake in time. "Don't worry, you don't have to tell me anything. If Eyden trusts you, that's enough for me. Although I am intrigued."

Eyden definitely didn't trust her but this wasn't a good time to raise that point. Lora was surprised Ilario wasn't more insistent, seeing as she was staying at his home. But she was grateful she didn't have to come up with yet another lie. "Thanks."

"Maybe one day, you'll tell me?" Ilario's smile was friendly, curious but respectful.

"Maybe," she replied. Strangely, Lora almost wished she could tell him. It might be his pleasantly cheerful attitude. Or maybe she just wanted to let it out. She was holding too many secrets in this world. It felt as if they were right at the surface, wanting to spill out. But she knew they would drown her.

"How are you liking Chrysa so far?"

"It's interesting." Lora searched for a piece of truth she could share. "We managed to get the crystal from Blue."

Ilario chuckled softly, emerald eyes sparkling. "Blue? That's the fake name he chose this time?"

"What name did he give you?"

"Phoenix." He looked at her dramatically. "Because like a phoenix, he'll always rise to party another day." Lora's laugh was true and it filled the room as Ilario joined in. "I've come to call him Nix. Flows easier off the tongue, don't you think?"

"Nix. Yes, I like it. I wonder how many fake names he has. It's probably a long list."

Ilario's eyes seemed to reflect her thoughts. "Possibly. He sure is a mystery."

"So is Eyden, right? You said so yourself."

"In some ways, yes. I've known him for years now but there's still a lot I can't get out of him."

Lora wondered if Ilario knew Eyden's family. Did they have dinner at his house too? Did they even live in or near Chrysa? She had never asked. It wasn't important to their mission, yet the thought wouldn't leave her.

Ilario played with the edge of the tablecloth. "I try not to pry too much. Although it's hard not to. I know I can trust him and with what we're doing, that's all that matters."

Trust made things a lot easier. If only she could trust Eyden as much as Ilario trusted him. Everything would be simpler. The lies wouldn't keep stacking up. She wondered why Ilario put all his faith into Eyden when he didn't know all his cards either.

"How did you and Eyden meet?" she asked.

"He saved me from doing something very stupid." Ilario let go of the tablecloth and folded his arms. "You know about the fae getting taken?"

"Yes. I went with Eyden yesterday to follow the guard."

Ilario seemed surprised but didn't comment on it. "Well, my boyfriend, he got taken three years ago. I was there when it happened. I was beside myself and without thinking, I grabbed a hold of one of the guards. He drew his sword and just when I thought I'd meet my end, Eyden pulled me back into the crowd. I wanted to take them all on." His eyes drifted from her face as his voice thinned. "It would've been suicide. Eyden saved me that day and he gave me something I could hold on to. He said he wanted to start investigating what's really going on here. I told him I was in and we've been working together ever since."

Lora was silent for a few seconds, taking everything in. "How did they discover him?"

A sad smile graced his lips. "Damir, he was adventurous. Reckless. That night, he pretended to be a royal and got us a free meal. It was dangerous and drew attention, but he loved the rush. It was hard to keep up with him sometimes but I loved him for it too. He could have given me a heart attack and I would have thanked him for it later." Ilario let out a laugh that got stuck in his throat.

Lora remembered Eyden's flyer. He wasn't just some fae after all. At least not to Ilario. "I'm sorry you lost him."

Ilario's faint smile was the only indicator Lora had that he'd heard her. He looked lost in thoughts, maybe stuck in an old memory.

There was a silence once more. Lora couldn't help where her thoughts turned to again. "Do you know what drew Eyden into the mystery of the missing fae?"

"I do," he answered. She looked at him, her eyes pleading with expectation. "But it's not my story to tell."

Lora nodded, failing to hide her disappointment. "Do you think he's still alive? Damir?"

"I don't know. Sometimes I have hope he escaped somehow. Other times I don't dare hope because what if I find out he's been dead all along?" He sought out her eyes. "Hope is a fickle thing, isn't it? It can hold you up yet also drown you completely in an instant."

"It is," Lora agreed. She clutched her necklace and looked down at the shiny reminder of home. "You can't live without it, yet it can kill you just the same."

CHAPTER 21

LORA

The guest room was not the same as Eyden's flat. Lora had changed in the bathroom in the hall and when she entered the room where they were supposed to stay, she found Eyden sitting on the edge of the bed. It was the only furniture in the room except for a small wardrobe. The room didn't leave much space to move about and there was nothing other than the bed to comfortably sleep on.

Lora closed the door and leaned against it, standing opposite Eyden, barely two steps away. When Eyden tilted his head up, the room seemed to shrink even more.

"Maybe I can sleep in the living room," she said, one hand on the door handle.

"There's no space there." He turned his eyes to the empty space between the bed and the wardrobe. "I was thinking the floor would do for two nights."

The wooden floor seemed anything but inviting. Even with a blanket underneath, it would still be a hard surface to sleep on.

"Are you offering to sleep there or are you telling me to lie on the floor?" She was guessing the second option.

Eyden smirked and the air in the small room became sweetly suffocating. "How about we gamble for it?"

"If Ilario is to be believed, I'd be a fool to take that gamble." She let her head rest against the door; the material felt cool and she tried to let the feeling overtake the warmth in her veins.

"What else did you and Ilario talk about?"

"Nothing much."

Eyden leaned forward, resting his arms on his legs, further minimizing their personal space. "What if you choose the game?" he asked.

She was tired from today and the thought of concentrating on any game was exhausting to her even though the room had an electricity about it that zapped her awake. "You really want to play for the bed?"

The teasing smile made a reappearance. "Unless you want to share?"

Lora blamed her tiredness for her slow reaction as she stared at him for a beat too long. Her mind conjured up images from their encounter at the club when he'd been even closer. The door didn't feel cool anymore at all. She lowered her eyes to the floor, escaping where her own thoughts were taking her. "How about rock, paper, scissors?"

"Is that a game?"

She looked up in surprise. "You don't know it? It's well known on Earth. It's quite simple."

"Teach me, then." The challenge in his eyes was infectious.

It didn't take long to explain the rules. Eyden listened to her attentively, probably already strategizing how he could beat her. Lora had never paid much attention to the strategic aspect of the game. It wasn't a serious game to her. Although this time it might be. The floor didn't look the least bit appealing.

"Okay, let's do this," Eyden said as he faced her. He was no longer on the bed. They were both standing, which made the space in between them almost non-existent. They couldn't fully outstretch their arms without touching the other.

"Best out of three?" Lora asked, pulling her fist closer to her.

Eyden agreed and Lora counted down from three. He chose rock, which she'd suspected, so she went with paper. Eyden's face didn't falter. He began counting and this round he chose rock again and Lora chose scissors.

They locked eyes before the last round. It felt as if he was attempting to read more than her next move, as if he was trying to find the answer to who she really was in her eyes. In the mix of blue and green, of lies and truths.

Lora's voice came out shaky as she counted down one last time. She found it hard to look away from his gaze. If only she knew what he was thinking. Who he really was.

She forced her gaze to their outstretched hands. Lora had chosen rock and he had chosen scissors.

She let her hand fall back to her side. "I guess luck was on my side this time."

"You think it's luck?"

"I suppose it's a mix of luck and strategy. You can think about what your opponent is most likely going to choose next but people can always surprise you."

"Yes, they can." Eyden's voice carried a certain wonder.

Somehow, it made her shiver and she crossed her arms as she took a seat on the bed, her prize.

Eyden turned towards her. "You want to play again?"

"Can't accept defeat?"

"The bed's yours. We don't have to play for anything."

Part of her wanted to sink into the bed but an idea formed in her mind. Her lips stretched into a teasing smile. "What's the fun in that? How about we play for truths?"

Eyden's eyes sparked at the challenge but it quickly dimmed, the enthusiasm dampening with it. "I can't promise to give you any truth you ask for."

"Neither can I. Let's try anyway." When he still looked uncertain, she added, "What happened to 'I never lose?'"

"That was about poker, not some silly human game."

"We play poker too, you know. It's not strictly a fae game. You can't claim ownership."

Eyden didn't answer, instead he settled down next to her on the bed and extended his fist.

Never could back away from a challenge, could he?

Lora won the next round of rock, paper, scissors and the sweet victory filled her with excitement. She pulled up her mental list of questions she was dying to ask but figured she'd better start with an easy one. "How old are you?"

Eyden relaxed a smidge, a subtle shift that could easily go unnoticed. "Twenty-seven."

Lora had assumed he was older but some part of her was delighted she was wrong. She made a fist and another round was quickly over. Lora lost but she didn't mind. She was curious to see what Eyden would ask her.

"What did Ilario tell you?"

A glimmer of disappointment took over her mood. He was only worried about what his friend had said in his absence. "He told me about Damir. That you saved him in more ways than one," she said.

The answer seemed to appease and trouble him at the same time. "I think he saved me too."

"How so?"

"Isn't that another question?" The light in his eyes was back and she didn't want to look away.

"If you answer it, I'll answer another one too," she dared him.

His eyes left hers as he exhaled slowly. "I wasn't in a good place when I met Ilario. I was...lost. Seeing his pain and his courage, it motivated me to start something. I don't know where I'd be if I hadn't met him. But I don't think it's enough anymore. I spend all this time being on watch. Waiting for something, anything to fall into place. But nothing happens when all you do is wait." There was a pause. "I don't think I was made for this." His voice sounded small in the tiny room.

"For what?" Eyden gave her a look. She had asked another question. Her curiosity only increased with each answer, it seemed. "Right, go ahead."

"Would you have crossed if your mother hadn't gotten sick?"

The question hit her very soul. It filled her veins with ice even though her skin was still warm to the touch. Lora didn't want to lie, so she considered her words carefully. "If I'm being honest, I don't think so. I took a risk in coming here. I wasn't sure it would work, but knowing my mum would die if I did nothing...it was enough to push me to try."

She wasn't sure what reaction she expected. Maybe disappointment in her lack of courage? Her lack of selflessness? But all she saw was understanding. Lora found it was the only thing she needed in this moment.

"How long did it take you to make that decision?" Eyden asked.

"I went the day after I found out my mum had the virus. But I decided in a matter of minutes," she answered before she even realised it was his second question in a row. His knee brushed against hers, probably accidentally, but he didn't pull back. Lora wasn't sure if he even noticed, but the light touch melted away the ice in her and started a fire.

Eyden looked unaware of the fire brewing beneath her skin. But his voice sounded raw, more honest than she had dared to hope for. "Sometimes I question what I'm really doing. I'm not taking action as much as I observe. I can tell Ilario wants to do more. To make sure no one else gets taken even if it puts him at risk. I keep holding back, sticking to the shadows. I don't think I was made for the light."

Lora thought back to last night. "I saw you trying to get to that young fae at the club."

"I wouldn't have, though, even if you didn't pull me back. I would have realised I can't get to him and stopped." There was no shame on his face, just honesty.

A question formed on her tongue. The same one she'd had before. If he felt like he wasn't made for this cause he'd been investing all this time in, then why did he start it in the first place? She knew Ilario's reason. But Eyden...had he lost someone too?

"The word you used in the closet," she said, not wanting

to upset him by saying it out loud when she'd promised she wouldn't, "what does it mean?"

Suddenly, the atmosphere changed. "I think that's enough questions for today." Eyden stood up abruptly. The space next to her felt empty, cold.

"I told you two truths. You owe me one more."

Eyden walked around the bed and touched the lamp on the wardrobe. The only light in the room went out. "I don't have it in me tonight to answer anything else," he said as he took a pillow and a blanket and lowered himself to the ground.

Lora laid back on the mattress, looking up at the ceiling in the faint light coming in through the window. She could barely see Eyden, but his presence was as if a spotlight was following him.

Exhaustion was taking over but a few words escaped her anyway. "Just tell me something real then," she said, echoing the same plea she had brought up yesterday.

Lora forced her eyes closed, knowing she wouldn't get a response. The image of Eyden looking at her, showing her a sense of understanding she didn't know she needed, was embedded in her mind. She couldn't shake their conversation. Her last question was still floating around in the air, waiting to find its answer. It made the room feel heavy, loaded with unspoken words.

When she finally felt sleep take her, a rustling noise brought her back to the edge of consciousness.

"Nahla was my mother's name." The words filled the quiet and as soon as they were spoken, the anchor that was holding Lora awake broke and she drifted off.

CHAPTER 22

AMIRA

The warmth of her caftee lifted the veil over Amira's eyes. Nalani had woken her up at an absurdly early hour, completely panicked about her being late to the temple.

"The ceremony starts at nine bells. Being late to the ceremony would mean bad luck for all the kingdom," Nalani said when she opened the curtains. The first rays of sunshine streamed in, bathing the room in a yellow light.

Amira sighed. She wasn't exactly the religious type and she wasn't superstitious either, but if she wanted Karwyn to appreciate her, she couldn't be responsible for the kingdom's lack of luck. She finished the last drop of her caftee and nodded at Nalani. The maid immediately jumped into action.

Nalani quickly brushed her hair before creating intricate braids that wrapped around her head. In between the strands of hair, she added turquoise silk ribbons that contrasted nicely with her dark brown locks.

While the maid was busy attending to her hair, Amira picked

up the now familiar bracelet that was lying forgotten on her vanity table. She hadn't worn it since her first event at the palace but today seemed like the perfect occasion. For appearance's sake, she would wear it and be the picture of a faithful believer. Amira wasn't looking forward to pretending to care about a goddess who clearly didn't watch over her. Her good luck had run out with the death of her father years ago.

Amira fastened the shiny silver bracelet around her wrist before looking up at the mirror. "Do you believe in Falea, Nalani?" she said, meeting the maid's eyes in the reflection.

She didn't hesitate in her answer. "How could I not? Falea has chosen our kingdom and has helped it prosper for centuries. The people in Turosian take great pride in honouring her each year, ensuring good luck and fortune for another year to come. I've never been able to go to the ceremony at the royal temple, but I've heard it's quite remarkable. Maybe you'll see my three sisters in the town square after the ceremony. They usually attend the royal offering."

"That would be very nice," Amira answered, no fake politeness needed this time.

"I have told them in my letters how lucky I've felt to have been chosen as your maid."

"Are a lot of fae going to be watching me?"

Nalani hesitated, pushing back her short black hair. "There will be some curious eyes wandering."

Amira's anxiety flared up, but she didn't say anything as Nalani started applying light makeup to her face. Amira's hand started trembling. She could already imagine all those eyes staring at her, detailing her physique and noting her lack of power. Nalani carefully applied a warm shade of pink to Amira's lips.

"And now, the final touch," Nalani said as she opened an engraved silver box that Amira had never seen before. She had to hold back her surprise when she saw the gorgeous tiara inside. The base of it was made of the finest silver, curling into delicate flower shapes. Instead of petals, the jeweller had used small, polished turquoise stones. Nalani carefully placed it on Amira's head, making sure it was secured in between the braids.

"There. It belonged to the last Queen of Turosian and the royal advisor thought it would be fitting for you to have it. It is going to be a strong symbol, as she used to wear it during Falea Night."

Amira's curiosity was triggered by the story of the origin of the tiara. She remembered the portrait in the book and Rhay's strong reaction.

"What do you think of this one?" Nalani said, showing her a formal dress. It was made of shiny silk. The iridescent silver colour made it look like a flowing river. Delicate, pale blue myosotises were embroidered on the bodice. Amira nodded and slipped on the dress with the help of her maid. She had never felt more regal.

Even though Falea seemed to have spared her any good luck, Bellrasae, who was looking after her home kingdom Allamyst, had at least given her beauty.

The carriage ride with Karwyn was painfully slow. Amira had

noticed the unpleasant look on his face when he had seen the tiara on her head. She almost felt sorry for him.

"It's your first Falea Night without him, isn't it?" Amira asked.

His eyes narrowed, annoyed by this tentative friendliness. "Yes. Thank you for the reminder."

"I'm sorry," Amira replied. "I know how hard it is to lose a parent."

Karwyn crossed his arms over his chest. "Our situations differ vastly. I lost both of my parents and my father's death was highly unexpected. His magic had only recently started to dwindle, he was not supposed to die for a couple years, at least. You were fully prepared for your father's death."

Yet it didn't stop the pain, Amira wanted to reply. Her father's life-source had been decreasing for a couple of years. He'd been 201 years old, so it was natural for his magic to start decreasing, and with it his health. He'd aged rapidly over the course of two years. Karwyn's father, on the other hand, had apparently only felt his life-source dwindling for a few months before he succumbed to it at the age of 199. It wasn't usual, but not unheard of either, for powerful fae who had used their power extensively.

Amira could see the veil of suffering in Karwyn's eyes and knew that his harsh words only meant that his grief was overwhelming. That, she could understand.

"I'm sorry you lost both of them," Amira said gently. "You were quite young when your mother passed, weren't you? That must have been difficult. I can't imagine losing my mother."

Karwyn stared daggers at her, his turquoise eyes burning. "Let me set one thing straight: My life—beyond court appearances—

is *none* of your concern. My mother was a selfish brat who does not deserve to be talked about. She is not to be discussed. *Ever.*"

Amira bit her lip and nodded. Yet a question formed in her mind and she couldn't help but ask, "How did she die?" She didn't remember anyone ever mentioning the cause of her death.

"Pathetically," Karwyn spat out before turning away from her, determined to ignore her.

Amira diverted her eyes from him to look out the window.

Along the streets, the people of Parae had lined up to wave at their king and his fiancée. Karwyn appeared to be completely disinterested by this mark of respect.

As the crowd increased, surrounding the carriage, Amira's stress flared up again. She didn't like the unexpected. What would people think of her?

The crowd grew more agitated and fae started putting their hands on the carriage while others were running alongside it. Amira could hear the excited screams of the assembly.

Karwyn let out an impatient sigh. "By Caelo, these people are truly animals. How dare they touch *my* carriage with their filthy hands?"

Amira was completely taken aback by his reaction. She would have expected more respect for his people from a king. Her father had always told her that a king was only as good as he treated his subjects.

Amira pressed her face against the window to get a closer look. Guards were pushing fae away, their hands wrapped around the hilts of their almandine swords. Amira felt a shiver run down her neck. Before she could see more, the carriage picked up speed.

The temple was larger than she'd expected. As Karwyn and Amira made their way across the marble stairs, she took in the delicate and ancient architecture. The base was a perfectly shaped circle crowned with a shiny silver dome. An intricate marble design resembling lace surrounded the walls. Large windows encased in silver made the temple look as if it was half up in the air, reaching for Caelo, the creator of Liraen. The God of the Sky. Every blessing had started with him. Even though each kingdom had their own protector, they all worshipped Caelo equally.

Amira was so busy looking at the building that she didn't notice the court gathered on each side of the stairs. It was only when she heard some fae whispering that she realised that what she had so dreaded was coming true. Everyone was looking at her and making discreet comments.

Her distress only seemed to fuel the rumours. Amira started imperceptibly shaking. She immediately felt Karwyn's hand tighten around hers, not for comfort but to make sure she wouldn't embarrass him. She was still grateful for it. Looking through the crowd in search of a familiar face, she was happy to encounter Rhay's cheery smile. He was waiting close to the entrance and he made sure to bow his head in an exaggerated manner as Amira passed by him. Her dress brushed against his hand and for a few seconds she felt calmer.

The first thing she noticed inside the temple was the carved marble altar in the centre. The writing on its sides was almost unreadable, showing its age. The walls were covered with ravishing paintings of Falea overlooking her kingdom. They were similar to the ones at the palace, only larger in size. The seats were placed all around the altar and there was a balcony with engraved silver railings.

Amira made sure to watch her steps as she followed Karwyn onto the balcony. He took a seat on the wooden throne and ignored her completely. She looked at the rest of the seats. Right next to Karwyn was a high chair upholstered with royal blue velvet. A queen's chair. But Amira wasn't the queen yet.

Before she had time to wonder about how presumptuous it would make her to assume this was her seat, Nouis tapped her on her shoulder. "You can sit next to His Majesty," he whispered in her ear.

Grateful, Amira gave him a warm smile before going to her seat. Around her, the most important members of the court took their seats. Amira recognised some of them in addition to Nouis. One of them especially caught her eyes. His face looked familiar but also foreign and his presence two seats from her made Amira feel uneasy. She was on edge without knowing why. Maybe it was his dark violet irises that looked as if they could absorb you into their void. They were always moving, on the lookout for something or someone.

A chill ran down Amira's spine. Maybe he was the man she had heard whispers about, Karwyn's shadow. The rumours she had heard said he was a ruthless spy, everywhere and nowhere at the same time, always there where you least expect him to be.

She shifted her focus to the crowd gathering around the altar downstairs. It seemed like everyone was wearing shades of blue and silver, giving the impression of a moving sea from above.

The chatter stopped once the priestess crossed the circle of fae to join the altar. Her dark skin glowed with a silvery shimmer and she was wearing a long teal dress with even longer sleeves.

The priestess raised her hand and everyone, including Karwyn, bowed their heads. Amira quickly followed.

The soft yet self-assured voice of the priestess filled the room. "My dearest people, my king, we are gathered here to celebrate Falea, our Goddess of Fortune. Blessed be her name."

"Blessed be her name," repeated the crowd. But Amira said it too late and she felt like everyone could hear her voice echoing through the temple. Maybe she was dreaming, but she thought she saw Karwyn grinning at her mistake. Amira straightened and smiled at Karwyn. She was determined to prove his preconceived notion of her wrong.

After a prayer sung by the crowd, begging Falea to bring them fortune for the year, the priestess moved closer to the altar. She took out a small glass jar filled with a suspicious substance and held it high.

Amira leaned towards Nouis who was sitting next to her. "What's in the jar?"

"A mixture made out of ground-up turquoise stones and liquid silver. Highly poisonous to everyone who is not fae," Nouis whispered to her, his eyes still focused on the mesmerising priestess.

"Those who are not worthy of Falea's blessing cannot consume this sacred potion. Those who are not as powerful and as strong as the fae. Cursed witches who live far from the Goddess' eyes. Unblessed humans who are not worthy of our Goddess' praise." The priestess' voice grew deeper and more threatening with each word. "May those who are beneath us never cross our path as we have Fortune on our side."

Amira's head started to buzz all of a sudden. The waves of pain hit her vigorously, one after the other, not letting her catch her breath. Her sight seemed to narrow.

"I will consume this substance to prove that I have been chosen, that I am truly blessed," the priestess announced.

The crowd was ecstatic. Amira could feel their violent instinct rising. Even though witches and humans were far from the same, they were both hated by the fae. If a fae was known to be the descendant of a witch, they were hunted for fear that the bloodline was now tainted. Being cursed instead of blessed.

The crowd cheered as the priestess drank the potion, tainting her dark lips with a silver shimmer. Amira's head suddenly felt as if it was going to explode, the cheers painfully echoing in her mind. Without thinking, she stumbled out of her chair and ran to the closest door.

The sun was high in the sky when she pushed the glass door open. Her escape had led her to a tiny balcony nestled in between the carved walls. Amira took a big breath and almost jumped when she noticed Rhay comfortably lounging on a bench. She realised she had never actually seen him inside the temple.

He smirked before taking a swig out of a highly decorated flask. "Fancy seeing you here, princess. I gather you're not the religious type."

"Not really, no," Amira said as she sat next to him. She couldn't help but notice the heady scent he was wearing. It was a mix of spices, exotic flowers, and extreme self-confidence.

"What would the king say about that?"

"What would your father say about your presence here?" she immediately replied.

"The secret is that good old Nouis isn't all that religious himself. Half of the people here aren't. It's all pretence and superstitions, even the so-called luck of the Turosian kingdom. If we were that lucky, the Dark King never would have taken over Liraen." He raised his shoulders. "Everything is about appearances."

Amira squinted against the sunlight as she detailed Rhay's sophisticated and over-the-top outfit. His clothes were brighter than the sun. "I thought you cared about appearances."

"I'm far too unique to always follow the rules. Plus, I can get away with it."

"I suppose *you* could say that," she sniped.

Rhay stared at her with wide eyes, feigning offense. "Princess, don't break my heart. It's very fragile."

"That's what happens when you offer it to anyone." Her comment was harsher than she meant, but her headache was still paining her.

Rhay looked at her, concerned. "The ceremony really did a number on you. You want some?" He gave her the flask and Amira took a sip that she almost immediately regretted. A wave of spicy alcohol hit her.

"I don't know how you can drink that this early."

"Well, I'm getting ready for the only interesting part of this day—the feast tonight."

"How is that different from any other day for you?"

Rhay jokingly joined his hands in prayer. "Because it's a party to celebrate a higher being. Someone superior to us all."

Amira's eyes darkened. "I always hated this idea of superiority and the crazy impulse it creates in fae. So many atrocities have been committed for so-called superior beings."

They stayed silent for a bit. Rhay took another swig out of his flask and contemplated the peaceful cloud passing in the sky. Amira's gaze was focused on the shiny reflection the sun created on her dress.

Suddenly, Rhay turned to her, an idea lighting up his eyes. "Do you want to learn a quick trick to block my powers?"

Amira was surprised he would offer to teach her such a thing. Most fae would do anything to keep their winning hand a secret. Yet she was curious about his offer even if Rhay's powers were not the ones she feared. "Okay, let's try it."

"If I'm right, and I'm always right, you're feeling extremely tense."

"Really?" she said sarcastically. "Anyone could have seen that."

"You're doubting my abilities? How dare you." The playfulness of his tone indicated that he wasn't truly offended. Amira let out a small giggle, putting a smile on Rhay's face. "You see, I'm so good that I've already changed your mood." He looked so pleased with himself that Amira laughed again, soon joined by Rhay.

The sound of someone clearing their throat startled them. "Are you completely incapable of behaving like a future queen?" Karwyn's angry voice was barely contained.

Rhay and Amira immediately stood up, facing their king. "I'm sorry, I was feeling unwell," Amira said in a small voice.

"You look perfectly fine to me. Embarrassing me seems to always make you feel better."

"I needed some air," she replied.

Karwyn gave Rhay an unequivocal look. "And some company, apparently."

"She had no idea I was here." Rhay's intervention only seemed to fuel Karwyn's anger.

"By Caelo, do you not realise how important this ceremony is? Nouis informed me you seek to take part in politics, but he seems to have been mistaken."

Amira's hand twitched. Her headache was back and tears were gathering in the corner of her eyes. Rhay noticed and took a step forward, moving in front of her. "Come on Karwyn, she's new to all of this."

Karwyn's face twisted, a flash of betrayal took over his features. "Watch yourself, Rhay. You barely know her, there is no need to take her side. She is clearly completely useless to the court besides the contest and appearances." Karwyn's insults dug deep into Amira's heart. How could he be so mean to someone he barely knew?

The toll of a heavy bell stopped Rhay's retort. Karwyn sighed impatiently before grabbing Amira's arm. "People are waiting."

Amira didn't resist and she let Karwyn drag her back inside. She turned her head just before the glass door fell shut behind her. Rhay looked troubled as he downed his flask and moved to follow them.

CHAPTER 23

LORA

Lora was barely awake enough to pay attention to Ilario's stories as the three of them walked through the woods in broad daylight. His constant chatter calmed her nerves as her mind switched between obsessing over whether their mission to retrieve the herbs would go smoothly and Eyden's last words in the dark. Had he actually spoken or had she already been dreaming, trying to fill the void?

Ilario stopped as they neared a new path that went uphill. "This is as far as I'll go—I need to head back and help out—but it's quite easy to find now. Just follow the path until you reach a clearing, then climb up the side to your left. The one with lavender growing on the ground."

Eyden lifted his chin in acknowledgment. "I'll see you later, then."

Lora gave her thanks and then they split paths, Ilario walking back and Eyden and Lora moving forward.

Walking uphill on uneven ground was not ideal, but Lora

knew it would only get more challenging once they had to climb. She tried to match Eyden's confident, fast steps.

The path became too narrow to walk side by side so she followed a bit behind. Her eyes scanned the ground as she tried her best not to trip. Every now and then, her gaze would travel up to Eyden, fixating on the back of his head as unsaid words haunted her mind.

"Do you have something to say?" Eyden asked as he looked over his shoulder and caught her staring.

Lora considered how to best phrase the question. Deciding to spit it out, she asked in a gentle voice, "What happened to your mother?"

She saw pain flash across his face before Eyden focused on the path ahead once more. "No more questions."

"Why?"

He didn't slow down or turn around. "Didn't we establish that we don't trust each other?"

He was throwing her own words back at her. Lora might have said something similar only a few days ago, but it felt as if it had been longer. She had been pulled further into the fae world than she had planned. Lora was certain it would be an impending regret, but she couldn't help herself.

Shoving that worry away, she asked, "Why did you tell me her name at all, then?"

"Temporary insanity?"

"Are you sure it's not constant insanity?" Lora replied, hiding her smile.

Eyden shook his head lightly. "I'm not the one insane enough to cross over to a completely different world." The coldness of his voice was slowly melting.

"Well, I don't gamble for people's lives," Lora retorted.

"I can always leave you for dead next time if you prefer." She couldn't see his expression but Lora liked to imagine a mischievous grin was plastered on his face.

The path became steeper and Eyden slowed down as he braced himself against the stone wall next to them. Lora followed his example. "You already know too much anyway. You know more about me than I do about you," Eyden said when the path eased up.

Lora searched her memory. He was probably right, but even so, it wasn't her fault alone. "You haven't really asked me anything that's not related to my secret."

"I didn't think you'd tell me."

"Here's your chance. Ask away." The words left her mouth before she fully realised what she'd said.

Eyden didn't take any time to question her offer. "How old are you?" he asked.

She couldn't withhold the smile as he repeated her question. "I turned twenty-four this month."

Lora thought he might stop there but he barely paused before he asked, "Besides your mother, who else did you leave behind?"

"The rest of my family. My friends."

"That's very vague. Who are you messaging every day with your phone device?"

She narrowed her eyes even though he couldn't see it, recalling all the vague answers he'd given her since she met him. Lora decided to answer anyway, intrigued where this conversation would lead. "My parents, my brother, and my best friend."

"You're close with your parents?"

"I'd like to say so. My mum married my dad when I was four years old. He's been a father to me ever since. We've always gotten along well." A sense of homesickness sneaked into her heart. What did her parents think now that she'd been gone for days? Were they losing faith in her?

Eyden's voice brought Lora back to Liraen. "Is he not your biological father?"

Not the direction she wanted this conversation to go, but she said, "He's my father in every other way that matters."

"What about your birth father?"

Take a hint. Then she remembered how Eyden avoided the topic of his mother. Maybe if she opened up a bit more, he'd tell her. "I've never met him. He wasn't interested in being my father."

A few seconds of silence followed, then he asked, "And your brother? Do you get along?"

The question brought her back to the day she'd found out her mother was sick and a feeling of dread and regret washed over her. "We used to be much closer before I left to study. I came back home when the virus took over my world. I told him I'd be there for him and now I'm not. He didn't want me to leave."

"He doesn't want you to get a cure?"

"No, he does. But he also wants me to be home and I can't do both. I probably made it worse by leaving without giving him any warning." Her brother's hurt face in the kitchen came back to plague her. The spoken promise she gave him was one of many she couldn't keep.

"He's your brother, he'll always forgive you," Eyden said. He seemed so convinced even though he'd never met Oscar. He still barely knew her.

"Do you have siblings?" Lora asked.

The pause stretched for so long, she started to accept he wasn't going to answer.

Eyden took an audible breath as he moved his head up, probably taking in the spotless blue sky of the warm, early afternoon. "My half-brother died at birth. I lost my mother at the same time."

Lora almost tripped as she fully took in his words. She stopped walking but Eyden continued, so she picked up her pace again. A piece fell into place and she felt sad that this was his story. Lora understood the pain she saw earlier but was surprised his mother had died during childbirth. Fae were almost indestructible aside from almandine.

As if he could read her thoughts, Eyden explained, "Birth is complicated for fae. It messes with a female's life magic—the magic that makes us strong and keeps us young until we near the end of our lifespan. Pregnancy can interfere with that magic and leave fae vulnerable. Sometimes there are...circumstances that no healer can save them from in time, after the child is born."

There were no perfect words for such an occasion but Lora quietly said, "I'm sorry that they couldn't be saved."

"I try to keep her alive in my mind as much as I can. I was seven when it happened. My parents had split up years before, but I don't think my father was ever able to get over her death."

Eyden peeked over his shoulder. His eyes were focused, the pain overthrown by layers of pretence. "Do you wish you knew your father?"

Lora eyed the ground, kicking at a tiny stone in front of her. "He chose to not be involved." Her mum had written him letters and he had responded...until she told him about her pregnancy.

"Doesn't mean you can't still wish it was different."

Wishing was as dangerous as hoping. Lora was spared from replying as they broke into a clearing and discovered the wall they were supposed to scale.

To their left was a short path leading out into an abyss. There were a few patches of grass and lavender blooming on the ground, falsely making the image less alarming.

Opposite the rather slick and high wall was only air, the cliff promising a painful death. Lora carefully spied over the edge when they walked onto the small trail. The fog hid how far the fall really was, but she could tell it was deep.

Eyden kept looking back and forth before his gaze settled on Lora. "If I asked you to go back and let me do this alone, you wouldn't, would you?"

She let out a short laugh that was more of a snort. "You want me to turn around now that we're almost there?"

"I can do this better by myself. You're human. If you slip and fall, you could die."

"I'm pretty sure you could die too even if you survive the fall." She pointed behind her to the dangerous cliffside. "If you get lost down there, I don't think a healer will find you in time."

"I'll be fine. I'm a good climber."

"And who says I'm not?" She actually wasn't, but that was beside the point.

"Look, it'll be quicker if I do this by myself. And I'll be safer if I'm not looking over my shoulder to make sure you don't slip and die." He wasn't totally wrong, but his tone was getting under her skin.

"Fine. Then I'm waiting right here." She sat down on a rock next to the stone wall and crossed her arms. "Go ahead."

She didn't know if Eyden could look any more annoyed. He seemed to grudgingly accept he couldn't completely win this argument.

Eyden took off his backpack and removed the equipment he'd borrowed from Ilario's home. As he secured a rope around his waist, Lora looked up to the top of the wall. It was high but the edge was visible. It was within her sight, barely so, but enough to give her hope.

Not quite an hour later, Eyden had reached the top and disappeared from her view. He had taken several breaks on ledges but never for long. Lora was certain if it wasn't for his fae strength, he wouldn't have been able to make the climb so effortlessly.

When he returned to the edge of the cliffside, he signalled that he'd gotten what they had come for. Eyden hooked the rope, which was attached to his waist, around a makeshift fixture. He had strategically been placing hooks as he'd climbed up, making sure he wouldn't fall too far. Lora had attached the other end of the rope to herself and it was also secured on another fixture on the ground next to her in case his weight overwhelmed her.

Lora positioned herself in a stance to keep steady and pulled the rope until it stretched tightly. Then Eyden started climbing down a few steps before he kicked off the wall as Lora tried to hold her ground. The first impact almost made her stumble but the rope was pulled tight, hindering Eyden's fall.

Lora loosened the rope bit by bit, enabling Eyden's slow descent. He looked untroubled by his uneven descent and soon enough his feet hit the ground.

"See, that didn't even take that long," Eyden said as he pulled on the knots that secured the rope around him.

"You have to admit my help did speed up the process." She looked him up and down, searching for the small bag he'd planned to fill with arentae.

"I would've been absolutely fine without you," Eyden replied as he shifted to look at her at the same time as the last knot unraveled quicker than expected. The movement pushed Eyden back a step and he lost his balance.

Time seemed to slow down. Lora watched Eyden blindly swing his arms to steady himself as he fell backwards, towards the cliff's edge. On instinct, she grabbed his outstretched hand to stop his fall. Both their arms stretched as far as possible and Lora stumbled forward until the rope that was still tied around her pulled tight, halting both of them in place.

Her right arm screamed in protest but before she knew it, Eyden had grabbed the rope with his free hand and pulled himself upright again. The movement brought them chest to chest.

Lora's hand still clasped Eyden's as they both tried to catch their breath.

Eyden dipped his head and if she had to guess, she would say she saw gratitude flicker over his face, mixed with something like confusion. She couldn't look away; she was drowning in blue, the wave sweeping everything else away.

Then a thought popped into her mind. "Tell me you didn't lose the herbs," Lora said, still breathless but not entirely from the fall.

Amusement lightened his eyes even more. "I still have it." Eyden patted his pocket with his free hand and the movement made Lora all too aware of their joined hands.

She pulled back out of her trance and untied her own rope once Eyden stepped back from the edge. He quickly packed up their stuff.

When she met his gaze again, Lora recalled their last interaction and the corner of her mouth pulled up. "The expert climber trips over his own feet. Guess it was a good thing I stayed after all, wasn't it?"

She didn't wait for a reply. Instead she grinned, turned around, and started walking downhill, assuming he'd follow. When Lora heard his footsteps and nothing else, her grin widened.

Eyden didn't have a smart comeback for that one.

CHAPTER 24

AMIRA

Walking through damp secret passages underneath the temple, Karwyn and Amira finally reached a heavily locked door. One of the guards who had escorted them took out a heavy bunch of shiny keys and began unlocking the door while the others stood guard around them.

Amira took a step closer to her fiancé and forced a smile. She wanted to ease the tension of their last conversation.

"Do not bother," Karwyn said without moving. "Spare me whatever you were about to say."

"Is this really how it's going to be until one of us dies?" Amira asked.

Karwyn's smile was savage. "I am doing you a favour, dear fiancée. Better to ignore someone than to tell them what you really think of them, no? Or do you want me to keep bruising your fragile little ego?"

Waves of annoyance raced through Amira's mind. "I'm sorry about the ceremony. But I really am trying my best."

"At seducing my best friend?"

Amira was shocked by Karwyn's accusations. She opened her mouth to reply but Karwyn kept talking. "You are aware that I am the one you have to marry, right? And that the contest heavily relies on my image. *You* are now part of that image. I cannot have you fooling around with Rhay."

She would never. She was only looking for friendliness, a pure connection, something her fiancé had been denying her. Was it so inconceivable for her to be friends with a man? Her intentions were pure, she was sure of it.

She was about to cast Karwyn's jealousy aside by telling him just that when a loud creaking noise assaulted her ears. The door was finally open.

As if he had practiced multiple times, Karwyn took Amira's limp hand and intertwined their fingers before stepping into the light.

The sun blinded her for a moment and she blinked a few times, trying to get used to being outside again. Her eyes were eventually able to grasp the size of the plaza and the crowd that was filling it. The houses surrounding them were three storeys high with flat rooftops and turquoise walls. Most of the buildings had stained glass windows representing Falea and Caelo, floating in the sky or looking over the kingdom.

The few guards who had accompanied them spread out around the wooden platform. One of them, a young, brown-haired fae, looked around the crowd, his lazuli-blue eyes searching for someone. Amira followed his gaze, intrigued by his attitude, but a veil fell over the guard's eyes and he became completely stone-faced. A true professional, committed to his duty.

The crowd was buzzing with anticipation and Amira could see it in their eyes. Fae of all ages were staring at Karwyn and her as they walked on top of the platform.

A metal gate was keeping the crowd away and alongside it, guards were posted. Amira wasn't sure if it was the gate or the menacing looks of the guards that were keeping the crowd at bay.

She noticed a group of three similar-looking women with small children. They bore a striking resemblance to Nalani, the same silky black hair and warm eyes. Amira was ready to wave at them until something caught her eye on their left.

Stuck on the door of one of the houses, Amira noticed a poster representing the man she had seen brought in by guards two nights ago. She was too far away to read what was written on the poster but she figured it could only be one of two things: a wanted notice or a missing person appeal. The first one would appease her worries and she could forget about the scene she had witnessed. After all, Parae was a big city, criminals were bound to exist there. But if it was the second, then something weird was happening in the kingdom.

She leaned towards Karwyn who was now looking at his nails, completely disinterested by the excited crowd screaming his name. "What's this poster for?"

She seemed to have triggered something in the king because his eyes immediately darted around the plaza. Realising his behaviour, Karwyn stared back at his nails. "There are no posters."

Amira pointed towards the door. "Right there."

Karwyn barely looked in the direction she was indicating. "Who cares? It is hardly any of our concern."

"As king, shouldn't you care?" She thought she saw a flicker of rage in his turquoise eyes, but Karwyn's answer was cut short by the arrival of multiple boxes overflowing with food.

The crowd cheered loudly as each box was piled up on the platform. But then the boxes stopped coming and Amira could sense some tension from the crowd.

Karwyn cleared his throat. "People of Parae, it is my pleasure as your king to offer you this food in honour of Falea Night. May we all be blessed by her fortune for the year to come."

Karwyn went up to one of the boxes and Amira followed him. "Where's the rest?" a voice screamed from the crowd. Amira saw Karwyn clench his jaw but he grabbed one of the boxes and carried it up to the gate. A bit hesitant, Amira did the same.

The representatives passed along the boxes to other fae in the crowd, creating a moving chain. Karwyn and Amira went back to get more.

"There's less than last year," another voice shouted through the noise of the crowd. Amira could sense them getting restless.

She leaned towards Karwyn. "Is everything all right?"

"It is as expected. These people are biting the hand that feeds them. They should be grateful they are getting anything at all," he said between gritted teeth.

They finished carrying the last of the two boxes. They seemed lighter than the previous ones. Amira gave her box to one of the representatives. The fae left the gate to go to the wooden table where the boxes had been piled up. The crowd was growing more agitated and fae were trying to climb over the gate. The guards unsheathed their swords and the crowd seemed to calm down.

Until a scream echoed through the plaza. "This box is practically empty!"

Chaos broke free. Fae started throwing themselves against the gates while families ran away, holding their terrified children against their chests. The guards tried to push back the angry crowd with their swords, sometimes drawing blood, violence fuelling violence. The injuries didn't stop the angry mob from climbing over the gates, overpowering the guards.

Amira looked around for Karwyn. He was already surrounded by guards who pushed their way to the tunnel access.

"Layken, get the princess," Nouis shouted. He hadn't been at the centre of the platform and was already moving inside the building by the tunnel access.

Her gaze locked with a guard—Layken, she presumed—who was fighting off the crowd but moved towards her. Blood splattered on her shocked face as he slashed an angry fae's arm. She froze completely, unable to get herself out of the situation. She saw everything happening as if she was in a glass box, violence erupting all around her. She was waiting for it to claim her as its prize.

Her mind let go of her body, abandoning it in its vulnerable state. She stood among the fighting fae. The turquoise uniforms of the guards mixed with the blue-dressed crowd.

She saw the slap coming but didn't even feel it; only the buzzing in her ear indicated that she had truly been hit. Layken pushed her behind him, his sword cutting through her attacker's chest easily. Amira watched the blood drip from his wound as he fell. A vision of someone else's blood took root in her head. It might have been her own.

Someone tore at the bottom of her dress, bringing her back to the riot. Layken kicked the fae in the face. "If you want to keep your hand, I suggest you stay back," Layken said, his tone strangely light for this occasion. Blood was smeared across his face. He rubbed his hand over his eye and forehead but it did nothing to remove the red stain.

"We demand more!" a fae shouted, his voice rising above the crowd. Amira looked over Layken's shoulder as he forced her to slowly back away, clearing a path for them to the tunnel. Her gaze found the fae as he screamed, "Caelo should take you off the throne!" The young fae looked to be a teenager. He held one of the half-empty boxes as he stormed forward, escaping the grasp of guards nearby.

The guards on either side of Karwyn stepped forward. She could see Karwyn's furious eyes as they fixed on the fae. The young man grabbed the mix of vegetables in the box and threw it at the king. The guards blocked most of it but a splash of spinach landed on Karwyn's face. The look in his eyes chilled her bones. It reminded her too much of Wryen.

"Amira!" Rhay's voice caught Amira's attention. He was running towards them, a bloodied guard's sword in his hand. Had he taken it from a fallen guard?

"Hold on," Layken said, barely avoiding the blade of a long knife as he pushed her a step back.

Amira tried to find Rhay again in the crowd but she couldn't see his tinted hair anywhere. Her gaze travelled back to Karwyn, who was now shepherded into the building where they had accessed the tunnel. Wondering about the teenage fae who had rebelled against the king, Amira scanned the area. She saw an unmoving body on the ground but there were too many fae blocking his head and upper body. She twisted her neck, trying to catch a glimpse of his features.

Finally, the fae moved and Amira's gaze travelled to the unconscious fae's head, which was now detached from his body.

Amira screamed. Everything else turned silent. Her feet wouldn't move. Layken turned her towards him. His lips were moving but she didn't hear anything. Screams tore through her. She couldn't tell if they were her own. They sounded familiar but distant in her head.

Amira barely noticed a sword swinging out of the corner of her eye before Layken abandoned his grip on her and raised his own.

The blood in her body froze and she felt her strength abandoning her as the screams froze and there was no noise at all anymore.

She felt herself lifted up. Strong arms holding her as they moved quickly. Her head fell back and she saw the peaceful face of Falea, Goddess of Fortune, looking over her from one of the stained-glass windows.

CHAPTER 25

◊

AMIRA

The bath was comfortably warm and the smell of crushed rose petals made her forget about the insidious scent of blood sticking to her body. When Nalani had helped her remove her dress, she had voluntarily omitted to comment on the dark red liquid sticking to the pleats of the silk-like fabric. The sight reminded her of the severed head. Another memory to add to her nightmares.

When she had regained control of her body, Amira had found herself in a carriage next to Rhay. He had been the one to carry her to the tunnel, Layken covering his back. Karwyn had already left in a different carriage.

Amira couldn't help replaying the whole day in her head. Leaving Amryne, she had expected to be far away from violence and madness. From all she had heard from her father and then her brother, Turosian was a very rich and stable kingdom. Nothing else could be expected from the home of the high king. But now it appeared that since Harten's death a couple months ago, things were starting to turn sour in Turosian. Amira wondered if her brother knew.

And what about the contest? If talks of a riot were to reach the other royal advisors' ears, Karwyn's chances at being selected for the High King Contest would fall. Rhay had called it civil unrest and had muttered something about his father handling it, but Amira wasn't convinced. What she had seen in the plaza indicated some kind of deep-rooted issue. And it could very well cancel the wedding if the right people got wind of it. A part of her would love to not marry such a cold-hearted man. But if she didn't, she would just have to go back to a man with no heart at all.

Amira was incredibly tired and for a second she considered falling asleep in the now lukewarm water. But instead she climbed out of the bath, her body glistening with the pale pink water, and wrapped herself in a soft towel.

Someone knocked on the antechamber door just as she finished dressing herself.

Expecting Nalani, Amira said, "Come in." She turned to see Rhay standing in the antechamber, a big smile on his face and a colourful book in his hands. She joined him by the door. Her gaze flickered across the hallway, making sure no one was there watching them. The last thing she needed was to increase Karwyn's suspicion.

"I have a gift for you. I think you deserve some distraction after what happened today." Rhay offered her the colourful book. On the cover was a beautiful young woman wearing intricate golden armour. The title was intriguing but unknown to Amira. A bit puzzled, she looked at Rhay.

"It's a human book, but they write about fae," he said.

"Oh, is it an historical essay?" Her father had made her read a few of them during her studies but they were, of course, written by fae. Amira wasn't particularly fond of them.

"No, no, it's completely fictional. The author has never set foot in Liraen. They're using their imagination and it's absolutely hilarious to see how they picture us." He paused for a few seconds. "It's also pretty scandalous, so I obviously love it, but maybe it will be too much for you." He pretended to take back the novel but Amira held on to it. She was definitely intrigued by the premise.

"I'm sure I can handle it. After all, I'm able to deal with you," she playfully replied. It felt nice to have a pleasant conversation for a change.

The sound of voices echoed through the hallway. Amira immediately tensed. It was best if no one saw Rhay at her door.

"Thank you for your gift, Rhay. It really means a lot. I should get ready for tonight," she said, knowing she still had to endure the dinner in Falea's honour.

"I offer you a present and you're kicking me out?" He feigned pain, putting a hand to his heart.

She couldn't bring herself to close the door. "What were you expecting in return?" Amira asked, half joking, half serious.

Rhay's mind seemed to wander as a grin formed on his face. "I was only joking." He did a pretend curtsy to relieve the tension. "I'll see you tonight, princess."

Amira spent what was left of the afternoon writing to her mother. Once again, Amira conveniently forgot to write about all the things that troubled her.

Amira hoped that her mother would soon write back to her. She had already sent a couple of letters and was still waiting for a reply. Worry took over her mind until Nalani opened the door, a long dress in her arms.

Amira showed the letter to her maid. "Would you be able to post it tonight? It's for my mother."

"Of course, my lady. I'll take care of it as soon as you are ready for the feast."

Amira sighed but she let Nalani undress her and put her in a new dress. The skirt was of tight, dark blue velvet. Hundreds of little turquoise stones were embroidered with silver thread.

Nalani reapplied Amira's makeup and looked proudly at her work. "Perfect. Now you need to choose something to burn for tonight, princess."

Amira shuddered at the thought of fire. Flames flashed before her eyes. A familiar scream echoed in her head. Amira shut her eyes tightly, blocking the memory. "Why do I need to burn something?" she managed to ask.

"It's a tradition for good luck and protection. You have to choose something precious that reminds you of a person you want to protect. Burning it in the sacred fire assures Falea's protection over the person."

"That makes a lot of fae to protect."

Amira's sarcastic remark didn't seem to dampen Nalani's excited mood. "What are you going to pick?"

Amira thought about it for a moment. She didn't have a

lot of people she wanted to protect. She would probably only put her mother in this category. One of the rare things she had from her were her letters. But burning one would mean that she would have to let go of it. Was she ready to do so when she had so few of them?

"I'm going to take care of your letter. His Majesty will pick you up in around ten minutes. Think about the object you will choose," Nalani said as she exited the room.

Left alone, Amira debated a bit more before settling on one of the shortest letters. After all, if it was to bring protection to her mother, Amira could relinquish one memory of her.

She had just screwed back the pillar after taking out the letter from its hiding spot when she heard a sharp knock on the door. Amira gave herself one last look in the mirror, making sure her braided ponytail was still in place.

She opened the door to face Karwyn. He was wearing a silver shirt with no visible button. Even though the cut was very simple, it was unmistakably expensive. His trousers were bulky enough to hide his frailer frame. Karwyn looked her up and down but gave her no compliment. So she did the same and ignored his fitting outfit.

Karwyn extended his arm, looking absolutely disinterested in the situation. Amira closed the door behind her and took his arm.

They walked in uncomfortable silence. The closer they got to the dining hall, the louder were the sounds of the feast, filling the empty hallway.

Outside the doors, Karwyn leaned in, provoking a difficult-to-hide shiver. "Behave and do exactly as I tell you," he said.

His orders made Amira feel like a soldier and she almost wanted to mimic an official salute, but she knew it wouldn't be taken well by Karwyn.

As the heavy doors opened in front of them, the voices inside immediately went quiet. A servant loudly announced, "His Majesty, Karwyn Adelway, King of Turosian, interim High King, and his fiancée, Princess Amira Rosston of Allamyst."

Amira disliked hearing her name associated with Karwyn's. But she knew she'd have to get used to it. Better to be an Adelway than shackled to her brother.

Nouis walked up to them with two delicate glasses of iridos in his hands. He bowed deeply before offering the drinks. Karwyn grabbed his quickly and Amira copied him with less confidence. She awkwardly held the glass in her hand, expecting her next orders. Her hand started trembling as she felt too many eyes on her.

Karwyn quickly grabbed her hand and straightened it. "Do not spill it. It would mean bad luck," he said.

Again with their stupid superstitions. It would definitely take her time to get used to that aspect of life in Turosian. Amira glanced at her bracelet. Somehow, it had survived unscathed by the riot. She wasn't convinced luck had anything to do with it.

Karwyn walked up to the large marble table overlooking the rest of the feast and Amira followed, her glass of iridos clenched in her fist. They stayed standing in front of their seats. The members of the court took their place behind the other tables. When everyone was ready, Karwyn raised his glass and everyone, including Amira, did the same.

"Esteemed members of the court, tonight we celebrate our

fortunate Goddess Falea. May she always protect the Turosian kingdom and its inhabitants." Karwyn turned to face Amira and linked his arm around hers in order for their drinks to be in front of the other person's mouth. All around them, fae did the same.

"Blessed be the fortunate Falea," Karwyn loudly said before gesturing to Amira to do the same.

"Blessed be the fortunate Falea." She hated how weak her voice sounded. The rest of the court repeated the five words. Despite the uncomfortable position, everyone downed their glass. The iridos coated Amira's throat, almost suffocating her with its sweetness. *Breathe,* she chanted in her head to calm her nerves. Then the feast started.

Sitting next to Karwyn and the rest of the guests, Amira must have looked like a child in a high chair. They seemed to have forgotten to put a wine glass for her. When she tried to catch the eye of one of the servants serving indigo wine, Karwyn lowered his head to say quite loudly, "I do not think you should drink any more. You are too frail to handle it properly."

Amira saw a few fae at her table laughed discreetly. Red with humiliation, she turned to Karwyn. "I forgot to thank you today."

Karwyn took the bait. "For what?"

"For leaving me all alone in the middle of a riot."

Karwyn gently took her hand and lowered his voice. Was he really going to apologise? "Dear fiancée, I am going to tell you a secret about me," he started softly, his voice almost caressing her ear. "I have never liked sarcasm in a woman." And he dropped her hand, not even giving her a chance to reply.

During the rest of the feast, Amira stayed quiet and barely ate anything. She felt Karwyn's eyes on her, commanding her to behave.

A burst of flames ignited the dining hall and Amira jumped to her feet instinctively, her heart pounding in her chest and dreadful memories plaguing her. In the middle of the room, servants were feeding a large pyre with logs of dark wood. Luckily everyone was too fascinated by the fire to have seen her panicked reaction.

Everyone except Rhay and Karwyn. The two friends were both looking at her, each with a different expression on their face. Concern radiated from Rhay and cruel enjoyment twisted Karwyn's grin. The more time she spent with her fiancé, the more he reminded her of Wryen.

Amira took a few deep breaths before settling back in her seat. She ignored Karwyn's smirk and focused on what was happening in front of her. Fae were dropping little objects into the fire. Once the flames consumed the objects, a dark blue smoke lingered in the air for a few seconds.

Rhay stood up and walked towards the fire. Held tight in his hands was a little leather handbook. Amira watched him throw it in the fire. It burned out quickly, giving out the now familiar smoke. Rhay turned around and smiled at his father with such fondness in his eyes. It was obvious that the notebook belonged to Nouis. Amira felt her mother's letter against her skin. She had hidden it under her dress, close to her heart.

She stood up, ready to go burn her letter. Karwyn immediately stopped her with one hand. "We go last," he said sharply. The sensation of his skin against hers made her sick. He quickly removed his hand. "I take no pleasure in it either," he said in her ear, "but you will have to hide your feelings about it better if you wish to remain here. Especially in front of my court."

Had he just read her mind? She stared at him, looking for an answer to her fears. Karwyn's face was void of any emotion. Impossible to read. It must have been a coincidence. Yet she couldn't shake the feeling of Karwyn lurking inside her head.

Amira sat down again. Her fork in hand, she played with the scraps of pie that were left on her plate. She felt a low rumble in her stomach but still decided not to finish the dessert. She didn't really know why. Maybe it was to feel something other than the constant anger she was in every time she tried to talk with Karwyn.

The king finally stood up, a little replica of the palace made out of turquoise was in his hands. "Follow me," he coldly said. Amira took out her letter and followed him.

As she walked closer to the fire, her heart started racing in her chest. A thin veil of cold sweat glistened on her skin. They reached the fire and Amira had to stop herself from running away. She bravely held the letter in front of her.

Karwyn snatched it from her hand. "What do you think you are doing? It is our duty to burn this statuette together to bring luck to the kingdom. Pay attention." He crumpled the letter in his pocket and forced Amira to hold the statuette with him.

A few members of the court watched them as they threw the replica of the palace into the flames. Amira didn't expect the smoke to be so sweet and heady. It almost felt like a drug. She stumbled, mesmerised by the smell and the scintillating colour. Karwyn turned to leave.

"Wait, my letter," she pleaded.

He turned back and put the crumpled letter in her open hands. "After your little escape at the temple, I did not think you believed in our tradition," he said mockingly.

Amira chose to ignore him and moved towards the pyre. The flames danced in front of her. It took her an unreasonable amount of strength to watch them. She threw her letter in the fire.

Through the smoke, she noticed that Karwyn was now on the other side of the fire, completely ignoring the few drunkards next to him. His gaze was focused on a small piece of sandy white paper. Amira caught a glimpse of drawings featuring stylised black butterflies. He mumbled a few words, much like a prayer, and threw the piece of paper into the flames.

When he raised his head, he noticed Amira staring at him. The love in his eyes quickly turned into hatred. The flames reflecting in his vibrant turquoise irises only amplified his anger. Fear coated Amira's heart. In her head, another pair of hateful eyes stared back at her. Only this time, they were lilac like a morning sky.

She squeezed her eyes shut but the flames increased, wrapping around her. A memory of burned flesh raced through her head. Long hair going up in flames. The crowd cheering as the fire took over the fae's body. Wryen's satisfied smirk. She felt bindings digging into her arms as the vivid memory took a hold of her.

A scream echoed through the room. It was only when she

opened her eyes and saw everyone staring at her that Amira realised that she had been the one screaming. She fell to the ground, breathing heavily as the smoke trapped her in the past.

Rhay ran up to her but Karwyn intercepted him. "Go fetch Saydren. I will take her to her room," she heard the king say. "Layken, take the princess."

A pair of strong arms grabbed her and raised her from the ground. As they moved across the room, she heard whispers coming from the few lucid fae. *I heard she's crazy. Is that why her brother locked her up in the palace? She's mad like the last Queen of Turosian.*

The doors closed behind them. Amira could feel her body burning up and she tried to free herself from the guard's strong hold.

"Amira, you need to calm down." For a second, Amira thought she heard concern in Karwyn's voice. She felt as if flames were clawing at her. Then there was nothing, just pure emptiness.

She regained control of her body when Layken dropped her on her bed. Amira rolled around, trying to escape the burning hands she could see out of the corner of her eyes.

"My lady, you have to stay still," said a voice she had never heard before.

"Who's talking?" she asked in a strangled voice as her eyes tried to see out of the darkness of her mind.

"I'm Saydren, the royal healer. I'm going to give you something to calm your nerves."

She could make out his tall silhouette but her vision was still blurry. A hand grabbed hers and dropped something small in it. Amira brought her hand right to her face to see what Saydren had given her. It seemed to be a tiny silver and red pill. She had never seen such medicine before.

A glass of water appeared in front of her. "Come on, take it. It will help you feel better."

Could she trust this man? She wished Rhay was here. She was longing for a familiar, friendly face.

Amira put the pill into her mouth but hid it underneath her tongue. When she drank the water, she made sure to not swallow the pill.

"That's good, now get some rest, princess." Saydren left her in the dark. Amira took out the pill and stuck it underneath her bed. She closed her eyes and tried to appease her chaotic breathing.

Suddenly, the door opened again. Amira pretended to be fast asleep, worried that the healer had come back to give her more medicine.

Her bed moved when the stranger sat down. Amira held her breath and squeezed her eyes shut, making herself see tiny dots of buzzing light. A hand landed on her face, softly caressing it with its burning touch. For a second the hand lingered on her throat as it often did, reawakening the painful memory that followed her everywhere.

"Don't act like a lunatic, Amira, or your chance at marriage will be ruined. My patience is running thin," a familiar voice hissed in her ear. A voice that occupied all her nightmares. But it was never just a dream.

CHAPTER 26

LORA

Lora never thought she'd one day willingly participate in a fae celebration, yet when they'd found Mrs Marsyn setting up the garden for Falea Night, she couldn't refuse the kind woman's invitation. She was still unsure if Eyden had wanted her to join and, if so, why. Lora had read the question in his eyes when Mrs Marsyn insisted they get ready for tonight, but she couldn't place the motivation behind it.

What she did know was that they weren't going to walk to Chrysa that day as they wouldn't make it back during daylight. So was there any harm in joining the event? It was the kind of research she'd never get access to again. For that reason, she could take being surrounded by too many fae one last time.

A knock on the door made Lora sit up on the bed in the guest room. She'd changed into the dress that was left for her and tried to style her hair by braiding part of it into a messy headband. A few dark-blonde strands fell into her face when she tilted her head up to the door.

"Come in." She got up on tired feet and fixed her dress. It flowed down her legs in a wave of light blue, glittering satin. It had a slit on both legs and small cut outs above her waist but overall it was quite comfortable.

Eyden opened the door. His curly hair was styled for once and he had changed into navy blue trousers and a matching shirt, the material shining where the light touched it. His eyes took her in quickly before stopping at her feet. A small smile played on his lips. The slit not only revealed part of her legs but also her black ankle boots that she'd been wearing ever since Eyden handed them to her. They didn't compliment the elegant dress but she didn't mind.

"If you want other shoes, I'm sure Mrs Marsyn has some," Eyden said.

"No, that's all right." For once, she kind of liked the idea of not fitting in completely. Lora sidestepped Eyden as she walked through the door. "Let's do this," she said as she held his gaze and took a step backwards.

Eyden nodded and off they went to the once rather empty garden that was now filled with silver tables and chairs. Each table was decorated with elegantly styled turquoise flower bouquets, silver threads circling the stems. A multitude of candles and torches sticking out of flowerbeds lit up the area. In the middle of the garden, a pile of wood was neatly placed together. She assumed it would make a spectacular bonfire once the sun had fully disappeared. The warm night wind brushed her bare shoulders in a comforting gesture.

The area was crowded with cheerful fae. Most were already seated. The tables were filled with food and bottles of wine, displayed on shimmering turquoise tablecloths. Lora caught sight of Ilario, who gestured for them to join him at his table.

Once everyone was seated, Mrs Marsyn tapped a spoon against her wine glass to get everyone's attention. "Thank you all for coming. I'm so grateful that we're all here to enjoy this meal and wine that was provided by the king himself in the name of our Goddess."

Lora looked at Eyden in surprise. The king gave them this meal? All of this, yet fae were still starving? Eyden's face was a perfect stoic mask. Ilario, on the other hand, looked tense. His mouth formed a tight line as he listened to his mother's speech.

Ilario caught Lora staring. "Scraps of food. Nothing else. The thanks should go to the community."

Lora almost missed his muttered words. If it wasn't for Eyden's subtle twitch, his lips curving upwards on one side, she could have sworn she'd imagined them all together.

Mrs Marsyn raised her glass and everyone followed her move. "Blessed be the fortunate Falea."

The gathered fae repeated her words and Lora moved her lips, pretending to follow their example. Eyden lifted his glass off the table and pointed to Lora's full one. She picked it up for show but had no intention of drinking it. To her surprise, when she looked across the table she saw fae linking arms and sharing their drinks with each other.

Intrigued, she returned her focus to Eyden; he was looking at her as if he was asking for her permission. Understanding his intention, Lora extended her arm and Eyden turned in his chair as they linked arms. He moved his glass towards her lips and

Lora mirrored his movement. One of her legs was in-between his as they both shifted closer to share their drinks.

Eyden took a sip first and Lora's breath hitched as she noted their closeness. Her bare knee grazed his thigh, the material of his trousers soft against her skin. When his eyes met hers, the intensity made her hand unsteady, but she held control and took a sip from Eyden's glass.

The wine was sweeter than expected, coating her tongue pleasantly, and her eyes drifted shut for a second. When she met Eyden's gaze again, she found him staring back with as much intrigue as she had hidden within her as well.

The reflection broke something loose inside her. She realised this was their last evening together. Tomorrow, they would get the cure and Lora would go back home. She would leave all of this behind her and never think of it again. So what was the harm if she enjoyed tonight? It would all disappear, turn into a faded memory of temporary insanity.

Eyden finished the glass and Lora stopped halfway through, afraid if she had too much it would make her truly forget everything. She'd rather lock it away than erase it completely.

The noise of clattering cutlery and chatter made them break apart and Lora dug into her food. She noticed this was the first time she was served meat since arriving in Liraen. Combined with the expertly prepared mashed potatoes, the dish was as exquisite as she hoped this evening would be.

The tables were moved to the side and a frighteningly large fire rose in the middle of the garden, yet no one seemed bothered by the possibility of it getting out of control. The fae apparently enjoyed the fire and stood dangerously close to it as they threw various objects into the pyre. They were instantly consumed by the flames and a midnight blue smoke gathered, mixing with the ashes floating in the wind. The smoke invaded her senses but Lora found she didn't mind the heavy scent.

"It symbolizes good luck," Eyden said, standing closer to her than she'd realised. "If you burn something that belonged to someone you care for, you're ensuring them luck for the coming year."

"I don't have anything." The only thing Lora had on her from her world was her rose gold necklace. Her mother had given it to her, but there was no way she could part with it. Lora could hear her mother's voice in her head, telling her to never take it off. It felt like an anchor to home. To herself. To her human side.

"It can also be something that symbolizes the person." There was an opening around the fire as a group of fae left. "I'll be right back," Eyden said as he walked to the spot.

Lora searched the garden and noticed a few irises growing on the ground. It was her mother's favourite flower. She took it as a sign and gently plucked one of them.

When she joined Eyden by the fire, he was about to throw something into the flames. Something small enough that she couldn't see it as he clasped it tightly.

Eyden slowly opened his hand but his eyes were focused on the flames. Lora wasn't sure he was even aware she was there. She caught a glimpse of his object before he threw it into the fire. It was a tiny silver flower ornament that reminded her of the one attached to his pen.

Maybe it belonged to his mother. The thought made her think of her own. Lora pictured her mum as she held the iris in front of her face. The purple flower looked bright and hopeful even against the flames raging behind it. Sometimes beautiful things had to burn to create something spectacular. With that in mind, Lora let the flower drift into the flames and watched as it burned until midnight blue smoke was the only thing left behind.

She turned to Eyden. The fire from the pyre was reflected in his eyes, red mixing with blue, turning his gaze to melted ice. Lora wondered what he saw in her reflection. If he noticed her emotions were a mix of conflicting colours.

Eyden quickly glanced away then back at her. "I'll be back," he said and with no explanation, he walked off. Lora imagined he might go to the house and come right back but instead he walked across the field until he disappeared into the woods.

"He does that sometimes," Ilario said. She hadn't heard him approach but she'd been distracted, looking at the spot where Eyden had vanished into the night.

Lora backed away from the fire and replied, "Does it not bother you?"

"Not really. I'm sure he has his reasons and it has nothing to do with me. He's always there when it counts."

"But doesn't it drive you mad? The not knowing?"

He gave her a half-grin. "I'm curious, sure. But that's Eyden. I can tell it drives *you* mad, though," Ilario said, a teasing light in his eyes.

Lora stared into the fire, now a healthy distance away from her. "I just don't like not knowing."

"That's all it is?"

"Of course."

"I think you care more than you'd like to admit."

Lora gave him a look as if to say the thought was absolutely absurd. She tried to find something to change the subject and spotted Ilario's parents holding each other as they watched their guests enjoy the festivities.

"Your parents seem happy," she said.

Ilario followed her eyes. A look of content washed over his face. "Yeah, they are. They've been married for almost 120 years."

"That's a long time." The reply slipped from her lips before she could reconsider. It was an impossible number for humans.

Ilario didn't seem to question her statement. "I suppose so. They had me quite young."

"How old are you?"

"Twenty-eight."

They couldn't have been that young then, but she figured fae had a very different way of looking at age. She wondered if it had anything to do with the complications of fae pregnancies that Eyden had mentioned.

Suddenly music started playing, elevating the joy in the air. Lora searched for the source and spotted a small band playing on the edge of the garden. Fae started gathering in the middle of the green lawn as they moved to the joyful music, enjoying themselves.

Ilario took a step forward and then back again as he knelt on the ground. A crushed iris was in front of him. He'd probably stepped on it by accident. Ilario cradled it in his hand and the flower righted itself, blooming brighter than before.

Lora stared in wonder and the expression was still written on her face when Ilario stood up and looked at her. "Earth magic," he said, his tone questioning.

She realised she shouldn't be surprised to see a display of fae magic. And she shouldn't find it fascinating either.

Ilario might not use it for anything bad, but he could. She knew from history books that high-level fae with earth magic could harm others easily. For instance, through dangerous earthquakes. "Right, of course. For some reason, I didn't imagine you having earth magic, considering you're a trader."

"I suppose you're right. I don't need earth magic for my work. I've never enjoyed gardening that much, if I'm being honest. My mum loves it. It brings her joy, the solitude of it. Just her and her garden. I would much rather be surrounded by people than plants." Ilario looked towards the flowerbeds and the fenced-off vegetable garden. "Although it does help every now and then. I sell a lot of things my parents grow here and sometimes I help my mother out when I visit. But for the most part, I let her do the gardening while I focus on the trades."

"That's a good system." The thought of them working together as a family and using their strengths to their advantage made Lora smile. An image took form in her head. Her mum was cooking in the kitchen at her Buffalo Diner, Oscar was by her side, dropping a healthy amount of spices into the pot on the stove, while Lora made the rounds, banished from the kitchen for good reason.

"It works quite well," Ilario answered before his gaze drifted over her head. "Look who's making a reappearance."

Lora turned around and her eyes immediately found Eyden. His eyes met hers and didn't move from her face as he walked towards her with a newfound urgency. She noted the shift in his eyes when he was in front of her. Something had changed, but she couldn't put her finger on it.

"I forgot to say something earlier," Eyden said, breaking his stare.

Lora looked to her left but Ilario was already walking away. "What is it?" she asked, unsure of what he was about to say but craving the answer.

"Thank you for what you did on the cliff," he said in a quiet voice.

Lora smiled at his words. "And what did I do exactly?" she teased, not letting him off that easy. Not when it was such delightful fun to watch him squirm.

"You're really making me say it?"

"I think you already know the answer to that one."

A slow grin stretched across his face. "Okay, only because it's Falea Night." He took a deep breath. "Thanks for not untying your end of the rope right away so you could stop my fall without putting yourself at risk."

She laughed and it ignited her heart as much as the flames ignited the pyre behind them. "That's the worst thank you I've ever heard." Her mind jumped to a new question as if on autopilot, to demand where he'd disappeared to. But when she looked into his eyes again, the question evaporated. The way he looked at her, with that teasing fire swirling in his light eyes, Lora didn't need anything else right now.

"But I'll take it," she said. This wasn't a night for questions. She suddenly didn't feel like talking at all anymore.

Eyden seemed to have the same understanding. Instead of speaking, he held out his hand.

Lora hesitated only for mere seconds. The feeling of his hand in hers was different than before. They weren't on a mission, this wasn't pretence.

Eyden led her to the makeshift dance floor until the euphoric music surrounded them, veiling them into their own world even as other fae danced around them. His hands drifted to her waist, fingers grazing bare skin and satin. Lora hooked her arms behind his head and stopped thinking, focusing on feeling this flicker in time that would only be theirs for today.

She'd blame it on the wine later. The heating of her skin. The way his touch burnt her in the best way. Her insanity for embracing this moment when she should turn away.

Eyden's carefully styled hair came undone as they danced slowly, loose curls falling into his face. Lora didn't stop herself and ran a hand through his hair, pushing it back to reveal his blazing eyes, a thousand questions swirling in a pale blue sea. Her breath caught slightly as the movement brought them even closer. She could've sworn she saw Eyden's eyes drift to her lips before finding her eyes again.

Without warning, the music sped up and became wilder. Fae started bumping into them and they were forced to drop their arms as the song turned into a group dance. Everyone around them was dancing freely, unbothered.

Lora was out of her element but when Eyden grabbed her hand and spun her around, her worries vanished again and soon they were lost in the mass of people. Two insane souls, dancing their hearts out under the stars, illuminated by flames that signalled luck would come their way.

Lora almost stumbled over her dress as she opened the door to the guest room. She turned from Eyden's amused, crooked smile and let herself fall onto the bed. The wine was still coursing through her system, turning her mind fuzzy. It might also be the dancing that had messed with her head. Or rather, her dance partner.

Shifting on the mattress, her eyes searched for Eyden. He'd taken off his jacket and when he untucked his shirt, her eyes got caught on the sliver of bare skin above his trousers. The wine was definitely at fault for her flushed skin. Nothing more.

She forced her gaze up until she met sparkling blue illuminated by a layer of starlight streaming in through the window. The smile playing on Eyden's lips did interesting things to her. Tearing her eyes away, Lora stared at the light patterns on the ceiling instead. She needed the feeling to vanish, to be washed away with this day. Tomorrow would catch up with her soon enough.

Even though she didn't see him, she could hear Eyden settling down on his makeshift bed on the floor. Lora should sleep, she knew that much. Exhaustion should override the low electricity rushing through her. Still, she found herself saying, "The stars are incredibly bright tonight."

She almost thought he'd already fallen asleep, but then his quiet voice filled the room. "It's a good sign. The story goes, the brighter the stars shine, the more present the Gods are. You see the big one next to the diamond?"

"Diamond?" Lora lifted herself up on her elbows, squinting as she took in the patterns in the night sky through the window. "I don't see anything like that."

"You're too high up."

Before she could rethink her insanity, Lora rolled off the bed and joined Eyden on the floor. She must have left her head on the dance floor. The look he gave her was a mix of surprise and excitement. Lora swallowed before she said, "Show me."

His eyes sparked with intrigue before his gaze left hers as he pointed out a structure of stars, creating a shimmering diamond in the dark. And there, to the right, a noticeably bigger star burned at the forefront.

The corners of her mouth pulled upwards. "I see it."

"The God of the Sky keeping watch," Eyden mumbled. His voice felt closer than expected. Their nearness made a shiver dance across her skin.

"Caelo. Of course." The religion of the fae left gaps in their human research, but for once, she wasn't focused on fae history.

"Some fae like to wish upon the stars. Especially on nights this clear."

Another superstition, but this one felt closer to home. The sky might be embracing the beauty of the night, but her mind was anything but clear. "Did you ever make a wish?" She regretted the question as soon as she said it. This wasn't the time for it. "Forget it. Never mind."

The silence wasn't unpleasant but it felt like the end of the night. Lora shifted, gripping the fabric of her dress to get up, but Eyden's words stopped her. "I used to."

She settled back down, somehow even closer this time. Her right leg brushed against his but she didn't dare move. "What for?" Lora asked, her voice a whisper.

He wouldn't look her way. "Always the same thing. That my mum had kept her promise. That she would be fine." Eyden turned towards her. "What would you wish for?"

That she could keep all her empty promises. Somehow fill them all up with hope and starlight. But there was no such option. "The same thing," she answered, her tone wavering, but her stare held firm.

Light danced over his face. Her eyes searched his but all she found were more questions. He was so close. His breath mixed with hers. The scent of sweet wine filled her nose. She felt as if they brought the fire with them to this tiny room, flames engulfing them in madness. She must be mad to feel this want—this need to move closer. Part of her wanted to encourage the voice in her mind that told her to shut off her fears.

Eyden tilted his head down, his mouth lining up with hers. A subtle shift and their lips would brush. An infinite second stretched between them. She was utterly aware of the slit in her dress that revealed part of her leg. Her bare skin brushed against his leg. She could see it in his eyes that he knew it too.

Eyden moved closer just as doubt washed over her like ice-cold water. She pulled back and let her eyes fixate on the steady stars. A shooting star flashed across the sky. Her lips parted in wonder. "Another good luck charm."

"Quite the opposite." He met her gaze briefly, now no longer reflecting fire, but rather burned out embers, before returning to the image of the star-filled night. "A falling star is the beginning of ruin."

CHAPTER 27

AMIRA

A cold hand brushed against her cheek. Amira opened her eyes, expecting to see the cruel eyes of her brother. Thank Caelo, she was faced with Nalani's warm eyes. The maid grabbed a glass of a sweet-smelling drink and pushed it to Amira's lips.

"Drink, this will make you feel better."

The syrupy liquid gave her just enough energy to start asking questions. "Do you know what happened last night?"

Nalani shifted, visibly uncomfortable with the answer.

"Is it that bad?" Amira insisted even though she dreaded the answer.

"There have been some rumours," Nalani said while avoiding Amira's eyes. "But I've told everyone that you were still in shock about what happened in the city plaza. Your brother was very worried about you."

Furious would be a more accurate description, Amira thought. Picturing his sullen eyes, she shivered. She had to prove to him that she was still fit to become Karwyn's queen.

Nalani reached into her pocket and handed her a note with familiar handwriting. "Mister Messler delivered this note while you were still asleep. He told me you should open it as soon as you wake up."

Her head still buzzing from last night's events, Amira opened the note.

"Dear Amira, if you are feeling up to it, you should join the council meeting today at eleven bells. This will be more educational than a history book. I'll see you there,

Your extraordinary friend,

Rhay."

This was her chance to prove her commitment to this marriage and to her brother's alliance with Karwyn. If Amira could impress her fiancé at the meeting, he might talk highly of her to her brother and they would forget all about her panic attack.

Amira's confidence left her as soon as she walked out the door of her room. Anxiously walking to the meeting room, she couldn't help but pull her side braid. The sharp pain didn't stop her until she reached the heavy doors of the council room.

No one turned their head when she entered the room. All the figures present, known and unknown, were focused on a gigantic map laid out on a round table made out of the trunk of an oak tree.

Amira stood awkwardly in the entryway before finally catching Karwyn's eye. He looked as displeased as usual to see her. Only Rhay's face brightened when he saw her. With a gesture, he invited her to join them at the table. The only seat still available was right next to Karwyn. Not the seat she would have chosen, but her life had never really been about choices.

She took a seat next to the interim high king.

"What are you doing here?" Karwyn whispered angrily.

"You know I want to help," she said, exuding optimism.

Karwyn snickered. "You know nothing of politics. Should you not be picking a dress for tonight's feast?"

Amira's bruised ego made her raise her voice. "I had an idea how to avoid the other kingdoms hearing about yesterday's incident." She met Karwyn's questioning gaze. "The riot," she added.

Karwyn's pale face turned red. "There was no riot. A little civil unrest is nothing to worry your head about. Stop disturbing the order of the council and go back to your room."

Amira noticed that all the men in the room were staring at them. In addition to Nouis and Rhay, she recognised the fae she had seen with Karwyn on her first night in the palace when she'd gotten lost in the creepy corridor. He had an ancient presence about him, yet his light brown skin was the picture of health and the short hair on his skull was an incredible shade of midnight black.

He was the only one to dare intervene. "I think Princess Amira should remain. In her position as the future Queen of Turosian, she can help us find out more about the other contestants. After all, if I recall correctly, her father had very good connections to King Tarnan."

Amira heard a few grunts of approval coming from the other advisors. She turned to the fae who had defended her presence. "Thank you, advisor...?"

The fae let out a quick laugh. "I'm no advisor. I'd like to think my position as the royal healer is far more interesting. We met yesterday, actually. Saydren is the name."

Amira felt blood rushing to her cheeks as she was reminded of her state the previous night. This must mean Saydren had been the one offering her medicine.

"Well, thank you for your help," Amira said. She felt Saydren's stare lingering on her face, making her uncomfortable.

Karwyn sighed. "Let us stop the chit-chat and go back to the matter at hand." For once, Amira was relieved by Karwyn's intervention.

Nouis took out a long scroll. "I've talked with most of the royal advisors from the other courts and the three candidates with the highest chance of being selected are yourself, Your Majesty, King Tarnan, and Queen Kaylanthea." Amira heard a few snickers at the mention of the last name. Apparently, the council didn't see Queen Kaylanthea as a worthy opponent.

Karwyn laid back in his armchair with a satisfied smile. "Quarnian is one of the poorest kingdoms. Kaylanthea has never been able to implement strong taxes. She is merely getting the sympathy vote."

"You should still be aware of her. Her water powers are quite impressive. I've heard she opened a passage through a powerful river," Nouis said with a serious tone.

Amira saw Karwyn's eyes darken. He obviously didn't like to be challenged. "Are you suggesting that my two powers are no match for Kaylanthea's single one?" Amira could hear the growing anger in his voice.

"Of course not, my king. I was merely putting everything on the table. We wouldn't want her to try to one up you during the public display of power," Nouis quickly added.

Amira saw the anger in Karwyn's eyes being replaced by

something quite different. Was it *fear?* Looking over at Rhay, the princess saw that the young advisor was intensely focused on Karwyn, as if trying to ease his friend's mind.

"Your Majesty comes from the longest line of high kings. I'm sure everyone can already see that you are the perfect heir to your family's legacy," Nouis said with the clear hope of breaking the tension.

Amira thought back on the history she had learned from her father as a child. The Adelway family had only secured power again once the Dark King had been vanquished. The one time another kingdom other than Turosian had been at the forefront of ruling Liraen, it had ended in disaster. Variel Sartoya had to be stopped. In doing so, it wasn't just the Dark King himself who had been overthrown. His whole kingdom, Rubien, had been abandoned by the Gods and therefore only seven kingdoms were now recognised in Liraen. Before the Dark King's reign, it had always been an Adelway sitting on the throne. Indeed, many must be glad to fall back into this tradition.

"What about Tarnan?" Amira dared ask. She had a few memories with the King of Carnylen, all nice ones. And she knew that he was a good amount older than Karwyn. Wouldn't that make him a more suitable choice?

"Tarnan is a worthy opponent. He's well connected and a very good diplomat. But he's older and probably too smart for his own good. The advisors want a high king who is going to rule as long as possible. And he has never showcased his earth powers, so I think it's safe to say he doesn't present any risk in the power competition," Nouis explained to her.

"I see you have a lot of faith in me, lovely fiancée," Karwyn said in an almost playful tone. But Amira could still hear the bitterness underneath it.

"I know my brother puts a lot of faith in you as his ally. I would never doubt his choice," Amira cleverly replied. She did know that her brother most certainly wanted the high king crown for himself, but no one ever took the kingdom that celebrated beauty as a worthy opponent. Her brother was forced to side with someone more powerful and more respected than him, someone who could provide him a drop of power.

"Your brother is not the only one. The King of Obliveryn, Quintin Nylwood, is another trusted ally of our court," Karwyn boasted.

The kingdom of Obliveryn was blessed by the God of Courage. Amira could only agree that King Quintin was a good ally to have, but looking at Karwyn's prideful glow, Amira felt the need to poke at his confidence.

"You said that Queen Kaylanthea's kingdom was the poorest. My only concern is that the advisors are going to assume Turosian is suffering after the...civil unrest on Falea Night." She had to hide her smirk when she saw Karwyn's pissed off face. His glow was definitely gone.

"Our finances are impeccable, fiancée. And if I were you, I would make sure not to spread hurtful rumours." His voice was ice cold.

Nouis chimed in, "Our silver supply remains intact, although we should be careful about its spending."

Karwyn gave Nouis a death stare. The advisor immediately lowered his head to pretend to look at a long scroll.

Rhay loudly closed the book he'd been reading. "Well, I'm

only spending a bit for my party. I give so much back to the people, it's definitely worth it," Rhay joked. Amira was surprised he was even talking as he had spent the whole meeting not so subtly staring at what looked like a similar novel to the one he had gifted her.

Nouis subtly hit his son on his shoulder. "Rhay, can you for once make a valuable contribution as a royal advisor?" he hissed under his breath.

Rhay straightened his back and put his book away. "What about the renewal of the treaty with the humans? I was thinking I could go with Karwyn."

Karwyn looked at his nails. "I had forgotten about that. I have been more focused on the contest than this meaningless treaty."

"What about their sickness, are we going to help them?" Rhay asked as Karwyn impatiently tapped his fingertips on the table.

"If they have something to offer us in return, I might consider it. But they seem too prideful to ask for our help." Karwyn stood up. "Let us conclude this meeting. I have other matters to attend to now."

All the advisors stood up and gathered their things. Amira stayed in her chair, trying to digest all the things she had heard during the meeting. So there was a sickness in the human world? That didn't surprise her. All she'd ever heard was that humans were weak and feeble. *Like you,* a voice murmured in her head.

Shaking away the thought, she stood up to leave when she felt Karwyn pulling her back.

"You need to be more careful who you spend your time with, Amira. Rhay is not a sensible choice of friend for you. Do not make me go to your brother to break off the engagement. We both know he would not take it well," Karwyn sneered. Amira's blood turned cold. She understood the threat perfectly. A burst of flame flashed before her eyes. "Be on your best behaviour tonight and I shall inform him that our engagement is going along nicely."

Without words, Amira just nodded before plunging into a deep bow. When she raised her head, Karwyn was gone. She knew her friendship with Rhay would bring her trouble. All her past friendships had ended tragically. Some worse than others.

But how was she supposed to survive this alone?

CHAPTER 28

AMIRA

Dinner had just started but Amira was already tired of the pretence. To her surprise, after the initial appetizers, the servants brought piles and piles of food that could have fed the entire kingdoms of Allamyst and Turosian. She had been wrong, the Turosian kingdom wasn't poor, it just kept its richness for the wealthiest of the court.

The meat quickly disappeared into the voracious mouths of the guests. Her hunger was long gone. How could they eat so carelessly when so many people had to struggle to find food? It wasn't the only reason for her lack of appetite. Karwyn's threat was too present in her mind for her to think about something as basic as food. She cast a glance around the room.

As a mere level one, she was surrounded by the most powerful fae of Liraen. Every king and queen was present for this dinner, which signified the start of the contest. Even though she was part of a royal family, Amira felt like she didn't truly belong here.

Sometimes she wondered if she would have been happier living just with her mother as a commoner, out of Wryen's reach.

Queen Kaylanthea Zhengassi's stoic attitude contrasted with the rest of her table. She never raised her voice and listened attentively to all the drunken talks around her, yet she gave off an impression of perfect authority and confidence. Her kingdom, Quarnian, was protected by the Goddess of Loyalty. Amira wondered if the queen followed her kingdom's sentiment, putting loyalty above all else.

Kaylanthea's short black hair was tied around her head in four tight braids ending in a small bun. The pale pink of her irises shone as she smiled at the man next to her. He was incredibly tall and strong-looking, perfect for the guards.

But Amira could sense a sweetness in him as he looked proudly at Kaylanthea. The love and respect between the two was obvious to anyone watching. Amira turned her head away, a flash of jealousy in her heart.

A few seats away from her, on Rhay's table, was the other main contestant, King Tarnan Ellevarn. Amira remembered Nouis' depiction of the Carnylen king. Quick with words, cunning, and always in the know—that was also the description her father had used once.

Nothing less could be expected from Tarnan, as the God of Wisdom was watching over his kingdom. Being curious and knowledgeable was highly valued in Carnylen.

During the ball for her thirteenth birthday, Amira had had a riveting conversation with Tarnan on the importance of learning about human culture to be a better negotiator at the treaty renewals. He had taught her some fascinating facts about the human land and had gifted her a human book full of colourful illustrations. When she had moved bedrooms after her father's death, she was unable to find the book. Jealous of such a rare present, Wryen might have stolen it.

She had encountered Tarnan on other occasions, the last one being her father's funeral. As they were burning his body covered in dark gold and purple, the King of Carnylen had moved from his seat to stand next to Amira's. Without saying anything, he had tucked a sunset orange handkerchief into her trembling hand. Her teary eyes had thanked him as he had gently pressed her shoulder.

Amira had merely picked at her food before the plates were carried away, replaced by an avalanche of desserts. She painfully ate a spherical pastry filled with an orange-flavoured cream. The sweetness left her completely unbothered. As everyone left the table to start dancing to the joyful music played by a group of court musicians, Amira stayed back. The only person she would enjoy talking to or even dancing with would be Rhay, but after Karwyn's comment she knew it would be foolish to be seen with him.

Silent and immobile, she stared at the fae dancing without a care in the world. She envied the smiles on their faces and the joy in their laughter. If she had any power, she would have used it to stop their silly happiness. Holding back tears, she fought this strange feeling of hate. The chair next to hers moved and she quickly composed herself.

"Princess Amira, I can't believe how much you've grown." Tarnan was sitting next to her, his amber eyes set on her face. He hadn't changed much in eight years, the same buzzed black hair and pale skin that would make anyone look sick but that seemed perfect on him.

He extended a hand and grasped Amira's shoulder with affection. "I remember you being more extroverted. Was it only childlike excitement or are you still as full of wonder?"

"As you've said, I've grown," she replied, more coldly than she would have wished.

"Well, it pains me that your wonderful spirit has been defeated by adulthood. Perhaps you just lack the proper conversation partner," he said, looking at Karwyn and Wryen plotting together.

"It is true that after my father's death, I have lacked intellectual stimulation." A wide smile curled Amira's lips upwards.

Tarnan let out a small laugh. "Maybe you're not that lacking in spirit after all. So tell me, Amira, what do you think of the current situation?"

"I've been through a lot of changes lately, so I'm afraid you'll have to be more precise."

"The human world and their sickness. With their deadly virus killing thousands, I think their leaders are going to want to do the treaty talk early this time."

Amira thought back on Karwyn's comment at the council meeting. So this was more serious than she had first assumed. "Karwyn doesn't seem to be jumping in to help. Do you think he should?" she asked. Fae healing magic worked easier on other fae but she knew they would be able to find a cure for humans if they tried hard enough.

Tarnan pondered for an instance. "Perhaps. I imagine the court will want to use this opportunity to once again show humanity that fae are superior. They will have to offer something in return at the treaty meeting."

"What could they possibly give us that we don't already have?"

"You know, they are quite resourceful. Our world would be widely different if it wasn't for them. And there's a whole black market dedicated to trading human items for ours."

"I've never really cared much for them—the objects and the humans." They were a different species. One that fae needn't spend any thoughts on.

"It's because you've never needed to, princess," Tarnan said, leaning in. "But your ancestors relied heavily on them. By Caelo, this palace wouldn't be the same if it wasn't for them. Hundreds of humans lost their lives to rebuild our cities after the tear in the universe opened the portal to the human world."

A sense of uneasiness overcame Amira. The war that had preceded the tear had always been a sensitive topic for most fae, even if hundreds of years had passed since the last of the combat. Wiping out generations of fae, the war had left them highly reliant on the Dark King's plan to rebuild their forces. That was the beginning of a new era for Liraen, the era of human slavery.

Questions she would rather not have to think about filled Amira's mind alongside vivid pictures of pain and suffering. In the end, they had used humans for their benefit. And when the Dark King had turned on the fae, they had depended on the people they had enslaved to help overthrow his reign. After that, fae had been forbidden from enslaving humans ever again and the border spell had been created. But that didn't mean the fae had accepted humans. They weren't fae, they weren't part of their society. Amira knew that however many humans were still in Liraen, they would never be blessed and, therefore, they would never be accepted.

Tarnan patted her shoulder. "Anyway, with the contest happening at the same time as the treaty talk, it makes sense that the fae have other priorities. Every royal in Liraen will have their own interest at heart." Tarnan's gaze burned through Karwyn's back.

"How unusual," said Amira sarcastically. Tarnan looked at her with an incredulous gaze.

"I knew you hadn't really changed." And he let out a thundering laugh, drawing everyone's attention to them. But Tarnan didn't seem to mind the attention. It wasn't that he was craving it, he merely seemed totally unbothered by the stares and the whispers.

"I have heard that you're in the lead for the contest this year. I'll take it that you'll also have your best interest at heart and won't get involved," Amira said.

"I think we both know your fiancé is the one who's going to win. How thrilling for you to be engaged to the future high king." Tarnan had no mischief in his heart when he said the last sentence, yet Amira's heart sank in her chest. She hated being reminded of what her life would be like from now on.

"And you're not mad about that? I thought it was the goal of every king and queen to win the contest," she said while staring at Wryen obnoxiously boasting to a young red-haired fae. The young woman's eyes were looking in every direction for a potential escape. Amira could only feel sympathy for the poor victim of her brother's inflated ego.

"You'd be surprised to know how many of us would rather

stay in the shadows. Being in such an important position can drain your strength. That's why the second part of the contest is a test of power."

"You don't think you'll do well in the contest?"

Tarnan's eyes turned dark for a second before he let out a low sigh. "My powers are quite limited, even for a king. In Carnylen, we rely more on knowledge and information than pure displays of raw power. There's great strength in knowledge."

Amira could only agree. She wished she had the opportunity to gain more insights. "I suppose you have heard what happened during Falea Night?"

Before Tarnan could reply, a glass of iridos appeared in front of Amira. Rhay winked at her and said, "I saw you had been deprived of a good drink."

Amira's hand reached out for the drink but stopped right as she touched it. Her eyes searched for Karwyn or her brother in the crowd, but they were busy talking with Queen Kaylanthea.

"Young Messler, I see you still like to make yourself useful. Even when it isn't the smartest move," said Tarnan with a knowing smirk. He raised his glass. "Let us toast to your future, Rhay. Your father has told me he wants you to start training to become the next head advisor."

Rhay's body immediately tensed up but his face remained perfectly even. He raised his glass and gave a little nod to Tarnan. Amira couldn't really pinpoint the two men's feelings towards each other. As much as he seemed annoyed, Rhay still had too much respect for the king to give one of his witty comebacks. And she was sure Tarnan's comment wasn't ill-intended.

"His wants and my wants don't always align, so I wouldn't

necessarily take his word for it," Rhay finally replied after taking a few sips of his drink.

"Well, I told him that I'm sure you'll make a great head advisor one day. You have all the talents necessary for it. And I know you and Karwyn are close."

"As long as it doesn't involve the ability to cook. That would put him out of the running," commented Amira, feeling a bit left out.

Tarnan and Rhay looked at her, surprised by her sudden intervention, then they both let out a cheerful laugh.

"By Caelo, I've missed you, Amira. You should visit me sometime," Tarnan said loudly. Loud enough for fae to turn around and stare at them.

Amira expected to see Wryen's angry lilac gaze among them, but he wasn't in the crowd. Her heart raced in her chest. Had he already left?

Hope warred with terror inside of her and she tried to bring herself back into the moment with Tarnan and Rhay, tried to convince herself that she was safe. But she never was. Not under Wryen's watch. And the longer she spent with Karwyn, the more she was sure she would never be safe with him either.

CHAPTER 29

LORA

Neither Lora or Eyden spoke much on their way back the following day. They hadn't talked any more last night either. Exhausted yet exhilarated, Lora had fallen asleep watching the stars on the floor. The last few days had been tiring, but it was all going to be worth it. At least for her.

The feeling of guilt was sitting like a rock in the pit of her stomach. The sinking feeling of knowing she was about to mess up any kind of trust the two of them had built. It was a conundrum. Lora couldn't trust Eyden enough to tell him the truth about how she'd crossed the border, so what other choice did she have than crushing the little trust he might have developed?

Maybe she could help him some other way to make up for it. Provide him with things from the human world instead of telling him how to cross. But that would mean keeping in contact. The thought made her anxious in a million different ways.

It probably was impossible anyway. She'd have to make a run for it across the border. Lora couldn't risk Eyden holding her back if he realised too soon that she wasn't able to hold up her end of the bargain.

She might have seen the kind side of him. The side that made Ilario trust him fully and his parents happy to see him. The side that cared about the state of his world. The side that played her for truths, whispering secrets in the dark. But it wasn't enough to risk the reason she came here. At the end of the day, he was still fae.

Lora was so close to ending this brief chapter in her life, to going back to an ordinary life without fearing for her family's health. She reminded herself that this would soon feel like a dream and eventually vanish from her mind—and the guilt with it.

They quickly retrieved the crystal and vial from Eyden's closet and Lora soon found herself in front of an apartment building across from the bar where she'd first met Sahalie.

Eyden raised his fist, about to knock on the door, but he hesitated and sought out her eyes. "Once we have the cure, you're leaving right away?" he asked.

She could tell he already knew her answer. "I have to. But I'll need to get my backpack with the rest of my stuff first." Bringing the bag would have drawn too much intention. Too many zippers to pass as a regular fae item and they were in the middle of the town. And maybe a tiny, barely existing part of her wanted the small detour.

Eyden lifted his chin in a quick gesture. No words, they were beyond them now.

Before he could knock, the door opened and Sahalie peeked her head outside.

"There you are. Finally. Come on in and make yourself at home as you usually do," she said, ignoring Lora's presence. She couldn't find any of Ilario's friendliness in Sahalie. How were the two cousins so different from each other?

Eyden swung the door open completely as he passed it, entering the flat and making sure Lora followed behind. Sahalie's gaze briefly travelled to Lora. She couldn't tell whether Sahalie truly disliked her or merely hated that she'd come here with Eyden. Her emerald eyes almost seemed as if they could unravel every hidden lie.

"Should we sit at the table?" Eyden asked, drawing Sahalie's attention.

"The couch is fine. I already gathered some things." Sahalie sat on one end of the couch and patted the empty space next to her, her green eyes never leaving Eyden.

Much to Sahalie's dismay, Eyden chose to sit in the sofa chair opposite her instead. Lora hid her smile at Sahalie's irritated expression, but then she realised this left her with the couch seat.

Keeping her expression blank, Lora sat down on the far end of the couch and decided to move things forward quickly. She pulled out the items from her pocket and laid them on the glass table next to the items Sahalie had prepared. "Green aventurine and the vial of infected blood."

Eyden emptied his bag of silver, shimmery herbs. "And, as requested, arentae."

"Well then, let's get right to it so we can celebrate after," Sahalie said, looking up at Eyden, who, in response, merely gestured to the items spread across the table. She reached for the vial of blood, briefly meeting Lora's gaze. That was all the acknowledgment she gave Lora before she set to work.

Sahalie poured half of the blood into a small bowl. She took a leaf of arentae and squished it in her hand, dropping the sparkly silver substance on top of the red one. After adding a dash of some other herbs Lora didn't recognise, Sahalie closed her hand around the green healing crystal and held her other open palm over the bowl.

The crystal started to glow, green light streaming out of Sahalie's closed fist. The fae closed her eyes in concentration and soon the blood mixture gleamed too.

Lora turned her eyes to Eyden, who was looking intently at the table as she had been a second ago.

She couldn't quite believe that they had come this far. They were moments away from reaching the finish line. She already imagined the message she would send her family. Lora hadn't told them that today was the day. She'd said soon, not wanting to get anyone's hopes up.

Yet her own hopes had never been higher than in this moment. Maybe luck really did come her way. Maybe in more ways than one. Eyden had been wrong. The shooting star wasn't a bad sign at all.

When Lora shifted her attention back to Sahalie, she noticed the fae was grimacing in pain. Her breathing was quickening, her outstretched hand shaking. Then the light went out.

Sahalie opened her eyes and turned to Lora first, a look of uncertainty taking over her features. "This is more difficult than I expected. I'll need more arentae," she said as she grabbed a few more leaves.

Lora didn't know whether she should panic. She felt like a wave of cold water hit her system. But when she found Eyden's gaze, she felt herself coming up for air. His eyes said to give it time, so Lora let her hope keep her afloat.

Sahalie's eyes closed as she tried again. The green light appeared instantly and this time Sahalie took her time. After a few minutes, Lora thought she saw her relax, but then she gasped sharply and dropped the crystal.

Emerald eyes found Lora's. "I can't do it." Sahalie leaned back on the couch, exhausted. "I wish I could, but this virus has a strange effect on my magic."

Lora's head emptied out. All that was left was white noise. She distantly heard Eyden say, "Can't you try again?"

"I don't know what else to do. You might need someone more accustomed to human diseases. Or a level five," Sahalie replied.

Lora wasn't looking at any of them. She was staring at her mother's blood on the table, riddled with the virus. Still infected. Not healed. Nothing. She was right where she'd started. She had accomplished absolutely *nothing*. Worse, she had wasted days. *Days.*

Suddenly, the walls around her seemed to shrink. Lora could hardly breathe and her hands quivered. She thought she might have heard Eyden speak, but she couldn't make out the words. Couldn't focus on anything.

Lora forced her eyes shut as she felt her skin burn with paralyzing fear, the cold water she felt earlier evaporating into steam that locked her into a state of panic.

She needed to move. Though the fumes in her mind

overwhelmed her, Lora managed to stand up, barely feeling the movement as if she wasn't even touching the ground.

Eyden and Sahalie were mere shadows as she passed them silently. Out of the corner of her eye, she saw Eyden reach for her.

But Lora headed for the door and didn't look back.

She stormed towards the alley next to Sahalie's place, her pace as fast as the panic racing through her body. The cool night air enabled her to catch her breath, but the crushing feeling shattering her hope didn't let up. She had put in days to get everything for Sahalie and it was an utter failure. How did this happen? Had she been naïve in having any hope at all?

She knew her mission wouldn't be easy, but the fae had magic at their disposal. There *had* to be a way. She had believed this was it. So much so that she'd followed Eyden's way, giving in to his plan. Should she have been looking for alternatives? Did she let herself get so sucked into this world that she didn't pay enough attention to all the possible outcomes?

Lora made it to the side of the building when Eyden finally caught up with her.

"Lora, wait!" Eyden shouted as he followed her into the alley.

She whirled around, catching his eyes. "Did you know this wasn't going to work?" The question left her lips before she had even fully formed it.

Eyden looked hurt and guilty at the same time. "I thought it would most likely work."

It wasn't good enough of a response to calm the feeling of

betrayal settling in her heart. "But you made me think it was definitely going to work." And here she'd been feeling miserable about her own dishonesty less than an hour ago. She should've focused on Eyden's instead. What excuse did he have to mislead her, give her false hope?

"I said it *should* work because I thought it probably would," Eyden said.

"Semantics." Lora could hear the hypocrisy in her words but she didn't care. All she saw was her mother's sickly face and a ticking clock next to her grave.

"Listen, I said I'd help you get a cure and I'll keep trying. Nothing has changed."

"Nothing has changed?" she asked, humourless. Lora turned to the darkened sky. "You gave me hope, Eyden. And now it's drowning me."

She heard Eyden take a few steps closer. "It's not all over. There's more than enough time—"

Her head snapped back to meet this gaze. "Are you really going to tell me how much *time* there is again? Can you really not see the urgency?" Lora let out a dry laugh. "I was right about you the first time." Eyden didn't have the same motivation that she had. She was doing this to save her mum, who would be so disappointed in her. He was doing it for *business*.

"What's that supposed to mean?"

"You're just like how I imagined fae to be. Cold—heartless—when it comes to humans."

Eyden took a step back as if she'd lashed out with more than words. "Right, because you can put us all in one box. We're all monsters just because I have no easy solution for you."

"That's not the only reason," she whispered.

"Why else?"

"I—" She didn't know how to explain it. She didn't want to elaborate on her complicated feelings towards fae. "Admit it, you don't give a damn about humans. You told me from the start that this is just about business," she argued loudly. She heard her anger increasing with each word. Fiery fury had filled her up and now it needed an escape. "Why did you even tell me anything?" Sudden realisation dawned on her. Could he have been leading her on a fool's errand? She didn't wait to let him answer for himself. "You went along with my questions to get me to trust you for your own benefit, didn't you?"

"What?" Eyden's face was the picture of perfect disbelief. Or of perfect pretence.

She was suddenly unsure if Eyden hadn't had an ulterior motive this whole time. Had she been stupid enough to put any amount of trust in a *fae*? "That's not a no," Lora replied.

Eyden shook his head. "You're not thinking clearly."

She only half heard him in her spiral into rage. It all came spilling out, raging fire swallowing her hopelessness. "Brilliant, take advantage of the human girl who's trying to save her family. Were you hoping I'd look into your dazzling eyes and spill all my secrets? Well, too bad, I still held onto my best ones."

Eyden looked taken aback, both furious and intrigued. "You were the one who started asking questions! Not me. I was perfectly fine keeping our distance."

"So you're saying you were never curious about me?"

"Yes." A hurt look crossed her face. Eyden seemed to sense

the implication she had conjured up. "No. No, that's not what I meant."

It didn't matter anyway if he wanted to get to know her. All that mattered was if she could trust him to actually fucking *try*. To see that she needed the cure as soon as possible and to *care*. "How do I know anything you tell me is the truth, Eyden? How do I know you're not wasting my time, thinking I'll give up my secret sooner or later?"

"By Caelo, can we stop this pointless argument and move on?" His tone was sharp, digging into her soul.

Lora couldn't let it go. Not with everything on the line. Anger and desperation was building up in her. "No, we can't. I don't bloody care if you think it's pointless. I need that cure, Eyden. I can't risk wasting my time, assuming you're actually trying your best."

Eyden searched her gaze. "I *did* try. This was me trying. You're worrying for nothing."

Nothing. *Nothing.* That's what the cure was to him, wasn't it? Nothing of importance. Just another trade that could take its time. "Right, how silly of me to worry. Such an unfortunate, human thing to do," Lora replied, venom in her voice.

"Has worrying done you any good ever?" His voice turned toxic in her ears. "It won't help you get that cure any faster either."

"Fuck you, Eyden."

His face relaxed as if he considered he might have gone too far. "Lora—"

Eyden's words were cut off as a force of air came out of no-where, roughly throwing him to the ground some distance away.

The wind went past her. Lora felt it lift her hair, partly obscuring her vision.

Turning her head, she noticed two dark figures had appeared in the alley, coming into view in the moonlight. She could make out their menacing stares in the low light and her heart threatened to give out.

She could kick herself. They had been so lost in their argument, they hadn't kept their guard up. And worst of all, she'd basically announced that she was human. Her heart beat faster as her anger quickly washed away, replaced by panic once again.

Lora turned on her heel and tried to run to Eyden, but one of the fae ran forward and grabbed her arm faster than she expected. He drew her back harshly. She yelped in pain and it seemed to evoke Eyden's attention, who was still on the ground.

A knife left his hand so quickly, Lora barely caught the flash of silver and red. But instead of hitting its target, a gust of wind rerouted the knife's path, returning it to Eyden. It hit his chest and Lora saw red.

Blood was pouring from Eyden's wound, but somehow, he got up and immediately tried to remove the knife. The fae, who must have air magic, forced Eyden's arms to his sides with another storm of air, stopping his movement, leaving the knife firmly in place.

Seeing Eyden's pained face, Lora kicked the fae holding her in a sensitive spot, unleashing her newfound anger. The fae yelled and dropped her arm but before she could take a step, he grabbed a fistful of hair and threw her against the wall. Her head hit stone and she immediately slumped to the ground.

Ignoring the pain as best as she could, Lora forced her eyes to remain open as she tried to look in Eyden's direction. But Lora couldn't make out anything, as if a heavy veil was draped over her face.

Her head felt funny. She distantly realised it was another good reason to panic, but all her thoughts turned to mush.

"Careful, now. We don't want her dead," a menacing voice said.

It was the last thing she heard before her vision turned completely black, drowning her in darkness.

CHAPTER 30

◊

AMIRA

Wryen was lounging on Amira's bed, drink in hand, when she returned from dinner after catching up with Tarnan. As she closed the door behind her, he raised his glass.

"To the sky, sister! We must celebrate tonight." He stared at her, waiting for her to take the bait.

Amira's frozen lips were unable to utter the question her half-brother was dying for her to ask. Growing more impatient, he downed his drink and rose from the bed.

He took her hand. "Let's dance. I haven't seen you dance in a long time." Wryen grabbed her by the waist and forced her to move.

Completely baffled by the situation, Amira followed his lead. They swayed in silence for a bit. Amira's distracted mind made her lose the rhythm a few times but Wryen didn't say anything. She tried to keep a clear head to be ready for when he would eventually attack. Like a predator trying to lure its prey under a false sense of safety, he made her twirl a few times, her long dress flaring out in a perfect circle.

The music seemed to come to an end in his head and he tilted her, holding her back with one hand. Looking deep into his eyes, she saw the fiery insanity that he kept hidden from everyone but her. He smiled slowly, his lips curling. And then he spat in her face and dropped her.

The fall lasted only a second but her heart dropped in her chest. Wryen turned his back to her. "I didn't think you were capable of failing at the only thing you're supposed to do, seduce a man." He stroked her silky bed sheets with one hand. "Actually, no, you're perfectly capable of seducing a man. Your stupid little brain just can't comprehend simple instructions."

He turned to her. An invisible hand grabbed her throat and squeezed so hard that she couldn't breathe. Wryen's face was completely distorted by disgust and hate. He lowered himself to her level and grabbed her hair to make her stand up. The sharp pain made her close her eyes. Tears were trying to escape but she forced them back.

Wryen drew his face close to hers. "This marriage will only happen on two conditions: Karwyn being selected for the contest and him still wanting to marry you. There are other princesses in Liraen he could select. If he doesn't marry *you*, I'll be very disappointed. And you know what happens when I'm not satisfied, don't you?" Amira nodded while avoiding his stormy lilac eyes. "So instead of trying to seduce a lowlife like Rhay, I want you to do whatever it takes to make Karwyn fall in love with you. You wouldn't want to bring further shame to our family by being rejected, would you?"

She nodded again, her head buzzing with pain. So Karwyn had talked with her brother, after all. Or maybe Wryen had informants of his own, secretly following Amira around.

He finally let go of her hair and started pacing around the room. "You'd be wise to remember that you're not the only one I can hurt. I haven't had a good opportunity to let my fire shine in quite some time. Far too few executions. Have you heard from your mother recently, by chance?"

The thinly veiled threat made her want to beg on her knees and rip his throat out, but she knew she was only capable of the first one.

"Please," she said with a hoarse voice. Images of flames clawing at skin quickly flashed through her mind before she could banish them.

A twisted smile appeared on Wryen's lips. Once again, he had aimed right where it hurt.

"I may be persuaded to let her be if I'm under the impression Karwyn is smitten by you. I've heard he's gone to Rhay's afterparty." He moved closer to whisper in her ear, "A smart girl would follow him there."

When Amira silently nodded, he finally left.

The minute he closed the door, Amira ripped out a strand of hair. Refraining from screaming, she undressed and threw away her dress. Digging her fingernails into her arms, she wondered what it would feel like if she tore the skin to her bones. She just wanted out, out of Wryen's control, out of her life.

Amira closed her eyes, letting a lonely tear drop from her cheek. And then she chose an outfit.

Restricting her movements, the dress lifted up as she climbed the stairs leading to Rhay's party. In the distance, she heard the murmurs of the seductive music. If she had been in a different mood, she would have been tempted to let her body follow the rhythm. Instead, her mind was ice cold and focused on her impossible task.

Bracing herself, Amira entered the room. She arrived later than last time and the guests were already intertwined with each other. Her instinct told her to run away, but the grip of her brother on her mind wouldn't let her.

She tried to find Karwyn in the depraved crowd. The more she looked, the more she was convinced that Karwyn wasn't there. The party was overwhelming to her every sense and it was all about losing control, something Karwyn never seemed inclined to do. Loud music, heavy drinking, bodies pressed against bodies, the sound of dozens of laughs in cacophony—it was all too much for Karwyn. And for someone like her, she thought.

But to Amira's surprise, her eyes fell on Karwyn coming out of one of the secret alcoves with Rhay. And the most surprising part was his joyful attitude. *Smiling.* Amira would have never guessed that the King of Turosian was capable of such a trivial thing.

As she approached them, another woman took her spot. A beautiful woman with striking golden eyes and short blonde hair whose presence Karwyn seemed to tolerate, if not enjoy. The blonde woman moved with the confidence of a powerful fae but it was the first time that Amira had seen her. She was sure that she would have remembered her if she had been at the court. Maybe she was from another kingdom?

Her light hair could indicate an Obliveryn origin. But the golden eyes were surprising. They looked around, filled with secret intentions. Was she one of Karwyn's rumoured spies or the reason her fiancé didn't seem to care for Amira's affection?

Shaking her head, she came back to her senses when she realised that Karwyn was missing. "By Caelo," she hissed, turning multiple heads in her direction. But everyone quickly lost interest and went back to their respective lovers.

Rhay had disappeared too and the young woman strolled around the party with a drink in hand, smiling at the busy couples. Intrigued by her, Amira decided to follow the fae, trying to be discreet.

To blend in, she grabbed a glass of iridos from a silver platter.

Even if she seemed to know everyone there, the woman didn't engage with anyone. Instead, she looked like she was taking mental notes of everything that was happening. All the affinities that were created, all the shyly exchanged whispers, all the embarrassments.

Amira realised she had downed her drink. A floating sensation took over her mind. *Focus*, she admonished herself.

Suddenly, the fae disappeared into one of the alcoves. Amira hesitated for a couple seconds before deciding to follow her. Maybe she knew where Karwyn had gone?

When Amira entered the room, the woman turned to her and handed her another glass of iridos. "My, my, I seem to have caught your eye. Lucky me," she said with a deep and sensual voice. Amira blushed. Completely caught off guard, she accepted the drink and let the iridos coat her tongue.

"Gathering courage to declare your feelings?" the fae joked before teasingly playing with a strand of Amira's hair.

Amira's face was burning. But she mustered her last strength to reply. "I think you already have enough attention from someone much more powerful."

The woman laughed and let go of Amira's hair. She sat on the velvety couch pressed against the back of the alcove. "You don't have to be jealous, princess. My interest in your fiancé is strictly professional."

"What do you mean?"

The woman pressed a finger against her painted lips. "I'm afraid that's something you'll have to find out later. But I'm sure we can find other things to talk about if you don't miss your fiancé too much." She laid an inviting hand on the couch and bit her lip.

Amira wasn't sure if she should try to get something out of the woman. At least learn of her connection to Karwyn. She caught the stranger staring at her, eyes travelling up and down her body. Wryen's orders lingered in her thoughts.

Amira fumbled with her words as she tried to back out. "I'm sorry, I have to go."

She bolted out of the alcove, the final words of the woman ringing in her ears, "Leaving so soon? How sad, we were just starting the real fun."

Almost running, she downed her second drink and almost dropped it when she bumped into Rhay. The one person she wasn't supposed to talk to. Her brother's threat echoed in her head. But another voice whispered in her ear, *Maybe he knows where Karwyn is.*

"Hey there, be careful with that," he said as he steadied her cup. "You wouldn't want to bring us bad luck. Or worse, damage my ravishing outfit." Amira's laugh sounded fake to her ears, but Rhay didn't seem to notice.

"I'm sorry, Rhay," she whispered as she lowered her head.

Rhay grabbed her chin in his hand and raised her head gently. "No worries, princess. Let's get you a new drink." He took her arm and led her to the bar. Gesturing the bartender, he winked at her.

Amira was still torn between stress and excitement, but the amount of alcohol in her veins favoured excitement. When she saw Rhay furrow his brows, she understood that he was trying to read her emotions. So she forced her mind to load up on happy memories, letting herself go into the ecstatic mood of the crowd. Rhay smiled as he picked up a shimmering blue drink.

Amira extended her hand but Rhay didn't let go. "Promise me one thing." Amira lost herself in the sea of his eyes. She nodded. "Promise me, you won't spill it on my clothes."

They shared a freeing laugh. Rhay let go of the drink and Amira was able to taste it. It was surprisingly sour, but in a pleasant way. The subtle sweetness came after a few sips. A drink as confusing as Rhay. "You created this, right?"

Rhay beamed with pride. "Yes. You like it?"

"It's definitely better than your cooking."

He punched her arm with little strength. "Come on, don't be rude or I won't give you my secret recipe."

Amira raised her hands. "Sorry, sorry, I'm listening. What's the secret?"

Rhay leaned in, his lips almost touching Amira's ear. "The secret is...a secret." He moved back.

This time Amira was the one doing the punching. "That's not fair, you can't tease me like that."

"But teasing is my specialty," he answered, voice low and inviting. Before Amira had a chance to react, he continued, "I'm sorry, princess, but this recipe may be my key to freedom."

"How so?"

"Well, if Karwyn and my father grow tired of my antics and decide to throw me out of the palace, I'll make my fortune as a bartender."

Amira took another sip of the drink and let it sit on her tongue. A pleasant tingle flowed through her. She was suddenly in the mood to tease too. She feigned disdain. "I mean, it's not that great. I'm not sure how much you'd make with it."

Rhay brought a hand to his heart. "How dare you?" He tried to take back her drink but she downed it and smiled. "Downing it? That's bold, given the strength of this drink. I like it."

She couldn't think straight. The three drinks she'd had were working hard on making Amira lose her focus. Drinking with Rhay was the wrong decision, she knew it, but at the same time, it was the only one that brought her joy. Didn't she deserve some joy after all the years spent under Wryen's control? And maybe she could learn a thing or two about seducing Karwyn by talking to his best friend.

The drinks kept coming. Nothing really made sense anymore,

one minute they were laughing about someone's overeager kissing, the next they were crying over their lost parent.

In a dark corner of her mind, Amira couldn't completely forget about her brother's threat.

They were lounging on a couch when she thought of Karwyn again. Half joking, half serious, she asked Rhay, "How do you seduce a man?" Hearing the question, Rhay seemed to immediately sober up. A shy blush even flushed his cheeks.

"I'm sure this man doesn't need any seducing from you. You're just too...perfect to need any effort."

Amira sighed. "Sadly, I think you're wrong."

"Well, maybe pay him a compliment. You have to make him feel special. Some physical contact is also good. You could touch his shoulder while you're talking to him." As he spoke, Rhay moved closer to her, but Amira was too drunk to properly process it. "Try to banter with him. Everyone loves a good laugh."

Amira stared at him in surprise. "Really?"

"Yeah, he'll love your sassy comebacks."

She didn't quite believe him, but the alcohol made her agree. "If you say so. I'll try."

Seeing a tray of food passing by, Amira stood up and left him wondering on the couch. After all that drinking on an empty stomach, she was famished. She followed the tray around and managed to grab a tiny vegetable sandwich. It wasn't much, but it made her want to drink again.

Stumbling back to the bar, she was going to order a drink when a young man approached her with a cheeky smile. His sleek black hair covered one of his dark green eyes. He felt strangely familiar. Amira smiled at him, unsure of his intentions.

"Good to meet you, princess. I'm Thyl. You look like you could use something to take the edge off," he said, showing her a small silver and red pill. "Take this and all worries will leave you."

With wide eyes, Amira reached for the familiar pill. But another hand took hers. She turned her head to meet Tarnan's eyes. He took the pill and crushed it under his heel.

"You have no right to offer or sell this," he sharply said to Thyl.

The dealer raised his hands and quickly left. Tarnan turned to Amira. "Are you all right, princess?"

Amira fluttered her eyelashes, her drunken state clearly visible. "What was that?"

"Fortae, a cursed drug born out of suffering. You should never take it."

"I...I don't understand. Saydren tried to give me these pills on Falea Night. It can't be cursed," Amira said, slurring her words.

Tarnan shook his head in disbelief. "Are you sure it was Saydren, the royal healer? I can't imagine he would do such a thing. It must have been a similar-looking pill."

Amira's memories of the end of Falea Night were still blurry. Maybe Tarnan was right, maybe she had confused the pill given by Saydren with this one, *fortae*.

A soothing hand appeared on her shoulder. "What happened?" Rhay asked as he joined them.

"You were with her?" Tarnan angrily asked. Rhay nodded. "You're doing a terrible job taking care of her."

Amira tried to move towards the door but the whole room was spinning. Rhay and Tarnan each grabbed one of her arms.

"We got you," Rhay said with a worried smile while avoiding the storm in Tarnan's eyes.

Slowly, they walked towards the door.

Amira turned her head and saw the woman from earlier staring at her with a mysterious smile. The beautiful fae winked at her right before the door closed.

CHAPTER 31

AMIRA

Amira's head still pounded with a hangover the next day as she headed to the painting session of her engagement portrait with Karwyn. She couldn't help but cringe as she remembered Tarnan and Rhay carrying her back to her room last night. She wasn't sure if she would ever be able to face the King of Carnylen again.

The first thing Amira noticed when she entered the cosy parlour was the enormous easel in the middle of the sunlit room. A blank canvas was fixed to it, hiding the face of the painter behind it. Amira could only see his shoes—practical black boots—and the bottom of his large black trousers. And then, a familiar face peered around the easel.

"Oh, hello." It was the mysterious woman she had met the night before. "I see you're the first to arrive, my lady."

"It's you," were the only words Amira was able to say.

The woman smiled and did a little curtsy. "I see you remember me. Varsha Marymlo, official painter of the Adelway family. Pleasure to see you again, princess."

Blood rushed to Amira's cheeks as she was reminded of their meeting at Rhay's party. The silence between the two women grew more awkward with each passing second. Actually, Varsha didn't look that uncomfortable. She had moved back to prepping her canvas and the different colours she was going to use for the portrait.

The door finally opened and, for the first time, Amira was relieved to see Karwyn enter the room. A very excited Rhay accompanied him.

"You should definitely read the book I just got from the black market. It's...daring," Rhay said.

Karwyn turned to him and said without blinking, "You are aware that the black market is not officially sanctioned by my authority?"

Rhay didn't look guilty at all. "Come on, you've seen my outfits. You know it's not coming from Liraen."

"Yes and I hate them," said a frowning Karwyn. Rhay gave Karwyn's arm a little playful punch. Amira wasn't sure if Karwyn's irritation was real or fake.

The only thing she was sure of was Karwyn's annoyance towards her. "Amira, such a pleasure that you are gracing us with your presence," he said in a mocking tone.

"Were you planning on doing an engagement portrait on your own?" Amira hit back, provoking Rhay's laughter.

"Hello, princess. I see you're full of spirit today," Rhay said, ignoring Karwyn's gaze. He looked her over. "I love the dress you chose." Rhay grabbed Karwyn by the shoulders. "Karwyn could learn from your sense of style. You've never seen how he dresses on his own. Luckily, I'm always there to give him fashion tips."

Karwyn's cheeks were bright red like Amira's had been a few minutes ago. In the corner of her eye, she noticed that Varsha was hiding a laugh. When she caught Amira's eyes on her, the painter put on a serious face but still winked at her.

"Varsha, always a vision. I'm a bit sad you're not wearing your famous *paint dress* today," Rhay said with a mischievous smile.

"I save it for your parties, dear," she teasingly replied.

Visibly annoyed by their flirty exchange, Karwyn removed Rhay's arm and turned to Varsha. "Shall we start? I have more pressing matters to attend to."

"Let's place you, princess, on this chair," Varsha said as she gestured for Rhay to bring the chair in front of the easel. Amira sat, not really sure about how to hold herself. But Varsha was focused on Karwyn. "Your Majesty, could you stand next to her with maybe a hand on her shoulder?" Amira felt Karwyn moving closer but she noticed that his hand didn't touch her. Instead, it hovered over her shoulder. Varsha was about to add something, but looking at Karwyn's face, she closed her mouth.

The painter lowered herself to Amira's feet and started fluffing out the bottom of her dress. The movement made Amira shiver. Or was it because of Varsha's warm breath on her ankles? She wrestled to stop her thoughts. Satisfied with the placement of the dress, Varsha went to her easel.

"Perfect. Now if you could avoid switching positions until I at least get the sketch done." She started scratching at the canvas with her pencil. The sound of her drawing was soon the only noise in the room.

Amira sat completely still. She could sense Karwyn behind her, doing the same. On the other hand, Rhay had curled up on an armchair and was reading his book. She wondered what it was about. The book Rhay had gifted her was still hidden in her wardrobe, the strange cover drawing her attention every time she opened the door to look for an outfit.

Now she could feel Rhay's intense eyes on her. He was watching her as if he was on the other side of a two-way mirror, with such carelessness and confused feelings. No man had ever looked at her like that. All the men she had encountered, the men who had lusted after her, had looked at her as if she was nothing more than a desirable body. A lifeless puppet they could control to their satisfaction.

Rhay's look was softer and respectful. He was truly embracing her as a person. At this moment, she felt like she could ask him anything and he would do it. Sensing Karwyn's hand above her, she wondered if her fiancé threatened her life, would Rhay come to her rescue?

She could sense the tension in Karwyn's body. She felt an urge to raise her head to see what had made Karwyn so mad, but her tendency to follow the rules stopped her. He couldn't have read her mind, could he?

Amira focused her attention on the painter. Varsha's face was twisted with concentration yet it remained beautiful. Amira was completely puzzled by the painter. A strong light in her eyes indicated that she was probably a level four, and still she was just a painter? Most painters were from Allamyst and they usually were only level twos. You didn't really need a high power level to be a good painter. An observant eye, a feel for colours, and a creative spirit were the most common traits Amira had encountered in the painters of Allamyst's court.

Varsha seemed to be finally satisfied with her sketch and she started mixing colours with a precise hand. Amira had always been impressed by some painters' capacity to represent fae with such vivacity. Fae, especially powerful ones, radiated a pure and raw energy that was hard to replicate on a canvas.

Amira had tried her hand at painting when she was younger following her father's encouragement for the art. She had failed so miserably at replicating a portrait of her father that he wasn't even able to lie convincingly.

Karwyn sighed, drawing Rhay's attention. But the young fae's intense eyes slowly drifted to Amira again. The air from her lungs escaped her and she went into a coughing fit.

"Are you all right, princess?" Rhay and Varsha asked at the same time. Finally able to take a deep breath, Amira gestured that she was fine.

"Always looking for attention," she heard Karwyn mumble under his breath. She pretended not to care but her body still tensed up. Why couldn't he at least try to be nice?

She could feel him growing restless. Karwyn's hand was twitching above her shoulder, sometimes even grazing the delicate fabric. Varsha was too focused on her painting to notice anything. On the contrary, Rhay had noted his friend's strange attitude and was visibly trying to communicate with him through gestures and eye contact. But his best efforts failed.

"I am taking a break," said Karwyn and without waiting for Varsha's reaction, he stormed out of the room.

Rhay quickly followed him.

"What in Caelo's name are you doing?" Amira heard Rhay say before the door closed behind them.

And then it was just the painter and her, back to their awkward silence.

Varsha smiled at her. "Do you want to see how it looks?"

"Aren't we supposed to only see it when it's done?"

"Come on, I won't tell anyone," said Varsha playfully.

Amira hesitated. She was curious to see the painting, but that would mean interacting with Varsha.

She stood up, happy to be able to stretch her legs on her short walk to the easel. An explosion of colours welcomed her when she saw the canvas was no longer blank. At first, she wasn't able to see the whole picture. It looked like pools of vibrant colours intertwined with each other.

"Take a step back," whispered Varsha. Amira did what she was told and she could finally see it. A strange feeling overcame her when she looked at herself in the painting. She could recognise the traits she had seen multiple times in the mirror, but something was different—special.

Her hand moved towards the painting and she almost touched it, but Varsha stopped her.

"It's not dry yet," Varsha said. Amira stayed still.

Varsha grabbed one of her brushes and applied some paint to the canvas. That's when Amira realised Varsha's power. The water she was using with the paint created perfectly mixed colours. When she applied it on the canvas, the strokes were precise and vivid, blending perfectly with the rest of the paint already on the portrait.

"You have water power, right?" Amira asked.

Varsha looked a bit surprised by the question. "I do, but I only use them for my paintings. Most fae don't notice."

"I always wanted water powers," she whispered to herself. "Why?"

"Water is the source of creation, everyone and everything needs it to grow. It's nurturing instead of devastating."

"You do know that the most powerful water fae can use it to provoke crashing waves that destroy everything on their way?"

"I wouldn't do that," Amira said with a serious face.

Varsha squeezed Amira's hand. "I know you wouldn't." The door opened and Varsha quickly let go of Amira's hand, leaving the princess with just the impression of warmth and comfort.

Karwyn and Rhay stared at them for a second before Karwyn exclaimed, "Let us finish this." Everyone regained their previous positions. Amira on the chair, Karwyn standing next to her, and Rhay completely spread out on his armchair, the book in his hand.

Varsha started painting again and Amira quickly felt her mind being plagued by thoughts and boredom. She didn't care to entertain either of them so she just tried to focus on what was happening around her. But, except for Rhay's not so discreet reactions to his novel, nothing much was going on. Her arms started to feel numb. She discreetly stretched them, but Karwyn still noticed and scoffed. Amira's anger rose in her stomach. Who did he think he was to police her that much?

"Keep still, do not prolong this. As the future high king, I do not have all day," he hissed. Amira realised that his hand was now fully on her shoulder. She almost slapped it away. Instead, she removed his hand by shaking her shoulder.

Noticing the tension, Varsha tried to diffuse it. "Maybe you could talk to each other to create a sense of intimacy for the portrait?" Karwyn looked at Amira with utter disgust. "Maybe you can recall the first time you met?" tried Varsha.

"She was thirteen. I accompanied my father to a trade talk in Allamyst. I met Amira at a ball and she was an insufferable brat who would rather dance alone than with the son of the high king."

Before Amira had time to reply, Rhay jumped to her rescue. "In her defence, I've seen how you dance. It's not glorious."

Amira couldn't help but gloat when she saw Karwyn's infuriated face. She remembered Rhay's advice and was determined to try it. "As I recall, we barely exchanged two words, so I don't know how you decided that I was a brat. You were the one who asked me to dance with the face of someone who would rather die than waltz with me."

"My father instructed me to ask you. It was common courtesy," Karwyn replied.

Amira rolled her tense shoulder. "So you do whatever your father tells you?"

Karwyn snapped back immediately, "And you do whatever your brother says, no? We make a great pair."

Her attempt at seduction had clearly backfired. She turned her head to see her fiancé's face was paler than usual. She knew she had gone too far when she had mentioned his father.

"I'm sorry," she said. "I shouldn't have mentioned your father. That was disrespectful of me." Her apology was heartfelt; she remembered Karwyn's strong reaction when she had brought up his parents' deaths on Falea Night.

She thought Karwyn was going to say something, but he just turned his attention to the painter. Rhay, who had observed the rest of the exchange with wide eyes as he sat next to Varsha, leaned towards the painter and whispered quite loudly in her ear, "I guess small talk isn't really their thing." He winked at Amira when he saw her smile at his remark.

"I can finish the rest of the painting on my own, you are free to go back to your duties," Varsha said as she smiled at Amira.

Blushing, Amira stood up and walked awkwardly towards the door. Something was pulling her back and she turned around to see what was happening. Karwyn had grabbed one of the ribbons of her dress.

"Stay. We need to talk," he said, calmly for once.

"Okay," she replied, a bit unsure but also curious to see what Karwyn wanted.

The interim high king gestured to Rhay and Varsha and they both quickly left the room, Rhay with his book and Varsha with her painting. They both brushed against Amira's arm when they passed her. A confusing shiver ran down her spine. Then it was just Karwyn and her.

She walked around the room, finally paying attention to the décor. With her hand, she caressed the petals of a strange silver rose that was held in a precious vase.

She turned to Karwyn. "What do you want to talk about?" He was being civil, which worried her more than calmed her. Was he luring her in as Wryen often did just to completely crush her?

"Come here," he demanded.

She furrowed her brows and showed her back to him. She wanted to avoid whatever was waiting for her.

"Come next to me, please," he asked this time.

Would he get angry if she refused? Amira hesitantly joined him in the centre of the room.

His bright turquoise eyes were searching hers when he asked, "What do you feel for Rhay?"

She hadn't expected his question. He wasn't outright accusing her of seducing Rhay this time. Instead he was asking about *feelings*. Was Karwyn jealous? Of whom? Rhay or her? Either way, she needed to get out of this conversation. Her hand discreetly pulled at a strand of her hair. She'd been so stupid to drink with Rhay last night. If Karwyn knew, Wryen would know soon too.

Karwyn pressed her before she could spiral further, "Do you feel for him as more than a friend?"

"Of course not," she simply said before even considering if it was true. She was confused about her own feelings all the time.

"Then you won't mind me reading your thoughts to confirm," he said as he tried to grab her arm. She quickly moved away and aimed for the door, her heart beating fast in her chest. But Karwyn was faster than her.

She found herself with her back pressed against the wall, prevented from moving by Karwyn's hold on her arms. So his mind reading power was indeed real. She hadn't been sure until now even though Rhay had said as much. Karwyn was getting more dangerous the longer she stayed at the palace. How far would he go?

This time, she was able to feel Karwyn's grip on her thoughts. It was as if invisible fingers were clawing at her mind, trying to tear down her walls to find the truth. A strange darkness started to build up in her core. She could feel something trying to escape. She struggled to get away from Karwyn.

Confusing thoughts ran through her, apparently making it harder for Karwyn to get his answer. She could feel him getting angrier as he tried to invade her thoughts, to hunt down each one of them.

"Did you train to block my powers?" he roared.

Amira's heart sped up in her chest. She hadn't, but the pain Karwyn was currently putting her under made her wish she had. Tears flooded her eyes as pain and fear mixed in her heart.

"No," Amira bit out.

"Then let me read you. Think only of Rhay," he demanded.

Amira let herself go limp. *Rhay, think of Rhay. Give Karwyn his answer.* She closed her eyes, immerging herself in her wave of thoughts. *Please let this be over.*

Finally, she felt Karwyn's grip loosen on her thoughts. "I see you are not lying. For once, you do not disappoint me, fiancée." He let go of her arms and stepped back. "We might be able to get along after all," he said with a knowing smile before he exited the room.

Amira shuddered, wondering what Karwyn had seen in her mind. At least, he seemed satisfied with her feelings towards Rhay. Would he demand proof like this every time?

She slid down the wall, her brain in shambles. How could she know rest when Karwyn was able to hunt down her most intimate thoughts? Wryen's control had been invasive, but nothing like this. With Karwyn's ability, how could she ever be free?

CHAPTER 32

LORA

Something cold and sharp dug into Lora's back. She moved slightly and was rewarded with a splintering headache. The sharp pain woke her up completely and she opened her eyes to a dimly lit, bleak stone ceiling.

Lora sat up faster than she should have. Her head spun. She was sitting on a cold stone floor and discovered a rock had been under her back, probably bruising her. But that was far from the worst part of her situation. While two of the walls around her were stone, the other two were made of metal bars.

She was in a literal cage. Earlier she had thought she couldn't feel any more hopeless. Apparently, there was drowning, and then there was the feeling of drowning over and over again, each time worse than the last one.

This was undoubtedly worse.

There was a wooden door at the end of the cave-like room. It was shut tightly and the only light illuminating the room were two torches on either side of the door.

For one second, Lora imagined this was a dream. Not because she couldn't imagine something this terrible happening to her, but because it didn't make sense. Who were these fae who had attacked her and Eyden? Why would they lock her up? Why not just kill her?

They couldn't keep her as a slave, it would go against the binding agreement humans had with the fae. Shortly before the border spell was put in place, the high king signed an agreement that hindered all fae from binding humans to slave contracts ever again. To Lora's knowledge, only witches were bound by such life-sentencing contracts nowadays. Witches were not seen as fae, but they weren't human either. They belonged to Liraen, so they weren't part of any human negotiations.

A fleeting thought went through Lora's mind like a whisper. If she was here alone, did that mean they left Eyden behind? Or was he dead? Her breath hitched but she quickly erased that last thought. If there's one thing Eyden was good at, it was disappearing. He probably left her and made a run for it. Most likely, he even embraced the idea of finally being rid of her.

He couldn't possibly be dead.

The creaking sound of the door made Lora take a step backwards, away from the bars. She steadied herself against the chilly wall.

A fae appeared before her as he walked into the room, stopping in front of the bars. He carried a cup of what she assumed was water. Lora racked her brain and decided he must be the fae who had attacked her earlier.

"Ah, she finally wakes. I thought you'd sleep away the whole day and we'd have to carry you outside," he said, a foul smile on his face. His expression reminded her of their previous encounter, confirming that he was indeed the same fae responsible for her head wound. Her hand drifted to the spot on her head, the blood now dried in her hair.

Her whole body screamed in anger. She wanted to charge at him, but the bars wouldn't allow it and she was sure her head wound would not agree with her. "Where's Ey—" She caught herself, not wanting to give away his identity. "Where's my...friend?"

The fae shrugged. "Beats me. He's of no interest to us."

A brief flash of relief went through her until she realised she'd been right. He left her behind. Shaking the thought, she asked, "What do you want?"

"Isn't it obvious?" he asked, puzzled.

"Would I ask if it was?" Lora bit out.

"Not a smart human, are you? Let me give you a summary. We overheard you fighting with your boyfriend and decided to take a chance with you. It was a dumb move on your part. You were practically begging us to take you. And what can I say, it's been a slow summer. But the last few days have made up for it. You're just our latest little addition. Young and healthy that you are, we'll get a good price for you."

Her thoughts briefly got caught up on the word *boyfriend*—very inaccurate—but then skipped to the important part. He had definitely said "price." She was to be sold. *Sold.* "You're selling me? Like a slave?" How was that possible? Did the agreement not work as well as they thought?

Her captor shook his head in a mocking manner. "You're not a slave. You're a blood bag."

"Blood bag?"

"Gosh, maybe I did throw you against that wall too hard."

She showed him the middle finger. The fae laughed, the ugly sound vibrating through Lora's body like a snake writhing beneath her skin.

"You must be lucky to have escaped this so far." He looked her over, stopping at her skull where her dark-blonde hair was now coated with dried blood. "Some fae like to get high off human blood. They'll pay good money to get their hands on a good blood source to make fortae. The drug is our top sold product. You'll join our other haul later tonight. We're waiting for the carriage, so don't get too...comfortable here," the fae concluded.

Lora was too occupied with this revelation to respond right away. They weren't killing humans instead of enslaving them, they'd found a new way to use them. She was utterly disgusted. She was to be used for her blood. All for a drug? The fae's priorities were royally fucked up. Maybe Lora did have some sort of brain damage and this wasn't real, after all. The longer she was awake, the less real anything felt.

"Well then, now that I see you're still alive and don't seem to be near death, I'm out of here. This place is depressing," the fae said. He left the tall cup of water by the bars and walked out.

Lora stared at the door for what felt like hours. She may have been in shock. A part of her had always known there was a real possibility she'd meet her end here. Being used as a blood bag wasn't what she'd imagined, but life rarely was. She came here seeking a cure, carrying her mother's blood, and now it was her own blood that would spill.

The irony made a laugh escape her. Suddenly, she couldn't stop. It was maddening. This was not a situation to laugh at. But she was in a cell in the fae world and she was all too aware that it was all because of her fight with Eyden, because she couldn't stop arguing.

The fae was right. She really was dumb. Lora had let her feelings and temper get the best of her and it would be her ruin.

The laughter turned into tears in a matter of minutes. Lora sank to the floor as the tears kept coming. First, she angrily wiped at them, but then she realised there was no reason to pretend. There was no one here to deceive.

Lora let her tears fall as her loss of hope drowned her completely and she slipped under water.

When she finally felt that she could compose herself, Lora took a deep breath and forced a mask of calm back over her expression. Her right hand gripped her phone, which had still been in her pocket, as well as the WiFi cube. She was glad the fae apparently saw her as such a small threat, they hadn't bothered to search her.

Sitting in the corner of her prison, Lora called her mum's number and pressed the phone to her ear.

It rang once. Maybe they weren't home.

Twice. Maybe it was a sign she should stay silent.

Third time. Maybe...

"Lora?" Her mum's voice came through the speaker and Lora choked on a fresh wave of sadness. "Is that you?"

Trying to keep from trembling, Lora replied, "Yeah, Mum. It's me."

She could hear a relieved sigh and possibly tears on the other side. "Honey, are you okay? What's happening? Why are you calling—I'm glad you did."

"I just needed to hear your voice."

"Are you hurt?"

Lora hesitated only for a second. There was nothing her mum could do to help. She would spare her the heartbreak as long as possible. "No, I'm okay. I just need a bit more time." She was met with silence on the other end. "But I'm close," Lora said to fill the void.

"You are?" her mum asked quietly.

"Just a minor setback," Lora added as she looked around the cell.

"You can come back anytime. I hate that you're out there. You belong home with us."

"I do. And I will." A promise rooted in nothing but lies.

"Are you truly okay? You didn't...you didn't explore anything fae-related, did you?"

A broad statement, but Lora knew her meaning. Did she explore her fae side? Not in a physical sense, but she couldn't deny that she had started to get curious. *No.* She shook her head. It was a dangerous path. She shut down her train of thought immediately; even thinking about it made her feel like she was betraying her family, especially her mum.

"No, of course not. I'm careful, don't worry," Lora insisted.

"Good. I wasn't trying to imply that you would. I wasn't sure how it would affect you, being over there."

Lora wasn't even sure how it really affected her. Would this experience change her? Surely, even if she did escape somehow, being sold and used as a blood bag would have to leave some scars. The thought made her shudder, but her voice sounded calm as she said, "I know. How's everyone?" Another silence. A heavier one. "Mum?"

"I...they are fine."

"Want to try again and convince me this time? What's going on?"

"I didn't want to trouble you. But since you said you're close..." Lora could hear her exhaling loudly. "Your dad...he tested positive. He has the virus."

And there it was again. That feeling of drowning, of being pulled under muddy, terrifying water. No hope in sight. Nothing to pull her up. But she needed to be the hope for her parents. To keep them fighting as long as they could.

"Lora?" her mum asked, worry carrying her voice.

Lora's eyes were watering. She was on the edge of breaking down for the second time. She couldn't do that to her mum. Not now. "Yes, I'm here. Sorry. I can't talk much longer. The data. I...I'll try my best. Just rest, okay? And tell everyone I miss them."

"I should have never doubted you, Lora. Come back as soon as you can."

The words were a slap in her face, like an icy wave taking her breath away. "I will. Bye, Mum. I love you."

"Love you too, honey."

Lora hung up quickly as fresh tears rolled down her cheeks and a muffled cry escaped her. Her phone was still in her hand, her fingers hurting from clutching it so tightly.

What was going to happen to her parents if she didn't show

up? Would they cling to the false hope she gave them until their last breath?

And what would happen to Oscar if both her parents died and she didn't make it back to Earth? He already felt abandoned by her now. He would forever hate her if she left him alone for good, especially considering she just gave her family hope that a cure was coming. Lora would hate herself too.

She wasn't sure at all if she'd made the right call. She knew if she had been in her mum's place, she would have rather heard the truth. But she couldn't bring herself to say it out loud. Maybe that made her a hypocrite. Maybe she was the worst liar of them all.

The endless pit of sadness slowly turned into anger. Lora blamed herself, but when she tilted her head up and her gaze snapped on the bars, the fury intensified. And this time it was directed at the fae who kidnapped her.

Her skin felt like fire as her veins burned in frustration. Something clicked in her mind and she knew she couldn't go down easily. She would fight even if it killed her. She had to try. For her family. For all the promises she had made that were waiting to be fulfilled. And if she didn't make it, at least she wouldn't be used as a blood bag. Lora was aware that that could end badly for entirely different reasons, since she wasn't fully human.

The thought of being experimented on made her shiver. Her fate couldn't end in her mother's worst nightmare. She'd been trying to protect Lora from this her whole life.

Lora stood up and examined her cell. Her eyes settled on the stone she'd slept on and she put it in her free pocket. She moved her other hand which was still holding onto her phone, thinking she should hide it again, but then another thought hit her.

Someone should know. That there was a real possibility she'd never make it back home. Lora unlocked her phone and clicked on Maja's name.

The sound of a key turning in a lock made Lora's idea vanish. She slipped her phone in her pocket and stood tall, not forgetting her other plan.

This time both fae entered the room. And they were both looking at her as if she wasn't worth anything and worth too much to lose at the same time.

They were taking her outside. She noticed it was quite dark already, almost a full day must have passed. Her hands were bound in front of her. Lora had considered throwing the stone at the nearest fae, but she knew the air magic wielder could use her own move against her. So she waited for her opening, going through different scenarios in her mind.

Lora could see the carriage through the open door in front of them. It was small. Another fae was sitting atop the bench, holding the reins, not even glancing their way. As they walked through the door, the fae who had attacked her guided her forward while the other fae stayed behind. She assumed the other one must be the air magic wielder. He looked familiar even though Lora hadn't been able to get a good look at him during the attack. She saw him gathering things in the adjoining room.

The fae who had a hold on her pushed her forward more sternly, almost making her trip. Her eyes scanned her surroundings in the moonlight. All Lora could make out in the dim light of the street lamp was the carriage, the shapes of a few buildings, and a narrow street leading into the woods.

She still had her phone. With her map, she could find a way back to Eyden's flat—assuming she didn't run into any more trouble. But the farther away the fae moved her, the harder it would be to get back on her own. She needed to get away *now*.

The carriage door was already open and Lora turned around, attempting to see where she could run to, but as she moved, the fae shoved her into the small space. Her back hit the floor hard and her head must have barely missed the bench. The fae lifted one foot to the carriage floor and leaned forward.

Lora kicked out with all her strength and anger. The fae gasped as he stumbled back and put a hand to his stomach. Lora didn't waste a second. She turned and scrambled forward, trying to reach the other side of the carriage. The other door.

She had grabbed the handle with her bound hands when the fae grabbed her foot and pulled. Her chin hit the wooden floor and she gritted her teeth against a new wave of pain. The fae yanked on her foot, pulling her back to his side.

Lora instinctively grabbed the first thing in her reach, the bench, and struggled against the fae's superior strength. Her eyes travelled over the goods stored beneath the bench. Bottles filled with shiny liquids and pills. Bags of blood sat on top of buckets filled with ice. Recoiling, she lost her hold. Lora quickly turned on her back just as the fae hauled her to him. She tried to kick again but he held both her feet, making her immobile.

"Bitch. I'll break your legs if I have to. You ensured yourself a very unpleasant journey," the fae snarled as he started twisting one of her ankles. A scream of pain escaped Lora's lips and her eyes squeezed shut.

"Fuck!" her captor shouted. The grip on her ankle loosened unexpectedly.

Lora opened her eyes in confusion. She didn't understand why he stopped until she followed his gaze to his shoulder, where a throwing star was now firmly embedded. The fae reached for the weapon, one hand leaving Lora's ankle. "Is that—"

"Almandine?" a female voice behind him said. He whirled around and Lora caught a flash of red curls. "It sure is."

Then a fist, knuckles clad in silvery red, hit the fae square in the face.

CHAPTER 33

AMIRA

Amira couldn't believe what she was reading. Blood rushed to her cheeks as she turned the pages. Rhay wasn't lying when he said that this human book was scandalous. Amira was glad Nalani wasn't around this evening to ask about her reading material.

Suddenly, she heard someone walking up to the door of her antechamber. She waited, expecting a knock, a sense of dread slowly coating her heart.

Instead, a piece of paper slid under her door. Surprised, she put her book aside and went to pick up the note.

Inside, a delicate and familiar handwriting read, "*Want to have an exclusive party?*"

Intrigued by the offer, Amira scurried around the antechamber to hide her book before she opened the door to her rooms and faced Rhay.

"I've brought the ingredients to make my signature cocktail," Rhay said gleefully as he showed her the multitude of bottles in his hand. "I thought we could have a small party in the drawing room at the end of the hallway," he added, cautiously looking around.

Amira hesitated. "I'm not sure that's wise." She was all too aware Karwyn would disapprove. "I'm quite tired. I'm not going to be good company."

"Nonsense, you're always good company, princess. Join me. Or I'll have to drink all of this by myself—and you know how much I hate hangovers," he said with a knowing smile.

"I'll have to think about it," Amira replied.

"Come on, princess. The drawing room will be empty. No one will look for us there." Rhay glanced at the bottles in his hands. "On the contrary, someone might see me standing in front of your door, so you better stop arguing." His smile slipped. "Unless you really want me to leave?"

Did she? It had been an intense day and she craved a distraction. She knew she was playing with fire, but Karwyn seemed to have lost his suspicion and Rhay insisted no one would know. Her heart answered for her.

Amira sighed. "Fine." Rhay's answering smirk clouded her worries.

"Follow me," he said. Amira closed her door and looked around the hallway before following Rhay. She crossed the hallway like she was swimming in an unrelenting ocean.

"Let's see those drinks you promised me," Amira said to Rhay as he closed the door to the cosy, unoccupied drawing room. She hoped once she had alcohol in her veins, the anxious feeling in her chest would disappear.

"Oh, I never forget promises involving alcohol." He winked.

They spent the next half hour mixing different types of

alcohol, spices, and fruit juices. Rhay's recipe seemed to involve a lot of guessing and randomness. At the end, they had made eight rainbow drinks and Amira was pretty sure that each one was different.

Rhay offered her a glass and grabbed another one for himself. "To the sky," they cheered. The drink tingled a bit, as if she was biting into something very bad but also very tempting.

She took a seat on a blue velvet sofa while Rhay respectfully sat on a chair. An awkward silence settled between them. Amira sipped her drink while avoiding Rhay's vibrant eyes.

"I wonder how it's going to look," Rhay said, breaking the silence.

Amira raised her head, intrigued by the statement. "What are you talking about?"

"Your engagement portrait."

Amira's interest immediately dropped. "The painter is very talented."

"Oh, yes she is," replied Rhay with a strange smile.

Amira wanted to press him with questions, but she wasn't sure that she would enjoy the response. "Have you ever had your portrait done by her?"

"By her, no, but one of my most prized possessions is a portrait of my parents and I. I was barely a year old when they made it so I don't really remember the posing time, but it's one of the last images of my mother."

Amira smiled gently at Rhay. She could feel the pain of his loss. "I'm very sorry. I know how hard it is to lose a parent. And you were really young, right?"

Rhay looked at the bottom of his drink when he replied. "I

was only six. She died in an attack while travelling back from her sister's house. There was a lot of instability in Sapharos back then."

Amira couldn't find the proper words to express her compassion. She decided to keep the conversation going. "Did you leave Sapharos soon after?"

Rhay downed his drink and grabbed another one. "Yes. My father was an advisor for Queen Kaede, but Harten Adelway had offered him a position a long time ago. He had said no at the time because my mother wanted me to be raised in Lazuli. But after her death, it was too hard for my father to stay."

"So you've grown up in the palace?"

"Yes, right along Karwyn. We were the same age." He paused for a second. "It helped, having someone who knew what it felt like to lose a mother. Karwyn had lost his mother barely a year before I moved to Parae." Before Amira could intervene, Rhay hastily added, "Plus, Karwyn also had quite a complicated personality. He was never interested in making a ton of friends."

"That part hasn't changed," Amira replied dryly.

Rhay's lips parted in an agreeing grin. "Can't really prove you wrong after today." His face suddenly turned serious. "It wasn't easy for him, you know, growing up in his brother's shadow."

Amira almost spat out her drink. "He had a brother?"

Rhay avoided her inquiring eyes. He looked so regretful, like he had just broken a very important promise. "Please don't ever mention this to Karwyn." He had never sounded more serious.

Amira put a hand to her heart. "I promise. But how come I've never heard of him?" She thought back to the portrait she had seen of the Adelway family before the Dark King had killed most of them. Had one of the two children pictured been Karwyn's brother?

"It's not a complete secret. His brother died in the fight against the Dark King almost 75 years ago. You're too young to have heard of him, but he is quite famous in Turosian. The king was very proud of his son and when he died, no one knew who would replace Harten on the throne when the time would come."

"But then he had Karwyn."

"Yes, and he has always compared the two. But how could Karwyn compete with a dead man? Only his greatness had stayed as his legacy, none of his faults."

Amira took in all this new information. In her head, she could see a young Karwyn desperately trying to gain his father's approval. It made him appear so...vulnerable.

Rhay shook his head in disbelief and looked at his empty drink. "I really made them strong this time."

"I thought it was a fool-proof recipe," Amira joked to lighten the mood.

"I shouldn't have told you all that. You're just so easy to talk to."

"Are you sure it's not just the drinks?"

Rhay laughed. "Well, that too. But I mean it, you're a good person, Amira. There aren't many fae you can have a genuine conversation with here at court."

She could feel her cheeks turning red. She wasn't used to such pure compliments. A bit of sadness sank her heart as she remembered the feeling of Karwyn invading her thoughts. "Karwyn doesn't think so," she whispered.

"Karwyn has always been very private about his feelings. I've known him for over twenty years and I've never seen anyone pierce his heart. It will take time," declared Rhay.

"Can I ask you something?" Amira started. Rhay gave her an encouraging nod. "Can you teach me how to block Karwyn's powers?"

Rhay froze. She could read his internal struggle on his beautiful face. "I could, but I don't think it'd be a smart move." He stopped for a second as a thought seemed to cross his mind. "Would be fun to piss off Karwyn, though. I like to keep him on his toes."

Amira thought back on Karwyn piercing through the veil of her mind, seemingly awakening something she wanted to forget. "Please, don't you think I'm entitled to some privacy?" It was her only shot at levelling the playing field with Karwyn. She shuddered, imagining a future in which even her most private thoughts were laid bare.

"I'm not sure..." He slurred his words.

Of course, he was drunk. It was a given after all the drinks he had downed tonight. Maybe she should try another way—a more honest one.

"I'm sure you know, as everyone else probably does in this palace, that I'm a level one. This relationship is completely unbalanced. After the wedding, I'll be completely powerless. Help me bring some balance to this. Help me show him I can be useful," Amira pleaded.

Rhay shifted on his chair, almost hitting the ground. "All right, I guess I can teach you some techniques." He fell off his chair, making Amira laugh.

"You're very drunk right now, so don't forget your promise tomorrow."

Rhay chuckled and came to sit next to Amira on the sofa. He was so close that their thighs almost touched. The sweetness of his breath was caressing her cheek. A shiver ran down her back. He looked completely out of it. A faint voice in her head told her she should move, but her drunken voice won.

"You know love can be many things, Amira. For some, it's lightning hitting you right in the heart but leaving you quickly. For others, it's a quiet storm, slowly building its strength. I've always been more of a lightning type of guy." He whispered the last part as he looked straight in her eyes, "And look where it got me..."

Amira's chest tightened. "Have you ever considered getting married?"

Rhay's eyes glazed over. "I..." He shook his head. "No, it's stupid." He looked straight at Amira. "You know I'm a free spirit. I'm not sure I'll ever be able to commit." Amira wasn't sure if it was disappointment or relief she felt in her heart. Rhay lowered his voice without noticing, probably too intoxicated to care. "What about you, Amira? Have you ever been in love?"

The question lingered in her mind. She knew the answer, but was she ready to share it? A pair of emerald eyes stared at her with such joy and childlike wonder. In her chest, her heart started pounding again. Her lips parted and her answer quickly made its escape, facilitated by her drunken state. "Once. It was such a wonderful feeling. So pure, so full of hope. And then it was ruined."

She only felt her tears when Rhay wiped them with his soft

hand. His eyes were full of tenderness. Lost in the ocean, she gasped for air. A burning sensation took over her lips and she noticed that Rhay was staring at them with a determined look. His face inched toward hers.

Everything slowed down, but Amira's thoughts were going at the speed of light. Was he really going to do that? Would he dare? Did she want him to? Would it help her forget? He was her only friend here, refusing him could make her current situation even harder. But the only person she truly wanted to kiss was long gone, merely ashes in the wind. She searched Rhay's eyes, trying to find the hint of emerald green she still longed for. As blue as the ocean, Rhay's eyes were not the ones she wished to encounter.

His warm breath caressed her face. She closed her eyes, immobile. He kissed her on the forehead. A sweet and gentle kiss.

"You'll find love again, princess. With Karwyn. And this time it will last," Rhay said.

She held her eyes closed, furious at what he had said. Deep in her heart, she knew that her feelings towards Karwyn would never evolve to real love. Not that her fiancé would mind; he had made it clear that he had no interest in her.

She heard the door open and close. When Amira opened her eyes, Rhay was gone and there were only a couple of empty glasses left to prove that he had been there. A fleeting thought passed through her mind. Would Karwyn ask her if she'd spent any time with Rhay? Would he read her mind?

Amira shook her head as she stood up, chasing away the worries. She quickly downed the last full cup. Soon after, a headache took over her mind. Her whole body was shaking and she could feel pins and needles in her arms and legs. Amira stumbled back to her room.

She fell on her bed. In her head, she saw strange figures with changing faces, sometimes familiar, sometimes unknown, all too painful to look at. Her body spontaneously started to convulse. She opened her mouth to scream but she was unable to make any sound. She tried to conjure a happy memory. Her mother smiling at her during her first official event. Walking in the streets of Amryne with her father disguised as a commoner.

Her breathing returned to normal and Amira quickly fell into a drunken slumber, populated with strange nightmares and even stranger memories.

CHAPTER 34

🔥 LORA

The fae stumbled to the side of the carriage, giving Lora a better view of the attacker. The girl looked young, maybe late teens. Her eyes were determined, loose red curls coming out of her high ponytail, framing her face. Her fist was raised for another hit. She was so small compared to the fae. But she didn't back down, brass knuckles digging into the fae's face.

The fae seemed to snap out of the girl's surprise appearance. He caught her fist mid-swing before it connected with his cheek again. His face twisted in a cruel smile. The girl spun and kicked him between his legs, grabbing the throwing star from his shoulder as he doubled down. The movement slowed her down and he reached out, landing a punch to her stomach that seemed to knock the wind out of her. He swept her feet from under her and she fell.

Lora tried to get up from her position in the carriage, but the smallest movement induced a pounding pain in her ankle. Her hands were still bound, which made it hard for her to shift her weight off her feet. She watched in horror as the girl hit the ground.

The fae leaned over her and just when Lora thought she'd be lost, the throwing star struck the fae's forehead. The attacker kicked at his legs and swiftly rolled to the side as the fae lost his balance and dropped to the ground.

The girl sprang to her feet, another throwing star in her hand. She pushed him onto his back with her leg and placed one foot on the fae's upper body as she pressed her weapon into the left side of his chest. The fae snarled in pain but barely moved against her hold.

It was quite the sight: the fae on the ground, one star embedded in his forehead, the other close to his heart, and the redhead standing over him, fae blood staining her brass knuckles.

She turned to Lora, breathing heavily, brown eyes looking up at her. "Are there others with you?"

Lora shook her head. Her voice seemed to have left her. Right, she wasn't here for her. There were more humans captured. Lora sucked in a sharp breath. She had been too preoccupied by the fight to fully realise that this girl looked *human*. She didn't look fae at all. Her eyes held no otherworldly shine to them or unique colour.

"Where are the others?" the girl demanded, pressing the star further into the fae's flesh as she leaned in.

His face constricted in pain. "Like I'd tell you. Go ahead, kill me. I bet you don't have the guts to go through with it."

The girl laughed, her voice carrying threats. "You have no idea what I'm capable of."

"He said they would sell them somewhere," Lora said as she finally found her voice.

"Is that so?" She put pressure on the wound in his chest and the fae coughed blood. "Tell me where or I promise, you'll wish I already killed you."

The fae remained quiet. The girl had placed a hand on the star in his forehead when a loud shriek caught her attention. Her gaze shifted, turning every direction to whatever was happening close by. Lora realised she had tuned out all the noise around them. There was another fight happening. People shouting, curses traveling in the air. There was a ringing in Lora's ear that made it difficult to make out concrete sounds. Her head felt hollowed out.

The girl grabbed the fae by his hair and knocked his head against the hard ground. The fae went limp, but Lora assumed he couldn't be dead. Not yet.

A young face appeared in her vision. The girl's eyes travelled over Lora before settling on Lora's hands. She stepped into the carriage and moved to unbind them. "Sorry, I probably should've done that sooner."

Lora looked over the girl's shoulder to the unconscious fae. "I think you were kind of busy saving my life and all."

"Ah, it's nothing. Trust me, I enjoyed punching the smile off his face."

Lora's hands came free and she rubbed at her irritated skin.

"Can you walk?" the girl asked.

Lora braced her arm against the bench next to her and pulled herself up. She hissed in pain as her ankle protested and her skull threatened to explode.

She hadn't realised she was so close to losing her balance until she felt an arm bracing her, guiding her to the bench.

There was a loud crashing noise in the distance again. The girl glanced between the door and Lora. "Did someone shout something?"

"I'm not sure. Maybe?"

The redhead angled her head back to get a better glimpse of the outside. "I hate to do this, but it seems like some ass kicking is needed. I'll be back, okay? Take a breather." She turned her gaze to Lora, then to the unconscious fae. "He'll be out for a while. I'm not done with him yet. I promised him a painful death."

Lora merely nodded. Her whole body felt heavy, as if being dragged down by weights. She followed the girl's movement with tired eyes. The redhead took the rope and bound the unconscious fae's hands before running off to join another fight.

Left alone, Lora felt like she was moving under thick water. She couldn't think clearly anymore, but she could think enough to realise that that was a bad sign. Glancing at her captor's face again, Lora decided she couldn't stay here. If he woke up, how much would the rope and throwing stars slow him down? She didn't have much strength left and she couldn't run. She needed to get away while she was still conscious and the fae wasn't.

Bracing herself for the pain, Lora gripped the doorframe and stood up, shifting her weight to her left foot. She carefully stepped out of the carriage. Her body was screaming, making her skin feel icy. Her eyes landed on the fae, now directly in front of her feet. Lora leaned against the carriage as her hand slipped into her pocket and curled around the stone.

Noises drew her eyes to the front of the carriage and further off. She could make out figures encircling someone, maybe the fae who had been driving the carriage. The seat that had once been occupied was now empty. He must have left before the redhead had shown up.

Lora could feel her focus slipping. She used her free hand to steady herself as she slid forward, her weight on her left leg, heading in the opposite direction of the commotion. Every step felt like agony. Her hair was falling into her face but she didn't have a free hand to pull it back. She neared the end of the carriage and noted the distance she'd have to cross to get to the nearest building. Maybe she could find a hiding spot in the alley. Somewhere. Anywhere. The carriage was too risky. If Lora passed out, she'd make it easy for them to drive away with her.

Her ears picked up rushed footsteps within the chaos of her mind. She turned as fast as she could without falling, setting her injured food on the ground even as pain shot up her leg.

The stone left her hand before she even took a good look at the figure heading straight at her. It barely missed his face as he ducked out of the way, dark curls falling into his familiar face.

"By Caelo, that's not the reaction I imagined." Ice blue eyes found hers as a smile started to form on his lips. "Actually, I shouldn't have expected anything else."

Lora's head was pounding. Was she imagining things? Did she actually pass out and create this scenario in her mind?

"Lora? Are you okay?" the figure who looked like Eyden asked, worry etched into his features.

She took a tiny step back but realised too late she wasn't holding onto the carriage anymore. Her right leg almost gave out and Eyden rushed forward, steadying her. Lora's gaze swung to where his hand touched her arm. It felt real. He *was* real.

"You came back," Lora whispered, her voice sounding raspy. She never did drink what the fae had left at her cell.

Eyden looked hurt but then the emotion swiftly left this face. "You thought I wouldn't?"

"I thought that maybe...maybe our deal wasn't worth the trouble anymore."

Something flashed in his eyes, but she couldn't read it, not when everything was so hard to focus on. Movement drew her eyes behind him. "Shit. Eyden—"

He spun sideways, one arm never leaving Lora. The fae had gotten up from the ground, fury burning behind his eyes. The rope was lying at his feet. He removed the throwing star from his chest, his lips curling into a cruel smile as his eyes locked on Lora. She wished she still had that stone to throw to wipe that grin off his face forever.

Then a knife flew through the air and hit its target with precision. The star dropped from the fae's hand as he stared at the knife in his chest, a new wound atop his old one. But this one was deeper. Iron mixed with almandine piercing his heart, draining his life source. No fae could survive without it. The magic that kept him alive and made him powerful was dwindling fast.

The fae clutched at the knife as blood ran down his chest. His eyes widened in panic, the grin long gone as he fell to the ground.

Seeing the life slowly leave his eyes, all Lora felt was relief and an odd sense of satisfaction. She wasn't sure what that said about herself, but there was no time to dwell on it now. She looked to Eyden, his hand still outstretched from when he threw the knife.

She finally took him in fully. His shirt was torn at the collar and stained with blood. There was also dried blood on one of his cheeks. He must have been part of the fight.

"Most of it isn't mine," he said, catching her gaze.

"Whose is it, then?"

"The one with air magic. I went into the building first, trying to find you. I found him instead."

He didn't need to say the rest. Lora already knew how that fight had ended. His eyes seemed to be trying to tell her too many things at once. *The fae got what he deserved. I came back for you. This isn't just about some deal. Please tell me you're okay.*

Or maybe it was her mind playing tricks on her and he wasn't trying to say half of those things. Probably the latter.

The sound of footsteps pulled her out of her thoughts. Eyden's eyes left hers as he looked towards the group of people approaching them. The girl from earlier reached them first. Two others were trailing her, dragging the unconscious third fae with them.

The redhead took in the dead fae, then focused on Eyden, a deadly glint in her eyes. Lora opened her mouth to explain that Eyden wasn't one of the fae who had captured her.

"For fuck's sake, Eyden. I told you no killing unless we have everyone," the girl said.

Lora's mouth closed in surprise. How the hell did they know each other?

"The knife must have slipped out of my hand. You know how it is," Eyden answered, a hint of a smile in his voice. He helped Lora lean against the carriage wall.

"Was there someone in the building?"

"Yes, but he's dead too," Eyden answered as he stepped away from Lora.

The girl groaned. "Great, now there's only one fae who could tell us where the others are."

Eyden turned to Lora. "Did they tell you anything?"

Lora stared at him for a beat too long before she pushed aside all her questions. "He only said I'd be joining their haul."

Eyden cursed under his breath. He looked towards the path leading into the woods before seeking the girl's gaze again. "He's not going to talk, Elyssa. I bet they've taken them to the Void. That path leads to Rubien. He must have blood sworn not to reveal the location."

Rubien, the lost kingdom? In Lora's research, it was always described as a wasteland. It wasn't accepted as a kingdom in Liraen anymore as it was believed that the kingdom's god, the God of Justice, had abandoned the land after witnessing the Dark King's sinister behaviour and misuse of his beliefs. Rubien had been completely deserted after the Dark King was destroyed, leaving only seven remaining kingdoms. Or so she'd thought.

Two humans stopped next to the girl, Elyssa. A man, who Lora guessed was in his mid-thirties, pushed the fae to the other man and stepped forward. "Just as I suspected. We helped you get your girl and we got nothing out of it. Typical fae." The younger man struggled with the weight of the unconscious fae and then let him drop to the ground.

Eyden moved forward quickly, facing the man. "There's no point in torturing him when I know he won't talk. I said I'd help you get everyone so that's what I'll do." His eyes briefly shifted to Lora before returning to the human. "I keep my promises."

His voice was reassuring, yet it made Lora's heart ache. Was this really about keeping his end of the deal? A list of promises she couldn't keep whirled in her mind, increasing her migraine. Not to mention, this whole scenario was absurd. Why was Eyden working with humans?

"We could hide. Wait until he wakes up, follow him, and then finally give him what he deserves," Elyssa suggested, pointing to the fae on the ground. The girl must have also noticed the items in the carriage that begged to be sold. If the remaining fae was as desperate as his companions, he would surely make his delivery even without them.

"You were just in a fight and are exhausted. If they've really taken them to Rubien, it will probably be a long journey there and the market will be crawling with fae. I can go by myself," Eyden answered.

"As if we'd trust a fae to save our people," the man sneered.

Eyden's brows furrowed in anger. "You want to go yourself, Jaspen? Please, be my guest. But don't drag my sister with you."

Sister? Lora wasn't sure she was following the conversation correctly. How could Eyden, a fae, be related to a human? And how could he care for Elyssa when he didn't seem to care for the fate of humans?

Elyssa interrupted Eyden and Jaspen's staring match. "I'm not staying behind, Eyden. We should all go. Strength in numbers."

"It's not smart to go now. It won't help Farren and your friends if we all end up dead," Eyden said.

"I can handle myself, you goddamn know it. We're not gonna

be the ones ending up dead—not if I have anything to say about it. But we can't miss our chance to finally find out where exactly the Void is."

Lora could tell Elyssa was furious but the girl turned away, holding back further curses.

An idea formed in Lora's splintered mind. "What if you could track him without actually having to follow him?"

Heads turned to her, curious eyes sizing her up. Jaspen and the young man next to him, whose name she didn't know, glanced at her for the first time.

The attention made Lora feel uneasy, but there was no going back now. She pulled her WiFi cube out of her pocket. "This connects to my phone. As long as it's on, I can track it on my digital map." Lora turned to Eyden. "Assuming I can get another one. A second WiFi cube from the black market here?"

Eyden met her eyes, the blue of his eyes shining with something like gratitude. "I can get you another one."

Elyssa smiled at Lora before addressing Eyden. "I don't fully understand that, but if you think it works, let's do it. As long as we still get to follow him and kick the jerk into another dimension."

"It'll work. I've heard of tracking with phones before," Eyden answered.

"If it doesn't work, we're going to have an issue," Jaspen said, wary eyes landing on Eyden then Lora.

"I think we already have an issue. Lots of them, actually," Eyden bit out.

Jaspen took a step towards Eyden, but Elyssa stepped into his path. "Jaspen, we need Eyden's help. You know that."

The man gave Eyden one last dirty look before he turned and crossed his arms. Elyssa's gaze travelled to where Lora heavily leaned against the carriage. "Lora, can you give me this cube thing?"

Surprised she knew her name, Lora held out her hand. Elyssa took the WiFi cube and turned it over in her palm. "It's on now?"

"Yeah, it is," Lora replied, nodding.

"Excellent. I'll hide it in the carriage." Elyssa disappeared inside the carriage before she even finished her sentence.

Eyden moved closer to Lora, standing next to her. "Are you okay?"

Was she? No, in so many ways, no. But she knew he was asking about her physical pain. "I think my right ankle is sprained." She moved her hand to the back of her head. "And my head has seen better days. But I'm fine."

"You don't look fine." Under other circumstances, she would have felt offended. But she thought she saw genuine concern in his eyes. "I'll get you some medicine from the market as soon as we get back to camp."

"Camp?"

"The human camp. El and—"

"It's done." Elyssa peeked out of the carriage doorway. "Let's get the hell out of here."

Lora had no idea what camp Eyden was talking about, but anywhere was better than here. That much she was sure of.

CHAPTER 35

LORA

Lora woke up with a start, her eyes frantically adjusting to the light as she searched for the cave bars. But she wasn't there anymore. She was lying on a couch in a room that looked like a tent. The rectangular-shaped room had walls made out of thick beige fabric. Her right ankle was packed with ice and propped up on a sapphire blue cushion. A second ice bag was next to her head. It must have slipped off in her sleep. Elyssa was standing in the corner of the messy room, washing the blood off of her knuckle rings.

The last few hours rushed back to Lora. Her ankle had slowed them down so much that Eyden had carried her to speed up the process. She'd had so many questions burning on her tongue as she had looked up at him, her arms around his neck. But even though she had tried to keep as still as possible, her head had still moved with each of Eyden's steps and it made her skull throb, turning all her questions into ashes as she drifted into sleep.

The place she found herself in now was lived in; piles of

clothes were on the floor, empty plates on a small table. The mess didn't bother Lora. It was inviting and beautifully ordinary. She assumed it must be Elyssa's room. There was a basin of sorts, a bed, a wardrobe, and the blue couch Lora was currently occupying.

Elyssa removed her weapons from the bucket filled with water and put them down on a towel. Her eyes caught Lora's as she looked over her shoulder. "Hey, you're awake. How are you feeling?" The young girl moved closer, sitting in the chair closest to the couch.

In this light Lora noticed the girl's eyes were more hazel than brown. But they were still human eyes, no hint of fae magic.

"Better. I think," Lora replied as she tried to sit up more. She gave up. "Where's Eyden?" She was still surprised he had shown up at all. But from what he'd said to Jaspen, she gathered he had a promise he needed to fulfil.

"He went to the black market, but he'll be back soon."

"Not the market in Rubien, right?" That's what Lora had understood from their conversation. That the fae had taken the humans to another market in the abandoned kingdom.

"No, we're going to follow that neat tracker of yours. We'll see if he's really going into Rubien, but it seems likely. The Void is the most hellish place they could take them to. That's where the *really* dark trades are being made."

If they were trading humans there, then Lora could only agree. If it wasn't for Eyden and Elyssa, she would've been dragged there too. "I think I said it before but in case I didn't, thank you for saving me."

Elyssa's face stretched into a grin. "You don't have to thank me. There's nothing quite like getting in a good punch. And it's what we do—help fellow humans. If anything, thank Eyden. I have to admit, I'm really curious about you two."

"You're curious? I didn't even know he had a sister. He never mentioned you."

Elyssa didn't seem hurt by that statement. "You could say I'm his biggest secret. Or one of them, at least. He carries too many. It's not you, Lora. There's a lot of danger here. Eyden learned pretty early in life that trust can be fatal."

She could understand the need to protect his sibling. It was the human part that had caught her off guard the most. Her assumption that Eyden cared for no human life had cracked.

"If you don't mind me asking, how are you related?" Lora asked.

"We're clearly not blood-related, if that's what you're asking. Eyden's mother was close to my family and we took Eyden in when his parents were, well, gone. He's the only family I have left now." A short pause, then Elyssa added, "So, you and Eyden? There's a story there, I can tell."

Lora shrugged. "There's not much to tell. We made a business deal. He's keeping his promise."

Elyssa nodded as a small smile played on her lips. "He told me about that. Vaguely. Said you came from the human world to find a cure and he promised to help you."

Her blood stilled, iced over. "He told you I'm not from here?"

"It'll be our secret, I swear. Trust me, I know how to keep a good secret."

Lora wanted to believe her, but she was scared trust would be fatal for her too. "No one can know about this."

"No one else will," Elyssa reassured her.

There was nothing more Lora could do, so she moved on. "You're not going to ask me how I did it?"

Understanding washed over Elyssa's face. "That's what Eyden asked, wasn't it? In return for his help?"

"Yes. For his trading business. I'm a business opportunity to him, so to say."

"I don't think you are. And I don't think he had his goddamn business in mind at all."

"Why else would he want to cross?"

"He doesn't. He wants me to go." Elyssa laughed under her breath as she shook her head. "That idiot. He knows very well I'd never cross. No chance in hell."

Before Lora could question her further, she heard footsteps coming closer. She looked towards the door and Elyssa quickly followed her gaze.

The flap of the tent opened and Eyden walked in, looking between Lora and Elyssa. "Did I interrupt something?"

"Lora and I were having a riveting conversation about your honest intentions."

"What now?" Eyden asked, eyebrows raised in curiosity.

Elyssa glanced at Lora. "It can wait. I'm gonna go have a shower." She picked up a pile of clothes, then scampered off to somewhere Lora couldn't see before the door flap fell back into place.

"Okay, then," Eyden said as he moved to kneel next to the couch. "I got this healing paste. It doesn't work for..."

"Viruses," Lora concluded. Heavy unspoken words hung between them.

Eyden sighed quietly. "No, it doesn't. But it will help with bruises and such."

"Like scraped knees?"

"Yes, for example. Can I see your head wound?"

Lora nodded and turned to her side to give Eyden better access to the back of her head. Since she had woken up, her wound hadn't been bothering her as much anymore.

She felt his fingers move her hair, stiff with blood, out of the way to reveal the spot where her head had hit the wall.

"It's not as bad as I feared," Eyden said as he gently applied something to the wound. It felt cool on her skin and she instantly felt lighter.

"What about your wound?" Lora asked, remembering the attack in the alley.

Eyden moved away and Lora sat up so she could look at him and keep herself from leaning against the cushions. "I heal fast. Don't worry about me."

He removed the already warmed ice pack from her ankle. "That was a good idea, by the way. The WiFi cube. Saved me from convincing El not to run off unprepared."

Lora mock gasped. "Did you just admit I'm smart? Again?"

Eyden laughed and the sound filled the emptiness in her heart, temporarily washing away the sadness she'd been carrying for the last day. Or longer. "I never admitted such a thing. All I said was the idea didn't suck."

"No, you said it was good," Lora corrected.

"Even with a head wound, nothing much escapes you," Eyden replied, the start of a grin lifting the corner of his mouth. He applied gel to her swollen ankle. The pressure hurt but not like it had felt earlier.

"I'm keeping count of your compliments," Lora said before a yawn escaped her and her head fell against the cushion again.

Eyden started to back away. "The medicine will make you really tired. You should rest."

"Wait. I have so many questions," Lora mumbled even as her eyes fell closed.

"We'll have time to talk tomorrow."

She assumed he'd left her, but when she heard Eyden's voice again, he was still close by. "I'm glad you're okay, special one. You can take that as a compliment."

CHAPTER 36

AMIRA

The morning had been slow. For once, no one had come to snatch Amira away from her room. She had stayed in to finish reading her book. The ending was a bit disappointing, but there was a sequel.

As she put the novel aside, she wondered if Rhay had the second book. If he didn't, maybe she could convince him to buy it for her at the black market.

As the sun stood high in the sky, she decided to go see Rhay to talk about the book. She was a bit unsure about how he'd react given what had happened the night before. Due to Rhay's strong cocktails, her memory of the evening was incomplete, but the fragments she had were pretty embarrassing. She couldn't believe that she had mentioned her past love to Rhay. Hopefully, he had been as drunk as her last night and wouldn't remember much either.

After a few moments of hesitation, Amira opened her door, leaving the peaceful room.

A flaw in her plan quickly appeared. The palace was huge and she still had no idea where Rhay's room was. She wandered around the palace, trying to find a servant to ask for directions. But the corridors were deceptively empty. She was ready to give up when she encountered Nouis, a heavy pile of documents in his hands.

He still managed to bow before her. "Good afternoon, Princess Amira. Did you have a pleasant morning?"

"I did, thank you."

"Good to hear." He paused for an awkward second. "Well, I must leave you, princess. I have some professional matters to attend to. But I will schedule another history lesson soon. I apologise for making you wait. With the contest, I am very busy these days, and we both know Rhay is not an acceptable replacement." Nouis was about to go on his way. "Begone in fortune."

Amira stepped in front of him. Nouis stopped in his tracks and smiled at her. "Yes, princess?"

"I was wondering where I could find your son," Amira asked. "I borrowed a book from him and I would like to give it back." Nouis looked at her strangely and she realised that she didn't have any books with her. "I mean, I wanted to ask him to lend me another one."

"I see. Rhay must be in his room on the second floor, first hallway, the door painted in silver."

"Thank you," she replied, a faint smile on her lips.

"You know, princess, my son can be quite fickle with his friendships," Nouis said. "I wouldn't get too attached."

Amira welcomed Nouis' cautionary words with a serious face even though she didn't really believe them. At least, she didn't want to believe them. Rhay was her only close friend at the moment. What would she do if he abandoned her?

"Thank you for your advice. I'll let you go on your way." They both bowed and Amira walked to the stairs, Nouis' words still running through her mind.

Finding the door wasn't that difficult, the sparkling pearly colour was visible from afar. But as she was about to knock, she heard two voices arguing inside, Rhay's and Karwyn's.

Curious, Amira put her ear against the door. "He saw you knocking on her door in the middle of the night," said Karwyn.

They were talking about her. How much did Karwyn know about last night? Amira's palms started sweating and a cold shiver ran down her back. She sensed the jealousy in Karwyn's voice. It was deadly. What was he going to do to Rhay? To her?

"It was just to cheer her up. Don't be jealous," Rhay replied.

"I do not appreciate you spending that much time with her. You are supposed to be the one person I can trust."

Rhay's voice wasn't as confident as usual. "I can be...friends with her too. I swear, nothing happened between us. I wouldn't cross that line with your future wife."

Amira had difficulties repressing her scoff. Rhay flirted with everyone, including her, but she had figured that he just couldn't help it.

"Appearances matter. I know you are my advisor in name only, but that much you should respect," Karwyn said. "She is weak and will get attached easily." The words cut deep into Amira's heart.

"She's stronger than you think," defended Rhay. "But she needs a friend here. Why does it bother you so much?"

Karwyn scoffed. "You know why. If she starts challenging my image in front of the court, who knows what would happen with the contest? The royal advisors might end up choosing someone else. My father might be dead, but I can assure you, he would rise from his slumber to kill me if I am not selected."

"Don't doubt yourself, you're going to be selected. No one is better suited to be high king than you," Rhay said.

"Not even Tarnan?" Karwyn asked, voice strangled by emotion.

"Not even him. It's *your* destiny."

"Of course, you are correct," Karwyn replied. "Being high king is my destiny and no weak little girl is going to stop me."

"Yeah...that's the spirit. Listen, you should really try to get to know her. Amira's a great girl," Rhay said.

"I am already making a great effort to tolerate her presence. Do not expect me to start chit-chatting with her. I have no intention of making new friends. And you should dismiss her friendship. I do not want her going to your parties anymore," Karwyn said in an angry tone.

"My parties are harmless," Rhay said in a light tone. A pause. Amira pressed her ear harder against the door. "Fine, so be it," Rhay continued. He sounded annoyed, but not enough to argue. "You know what, how about we go train together like old times? It'll cheer you up. I miss our training sessions," Rhay added.

Amira quickly retired to a nook in the hallway to hide from the opening door. She saw them leave, exchanging friendly remarks. She waited for them to turn to the stairs to properly breathe again.

So they thought she was too powerless to change Karwyn's

destiny? Anger was now boiling inside of her, slowly making its way to her heart and mind. Well, she was going to show them how resourceful she could be even without fae powers. Karwyn was worried about the contest, that could mean that he had things to hide. Things she could find out to prove that she was also capable of playing power games.

A plan was slowly forming in her head. She just needed to gain access to Karwyn's room. That would require some finesse, but she was ready to prove how important it was for Karwyn to have her on his side.

As Rhay and Karwyn were busy training together, she figured it was the perfect time to snoop around. She had heard that Karwyn's bedroom was on the second floor, not that far away from hers. It was easy to find, given the two guards patrolling in the hallway.

Amira wasn't sure of the best way to divert their attention. She knew they wouldn't believe her if she said that Karwyn had asked her to retrieve something from his bedroom. Observing the door from the nook of the hallway, she jumped when a hand landed on her shoulder.

"Are you having a secret romance with one of those guards?" Varsha whispered in her ear.

"What? No," Amira furiously replied.

"Oh, so both of them, then?" Amira could hear the repressed laughter in Varsha's voice.

"Who do you think I am?"

"Someone who has spent the last five minutes suspiciously staring at two handsome guards," Varsha said. "I'm not judging you, by the way. I understand that things with Karwyn are not running smoothly. I wouldn't blame you if you were looking for some distraction on the side."

Amira's cheeks were now bright red and she couldn't help but be disturbed by Varsha's closeness. She tried to clear her mind by moving away from the painter. "That's not what I'm doing. I don't care about the lack of romance between Karwyn and I."

Varsha looked at her pensively. "It's funny, I would have put you as the hopeless romantic type. It would contrast nicely with Karwyn's attitude towards love. But I guess you're as practical as he is."

Amira felt offended by Varsha's comparison, yet she didn't want to waste time explaining her vision of love to someone who was basically a stranger.

"Tell me then, what *are* you trying to do, staring at Karwyn's bedroom door like that?" Varsha asked.

Should she tell her? She barely knew Varsha and her allegiance was hard to pinpoint. She was the official painter, so her livelihood depended on Karwyn's will. Yet she didn't really seem concerned about Karwyn's approval.

As if she was reading her mind, Varsha said, "Whatever you're planning on doing, I won't tell Karwyn. I find it much more enjoyable to be in the know when he's not."

"I want to search his room." The words burst out of her like an overflowing river.

Varsha smirked. "I knew you'd be interesting. But I can already tell you, there's nothing interesting in there."

Amira furrowed her brows. How could Varsha know what was inside Karwyn's room? "Are you sure?"

"If you had secrets, would you hide them in the first place people would think to search?"

Amira discreetly pointed at the guards. "What about them?"

Varsha let out a little laugh. "Everyone can be bought. What's your price, princess?"

"I'm not worth anything." The words sounded bleaker than she intended. It was true though, wasn't it?

The painter took her hand and pressed it gently. "I disagree. Would you do something for me, Amira?"

Questions and confusion swirled in Amira's mind. Her eyes wandered over Varsha's friendly face. "Sure," she said without thinking of the consequences.

CHAPTER 37

LORA

The cold water felt heavenly on her skin. When Lora had woken up, Elyssa's room had been empty. Lora had eyed the pitcher of water next to the makeshift sink and hadn't wasted a moment to finally rub the blood and grime off her face and hands. Now that her wounds felt healed, her current state of sweat and dirt was hard to ignore.

When she finished cleaning up as much as she could, Lora tentatively opened the flap of the tent and peeked outside. She saw tents everywhere. They were not simple like the ones Lora knew from the camping trips with her family. No, these were real homes, almost like tiny houses with walls made out of thick fabric in various shades of white or brown. In the distance, she could make out the woods.

But what really drew her attention were the intrigued human faces that glanced her way. This really was a base for humans. Lora wondered how they were able to stay hidden when the fae were literally hunting them.

"Hi. It's Lora, right?" a young woman to her right said as she walked up to Lora.

Lora shifted uneasily. Was she scared of humans now too?

She fully stepped out of the tent and turned to the blonde girl. "Yes. Uhm..." She wanted to ask about Eyden, but Lora wasn't sure if everyone here knew who he was or that he was even here.

"Elyssa wanted me to tell you they went for dinner. I can show you to the dining tent if you feel up to it?" the girl asked.

Dinner? Lora looked up at the sky and realised the sun was already setting. She had basically slept away the last two days. And a whole week had passed since she had crossed over. The clock was ticking aggressively, reminding her she had to move fast.

Lora forced a grateful smile onto her face, pushing the worry away. "I'd like that, yes. Thank you..."

"Iris," the woman said, offering her name as she walked off, leading Lora further into the heart of the camp.

Lora must have seen at least twenty questioning human faces before voices travelled towards them. She recognised Eyden's sarcastic tone. "Remind me again what *your* brilliant plan was, Jaspen?"

As she and Iris stepped away from the last tent blocking their view, Lora took in the half-open one before them. The fabric was pulled up on one side, letting in the last rays of sun. Although the space was big, it was almost completely taken up by a large table in the middle. The floor wasn't like Elyssa's room, it was left bare, the grass blooming a bright green.

Everyone grew quiet as they entered the dining area. The group was sitting around the table, empty plates in front of them. Lora's eyes wandered from one end to the other, taking in the familiar faces of Elyssa, Jaspen, and the other man she'd seen yesterday before landing on Eyden. He returned her gaze, pulling back the empty chair next to him.

Iris offered Elyssa an awkward smile before she disappeared in the direction they came from.

"Great timing. We were just talking about you," Jaspen said. His shoulder-length, unruly hair was bound in a tight ponytail. He got up and shook her hand. "I'm Jaspen, I run this camp. You're welcome to stay here. We're always keen on helping other humans."

"Oh, thanks," Lora answered. His words were friendly yet his firm handshake made her feel uneasy. She dropped his hand quickly and took a seat at the table. Elyssa had gotten her a full plate of food and sat it down in front of her.

Lora gave the younger girl a thankful smile as she inhaled the delicious smell and dug in. She felt Eyden's gaze on her, but it was Jaspen who spoke up again.

"We were talking about how we need you to track the fae," Jaspen continued, sitting at the head of the table. He pushed his empty plate to the side then gazed at his empty drink, seemingly waiting for someone to refill it.

Eyden beat her to the answer. "As I said, she can look up the location here and then I can track him going from there."

Jaspen's dark brown eyes bored into Eyden's lighter ones. "I've already pointed out that we need to leave before the fae has reached his final destination. We need her—or at least her phone device."

Lora dropped her fork unintentionally, the noise startling her. "Excuse me?"

Jaspen's intense gaze settled over her. "It'll be hard to follow this fae if we can't take the map with us, won't it?"

Lora gulped. She hadn't considered this. Her phone was her lifeline, keeping her tethered to home.

Eyden leaned forward. "I told you, I'm a good tracker. I'll find the market or wherever he's going." He looked to his sister as if asking for her support.

Elyssa crossed her arms and glanced between the two men. "It's not ideal, but doable. It'll be harder, but Lora is already giving us a better clue than we had before. We got this."

"You must be joking. Yesterday you were ready to run after the fae and now you're willing to risk it all? The longer it takes, the higher the chances they will already be gone—sold—once we reach the location. We need the witch back."

"You have a witch?" Lora asked. She thought there might be a witch working at the black market; but here, with humans, that was unexpected, considering how rare they were. According to her research, the only witches in existence were bound by blood contracts to the crown. Some might call them slaves, much like humans had once been. Lora thought of Eyden's spelled closet and stove again. Was it the work of the same witch they were talking about now, or were there more witches in hiding than Lora imagined?

"Yes, and he's keeping this whole camp hidden. Once the spell wears off, we're all in a shitload of trouble. He's irreplaceable," Jaspen said in an almost harsh tone.

"More importantly, *Farren* is our friend," Elyssa added, her voice stern. "And I'm not willing to risk anything, *anyone*. Don't put words in my mouth. We'll get all three of them back. But we can't force Lora to go with us."

"I still think the best course of action would be for me to go alone. Rubien, especially the market there, is no place for humans," Eyden said. He met Elyssa's gaze. "And it would be faster."

Elyssa held his gaze as she replied, "Maybe so, but you're not invincible either, Eyden. And there are three people to rescue. It's not a one-person job. You know damn well I'm an asset."

"As much as I dislike the idea of spending even more time in the presence of fae, I can accept that we need Eyden. But we also need Lora to track the fae. And it would help having another person with us who can pass as fae," Jaspen said, tapping his finger against his glass.

"I agree with Jaspen," the young man sitting to his left said. He had been quiet for so long, Lora had almost forgotten he was there. He reached for the jug of water and filled Jaspen's glass.

Jaspen didn't even look at him, instead he turned to Lora. "We saved you, surely you'll repay the favour?"

She'd never felt this put on the spot. "I…"

"You can't make demands like that," Eyden said.

Jaspen shifted his insistent gaze to him. "I would hold my tongue if I were you, or my next demand will be to have your ass thrown out."

"I'd like to see you try." The corner of Eyden's mouth pulled up into a challenging half-grin.

"I'm going to throw both of you out of this tent if you don't behave," Elyssa said.

Lora had lost her appetite. She stared at her plate as a fog surrounded her mind, anxiety building up.

Elyssa must have noticed. She stood up and tapped Lora on the shoulder. "You want to go lie down?" she said. Then quieter, "I think you could use a breather."

Lora nodded, grateful to get out of this situation.

"This conversation isn't over," Jaspen snapped loudly as Lora got out of her chair.

"I say it's on pause and I'm not taking other requests at the moment," Elyssa said as she walked past him. "We're gonna try the tracking and report back."

Lora followed her, but her eyes were focused on Eyden. He was about to stand up until Elyssa shook her head. He nodded and reluctantly sat back down.

Lora couldn't help but feel a little bit disappointed, but she turned her back and matched Elyssa's steps away from the madness of this conversation.

"Where are we going?" Lora asked when they walked past Elyssa's tent. She'd figured they were going back to her room.

Elyssa kept going for a few seconds until she slowed down and looked over her shoulder. "Are you coming?"

"Are we not going back to your place?" Lora asked again as she picked up her pace to catch up.

"No, I made up one of the empty tents for you since I'm not sure how long you'll stay."

"I can't stay for much longer," Lora immediately answered. She was starting to feel restless not actively searching for a cure.

Although she had no idea where to go from here. All she knew was that she needed to keep trying.

Elyssa opened the flap to a smaller tent, not very far from her own. "I know you have your own mission," she said as she waited for Lora to enter the room. "That's exactly what I wanted to talk to you about."

This tent didn't leave much free space, but it was a space for herself even if only for a short period of time. Lora's eyes stopped at a familiar item. Her backpack was placed on the ground next to the bed.

"Eyden brought it," Elyssa explained.

Lora moved closer and noticed a new WiFi cube sitting on top of the backpack. It was a reminder that they needed her, but also that her family was probably waiting for another message from her.

Resisting the urge to take out her phone right away, Lora met Elyssa's eyes. "I'm sorry that I can't help you as much as Jaspen— and I'm guessing you—want me to. I really hope you'll get all your friends back and the tracking I can do here will help you enough to find them."

Elyssa sat down on the edge of the bed. "I understand your hesitation. Eyden told me you're doing this for your family. I would've done anything for my parents, too." A look of sadness came over her face. How long ago had Elyssa's parents passed away? Were they taken by fae? "I was talking to Eyden earlier and he filled me in on what happened with Halie. She said you might need a level five to figure this out, which is quite bizarre, really, but that's beside the point. You know that the king has his own healer? The most powerful healer in Turosian?"

Sensing where Elyssa was going with this, Lora asked, "So I've heard, but how would I get to him?"

"Well, here's the thing: I came across, or rather my fist came into contact with, some information a few weeks ago and I've been following Saydren, the healer, ever since. I know where he likes to hang out. Eyden didn't know any of this until today. He's more focused on trailing guards and keeping out of sight, as you might know. We usually share intel, so to say, but these past weeks have been busy and we haven't had time to properly catch up on all of our top-secret ventures. If I had known he needed a healer, I would have told him earlier, but the stubborn ass kept me out of the loop."

Lora stared at her, unsure how to respond. So this was what she wanted to talk to her about. "I see. Let me guess, you'll tell me where he is if I help you out first?"

Disappointment was taking over her feelings, but could she really blame Elyssa for taking advantage of the situation when Lora would've done—*was* doing—the same thing to save her own family?

Elyssa looked almost insulted at Lora's assumption. "No, I'm not gonna *force* you to help us. He's usually at River's Point every Monday and Wednesday evening."

Lora was taken aback by this free offer of information with no strings attached. Once the initial surprise wore off, she was already counting the days in her head. Monday was three days from now.

"I can show you the way once we've freed our people. Or I can show you before we leave and describe him to you. I do have to say, though, I don't think Saydren is someone who'll agree to help you without a price. Having back-up would be damn good. Eyden wanted to go with you, but he has to go with us to Rubien. Jaspen was right when he said our friends only have days left before they're moved and no one can track them anymore. Having you guiding us would save us time."

Elyssa looked at the door before catching Lora's gaze again. "Even Eyden knows this, but he'd prefer you stay here where it's safe. I can't blame him. He promised to help, but they're my friends, not his. Farren...he means a lot to me. I'd knock any door down to get to him. I'll understand if you decide you can't wait. But I hope you'll consider joining us even though it's dangerous and you might miss Monday's window."

"Why did you tell me all of this? If you really need my help, why didn't you offer me a deal?" Lora asked, genuinely intrigued by Elyssa's honesty.

"Because you should choose of your own free will. Everyone who is here, at this camp, is here because they believe in forging a better future. They're here to fight for the human lives in Liraen. I won't lie and tell you it's safe to go with us. We all know the risks and we take them anyway. If you're like me, you even walk into them blindly at times. I know you didn't choose to get mixed up with us, but you can choose whether you stay involved now."

Every possible response left Lora's brain. "I don't know what to say." Part of her wanted to say she would help, knowing she most likely owed them her life. At the very least, she could lend them her phone. But it was her only connection to her world. And the fae never used phones, neither did the humans here. Would they understand how it worked as well as Lora did? Was there another reason Jaspen thought they needed her, someone who looked enough fae and wouldn't attract attention?

Elyssa's hazel eyes sparked hopefully in the yellow light of the oil lamp. "Just sleep on it, will you?"

"I will."

"Grand. Now that that's out of the way, let's try tracking that bastard fae, shall we? And then I can show you to the showers. Not that this isn't a look, but I think you could use it," Elyssa said as she gestured at Lora's dirty clothes.

Her grin eased the tension and Lora couldn't help but laugh as she tried to smooth down her hair and her fingers got caught in a massive knot.

"I think you might be right," Lora replied. Maybe she was right about a lot of things.

CHAPTER 38

&

AMIRA

"I want you to pose for me. I need to finish your portrait," Varsha said and without waiting for a reply, she grabbed Amira's hand and led her out of the hallway.

They ran through different corridors until they stopped in front of a cobalt blue door decorated with orchids. Varsha pushed it open.

"Welcome to my humble studio," she said as she let go of Amira's hand.

Amira stepped inside the room bathed in sunlight. The messy appearance of the studio only lent to its charm. Pots of paints and canvases of all sizes were scattered everywhere. A few pieces were displayed on the walls. Most of them were official portraits of fae from the Turosian court, but a few smaller ones were more abstract. Amira couldn't help but shudder. It looked as if Varsha had painted her nightmares.

In an attempt to banish her dark thoughts, Amira looked at the easel in the centre of the room. On it stood her almost finished engagement portrait. The colours were so vivid that Amira was sure that Varsha had managed to put pure sunshine inside the painting. When she looked deep into her painted eyes, she could now see a glimmer of hope she didn't know was still in her.

"What do you think, princess?" Varsha was standing next to her, whispering the question in her ear.

"You seem to see things that I'm not even sure I still see in myself."

"It is easy to get your heart clouded by your mind. Thoughts are only the burst of an emotion. Your true nature lies in your heart and in your long-lasting actions," Varsha said, catching her gaze. "You have a brave, selfless soul, Amira. Don't let them take that away from you."

"I'll try," Amira said, not very sure of how long she could keep it up.

"Good," Varsha said with a smile. She gently squeezed Amira's arm.

Amira looked away from her own painted eyes and pointed at another painting. "Why did you paint that?"

Varsha followed her line of sight. Clashing prussian blue and burgundy red created shadowy figures on the canvas. "It's a feeling that I have here—in this palace, in this kingdom. There is something wicked around us, I've always felt it. Do you know that some fae just disappear in Turosian?" Varsha caressed the painting with her finger. "One day they're with their family and the next, they're completely gone."

Amira had never heard of any disappearances. "And the king doesn't do anything about it?"

Varsha shrugged. "He's never acknowledged it. It's never members of the court who disappear, so why would it matter to fae who are living in a palace? People talk though. Not the court, but fae outside these walls."

Amira could hear a hint of despair in Varsha's low voice. Without thinking, she squeezed the painter's shoulder. Varsha smiled at her and put the painting back.

"What were you trying to find in Karwyn's room anyway?" Varsha asked.

Amira hesitated, then carefully replied, "Nothing, really. I was just intrigued about Karwyn's mother."

"The late queen has always been a mystery. I wasn't alive back then, but my father told me that Harten Adelway brought her to the palace one day with no explanation. No one dared ask questions. Harten was in no way the Dark King, but he was still terrifying. Karwyn definitely doesn't measure up and I think that's what's eating at him."

Amira furrowed her brows. If what Varsha was saying was true, Karwyn was living in both his father's and brother's shadow.

"So are you ready to pose?" Varsha's question brought Amira back into the moment. She nodded absently.

Amira kept thinking back on what Karwyn had said to Rhay in his room. The interim high king was worried about something. Could it explain his coldness towards her? She had to find out more.

Amira had spent the rest of the afternoon with Varsha, posing and looking at her paintings before she returned to her rooms.

As Amira approached her door, she saw Rhay waiting outside.

He didn't smile at her as he usually would. Did Karwyn get through to him? Breathing slowly, she mustered a smile. She didn't want him to suspect anything.

"I was looking for you," she started, but Rhay didn't say anything. He just stared at her intensely as if he was trying to decipher her inner thoughts. "I've finished the book and I wanted to see if you had the sequel."

His expression remained the same. "The book?"

"The human novel. You know, the one you gifted me." She felt strange having to explain herself.

"I think one gift was enough," Rhay said in a surprisingly harsh tone.

"Is everything okay with you, Rhay?" Amira moved closer as she lowered her voice. "Is it because of last night?" *Or your conversation with Karwyn?*

Rhay searched her eyes. His stare bored into her. "What about it?"

Was he playing dumb or were her memories from their two-person party wrong? "It's just... You know what, it's nothing."

He avoided looking at her when he replied, "Actually, I think it would be better if we stopped spending so much time together."

Amira's smile crumbled. "Why? Did I do something wrong?" Was he really taking Karwyn's words to heart?

Rhay gestured vaguely. "No, but as you know, I'm quite busy. I can't spend all of my time with you. You're a bit clingy."

Clingy? Last night he'd practically begged her to spend time with him, and now this? He was the one who had kept trying to befriend her ever since she had arrived at the palace. Everywhere she went, he would be there, ready to distract her from the rest of the world. Now he was dropping her like a piece of dirty laundry?

"I don't believe you. Let's talk about it." She tried to grab his arm but he pushed her away.

"Stay away from me, Amira," Rhay said, stepping back. "I won't tell you again. We never should have been friends in the first place. It's only causing me trouble. And not the fun kind." Rhay walked away faster than she had ever seen him walk.

Still in shock, Amira stared at her door way too long before finally going inside. Rhay had decided to follow Karwyn's commands. Of course, what had she expected? Her friendship with Rhay couldn't last forever no matter how much she wished it could. Her fiancé, like her brother before him, had decided that she deserved to be alone, isolated from any happiness.

Tears flooded her cheeks. Her heart felt utterly hollow. Rhay, with his boldness and wits, had managed to make the transition into the Turosian world less terrifying. With her only friend gone, was there anything good left?

Amira grabbed the familiar strand of hair and pulled on it with all of her strength. She needed her pain to be translated into something physical or else she was going to explode. Something dark was growing in her chest, nesting right next to her heart, ready to devour her completely.

CHAPTER 39

LORA

When Lora returned from her shower, she didn't notice Eyden sitting on her bed until her eyes met his by chance. He was quiet, looking up at her in the dim light. Their previous fight stretched in the air between them. They hadn't had a chance to talk about any of it.

The fight. The current situation. What both of them would do moving forward. Lora had been waiting for the chance to talk to him alone but now that the moment presented itself, she almost wished they didn't have to talk.

He had come back for her. He did care about human life. At least for one of them, two if she counted her own. Lora was scared whatever they'd say now would ruin it. It would ruin this image in her mind that he cared more than either of them would admit.

But there was no avoiding it. She had a decision to make after all. Lora had activated the tracker on her phone and it'd shown her old WiFi cube was still in Chrysa, close to where they'd left the fae. Maybe the fae was trying to catch someone else. Either way, they needed to wait. It might take another day until they could set off. In that case, depending on how deep into Rubien, or wherever, the tracker would lead them, they would still be gone Monday night.

Elyssa had said that they would leave on Sunday no matter what the tracker said. They'd have to take their chances and go into Rubien blindly. It was their best bet. Which meant by Wednesday, it should be done. But Wednesday was still so far away. It would be a long break from her search for a cure.

"Hi," Lora said shyly as she dropped her towel and dirty clothes on the ground. She had changed into her other fae clothes that had been packed in her backpack. All her stuff was there just as she had left it at Eyden's flat. Except the vial of blood. She hoped Sahalie didn't still have it.

"Hey," Eyden replied, sitting too still.

Lora's eyes scanned the room as she moved her fingers through her wet hair. There was no other spot to sit, so she took a seat on the opposite side of the bed. She turned to avoid his gaze. The room was too quiet; it made the space feel suffocating with silent tension.

"So about—" Lora said at the same time as Eyden started with, "I'm sorry—"

"What are you sorry for?" Lora asked, tilting her head up. His vivid, light eyes struck a chord with her. There was a well of emotion hidden within the depth of blue.

He shifted, probably trying to find the words. Lora could relate, her own unspoken words were burning in her mind.

"That they took you. I said I'd help you and I failed," Eyden said, voice low.

His words hit her like a wave of pleasantly warm water. She hadn't even considered that he felt guilty. "You didn't fail. It was my fault. I was shouting, practically announcing to everyone in Chrysa that I was human."

"Yes, but I should have known better and found a way to—"

"Shut me up?" Lora amended. "I was on a roll, Eyden. You couldn't have stopped me."

He grinned, a lopsided grin that did weird things to Lora's stomach. "True. But I still wish it didn't happen."

"Me too." The memory of that cell froze over the feeling of warmth she'd felt only moments ago. "But you came back. You saved me. You don't have to be sorry. For *that*," she added with emphasis.

"So I have to be sorry for something else?" Amusement sparked in his eyes. "I'm not excused since I saved you? Your words, not mine."

"Too easy." Lora held back a smile.

Eyden shifted again, leaning in closer. "I never told you about Elyssa because I didn't think it'd be necessary. I don't tell anyone about her. Keeping her safe has always been my first priority."

It wasn't what was bothering her. She could understand protecting family and not trusting her with this specific piece of information. Lora was aware she only knew about Elyssa now because Eyden must have needed the humans' help to free her. It was a matter of life and death, not of trust.

"I was surprised to find out you have a human sister, but I understand why you put her above everyone else."

"It doesn't mean I don't care for other humans too. I do." Pale eyes travelled over her face before meeting her eyes. "For some."

The air seemed to charge between them. Lora felt the need to diffuse it even though her body told her something else. "Not Jaspen, I'm guessing?"

Eyden let out a curt laugh. "No, we've never gotten along. He's made up his mind that all fae are the villains in his story."

Something Lora had been led to believe as well. Her fingers stilled in her hair. It hit her then that she didn't think that anymore. Eyden was many things, but evil was not one of them. Neither was Ilario or his parents. Even Sahalie, though very unpleasant, didn't fall into that category. The realisation took her breath away for a second. Her carefully crafted image of fae was starting to crack.

"And Elyssa is still friends with him?" she asked, placing her hands in her lap, trying not to fall into a spiral as she pushed her realisation away.

"I wouldn't say friends. He's the leader. She sees his flaws, but she's all for the mission, and being part of his group is her way of making a difference. I have to admit, the risks she takes fucking scare me. Yet I also find it admirable."

"It is." She cursed herself for her next words but they wouldn't stay in. "You do know Elyssa has no intention of crossing, right?"

Eyden's gaze snapped to her. "She figured it out, didn't she?" He didn't wait for her to confirm. "She might not consider it now, but what if things got worse? What if their camp got discovered? It happened before, you know. It was a bloodbath. I want her to have the option to leave, to get the fuck out of there if worse comes to worst."

Her heart squeezed tightly. Elyssa would never be able to cross. An apology was lying on her tongue, but she couldn't say it. Couldn't admit the lie she had carried for so long. She pushed it down, drowning the lie so deep it was as if it never existed.

"I didn't know about fortae. I've heard rumours of humans being mistreated here. Fae looking down on them. But I didn't know they were used for their blood. Or that there was a whole camp of...rebels."

"I think your government doesn't care. There are so few humans here compared to Earth. They have their treaty meetings with the high king, pretend everything's fine, and turn a blind eye to everything else. It's easier that way, isn't it?"

She had turned a blind eye. Was she part of the problem? Elyssa wanted to change Liraen for the good of all humans. Lora was only thinking of herself and her family. But wasn't that survival instinct? Wouldn't most people do the same thing if they were in her shoes? "It shouldn't be this way," she said aloud.

"With a new high king or queen, maybe it won't have to be this way."

Lora went over what she knew about the other royals. Karwyn was the only one left from the Adelway bloodline, as far as she knew. If he wasn't king, who would be? Were the rulers of the other six kingdoms more suited for the responsibilities of the high king or queen? There wasn't enough information available in her world to properly judge them.

"Do you have anyone specific in mind?" she asked.

"No, but I'm trying to gather more intel. Elyssa and the others are too, for their own reasons. If Karwyn wins the contest and becomes high king...either nothing will change or it'll get worse."

"You're worried," Lora observed.

"I worry all the time." Reading her thoughts, he added, "I shouldn't have told you not to worry. You can't help it. Neither can I."

Hearing him say it melted the last bit of ice that barricaded her heart. Their fight seemed senseless now, words said out of anger and uncertainty. "I shouldn't have started a fight in the middle of the street in the first place. I guess we're even," Lora offered, the start of a smile playing on her lips.

"Yeah, that wasn't your smartest idea," Eyden teased, returning the grin.

"There has to be at least one bad idea to balance out all the brilliant ones."

For a moment, they merely smiled at each other. Eyden was the first to look away this time.

"I won't tell you again that there's time. I understand your urgency. Your family is your priority and I respect that. I want you to know that I would have gone with you to meet Saydren. If I didn't promise to help them and if my sister wasn't going as well, I would have gone with you and I'll be back as soon as I can to lead you back to the border."

"I know." She didn't know how or why, but she felt the truth in his words. "I don't blame you for helping your sister. We both have our families to look after."

He nodded, something like relief shining in his eyes. "I hope we can leave tomorrow, then I might be back before you leave to meet Saydren. In the meantime, I know Elyssa said you're welcome to stay here. Or you can stay at my place. I'll leave you a key. In case the shield drops."

"You mean the spell that keeps the camp hidden from fae?"

"From anyone who doesn't know it exists and doesn't know the password. Elyssa can fill you in on how to get in and out." His voice grew serious. "If the spell wears off while we're gone, promise me you'll run, okay? Hide at my place."

Lora wasn't about to make any more promises, so she danced around the question. "You think that will happen?"

"Probably not, but we can't rule it out. That reminds me, before Elyssa told me about Saydren, I went back to Halie's. She wasn't any more help, but I got the vial of your mother's blood."

Relief flooded through her. "Where is it?"

"I stored it in the closet. I thought it would be safest there, but I can get it before I leave." He found her eyes again. "Or I can get it now if you feel better having it close to you."

"No, it's fine. I trust..." *You,* a silent voice whispered in her mind. But did she? "The closet," she concluded.

Eyden's grin returned. "Okay, then."

Trying to ignore the feeling that grin invoked in her, Lora asked the question that had been on the forefront of her mind since they started talking. "You really won't ask me to go with you?"

Eyden's smile faltered a bit. "No, we don't need to endanger your life. Again. Jaspen will have to accept it. You'll be safer here. I'll stop by my flat tomorrow to get the vial and some silver. Elyssa thinks Saydren's services can be bought."

He really had thought this through, hadn't he? Thinking about what was safest for her. But was Eyden safer if she stayed behind? Was Elyssa? Could she turn a blind eye again when she knew her help might increase their chances?

Then again, it seemed wrong to spend time on someone else's mission, endangering her life, when her family was counting on her to come home.

Pacing in her room, Lora felt torn between the paths before her. She had tossed and turned all night, her mind spinning too fast to relax. She'd gone over all her options so many times she'd lost count. How could she choose one path when she didn't know how each would end?

When she looked at family pictures on her phone, Lora craved going back even more. The longer she stayed, the more difficult it would be to reconnect with her brother and assure her mother that her fae side was nothing she'd ever want to explore. When she'd first announced that she was studying Human and Fae History, it had led to one of their biggest arguments. But Lora had assured Karla it wasn't about curiosity concerning her own heritage. That's what she'd been telling herself too.

Elyssa and Eyden's voices were haunting her, reminding her of the critical situation they were in. What Lora really needed was an outsider's perspective.

After seeing the sun rise, Lora gave in and filled Maja in on her current predicament through multiple text messages, keeping it short but informative. Coming to an abrupt halt in the middle of her tent, Lora watched the dots appear and disappear for over ten minutes until her friend's reply finally came in.

"Damn, you've had an intense week. Keeping this short is difficult, but without further ado, here is my marvellous advice,"

Maja started. "As lame as it sounds, you have to go with your gut on this one. I know you like to create a thousand scenarios, but there is no way of knowing where each path will lead. There just isn't. You're right that your mum would say forget the fae. But isn't her opinion based on a single experience? No offense to your mum, I love her. It sounds like the people you met are not just fae. They're your friends—or more?? I need details! Do what feels right in this moment and ignore the never-ending analysis in your head. Otherwise you will definitely regret it. The only thing worse than taking risks is regretting never taking them in the first place."

Lora started pacing again, her messy dark blonde hair falling into her face. What would she regret more, never risking this mission or risking delaying her plan to get the cure? Maja was right. Lora would never know with full certainty how either path would end. What she did know was that she was here now, in this moment. And they needed her right now. Elyssa and the human rebels who'd risked their lives to save her. Eyden, who she cared for despite the lie she created that told her she didn't.

A soft knock brought her back to the present. Lora turned her head to the flimsy door and called out, "Come in."

The flap lifted and Eyden stepped into the room, Elyssa in tow.

"Good morning. Although it doesn't look like you got much sleep," Elyssa said. Eyden followed Elyssa's line of sight as Lora rubbed her eyes, trying to erase the dark circles that were most likely visible. Or maybe it was her dishevelled state that drew Elyssa's attention. "Any updates on the tracking?"

"It still wasn't moving outside Chrysa about twenty minutes ago," Lora said as she smoothed her hair behind her ears. Her eyes travelled between Eyden and Elyssa. Seeing them now, the unmade decision burned her from the inside out. Her eyes slid to her phone, Maja's message still on display. What did she feel in this very moment? What regret was she willing to risk?

She forced her thoughts to clear out, burning the unavoidable regrets to ashes. Her gaze snapped to Eyden. "I'm going with you."

Elyssa's face broke into a smile as she held out her fist. "Excellent."

Lora bumped her fist, but her eyes were glued to Eyden, who looked less enthusiastic and more shocked.

"You don't have to. You know that, right? You can stay and avoid all this madness. It would be smarter—safer," he said.

The ghost of a smile lifted the corners of her lips. "Well, someone once told me I'm insane. I guess they were right."

She could see the tension leaving his face, but it didn't last long. "Are you sure?"

"As sure as I can be," Lora replied.

Elyssa nodded, pleased with her answer, while Eyden dropped his gaze. Did he really not want her to go? Had she read him wrong or was he merely concerned for her safety? In some ways, he was still this closed book she'd barely opened. But then again, so was she.

"This is great timing. Jaspen has called for a meeting. We were stopping by to get an update but since you're joining us, you should come with," Elyssa said.

Lora nodded, forcing her eyes to leave Eyden's.

She was all in now. Risks, regrets...she'd take them all on, joining Eyden's mad mission. Even if unspoken lies still lingered between them.

"Absolutely not. That was not part of the plan." Eyden glared daggers at Jaspen, who casually leaned back in his chair. They were sitting around the big table again, talking through their strategy. The scent of caftee lingered in the air as the morning sun filtered in through the open wall.

"The plan was never finalised. Now that Lora agreed to join us, we can take our best shot at this. And I didn't ask for your opinion, Eyden," Jaspen announced.

Lora went through Jaspen's plan in her head, seeing the advantages even though irritation flowed through her. The way Jaspen had spoken made it sound final, although he hadn't yet asked for her opinion on the matter. Somehow, she had suspected as much.

Eyden placed his steaming mug on the table, the sound drawing attention. "You're getting it anyway if you want my help. If anything goes wrong at the Void or wherever else they do their trades, it'll be easier for me to get out of there on my own."

Jaspen's curt laugh was the definition of condescending. "We don't have the luxury of running away if things go south. As long as Farren is alive, we won't leave without him. We can't risk anyone finding my camp." His gaze shifted to Elyssa. "Anyone else."

Elyssa didn't back down from his stare. "It's working to our advantage now, isn't it? You said it yourself, we need Eyden. You should be goddamn thanking me."

"That doesn't mean he should be here. Don't think I've forgotten. We will discuss this later, you can count on that."

As Jaspen turned in his seat, Lora caught Elyssa rolling her eyes. The girl didn't seem all that worried about Jaspen's words even though his tone had been intimidating.

Lora couldn't make sense of Eyden's past with the humans. If he grew up with Elyssa, then why was Jaspen so against him being here? Why did he imply Eyden shouldn't know about this camp when he had supposedly been part of the community?

"If you want to be mad at someone, be mad at me. Leave Elyssa out of this," Eyden said.

Jaspen set his jaw. "Again, I don't need your opinion—on my camp or this plan."

"You should at the very least ask for Lora's opinion, seeing as it's her life you're risking," Eyden countered.

In response, Jaspen turned his stoic face to Lora. When he didn't say anything, Lora glanced at Eyden before she spoke up. "I'll do it." Eyden opened his mouth as if to disagree, but Lora continued on. "I know it's risky, but it's even riskier if you go in by yourself."

If she was going all in, then there was no backing down now.

"Finally, someone who sees reason. It's decided, then. Lora and Eyden will enter the trading location as buyers while Elyssa and I take watch close by. Ian, you will stay here and take care of the camp in my absence."

Ian, the young man who always kept close to Jaspen, looked up from his cup of caftee. "Shouldn't I go with you? I can help."

"No, I need you here. Someone needs to lead everyone to the emergency hiding spot should we fail. You're no use to us on this mission." Ian's face dropped, but he quickly recovered and nodded, dropping his gaze. "What does the tracker show now?" Jaspen asked.

Lora removed her phone from her pocket and activated the feature. It indicated her previous WiFi cube was on the move but still in Chrysa.

"The fae hasn't left town yet," she said.

Jaspen leaned across the table. "Can I see?"

Lora's fingers tightened on the device before she hesitantly slid it across the table.

Carefully picking it up, Jaspen's eyes followed their moving target on the map. "Fascinating. I've never come across anyone, human or fae, who possessed such a device. I've seen TVs, but this is certainly more useful."

"You can get pretty much anything at the black market now with some luck," Eyden explained.

"Apparently so," Jaspen replied, returning the phone. "Well then, we'll leave at first light tomorrow. No matter what."

Elyssa caught Eyden's eyes as they held a silent conversation. Lora's heart twisted at the sight, remembering the days when she and Oscar could communicate with mere looks, silently making comments in front of their parents with neither of them realising. In some ways, it felt like another lifetime ago.

"Well, we all know our roles. Ian, let's check on our supply," Jaspen said, pushing back his chair.

As the two of them walked away, Elyssa got up too. "I'll see you both later." She tightened the black string securing her high ponytail and gave Eyden one last meaningful look before exiting the tent.

Eyden twisted in his chair to meet Lora's eyes. "I know I'm repeating myself, but are you sure you want to do this?"

Was she sure? No. Lora had come to accept that certainty was like promises—nothing more than wishful thinking. "If I'm going to do this, then I want to give it a real shot. You can't get three people out of there on your own. They might all need help. And I'm the only one who can pass as fae."

"I could pull it off on my own."

A sigh escaped her. "You're not doing this alone, Eyden. Stop arguing with me, it'll lead nowhere. You should know that much by now."

"Oh, I know. But I had to try," he said, a grin lighting up his face. "Okay, fine, I'm done arguing. For now."

A small smile broke across her face. "Good. We agree, then."

Another agreement between them. Yet this one didn't feel the same. It seemed much less formal and more like an understanding between friends. And they were, weren't they?

The moment stretched between them until Eyden grabbed his mug and downed the last of his drink. "I have to leave for a bit. Get some supplies and ask Ilario to take over my shift."

Lora's gaze swung to the tents in the near distance, visible through the open door. "Does Ilario know about any of this?"

"No. I fill him in on any relevant information Elyssa shares with me, but he doesn't know who I get it from."

Lora searched his face. If he couldn't trust his best friend, then how could he ever trust anyone? How could he ever trust *her*?

Eyden seemed to read her silent question. "Everyone has a breaking point. The game we're playing...we both know we could get caught. And if that ever happened, I don't want Elyssa's name on his mind."

Lora wanted to reassure him that she'd never spill his secrets, but no sound would leave her lips. Nothing could be promised, not with the games they were stuck in, weighing them down in the murky water of uncertainty.

CHAPTER 40

LORA

Walking back to her tent, Lora took her phone from her pocket. Maja was still waiting for a reply. Lora hadn't had time to fill her in on her decision. But as she unlocked her phone, Lora noticed a flash of auburn hair in her peripheral vision.

To her left, a small path led into the woods and there was Elyssa, partly hidden by trees, walking away from the tent area.

Lora slipped her phone back in her pocket and headed towards her. She was intrigued where Elyssa was heading, but more importantly, she had more questions. If there was one person who could fill her in about Eyden's past here, it was Elyssa.

As she followed the path, Lora called out for the younger girl, but she didn't react. She might have been too far away. Lora increased her speed to make up the distance, almost running to not lose sight of her, yet Elyssa didn't turn around.

When she finally got close enough, Lora extended her arm, reaching out to gently tap Elyssa on her left shoulder. But her hand never connected.

Before Lora even knew what was happening, Elyssa slapped her hand away. She twisted Lora's arm behind her back with a speed Lora couldn't grasp. Lora cried out as her eyes darted to her side where a throwing star was putting pressure on her skin through the layers of clothes.

Lora didn't dare move, afraid of impaling herself. "Wait!"

"Lora?" The pressure eased, but Elyssa's hold was firm. "Shit."

Before Lora could catch her breath to reply, Elyssa released her arm. The girl took a step back, giving Lora space to move. Lora turned around slowly, stretching her arm.

Elyssa's eyes were wide, shock and guilt twisting her usually friendly face. "I'm so sorry. I saw something move behind me and I just reacted."

"It's fine," Lora said, dropping her arm to her side. It felt strained, but nothing to worry about. Elyssa's reaction did catch her off guard, though. She took in the path before them, leading into the woods. "Did we leave the shield? Is that why you...sort of attacked me?"

Elyssa cringed, meeting her eyes. She was more than half a head shorter than Lora, but her slim appearance was deceptive. Elyssa may look young and fragile, but she was anything but. Even now, as Lora looked her over more closely, she could see her athletic build, the strength she was hiding under baggy, worn-out shirts that had more than one hole.

"No, we're still protected here. I was just walking around to clear my mind." Elyssa's eyes scanned the woods as she pushed back a loose lock of hair. "I usually pay more attention to my surroundings. I have to. But sometimes it's nice to let your guard down."

"I didn't think I could sneak up on you," Lora joked, then immediately regretted it when she caught a flash of pain on Elyssa's face before her emotions smoothed out again. The deflection reminded her of Eyden.

"Here's the thing—since we're going on a mission together, I would have told you anyway—my hearing is not the best. As in, it's pretty shitty. A lot shitty, actually. Especially in my left ear."

"I'm sorry, if I had known—"

Elyssa's gaze was unwavering. "I know. I'm not blaming you. And it's okay. It's something I've learned to deal with. Everyone here knows how to approach me to avoid the reaction you got, but of course you wouldn't know."

Lora nodded, pressing her lips together to keep from apologising again. It didn't seem like Elyssa would want that. Knowing Elyssa's condition, Lora was even more impressed by how she had handled herself against the fae. But she did wonder why Elyssa didn't use fae magic to heal her. "You don't have to tell me, but..."

"How did it happen?" Elyssa caught her questioning gaze. "I was ten. I'm not sure what happened, exactly, it's not like we have a hospital for humans around here. But I had some kind of ear infection. It was bad. My fever wouldn't break for days and my parents were scared out of their minds. So was Eyden. He even snuck out to try and get some medicine, that fool." She smiled despite the shadows of her past. "Back then he was still so young and he wasn't used to being outside our camp. He had no fucking clue how to get any fae healing items."

Lora pictured a young Eyden, already so protective over his younger sibling, desperately trying to get medicine. She was sure he would've done anything for Elyssa even back then. But somehow things must have changed. There had to be a reason he was living outside these invisible walls now.

"And now? Eyden must have gotten you fae medicine later on, right?" Lora asked.

"He did once he started working for the black market. But by then, the damage was done. Irreversible, it seems." Elyssa shrugged, her face was devoid of regret.

"Did a healer try to recover your hearing?"

"No, actually. It would be a risk to expose myself to anyone and at this point, it's a part of me. My hearing isn't excellent, but I sure am. I don't need perfect hearing to fight my way out of any situation."

"I have no doubt about that." A knowing smile took over Lora's face. "So you've never met Sahalie, then?"

"Eyden won't tell anyone about me and vice versa. I got close to meeting Halie once, actually, by accident when I stayed over at Eyden's. It almost got real awkward..." Elyssa trailed off as she met Lora's eyes. "Anyway, the point is, it's better to not expose myself to any fae when I don't need a healer. Except for Eyden, I usually only acquaint fae with my fist."

Lora's thoughts were stuck on Elyssa's insinuation. The picture of Eyden and Sahalie bothered her more than she'd like. It shouldn't matter. Lora forced herself to focus on the first part of Elyssa's explanation.

Meeting Elyssa's gaze, she asked, "What do you mean you don't tell anyone about Eyden? Everyone at the camp must know him if he used to live here."

Elyssa pulled up her light auburn eyebrows. "Eyden really

didn't fill you in on how this all came about, did he? Typical. He probably glossed over the story, mentioning the parts that 'matter.'" Her gaze was knowing, as if Elyssa could read her, breaking down the walls of lies and denial. "I have a feeling it *all* matters to you."

The look Lora received was as if the other girl was trying to size up her reaction. But right now, all Lora felt was confusion. She couldn't say if it mattered when she was missing the actual information—vital information, it seemed. In answer, Lora took a seat on a tree stump close to the path, waiting for the blanks to be filled in.

Elyssa joined her, clearing her voice before continuing. "You heard about how our previous camp was discovered?"

Lora nodded. "I don't know the details, but Eyden mentioned it ended badly."

"It's my second most painful memory. I was only eleven. So much death..." Elyssa's eyes shifted from Lora's face to the trees. "When the survivors regrouped, they realised that the fae guards must have found us because someone told them about our camp. Or someone was goddamn careless and unwillingly led them there. Eyden was the only fae living with us. He was instantly blamed." Elyssa sighed, her eyes trailing a leaf as it fell onto the dirt path.

The pain reflecting on Elyssa's face tore at Lora's heart. "They all believed it was him?"

"There was a vote. I was too young to take part, but my parents fought for him—to no avail. Eyden was kicked out. He was barely sixteen. Hadn't lived outside the camp since he was a child. My parents were outraged that they would kick him out onto the streets with nowhere to go. We'd just lost my uncle when the camp was attacked. He was like a father to Eyden. He and Eyden's mother were...very close. It's how he came to live with us. Then, all of a sudden, he was supposed to be kicked out and lose my parents too."

"What did Eyden do? How did he survive?" Lora pictured a teenage Eyden, pick-pocketing to stay alive. She'd mocked him for his skill and now she wished she hadn't.

"My parents tried to help as much as they could, sneaking out food and other necessities. But back then, we didn't have as much as today. People noticed. Long story short, my parents decided we should leave with Eyden. But that didn't go as planned." A bitter laugh escaped her, eyes still trained onto the seemingly endless row of trees. "A year later, they died and I decided to live with Eyden. I wanted to be with family and without my parents, the camp wasn't home. I can't thank him enough for taking me in, but it wasn't easy. Always hiding, never really interacting with other humans. With anyone but Eyden. Eventually, I couldn't take it anymore. I needed to do something. For myself, for all humans. So about five years ago, I re-joined the camp. Jaspen, who hadn't been the leader before I left, let me in on one condition. Break all ties with the fae."

"But you didn't."

"I'd never. Eyden is my family." Elyssa stretched out her legs as her gaze moved to the tents visible in the distance. "I came back here because I needed a purpose. I needed to make my parents proud. And I found good people here. Friends. People who wouldn't judge me for staying close to Eyden. But Jaspen...he's convinced Eyden was the one who revealed the location of the last camp. He lost family in that fight. I can understand his reluctance to trust Eyden. But he needs to pull the stick out of his ass and accept that Eyden is on our side, fae or not."

Elyssa's story filled in some of her lacking knowledge, but there was still one missing piece. One piece that remained unanswered, even though Lora's suspicions were loud in her mind. She needed to hear it. "If you had to keep Eyden a secret, then how come you both came to save me?"

Wide hazel eyes met hers. "What do you think, Lora? He thought you were gonna die. He knew we were following the human blood traffickers and when he couldn't reach me, he showed up here. My brother—the guy who had been so goddamn careful to keep me hidden from the fae and himself hidden from the camp—just appeared. Out of nowhere."

Lora's breath caught in her throat as she struggled to work out Elyssa's words.

Elyssa's eyes didn't leave hers as a small grin stretched the corners of her mouth. "I walked out of my tent and there he was, surrounded by scared, angry humans with weapons drawn, ready to strike. I cooled them down just in time. I think Jaspen would have kicked us both out right then if it wasn't for our friends who got taken. We had a lead and were planning to strike even before Eyden told us about you."

Lora's gaze drifted to the ground as Elyssa's words fully sunk in. She was analysing every single one of Eyden's actions, going through his possible reasoning and coming to a terrifying conclusion that her heart was not yet ready to accept.

She thought back to that tiny room in Ilario's home. When

they'd played for truths. When they hadn't purely danced around lies.

Eyden's words were haunting her mind and her heart. Melting away the uncertainty, the worry that she was purely imagining things. *I spend all this time being on watch, waiting for something, anything to fall into place.*

He hadn't waited this time. He hadn't merely watched. *Why?* The answer was a whisper in her mind, making her heart flutter. She couldn't fully think it into existence. If she accepted the truth before her, what would happen?

Her own lies were holding her back, keeping her unmoving, waiting, but wishing *something* would fall into place.

The smell of smoke clung to the air as the bonfire warmed Lora's skin. The sun had set and people had gathered around the open flame, eating and drinking ale. Apparently, it was tradition for them before going on any sort of mission. Lora had seen lots of new faces. Most had been friendly, although some cut suspicious glances to the fae sitting beside her on an old log. Next to Eyden, Lora wasn't the most intriguing new face. Jaspen had filled everyone in, telling them Lora was human; otherwise, she was sure she'd be receiving suspicious glances too.

As the food disappeared and the bottles of ale were emptied, only Lora, Eyden, Elyssa, and Iris remained. Jaspen had been the first to leave, seemingly bothered by Eyden joining in on their laughter and joy.

It felt like a rare night. The calm before the storm. The laughter before possible pain. It reminded her of Falea Night.

Lora was drinking it all in, trying to bottle it up for when times would get harder again. She wasn't naïve enough to think tomorrow's mission wouldn't be difficult or dangerous. But tonight, her worries were laid to rest. They would still be there tomorrow.

She'd be lying if she said Elyssa's words from earlier that day didn't still sneak to the forefront of her mind every so often.

As they were laughing at one of Elyssa's jokes, Iris cleared her throat and stood up. "I think I'll go to bed. The ale is getting to my head." The smile she pointed at Elyssa was a little off. "Good night."

"Night," Elyssa said as Iris bit her lip before slowly turning away and walking off.

As her tall figure disappeared in the darkness, Eyden glanced over the flames to Elyssa. "Am I sensing something here?"

Elyssa exhaled loudly. Her hair, free for once, fluttered in the breeze. It was only a few inches shorter than Lora's. "So perceptive, are we?"

"I was thinking, since you and Farren aren't together anymore..."

"Wouldn't you like to know? I always have to force things out of you." Elyssa took a sip of her ale. Lora had barely touched hers. It seemed the other girl could hold her liquor much better.

"I tell you things," Eyden said, setting his empty cup on the ground.

Elyssa squinted as she pretended to think, leaning her chin on the palm of her hand. "It's more like I make brilliant guesses and sometimes you agree with me."

"That's because you are much more perceptive than me."

"Now you're talking." A smile broke across her face. "I can read you like an open book."

Lora leaned forward. The warmth of the flames felt pleasant against the cold night. "Can you fill me in on how to do that?"

Eyden gave her a curious look as Elyssa answered between laughs. "I'm afraid it took my whole childhood to get to this point. It was no easy feat. Harder than beating the crap out of an armed guard." She turned to Eyden. "But to answer your question, Iris and I are better off as friends. We kissed once and she's really pretty, but I don't see it working out between us. Not because of Farren. We're just too different."

The name sounded familiar. Lora recalled Jaspen's comment about Farren's role in their camp. "Farren is the witch, right?"

Elyssa met Lora's eyes across the flames. "Yes, he's been my closest friend ever since I returned to the camp. We tried dating for a bit, but we've moved on from that now."

Lora wondered how Elyssa became so open when Eyden was so closed off. They had much in common, but not this.

"Anyway, that's enough about me," Elyssa said. "I wanna hear more about what you two have been up to. Eyden mentioned you were at Ilario's. I've never met this 'best friend' of his. Is he real or a figment of his imagination?"

Eyden let out a curt laugh that almost got swallowed by the light wind. "By Caelo, of course he's real."

"It's hard imagining you with friends and not brooding alone in your closet at home."

Eyden opened his mouth to protest then closed it. Lora supposed even he realised he couldn't argue with that. The image of Eyden sitting in his closet, writing with that pen of his with laser-sharp focus, made Lora giggle.

"Although I couldn't imagine it either, Ilario is very much real. You'd like him," Lora said as her eyes drifted between Eyden and Elyssa.

Elyssa's smile had a tint of sadness to it. To lighten the mood, Lora said, "Did Eyden mention that I saved him from falling off a cliff?"

Elyssa's eyes widened with curiosity as she turned to her brother. "He must have conveniently left that out. Tell me more."

Eyden laughed, brushing a lock of dark hair from his eye. "I merely stood too close to the cliff. Lora was still secured by a rope, so she pulled me back."

"Stood too close to the cliff?" Lora's laughter was louder than before. She sought out Elyssa's eyes. "He left out the part where he tripped over nothing."

The other girl joined her laughter. "I wish I could've seen that. The invincible Eyden almost gets taken out by his own feet."

Lora was wiping tears from her eyes, her laughter ringing true. When her eyes met Eyden's again, she was afraid she'd gone too far, but all she saw in his eyes was joy. It calmed her laughter and invoked a different kind of feeling. She held his stare. "And for the record, I would've grabbed your hand even without the rope. I didn't even realise it was still there."

The intensity in his brilliant pale eyes made Lora second-guess her confession. Eyden swallowed. He glanced away, then back at her. "That would have been foolish." His lips tilted up. "Insane, really."

Elyssa's voice broke their eye contact. "Well, as glad as I am that you saved my brother's ass, he could use a dash of reality. Human or fae, he's not invincible either."

"I can handle a small fall off a cliff," Eyden said as he waved a hand.

Elyssa shook her head. "Exactly my point. Remember that card game we used to play?" She turned to Lora, not waiting for Eyden's response. "I had a lucky streak at first and he was obsessed with beating me. He could never admit defeat. When he finally won and I couldn't care less, he fucking lost it."

Elyssa's laughter rang in her ears as the fond memory warmed Lora's heart. Her eyes travelled to Eyden again. "And here I thought you never lose." A teasing smile lifted the corner of her mouth.

"Not when it matters." Eyden's voice was filled with unspoken implications.

Elyssa coughed lightly, getting up from her spot. "I think I still have that game. I'm gonna go get it and leave you two to continue talking in subtext."

Eyden grinned sheepishly as he watched his sister walk off. His smile increased the slow fire building inside of Lora. Left alone, just the two of them, she was hyper-aware of how close they were sitting.

"Are you worried about tomorrow?" Lora asked, breaking the tense silence. What she really wanted to ask was why he'd chosen to show up at the camp. Why he'd acted when so much was on the line. Why he'd tried everything to get to her when they hadn't even known each other that long. But was she ready to embrace his answer? To accept her own feelings that she'd tried so hard to brush off? It would completely ruin the image of fae she'd lived by.

Eyden stared up at the stars lighting up the sky, each one like a beacon of hope breaking through the darkness. "Honestly, a bit. I'm pretty sure Jaspen thinks we're both expendable."

The honest answer surprised her. Had they really moved on from pretence? "I thought their mission was to protect all humans."

Eyden tilted his head towards her. "It is. But protecting the camp is his priority."

Worry was sneaking back into her mind.

Seeing her anxious face, Eyden added, "If things go south, I'll make sure you get out of there. I promise."

Lora's mood sank further. She clasped her rose gold necklace, her constant reminder of all the wishful promises she'd made. "You can't promise that. Promises are...we both know there's no way of knowing with certainty how this mission will go."

Eyden was quiet for a moment, trying to read her expression. His eyes reminded her of a fair, hopeful summer sky against the dark night. "Okay, then I swear I'll *maybe* save you."

Lora's grin returned in full force. "I'll take that. *Maybe.*"

As Eyden turned towards the bonfire, the light of the flames danced across his face, illuminating his eyes. "You're not sure about this at all, are you?" he asked into the flames. "Yet you're still doing it."

Words from their night of truths flew through her mind once again, encouraging her on and banishing the thoughts that were holding her back. *No more holding back.* She'd done enough of that the night they'd watched the stars.

"Nothing happens when all you do is wait," Lora said, her voice a whisper of encouragement.

His gaze snapped to her. There was something special about the way he looked at her, as if she was the greatest mystery to be solved. His eyes held a spiral of emotions. She was sure the fire brewing behind them had nothing to do with the flames in front of them.

"I was right. The first time we met. I was right about you." The air between them was electrifying, charged with wonder and want. Somehow, they had both moved closer, their knees touching. "You are special. In more ways than one."

The corner of her lip turned up as her breath caught. "Go on. Just how special?"

His answering grin made her heart beat faster, increasing the fire in her veins. "You're...an especially special pain in my ass."

Laughter was spilling out of her, as free as the fire igniting inside of her.

Eyden's eyes wandered over her face as his expression changed into something different, something wicked. The heat in his eyes made her laughter fade, replacing it with anticipation.

His eyes stopped at her lips and the light feeling in her core began to tighten into something more. She could feel his breath on her lips as their heads moved closer, compelled by something unexplainable. Something magical.

Her eyes drifted to Eyden's lips as her own parted slightly. Lora felt the pull as they both froze. So close. The space between them almost non-existent. A moment of hesitation, of delicious anticipation.

Eyden's smirk undid her, broke the last string holding her back as the fire spurred her on.

No more waiting.

No more holding back.

Her lips met his in an explosion of sensations. The fire increased, overriding her every thought.

At the first brush of his lips, a piece fell into place. Lora didn't know why she'd been so insistent on holding back. It seemed ludicrous to deny herself this feeling of being a living flame.

She was melting under Eyden's hand as he touched her cheek and deepened the kiss. His lips parting hers, his tongue caressing her own. Her hand found its way into Eyden's hair, pulling him closer still, as she'd wanted to do so many times.

Her body tensed as his other hand drifted to her waist, under her jacket, scorching her skin through the thin fabric of her sweater. She leaned into the touch, embracing it. Encouraging it on. She was letting herself feel it all. His soft groan mirrored her thoughts and her hand tightened in his hair, wanting to keep him there forever.

Distantly, Lora realised she'd gotten her answer. She couldn't remember why she'd ever questioned it. How could anything be bad when it felt so right? When his touch invoked this fire within her that she didn't know existed?

In this moment, nothing else mattered. There were no lies, no unfulfilled promises.

Nothing was holding her back as she fully embraced this insane feeling fuelling the fire in her veins.

CHAPTER 41

AMIRA

Amira had spent the whole day thinking about Rhay's behaviour the previous day. Nouis had warned her that his son's moods were fleeting, but she had stupidly assumed that Rhay valued their friendship. Apparently, he didn't value it as much as he did his friendship with Karwyn.

She buried her head in her pillow. Her life in Parae felt dull without the presence of Rhay to distract her. Karwyn still considered her useless and had no interest in her. Once again, she was all alone. Same feeling, different place.

Amira squeezed her eyes shut, trying to keep the tears at bay. When she opened them again, she saw a figure towering over her. Frightened, she sprung up, almost falling off her bed.

"You're not ready yet?" said Varsha.

Amira tried to catch her breath. "Why? What for?" She tried to remember if she had made plans with Varsha, but nothing came to her.

"Rhay's party has already started. Let's go together," Varsha answered.

Amira rubbed her eyes. "I don't think he'd want me there. He didn't invite me." *Because of Karwyn.*

"Nonsense, he's your friend."

"Not anymore, apparently." His mind had been poisoned by his best friend.

Varsha sat on Amira's bed. "What did the bastard do?" Varsha said with a smirk. She had been living in the palace far longer than Amira and had probably seen Rhay's shifting behaviour before.

Amira pulled her legs close to her chest. "He said that I should stay away from him. That I'm too *clingy.*"

"Huh, that doesn't sound like him. The nerve of this guy," Varsha huffed before standing up. "You know what? You should go to his party looking fabulous and completely ignore him. That'll teach him!"

"I don't know. I think I should try to talk to him again."

"Fine. But if he's rude again, I'll have a word or two with him," Varsha said with a devilish smile.

Feeling confident in a vibrant amethyst dress, she entered the room with the beautiful painter at her side. The colour of her dress mirrored her eyes, bringing out the light in them. It felt nice to be in an outfit of her choosing. For too long, her brother had chosen all her outfits.

They made their way across the party room, craning their

necks as they hunted for Rhay. Varsha's eyes darted to Amira's left. "There he is. At the bar. Figures."

Amira turned around to see Rhay sitting on a bar stool, chatting with the bartender. He seemed so careless, far from the Rhay who had demanded she stay away from him.

"You ready?" Varsha asked.

Amira nodded, determined to get answers. "Thank you for your help. You can enjoy your night now."

"Always a pleasure to be of service to you, princess," Varsha said with a wink before disappearing into the dancing crowd, walking up to an incredibly attractive fae. Amira averted her eyes. She twisted a strand of hair between her fingers, the sharp pain bringing her clarity.

She joined Rhay at the bar without him noticing. As she sat on the bar stool next to him, she saw him tense up. "Can we talk?" Amira started.

Rhay turned to her, a large grin on his face, but it seemed forced. "Princess, I'm so glad you could make it. What do you wanna talk about?"

"You remember our last talk, don't you?" Amira asked, irritated by his pretence. She had half-expected him to tell her to leave him alone.

Rhay took a sip of his drink. "Of course, I remember. I wasn't that drunk."

So he had been drinking yesterday. Maybe that explained his strange behaviour. But from what she had gathered, drinking usually made him friendlier, not meaner.

He took her hand. "Don't worry, I'm gonna teach you how to

block my powers. I haven't forgotten about my promise. The key is to learn to balance emotions."

Amira had never felt more confused. Why was he helping her after their last conversation?

Rhay continued without paying attention to her. "I have to be honest, it's harder for low-level fae to learn to block mental powers. I'm not saying it's hopeless, but you need to have a strong grip on your mind. I want you to try something."

He pressed her hands and suddenly, all her anger was gone, replaced instead by a lingering feeling of nothingness. She was just...*fine.*

"Now that I've levelled your emotions, let's start with a simple exercise. Think of a single moment that made you feel a specific emotion. It can be sadness, anger, joy, fear...whatever you want. Don't tell me what it is. Just close your eyes, remember that time and how it made you feel. Do you have it?"

She wanted to ask him more questions about the previous day. Why was he acting as if nothing had happened? His eyes demanded her to focus and she wanted to learn more than anything, so she decided to play along.

Amira closed her eyes. Her mind wandered around her memories. She didn't know which one to pick. Her fifteenth birthday drifted to the forefront. She was surrounded by her parents, perfectly happy. And then her father had gifted her the comb. She remembered admiring the present, mesmerised by the changing colour of the nacre.

"Now try to level all the emotions of that memory," Rhay continued. "Use an opposite emotion for it. Disgust for pleasure, peace for anger, sadness for happiness."

It wasn't hard for Amira to turn the joy into sadness. Her birthday had been three days before her father's death. An image of her father's lifeless body struck her mind. She clenched her fist, trying to fight back the tears.

"Hold on to the balance." Rhay's voice sounded further away, a faint echo in her head. "Don't let either emotion take over. They have to cancel each other out."

But the heartache was too much. She could feel tears watering her eyes. Her heart was hollow. She was hollow. Just a pit of sadness. Everything seemed hopeless and empty. Nothing would ever change, she realised. She felt like a rock was crushing her, pinning her to the ground.

She heard Rhay's faint voice calling her. "Princess? *Amira?*"

She tried to speak, but her mouth had been stitched shut. Her scream echoed inside her head, but it didn't sound like her voice. She could feel two burning hands gripping her. Suddenly, everything stopped. She was floating in the ether.

"Amira, open your eyes," a voice called.

This time, she was able to obey the command. She could feel Rhay's concern before even looking at him. "I guess I failed."

Relief appeared on Rhay's face. He even gave her a half-smile. "Not exactly. You succeeded at first. But you let your counter emotion take over."

"It's hopeless, isn't it?" *I'm hopeless.*

"No, I don't think so. We just have to take it easy for now. You can start by practicing every day. Each time you start to feel a strong emotion, try to balance it out. Like you're disinterested in your own emotions. As for thoughts, try to imagine that they are in a jar whose glass has been darkened. Only you can see them.

If you focus, you can sense when Karwyn tries to get inside your head. Then, plunge your thoughts into darkness."

Once again, he pressed her hands and she felt her anxiety vanish. To try out Rhay's advice, she fought back a bit. Rhay's lips stretched into a proud smile. "I see you're learning fast after all. Come on, let's get a drink to celebrate."

An ice-cold voice interrupted them. "To celebrate what, precisely?" Rhay looked guilty as he faced Karwyn. But the king wasn't focused on his friend. Instead, he was angrily staring at Amira, who quickly let go of Rhay's hands.

"I cannot believe you had the nerve to lie to my face," Karwyn hissed. Even if she wasn't an empath, Amira could sense Karwyn's overwhelming rage. He grabbed her by the arm. "Come with me."

"Karwyn, it's not what you think," Rhay tried to intervene.

"Do not tell me what to think." Karwyn whirled around to stare at his friend. Betrayal laced his voice with ice, making Rhay lower his head.

Karwyn dragged Amira away from the bar. She didn't want to cause a scene, it always made things worse. She'd had time to learn that with her brother. Yet she couldn't help but whimper at Karwyn's strong grip on her wrist.

He opened the door to the terrace and pushed her outside. In a threatening motion, he marched towards her, forcing her to come closer and closer to the ledge.

"How dare you pretend that you did not learn how to block my powers. Pretend that you do not care for Rhay," Karwyn said, piercing her with his furious gaze.

Amira felt the railing pressing on her back. "I didn't lie. Rhay didn't teach me how to block his powers until tonight. I didn't know how to do it before. I'm completely untrained. And nothing *ever* happened with Rhay."

"Lies!" Karwyn screamed, inches from Amira's face. "You know I could crush you in an instant."

Fear rushed through her, but then another feeling took over. All these threats, Amira had already heard them a thousand times from Wryen. She had accepted them, letting her half-brother dash out his threats knowing he'd act on them. But unlike Wryen, Karwyn was all talk, nothing more.

"Reading minds is hardly lethal," she said, surprised by her own strength. "And I've never even seen you use your air powers. It's almost like you're not that powerful after all."

She gasped for air as Karwyn's hand squeezed her throat. "I do not like what you are trying to imply, dear fiancée," he said in a derogatory tone. Her breathing became erratic. Karwyn's fingers dug deeper into her flesh. The sounds of the nearby party were starting to fade.

"Do not ever try to deny my superiority over you. I can crush you whenever I want. To me, you are *nothing*. Your only use is to provide an heir to Turosian. Do not challenge me, or I will have to *force* you to behave."

Amira's head was buzzing from the lack of air. With the last of her strength, she tried to use her arms to push Karwyn away, but he just laughed at her pathetic attempt.

He leaned in, his breath tickling her ear. "Do you understand your place now?"

With tears in her eyes, she tried to articulate, "Yes. Please, let me go."

"Louder," he asked with an insane look in his eyes. Instead of mercy, he squeezed her throat even harder. Her head was pulsating and darkness appeared at the corner of her eyes.

"*Please,* Karwyn. I'm sorry," she screamed hoarsely. She could feel the cold night air brushing past her.

He let go of her and she had to grab onto the railing to not fall over it. She tried to catch her breath as Karwyn towered over her. "Pathetic little doll, do not make me ask for another toy."

He left her on the empty terrace. Amira stood up to try and leave. Her feet would take her to her room. She trusted them. But they suddenly stopped. Amira tried to take another step but they wouldn't move, completely stuck to the floor. She felt herself slowly sinking; her body felt as if it was absorbed by the stone floor. Gasping for air, she desperately tried to put her body in motion. One little move, just one little move, something to prove that she was still *real.*

Her body was so heavy, heavier than it had ever been. She had to battle against her own self to even breathe. A thought crossed her mind, how easy it would be to just give up. To let herself be swallowed completely by the palace. To just fuse with the stones. Amira closed her eyes and let herself drown.

As she was about to lose herself completely, a hand brushed against her skin, bringing her back to reality.

Amira opened her eyes and was met with Rhay's worried face. Her lips trembled as she spoke. "Please, take me out of here."

CHAPTER 42

AMIRA

Amira found herself underground, walking between cold stone walls. After her panic attack, Rhay had led her to a secret passage hidden behind a fresco representing Falea looking over the Adelway bloodline.

She had never suspected that a whole maze existed underneath the palace. The dark path was sparsely illuminated by torches and appeared to be endless. It seemed to lead outside. The air grew colder the farther they walked.

Amira's head was still pulsating and her breathing wasn't completely back to its normal pace, but the warmth emanating from Rhay's hand calmed her mind. When she saw his tense face, she understood that he was fighting her dark mood with his powers and that the battle wasn't an easy one.

She dimly remembered that she shouldn't be with Rhay. It was the reason she was in this situation in the first place. But she needed something—*someone*—to remind her she was still *alive*.

Finally, after a few turns, they reached a door that seemed to defy time itself. The wood had been deeply attacked by termites, yet it was so heavy that Rhay had to let go of Amira's hand to open it. It made a very loud creaking sound and Amira feared that whoever was on the other side could hear them. It led them out into the woods.

Amira turned to Rhay, concerned. "Where are you taking me?"

He winked. "Don't worry, princess, we're not there yet." Rhay extended his hand again. "Do you trust me?"

Did she? After their conversation the night before, Amira was still confused about her relationship with Rhay. Who was he to her? A friend? A confidant? Or a particularly smart enemy? Still, she thought, he seemed to care about her. Maybe she should have some faith in him even though she couldn't understand why Rhay was friends with Karwyn. Did Rhay know what Karwyn was capable of?

She took Rhay's hand and followed him through the trees. Their journey was short and soon Amira could admire the charming little town at the foot of the hill. She turned her head and saw that the palace was far behind them.

"This is Chrysa, the town right next to the border." He leaned in as he whispered the last words, "Home to the famous black market."

Amira shivered and Rhay misinterpreted it. "Are you cold? Do you want my jacket?" He removed his shiny pale blue jacket.

"Oh, no, I'm okay."

Not listening to her, he put his jacket around her shoulders. "Take it. I don't want you to be cold."

Amira smiled at him and put on the jacket. The inside of it was made out of the softest fabric she had ever felt.

"It's a really nice jacket," she said.

"Right? I ordered it at the black market." His face was the one of an excited child who had just received the present he'd been waiting for. Amira found his enthusiasm endearing. It chased away the dark thoughts still swirling inside of her.

This time, she was the one offering her hand. She needed the distraction from what had just happened with Karwyn. "Take me somewhere fun," she said.

Rhay led her to the town centre. Groups of friends had taken over the streets and the atmosphere was filled with laughter and animated voices. Amira couldn't believe how happy everyone around her seemed to be. She had long forgotten about the easy joy of spending time with friends.

They came across another street and Rhay stopped. Excited to see where he had taken her, she turned her head to the right. Her smile immediately left her lips when she saw the blackened windows and the scantily dressed fae kissing in front of the building. She witnessed a couple of drunk male fae being ushered through the door, the guard at the entrance lifting a heavy velvet curtain. Amira caught a glimpse of the scandalous business going on inside. Her cheeks flushed red, with anger or with shame she wasn't sure.

She did something very unladylike and punched Rhay's arm, not expecting it to be as solid as a rock. "Dammit," she said while moving her hand slowly to regain the feeling in her limb.

Rhay looked at her, utterly confused. "What did I do?"

"You're taking me to a sex club?" she said louder than

she intended. A few fae turned around, totally amused by the situation.

Rhay's eyes widened when he saw the building behind Amira. "No, no, I completely forgot it was right across the street." Amira had never seen him so apologetic. "I would never take you to a place like that." His smile came back as he saw Amira's angry eyes soften. "Unless you asked me to." He dodged Amira's next punch.

"That's not funny, Rhay!"

"Well, your face certainly was. I thought I saw my 200-year-old great aunt for a second."

Amira raised her fist. "Don't make me aim for your face next time."

Rhay looked horrified. "Please don't, you'll ruin the moon dust I spent hours carefully applying. That shit doesn't follow directions."

Amira couldn't help the smile taking root. Of course, Rhay had spent hours getting ready but still looked effortlessly cool.

He pointed to the club opposite the whorehouse. This one definitely looked tamer. A bunch of reasonably dressed fae were talking outside with drinks in hand. Amira read the name displayed in copper letters, Caligo.

"It's one of my favourite clubs. Very versatile, like me. And they love a good theme night. Again, like me," Rhay said proudly.

Amira stopped herself from rolling her eyes and followed him inside. She immediately noticed the stage in the middle of the room. Some tables and chairs were placed around it. Most of them were already occupied with groups of fae drinking wine and ale. The lights emitted an orangey glow, creating an intimate and cosy atmosphere.

A bar made out of panels of light-coloured wood was tucked in the corner of the room. Behind it stood a young fae with multiple rings in her ears and tousled short brown hair.

Rhay immediately went to the bar and embraced the young woman as best as he could over the bar. Amira awkwardly joined them.

"Amira, this is Gadrane, a good friend of mine," Rhay said. "She pours drinks almost as well as me."

"I'm always surprised by the ego of this guy," said Gadrane with the hint of an accent.

"You and me both," Amira replied and the two girls let out a short laugh.

"What can I get you guys?"

"A glass of indigo wine for me," Amira answered.

"Vodka indio for me, love," added Rhay with a cheeky smile.

Gadrane poured their drinks and slid them across the counter. "Here you go."

Behind them, a fae climbed on the stage and started playing a sweet melody on the guitar. Amira turned around to watch him. He picked up the pace and fae started cheering.

"Remember, it's an open night. Everyone's welcome to join me," the guitarist said.

A couple of fae climbed onto the stage and picked up spare instruments. The joyful and strangely still melodic music filled Amira's ears.

Rhay smiled at her. "Wanna join?" he offered.

"Oh, I don't know how to play any instruments."

"I'm sure you have other talents," he said without any innuendo this time.

Amira shook her head, too self-conscious to join the other fae on stage. Rhay, on the other hand, took a chair and put it next to the guitarist. He grabbed a small tambourine and started shaking it while singing about the happiness of being young and carefree.

His singing was definitely more pleasant than his cooking, but Amira had to disagree with his lyrics. Youth didn't necessarily equal an easy and worry-free life. She was the living proof of the opposite. Still, she smiled at Rhay's blissfulness. And when he gestured to her for the third time, she let herself be won over by the lively tune and joined them on stage.

She danced with other fae, her body taking over. In this instant, Rhay's song was true, she was carefree. A wave of happiness shed her worries. She didn't mind that fae were watching, she was dancing for herself, for the pleasure of moving alongside the fast rhythm.

They stayed on the stage for a couple more songs before stepping back and finding a cosy table to finish their drinks. A few fae stayed on the stage and started playing a slower, more melancholic song.

Amira took a few sips of wine while the euphoria of being on stage calmed down. She was still uneasy about their encounter the day before. "Rhay?" she started, her voice shaking more than she would have liked.

His lips curled into a half-smile. "Yes, princess?"

"I was thinking about what happened yesterday. You seemed so cold and distant without any reason...I don't understand why you were so different tonight."

Rhay looked utterly confused and for one second, Amira thought that she had completely lost it and that the conversation they had had yesterday was purely in her head. But before she could confirm her suspicion, she felt the strong grip of a hand on her shoulder.

She froze, her brain going into high alert. Had Karwyn followed them here? Was he going to finish what he had started earlier? Her body tensed as if it could still feel the king's hands on her throat.

A warm and heavy breath grazed her cheek. "You dance well, girl," a drunken voice said in her ear. She almost jumped and quickly removed the hand of the man who was now facing her. His glassy eyes and precarious stance indicated that he'd had too much to drink. The man tried to come closer and stumbled against their table.

Rhay grabbed him by the arm and helped him stand up again. "Hi there, my friend. I think you'd better go home."

"I'd like to go home with this fine piece of ass," he slurred as his grabby hand landed on Amira's shoulder again.

She froze as she felt the disgusting warmth radiating from the man spreading on her body. Her mind shut off, overwhelmed by fear. The pressure intensified on her frozen skin, a twisted touch trying to dominate her. Amira wanted to fight back, but the memory of a burning hand held her back, silencing her once more. The only thing she had enough strength to do was wish to be removed from the situation.

She saw Rhay stand up in a blur. "Don't talk to her like that," Rhay snapped back at the drunkard. Rhay was taller but the other fae had a meaner look in his eyes.

"I'm just complimenting her," he said while his lustful eyes undressed Amira.

Suppressing a gag, Amira sprung up. "Let's go," she said to Rhay. She tried to get around the drunken fae, but he grabbed her by the waist. She let out a soft cry and Rhay immediately tore the fae away from her.

Instead of punching him, he held his arm in a tight grip and his face switched into a deep focus. Amira quickly realised that he was trying to change the drunken fae's mood. A few fae had started to notice the commotion and were looking at the scene without intervening.

The fae pushed Rhay away. "You have a problem? Fight me, then," he yelled before planting a long knife on the table. The whole room went silent. They all understood what the gesture meant. A challenge had been placed, a duel of honour.

Rhay turned around to look at the crowd that had gathered around them. "Who has a knife?" he shouted with too much excitement in his voice. A tall and bulky man stepped out of the crowd and gave his knife to Rhay. Rhay stared at the drunkard before plunging the knife into the wood. The crowd cheered. The challenge had been accepted.

Crushing her like a boulder, the tension in the room made Amira completely panic. Rhay and the drunk fae were still staring at each other, each of their knives planted deeply into the table. The sight of the two blades cutting deep into the wood changed into a vision of a blade cutting deep into Rhay's skin. She knew that as long as the blades were not made out of almandine, he'd be fine, but she couldn't stop her heart from beating fast.

Amira leaned in and whispered into Rhay's ear, "Are you sure this is wise?"

"Don't worry, I have experience. I also know this type of guy and he won't stop until he gets a good beating. Plus, I can't let him insult you like that," Rhay whispered back.

She wanted to say that she was used to insults and that this one wouldn't cut deeper than the hundred her brother, or now Karwyn, had said to her. But the crowd started to cheer loudly, excited by the perspective of combat.

Amira felt a presence to her left. She turned her head and witnessed Gadrane coming to stand next to Rhay.

The bartender raised her hands. "I don't condemn fighting, but if you really have to take out your excess of violence, then please do it in the indoor courtyard," she said while staring at Rhay.

Rhay took his knife out of the table and raised it above his head. "Well, you've heard the lady, to the courtyard," he roared before leading the crowd to the back door.

Amira followed with fear in her heart. Rhay seemed to be enjoying the situation a little too much and she worried that he would make a stupid move.

The small indoor courtyard quickly filled up with the curious crowd and a circle formed around Rhay and his opponent. A fae in the crowd created little fireballs to illuminate the duelling ground.

Rhay and the other fae stood still, their long knives in hand. Rhay exuded confidence while the drunkard could barely stand still. Someone counted down from ten to zero and then the duel started.

Amira quickly noticed that the fight was at a disadvantage. Rhay was vastly superior in terms of strength and speed. Everyone could see that he had practiced hundreds of times before and he quickly got the upper hand.

Dancing around the other fae, Rhay inflicted multiple tiny cuts on his opponent. Instead of stopping him, the lacerations fuelled his anger and his attacks became bolder and more erratic. A few times, Amira had to hold her breath as she saw the drunkard charging Rhay, his blade raised high. But every time, Rhay swiftly avoided the knife, taunting his opponent with his sly grin.

She was relieved to see the assailant growing more and more tired with each failing attack. Rhay managed to grab the man's arm and twisted it enough to make him groan and drop his weapon. The crowd cheered loudly and Amira let out a relieved sigh. The fight was over when Rhay pinned the fae to the ground, his tall figure towering over the immobilised fae. Amira heard a few shouts encouraging Rhay to hurt the fae more, but she knew that he wouldn't listen to them.

As he was about to let go, a sudden gust of wind pushed him far away from the drunk fae. The strength of the wind made Rhay stumble before falling on his back. Amira noticed a dark-haired woman in the crowd making hand movements just as a second wave of wind pinned Rhay to the ground.

Before anyone could stop him, the drunk fae took out a small knife with an unmistakable red tint from his boot. *Almandine*, a voice whispered in Amira's ear. Her heart shrunk in her chest.

The assailant threw the knife. It sunk into Rhay's hand, drawing a distressed cry from his throat. The drunk fae stumbled and Amira understood that the woman with air magic had helped his perfect shot. Luckily, she hadn't aimed for Rhay's heart or he would be lying dead in front of her eyes.

"He's cheating," Amira screamed but the loud cheer of the crowd covered her voice. They wanted a show and they were getting one.

Amira tried to get to the front of the crowd, but she was pushed back. In between the cracks of the crowd, she saw the drunkard pick up his iron knife from the ground while Rhay stood up and removed the almandine knife from his hand. Droplets of blood fell to the ground.

The cheating fae launched himself at Rhay, who was clearly still in shock over his injury. Rhay still managed to knock the iron knife out of the drunkard's hands.

They wrestled on the ground, each trying to grab a knife. Just as Rhay almost reached his weapon, the other fae punched him in the face. Rhay immediately retaliated, delivering a right hook that surely hurt. In the heat of the action, the drunk fae's hand desperately searched for his knife. Just as Rhay delivered another punch, the drunkard grabbed the first knife he could get without looking.

But it wasn't the iron knife. Amira saw the dreaded red tint just as it plunged into Rhay's chest.

Time slowed down. Amira watched in horror as Rhay's hands fell to his sides, no longer able to hit back.

The woman with air magic screamed, "Mylner, what have you done?"

Mylner stared at the knife in Rhay's chest with disbelief and sobered up immediately. Horror and fear crossed his face. He removed the knife, cursing loudly. "Shit! I didn't mean to!"

Amira tried to get closer to Rhay, her eyes set on his wound. He seemed to have missed Rhay's heart, but her fear for his life didn't let up.

The fae, Mylner, looked around, panicked. The bloody knife still in his hand, he used his free one to press on Rhay's chest. "I'm—"

Suddenly, the blade flew out of the hands of the assailant. Was the air wielder trying to clean up their mess? But when Amira turned her head to where the crowd had parted, she was shocked to see a hooded figure holding the knife in his raised hand.

"What on Liraen is going on here?" thundered the man.

Amira would recognise his cold tone anywhere and she wasn't surprised when the man removed the hood of his cloak. Karwyn turned to the guards stationed behind him.

"Seize him," he ordered with his finger pointed at the drunk fae. The crowd immediately scattered as they recognised the guards' uniforms. Some ran away to the nearby streets while others, probably too inebriated to function, went back inside the bar, their drinks still in hand.

The air wielder tried to run away, but Karwyn grabbed her

by the arm. "Where do you think you are going?" he said with a sadistic grin. He twisted her arm with so much strength that Amira heard the fae's bones crack from where she was standing. The woman yelped, the pain too intense to even let out a proper scream.

Now that the crowd had finally parted, Amira ran up to Rhay, who was still on the ground. She caressed his damp forehead. "Rhay, can you hear me?" she whispered.

Rhay coughed and opened his eyes. He looked more shocked than truly hurt. "I'm fine, but I can't stand up."

"Did you hurt your back?"

"No, but I'm pretty sure I ripped my trousers when I landed on the ground and I'm not wearing any underwear." They both let out a relieved laugh that drew Karwyn's attention. Amira saw his eyes going from a concerned look when facing Rhay to a profoundly angry one when he noticed Amira holding his uninjured hand.

"You have made quite a mess," Karwyn said. Amira didn't know if he was talking to her or Rhay, but she wanted to say that Karwyn was at fault too. If he hadn't assaulted her earlier, Rhay wouldn't have found her in such disarray.

Karwyn walked towards them, avoiding the whimpering drunkard held by the guards. He lowered himself and discreetly pushed Amira aside, making her fall on her behind. "I am glad I came just in time. I knew if Amira was involved, only trouble could await. Do not worry, I will make them pay heavily for what they have done to you." Rhay's face dropped, but Karwyn didn't seem to notice.

With one flick of his hand, Karwyn gestured to the guards

to move away from the assailant before sending a gust of air that crushed the man to the ground with an intense force. The interim high king stood up and put his boot on the fae's face.

"You see, Amira," Karwyn said, "I do have air powers. I just do not like to waste them." His boot pressed harder on the skull of the now powerless fae while Amira watched in horror.

CHAPTER 43

LORA

As Lora crossed the woods the next day, she couldn't help but take note of the portal shimmering through the trees to their left. The tear was at the edge of Chrysa. It didn't only serve as a magical border to Earth, it was also very close to the border to Rubien.

The fae they were tracking had a headstart on them; he had left Turosian late the night before. Eyden had been right in his assumption that the fae would be leading them to Rubien. They were surer than ever that the other humans were held at the Void, waiting to be sold.

History books said that there used to be a large temple on the border between Turosian and Rubien. It was there that the Dark King had decided to rip a tear in the fae's universe to find willing slaves, leading them to Earth.

Lora held onto her phone with one hand and shielded her face from the low-hanging branches with the other. Walking through the woods was less than ideal, but it was the only way to discreetly enter Rubien, avoiding the run-down roads that traders could be using. It didn't help that after a few hours, the pleasantly warm Turosian weather turned uncomfortably hot.

Nearing Rubien, the trees became scarcer, the ground drier. Soon enough, Lora's feet were kicking dust and sand. They made their own path through land lined with trees and plants or hidden by stone structures. Lora wondered how the lush green trees survived in this heat. Then again, they looked different than what she was familiar with. She was glad for the cover from the unrelenting sun—and potential danger.

Lora glanced behind her where Elyssa and Jaspen were talking before shifting her attention to Eyden. He was keeping close to her, helping her guide them forward safely. His eyes were focused on the desert stretching before them. They hadn't talked about what happened last night. Lora wasn't sure what the kiss meant to him. The only thing she was sure of was that for her, there was no going back to who they were before. They'd stepped over an invisible line and Lora couldn't imagine taking it back. The memory of his lips on hers, his hands drawing her closer, was still burning in her mind.

As if reading her thoughts, Eyden turned his head, his eyes meeting hers. A slow grin spread across his face. His brown skin gleamed in the sun and the pale blue in his eyes sparkled. It was a sight Lora would have tattooed in her mind for quite some time.

She bit her lip to hold back the goofy grin that was surely breaking free. Eyden noticed and his grin became daring, as if he wished they were in a different kind of situation. Alone. Not walking through a forgotten, lawless country.

Thinking of what they could do if it was only the two of them, what they could've done if Elyssa hadn't returned with a deck of cards last night, Lora blushed and broke their stare. It probably had been for the best. It had been a fun night after all, laughing with Elyssa as Eyden lost the first round, out of practice, it seemed.

Lora forced her attention to the digital map in her hand, hoping her tracker was leading them in the right direction. It seemed the fae was now keeping close to an area some hours away from Rubien's capital, Cinnite.

Just as the thought left her, buildings became visible in the distance.

"It's Cinnite, isn't it?" Eyden asked, peeking at her phone screen.

"I think so," Lora answered.

The closer they got, the clearer it became that the city was abandoned. Collapsed buildings and ruins were all that was left. The desert was quiet, as if every soul had fled, which was probably true for the most part. After the battle in Cinnite that ended the Dark King's reign of terror, fae and humans alike quickly sought refuge in their neighbouring country, Turosian.

Lora wondered how the city had looked before the battle. Judging from what was left, it had been a grand city, shining bright with potential before it was all torn down. She glanced at her shoes, covered in copper sand. It had a uniqueness to it, the shade of red fitting for the Ruby Kingdom as it glistened in the warm sunlight.

Elyssa appeared at her left, snapping her out of her thoughts. "Cinnite?" When Lora nodded, the other girl continued. "Never thought I'd see it for myself. What a fucking mess. No wonder people say it's haunted."

"Haunted, really?" Lora turned to the shorter girl. Her auburn hair, gathered in a high ponytail, appeared lighter in the sun, and her few freckles were more prominent. She hoped Elyssa's fair skin wouldn't get sunburned.

"If you believe in those things, then I guess it's a valid fear. Their so-called God of Justice did leave them after all, or so the story goes."

"A kingdom without a god looking over it is no kingdom at all in Liraen," Eyden said, meeting Lora's eyes. "That's why it's lawless territory now."

"Some people believe it's the wiped-out Sartoya bloodline that's haunting the city. The Dark King still roaring even in death. The last remains of his dark magic still lingering. His whole family deceased but still trapped on Liraen, repelled by Caelo." Elyssa screwed up her face. "Better we stay the hell away. Though if Variel Sartoya's ghost is haunting this place, I'd like to give him some payback on behalf of humanity."

The thought made Lora shudder. She was glad that she didn't have to live through all the destruction and fear Variel Sartoya had brought to Liraen. If it wasn't for him, humans would've never been roped into the fae's world. The tear in the universe would've never happened. Using that kind of dark magic had messed with the whole Sartoya bloodline, giving them the dangerous power of compulsion—at a cost. The Dark King had grown weak, his life source draining much too quickly, the dark magic twisting his very being. It had given him the ability to feed on other fae's life sources to stay alive while his family became casualties of dark magic.

The fae's weakness, being unable to resist the Dark King's compulsion, had been the only reason humans were seen as an advantage. The fae had needed their help, their human minds that stayed unaffected by the Dark King's compulsive magic. Only together had they been able to bind the Dark King's power and destroy him once and for all.

"We should walk around it," Eyden agreed. "There are rumours Harten Adelway liked to exile fae to Rubien. Better we don't find out they're hiding in Cinnite the hard way."

Lora glanced around the desert towards the run-down, broken buildings. "Would they have stayed here?"

"In Rubien? I'm assuming if the rumours are true, they probably signed a blood contract which would make it impossible for them to leave."

Another shudder went through her. The principle of blood contracts had always freaked Lora out. It's why she hadn't mentioned the vial of her mother's blood until she had to.

"Of course. Fae and their blood contracts," Jaspen said, joining their conversation as he appeared next to Elyssa. "Harten Adelway was no better than the Dark King. He took advantage of us, used us to overthrow Variel Sartoya. He promised us freedom, yet here we are, still living in fear."

Eyden glanced in his direction. "As much as I hate the Adelways, I'd have to disagree with you there."

"Coming from a fae, I'm not surprised."

"Don't get me wrong, the reign of the Adelways needs to

come to an end. But the dark magic Variel Sartoya brought to Liraen...I don't think there's anything worse than that."

Jaspen walked a step ahead, making it easier for him to meet Eyden's gaze. "Because the magic the current king possesses is so peaceful? The whole logic of choosing kings based on how powerful, how supposedly blessed they are by the gods, is ludicrous. Strong minds are what matters. A clear vision for a future."

Eyden kept his pace next to Lora, unbothered by Jaspen's comments. "I don't believe a fae's high level means they are more blessed. I can agree with you there. But dark magic is a different beast, an unpredictable one with costly consequences."

"And that belief has nothing to do with the fact that you're a level one, right?" Jaspen's laugh was dry, mocking.

Eyden merely shook his head and turned to Elyssa, silently pleading with her to take over before he lost it. Even though he wasn't looking at her, Lora knew she'd interpreted his intention correctly. It struck her then how familiar she'd become with him.

Elyssa exhaled slowly. Catching Lora's gaze, the corner of her mouth turned up as if to tell her *it never ends*. "Let's focus on passing by Cinnite quietly, okay? Besides, we're all on the same side here. We all want Karwyn Adelway off the throne." Elyssa met Jaspen's stubborn eyes. "Try to keep that in mind. Allies can be found in unexpected places."

"Temporary allies," Jaspen said. "Eyden's still our enemy. Try to keep *that* in mind, Elyssa."

Elyssa rolled her eyes and turned to Jaspen. "Eyden was never our enemy. If you gave him a chance, you'd know that. This rescue mission should prove my point, if nothing else. It's time you stop your pointless arguments and get on board."

Jaspen turned to Eyden before his eyes landed on Elyssa again. "You do know that your uncle would still be alive if it wasn't for Eyden? So would your parents. If they hadn't been so attached to him, they wouldn't have had any issues at the camp. They wouldn't have looked for ways out. You're a disgrace to humanity, just like your uncle."

Elyssa gaped at him, a murderous glint in her eyes, while Eyden remained deadly silent. His lips pressed together in a tight line.

"My parents died because they wanted a better life for me and Eyden," Elyssa said, her voice razor sharp. She stepped in front of Jaspen, forcing him to halt. "They wanted us to be unafraid of being discovered again, being killed by guards, or killed by human infections that modern medicine could cure. They believed the old camp was forging the way for a better future. My uncle died protecting *that* camp. But everyone who voted Eyden out, who showed disrespect to a family losing their son, took that belief from them."

"No one forced you to come back, Elyssa." Jaspen tried to move past her, but Elyssa held her ground. Lora had stopped next to Eyden. He stood frozen in place, clenching his jaw.

"No, but you know damn well you need me," Elyssa said.

With no warning, she shot forward, kicking Jaspen's legs out from under him. Lora saw his eyes widen in surprise just before the back of his head hit the sandy ground. A wave of copper dust settled in the air. Lora thought she heard Eyden chuckle beside her.

"I'm the best fighter you've got," Elyssa said as she knelt next to him and pointed her throwing star at his neck, far enough to not draw blood but close enough to appear threatening. "And I'm committed to the mission for the sake of all our futures. But don't speak badly about my parents or my uncle *ever* again. We had this conversation five years ago and I'm not goddamn having it a third time. You can dislike him all you want, but don't you fucking *dare* blame my brother. If it's his fault, then it's my fault too. And everyone's at the camp—including *yours*."

Jaspen swallowed, at a loss of words, it seemed. The desert was quiet, eerily so. Elyssa and Jaspen were locked in a staring match, then Elyssa swiftly rose, turned on her heel, and walked ahead. Lora noticed the throwing star was still in her hand, ready to strike for real should any danger or insults come her way. Jaspen glanced at Eyden, his eyes still holding on to a lingering hatred, before he got up, dusted himself off, and followed Elyssa. He stayed a few steps behind as if he didn't dare get too close.

Lora turned to Eyden as they both fell back into their pace. She broke their silence. "I don't quite understand what happened, but now I dislike Jaspen even more."

"Yeah, me too." A sad smile grazed his lips. "Didn't think that was possible."

Lora sought out his eyes, still radiating anger behind the striking ice blue hue. It seemed she was still looking for missing pieces even after she had the most important one figured out. Eyden's past was a tough puzzle to put together, but she wanted to get there.

The next breath he took was shaky, as if Eyden just now fully took in the painful memory Jaspen had brought up. His eyes left hers as he tilted his head to the spotless sky.

"Elyssa's parents...they died crossing the border."

The day passed without any more arguments. They all stayed quiet as they passed by the ruined remains of Cinnite and other smaller cities.

The silence gave Lora too much time to think. Hearing how Elyssa's parents had perished rattled her. She didn't know the details, but assumed they must have thought they'd found a way to cross safely. And it failed. Of course. As it would now.

Eyden thought he finally found a way, through Lora. A way to achieve what their parents had wanted for them. A safer life beyond the border, in Lora's world.

Lora knew she was giving him the kind of false hope she'd never want. The kind that lifts you up just to drop you off a cliff.

Nevermind that Elyssa had no interest in crossing. Lora could understand why she'd be hesitant. Still, Eyden was right. It was all about options. Elyssa's parents wanted them to have this opportunity. And Elyssa might refuse now, but from what Lora had learned about Liraen, maybe she would change her mind soon enough.

The lie that had kept Lora's mission going was pulling at her heart. Would she lose Eyden if she came clean now? Would whatever trust they had gathered crumble into dust? Would she lose the friendship she'd started to build with Elyssa?

And would they abandon her before her own mission was complete? She still couldn't say for sure. But if she kept this secret until the very last moment, Lora knew she'd definitely lose Eyden. It would be a betrayal he'd be unable to overcome.

And then that would be it. The end of their story. She'd be

back in her world and no one would ever know of her time in Liraen. It had been the perfect plan, hadn't it? Except now she wasn't all that sure she wanted it to end.

Looking at his side profile, Lora studied Eyden's features. The striking eyes. The slight curve of his lips. The messy, dark curls, kissed by the sun. She didn't want their story to end this soon. There was more she wanted to learn about him. More she wanted him to know about her. Most of all, she wanted more of this warm feeling that got under her skin every time she looked at him.

Lora had never quite felt it like this. She had been in one serious relationship before, but it hadn't felt the same. The thought of never seeing him again felt as if it could drown her. One look was all it took and she was drowning in a different sense, while the flames beneath her skin kept burning as bright as ever. She knew they hadn't known each other for long, but she couldn't deny the crush building between them. Was it so wrong to want to keep exploring it, even if only for a little while longer?

Eyden turned his head and found her staring at him. A smirk lifted the corner of his mouth.

What words could possibly describe how much she hated keeping this lie to herself? Even if she found the words, this was not a conversation to be held in front of an audience, especially not Jaspen.

Lora glanced at the tracker in her hand as she pushed back a strand of hair that had escaped her loose braid. "We're close. Less than an hour away, it seems."

Eyden held her gaze for a while longer, like he sensed that she wanted to say something else entirely. "Okay, good." He looked to where the sun was setting ever so slowly. "I think we should stop for today. Better if we don't have to flee the market in the dark when we're blind to any dangers lurking around."

Elyssa, who had been completely obscured from Lora's vision by Eyden's taller frame, said, "The area up ahead seems good to stop at. I think that might be a small cave." She pointed to their right where a stone structure stretched next to them. Some distance away, it appeared there was indeed an opening.

The trees surrounding them provided cover as they veered off track to take a look at the cave. Eyden walked in first, knife in hand. Less than a minute later, he returned, telling them it was unoccupied. Lora and Elyssa joined him.

Jaspen walked in last, taking off his backpack on the way. "I suppose this will do."

Elyssa's eyes almost rolled back in her head before Eyden caught her gaze. He put two fingers behind his ear and she nodded, returning the gesture.

Lora wasn't sure what that was about, but she didn't have time to get to the bottom of it as he turned towards her. "I'm going to get some firewood," Eyden said.

"In this heat?" Lora asked. A fire was the last thing they needed. Although the weather had gotten more bearable now. The sweat lining her skin had dried. She unbound her braid, shaking her wavy hair and enjoying the soft breeze.

"It's warm now, but at night the temperature drops immensely." Eyden dropped his gaze for a second, feet dusting up sand.

He had handed her the perfect opportunity to talk. "I'll go with you," she said before she could change her mind.

When he looked back at her, something in his eyes had shifted. "Do you want to make sure I don't get lost?" The ghost of a smile lit up his face.

"Sure." Her stomach was in knots as she thought about how she was about to wipe that smile off his face. She glanced at Elyssa, but she had busied herself setting up the sleeping bags while Jaspen merely watched.

Eyden waited until Lora turned back around before he led the way. Following, Lora untied the jacket hanging around her waist and slipped it on so she could store her phone securely in her pocket.

Both of them walked silently, yet inside she was screaming with fear and dread.

CHAPTER 44

AMIRA

Amira thought that Karwyn was going to crush Mylner's head with his boot. But instead, he ordered his guards to take him and the fae woman back to the palace.

The sun was already starting to rise when Amira found herself in a carriage with Karwyn and Rhay. The silence was deafening. The injured fae was lying on his back with his head on the king's knees. The bleeding had stopped, but Rhay was holding his hand to his heart, in a very dramatic gesture. Amira was more than glad that the blade had avoided Rhay's heart. It could have been much worse.

A rock on the road shook the carriage and Rhay yelped.

Karwyn banged on the wall behind the driver. "You better be more careful," he roared. His usually smooth forehead now showcased a deep crease.

Rhay opened his eyes with difficulty. "Please, Karwyn, don't scream."

"I am sorry, Rhay." It was probably the first time she had ever heard her fiancé apologise to anyone.

She didn't know he was capable of such a thing, but as she watched Karwyn softly caress his friend's forehead, she realised something. Rhay was his soft spot and probably the only person that could stop him from his madness. It was now clear to Amira that Karwyn saw Rhay as more than a friend. The question was, did Rhay reciprocate the feeling?

She carefully examined the pair during the rest of the journey. The more she watched them, the more her heart ached. She longed to have the same closeness with someone that Rhay and Karwyn shared. The injured fae kept trying to lighten the mood by making stupid jokes about his wounds. He even managed to make Karwyn crack a smile.

Rhay painfully turned his head to face Amira. "Am I that unfunny? Don't you have enough pity to laugh at the terrible jokes of an injured man?"

She extended her hand but immediately put it back on her knee when Karwyn's eyes burned into her flesh. "I'm sorry. I'm still in shock." She dared to look at Karwyn when she spoke.

He scoffed at her comment. "Like you should be the one in shock," he sneered.

Furrowing his eyebrows, Rhay tried to rise on his elbows but failed. "Amira was assaulted tonight. That was the reason for the duel. I had to defend her."

Karwyn gave her a death stare. "Then you are the one to blame for Rhay's injury."

"Actually, I think the other guy is to blame for that," Amira replied, holding Karwyn's stare.

"Well, everyone who is responsible, directly or indirectly, for Rhay's injury will be punished." His ice-cold voice sent a shiver down her spine.

Rhay averted his tired eyes, apparently unable to defend Amira any longer. Just as she was going to talk back, the carriage stopped and a couple of guards opened the door to take Rhay away.

Karwyn got out of the carriage and turned to Amira. "Go to your room and stay there. We do not need Rhay to go on another rescue mission."

"I can't check on him?" she asked even though she knew the answer.

"Are you a healer?" Karwyn snapped back.

"You know I'm not."

"Yes, right, you are *useless*. I do not see why Rhay would need you, then. I told you to stay away from him. I am at the end of my patience." Karwyn slammed the carriage's door in her face.

On her way to her room, Amira couldn't hold back her tears. And once she opened the door to her bedroom, the cries only intensified. Tears hurtled down her red cheeks, staining Rhay's jacket. She hadn't even noticed that she was still wearing it. Thinking she could use it as an excuse, Amira took off the jacket and went to open the door again.

Her feet crossed the threshold, but a gust of wind pushed her back inside. She tried again, but an invisible wall prevented her from leaving her bedroom. At the end of the hallway, she noticed Karwyn's right hand raised in front of him.

Maintaining his control, he walked towards Amira. With a single motion, he pushed her further into her room.

"You may have learnt to block my mind power, but there is nothing you can do against air magic," Karwyn said.

She wanted to slam her door in Karwyn's face, much like he had done earlier, but his magic air kept her body completely still. It was infuriating.

"Have I not made myself clear?" Karwyn's lips twisted into a cruel smile. "Should we find another terrace for round two?"

"I wanted to give Rhay his jacket back," Amira stuttered. Karwyn's eyes noticed the shiny apparel in Amira's hand. The sight troubled him enough for his power to stop working. Free from the wind, Amira fell to the ground.

In one stride, Karwyn was next to her. He tore the jacket from her hands. "I will return it."

Amira stood up, trembling. "I'd rather do it myself, to see how Rhay's feeling."

"How do you think he is feeling?" Karwyn asked as he looked at Amira's trembling hands with delight. "Thanks to you, he was attacked. Luckily, the almandine did not get to his heart, but all this commotion could have easily been avoided if you had followed my order and stopped dragging him into your mess."

Amira balled her hands into fists to stop from shaking. "I never asked him to become my friend. He made his own decision."

Karwyn snickered. "Friend? Is that what you think he is to you? You are just a broken doll he would like to fix. He cannot resist playing the knight in shining armour. But eventually he grows tired of his broken toys."

Hiding the pain in her voice, she snapped back, "So why is he still friends with *you*, then?"

The slap took her by surprise. She didn't even see Karwyn launch his hand, she just felt the dry pain on her cheek. Her vision blurred for a few seconds. Was this how it was going to be from now on? Karwyn not only using his voice, but also physical violence, to strike her?

"Your brother assured me you were accustomed to following orders. I will surely write to him about your behaviour. We will see what he will make of it." Karwyn stormed out of the room, the shiny jacket in hand.

Amira stood there, her cold hand on her cheek to soften the burn. Coming to Turosian, she had thought that she would be able to leave the violence behind. But pain seemed to be following her along the way and now she was going to marry it.

It was dawn when Amira decided that everyone must have gone to sleep or was not awake yet. A dressing gown wrapped around her, she carefully moved around the palace until she reached Rhay's room. She was relieved to see that no guards were standing in between her and the door.

She knocked twice and entered before hearing a reply, as she was worried someone would catch her in the hallway. The bedroom was dimly lit, but Amira could still make out the general layout of it.

Instead of paintings, the walls were covered in strange pictures that Amira quickly understood were representations of fae made by humans. The room was a complete mess with clothes, books, and weird-looking objects scattered everywhere. She noticed a large square box surrounded by what looked like very flat books. On the strange surface, she saw people moving around, living their life like they weren't imprisoned in this tiny box.

But what truly mattered to Amira was Rhay lying peacefully in an extravagant canopy bed. His back was raised by an abundance of silky pillows and his pale pink hair was swooped to one side.

She sat down on the bed beside him. "Rhay, how are you feeling?"

"He's better," said a voice that wasn't Rhay's. That's when Amira noticed the man sitting on the other side of the bed. Half hidden in the dark, she couldn't make out his figure at first.

"I'm sorry, I thought he was alone." She stood up, completely panicked by the stranger's presence. At least it wasn't Karwyn. "I'll go now."

Rhay grabbed her hand. "Stay," he softly pleaded. He turned his head to the mysterious man. "Saydren, could you leave us for a bit?"

Saydren. Amira remembered her encounter with him at the court meeting.

Saydren turned his iron-grey eyes to her. "She can stay, but don't forget to get some rest, Rhay. You had an eventful day."

"Thank you, Saydren," said Rhay. Still a bit uncomfortable, Amira once again sat down next to Rhay while still maintaining an appropriate distance between them. They both watched Saydren gather vials of ointments and medicine in silence. He left one tiny clay jar on the nightstand.

"Don't forget to put this cream on before you go to sleep," Saydren said as he made for the door.

"It's engraved in my head," Rhay joked. Saydren left and then there were two.

Amira turned her gaze to his injured hand before moving to his chest wound. "I'm really sorry, Rhay. I could've gotten you killed."

Rhay took her shaking hands. "Nonsense. Do you think I'm made out of glass? I don't break that easily. Plus, I love that everyone's taking care of me. Including you," he said the last words with fire in his eyes.

Amira tried to defuse the lingering tension. "Still, I should have convinced you to just drop it. It wasn't worth it."

"Yes, it was. The only thing I regret..." His eyes met hers. They were burning with something that resembled fever.

"Yes?" she said in a heavy breath. What was he trying to imply?

"Actually, could you put the cream on? I worry I'll forget."

Amira snapped out of her thoughts and stared at the angry red scar on Rhay's exposed chest. She couldn't help but blush.

Rhay let out a laugh that turned into a coughing fit. When he caught his breath, Rhay raised his injured hand. "I'll just need some on here."

"Oh, sure," Amira said before grabbing the jar of cream. She carefully took out a dollop of product and slowly applied it to Rhay's injured hand. The flesh had already started to heal and the wound was clean and not as gruesome as Amira had expected.

"I regret," Rhay resumed. Amira focused her attention on his hand, too scared of the words that might come out of his mouth. "I regret ripping my favourite pair of trousers. They're beyond repair."

Amira let out a relieved laugh. "I'll buy you new ones."

A large grin took over Rhay's lips. "Princess, you can only get them through the black market."

"Right, you're probably better off buying them yourself."

They stayed in silence while Amira finished applying the cream. It's only when she raised her head from the wound that she noticed Rhay's pained expression.

"Did it hurt?" she softly asked.

"A bit."

Amira could hear in his voice that he was reluctant to acknowledge his own pain.

"I'm really glad you're okay now. And thank you for fighting for me."

"Anytime, princess," he said with a wink.

"I might give you a few days to rest before getting myself into trouble again," she teased.

But Rhay's deep blue eyes were incredibly serious when he replied, "You do know that you did nothing wrong, right? That guy was an asshole and he deserved to be punished."

Rhay's words made her think of Karwyn. The fire on her throat and on her cheek came back. Instinctively, she rubbed her hand on her cheekbone to appease the pain. Rhay didn't seem to notice; his eyes were fighting to stay open.

She wondered if she should tell Rhay about Karwyn's violence towards her. The words left her throat before she had time to talk herself out of it. "Karwyn strangled me today. That's why I had the panic attack." Tears flooded her eyes. "I'm scared, Rhay." There it was, the cold, hard truth. She had avoided looking at Rhay, but the absence of any reply hurt more than facing him.

"You're not going to say anything?" she angrily said as she turned her head.

Rhay's eyes were closed and his even breathing indicated that his mind had left for the land of dreams.

"Great timing," she mumbled. Rhay's hand was still on her lap. She carefully put it back on the bed and left the jar of cream on the nightstand next to him.

Going back to her room, she kept replaying the night's events. The disastrous party, her short-lived escapade with Rhay, and all that violence. Leaning against a wall, she closed her eyes for a second, trying to fight back the knot that was tying her throat. But it refused to go away.

When she opened the door to her room, Nalani was waiting for her. "My lady, I was worried. I heard you were attacked. Are you all right?"

Amira sat on the bed. Tired, she was so tired. "I'm all right, Nalani. I wasn't the one who got hurt." At least not officially, she thought to herself. Everyone around her always got hurt because of her.

The maid sat next to her and gently brushed away a strand of Amira's hair that was covering her face. "It's over now, my child, you can rest. They're going to be punished. The judgement is in the afternoon. They'll never hurt you or anyone else ever again."

Amira pulled away from Nalani. "Are they going to be thrown in prison? For life?"

"Don't worry," Nalani said, taking her hand. "Knowing His Majesty, they'll be executed."

CHAPTER 45

LORA

Every step was one step closer to the possible end. Could Lora really tell Eyden the truth now? The lie was a safety net holding them together. It's what had brought them together in the first place. Would Eyden have ever helped her if he had known the truth right away?

Lora hadn't paid much attention to her surroundings as they walked. When she looked up, they had broken into a clearing. The sweet smell of flowers rose in the air. Her eyes drifted to the ground, taking in the blooming plant. Lora had never seen flowers like this. The peach colour was dusted with flecks of sparkling red. Utterly unique.

If Lora and Eyden's relationship could be described in one word, unique would be a good one.

"It's pretty, isn't it?" Eyden asked, watching her kneel next to the beautiful flowers.

"Yes. At least they survived the war," Lora answered. As she regarded the flower, she reached for the phone in her pocket.

Unlocking it, she took a quick picture of the foreign plant. She was about to add more to her research notes about Turosian, but her eyes drifted up to Eyden instead. He looked at her in confusion.

"I was taking a picture. For memory," she said. Before he could ask, she added, "I haven't photographed anything else. I've taken some notes about Turosian, but your secrets will stay with me."

He crossed his arms but didn't appear all that worried. "And I should take your word for it?"

About this, he could. About her own secret, he couldn't. Her stomach was in knots as she answered, "Maybe." The light tone of her voice didn't fit her mood.

A sly grin spread across Eyden's face. "Why are you taking notes anyway?"

"Why wouldn't I? This is fascinating. The history we've documented doesn't capture all of *this*." She gestured at their surroundings before focusing on the unique flower again. "I didn't even know anyone still lived in Rubien. Or about the Void."

She looked up at him, her hand still lingering on the soft petals. "Do you think Rubien will ever return to its former glory?"

"It seems unlikely. I'm more concerned about Turosian right now, but I do hope eventually all kingdoms can be rebuilt into something better, something great."

"So you don't think their god left Rubien? Or do you not care?" Lora asked as she stood up, pocketing her phone.

"I think none of the gods intervene. I don't think they ever left so much as they never stayed here to begin with. They exist somewhere beyond our plane."

Lora nodded. She was holding in words, her confession

swirling in her mind, still locked away. The lie flowing through her like waves of cold water.

The buzzing of her phone interrupted them. She fished out her device and opened the new message.

"Mum asked me to check in on you," Oscar wrote. Then a few seconds later, "I'm doing okay btw. In case you wanted to know."

Lora grimaced. When had she last asked how he was doing? She had purposely avoided it, she had to admit. The pressure of her parents' sickness was already too much without putting her brother's mental wellbeing on her shoulders.

"Everything okay?" Eyden asked, drawing closer.

"Yes," she said quickly. Another lie. Hadn't she decided it was time to end this twisted mess of lies she had created? Lora looked up from her screen. "No, actually. It's not fine. It's my brother. I...I found out a few days ago that my dad has caught the virus too. My brother has to take care of both of our parents now and I haven't been checking in enough."

A concerned look flashed over his face. "Your father is sick too? By Caelo, I'm sorry, Lora. I shouldn't have asked you to come with us."

"You didn't. And I didn't tell you because you'd feel bad. I...I've been trying to ignore it. It's all too much." Lora sighed, her lips quivering as she hung her head. "He must be so angry with me. He didn't want me to leave in the first place. Now Oscar has to deal with this all on his own and I'm not even checking on him."

"I don't know your brother, but I do know the only reason you came to Liraen is your family. To take care of them. To make sure your brother isn't losing his mother." He lifted her chin, meeting her sad gaze. She didn't know when he'd moved closer. "You're a good sister. Oscar will come to understand that. Sometimes you need to leave, but it doesn't mean it isn't a sacrifice on your part too."

"How did you feel when Elyssa left to re-join the camp?"

Eyden's hand left her face. For a second, Lora thought she'd overstepped, but then he said, "Lost? I thought I'd failed her. El, she deserved more than I could give her. Hiding at my place, only really interacting with me... It was fine for a few years, but the older she got, the more I could see her restlessness. She needed to get out there, be proactive. I couldn't give her what the camp offered her. I encouraged her to go find her own path. I never told her, but I was hurt for a while, until I realised her leaving wasn't because of me, it was *despite* me. And even though we didn't live together anymore, I realised she would always come back to see me. She would never forget about me."

"No, she wouldn't." Their bond was special. Lora was hoping someday she'd be able to get back to that place with her own sibling.

"And neither will your brother."

Lora gave him a grateful smile before she sent off a text to Oscar, apologising for not being there and telling him she loved him and hadn't, nor would she ever, forget about him. Teary-eyed, she locked her phone, but then seconds later it buzzed again.

"Your brother again?"

She quickly skimmed her notifications. Maja had messaged her. "No, I don't think he saw my message yet."

"Is there...did you leave someone else behind?"

The question threw her off a bit. Somehow Eyden's interest lifted her spirit again. "What kind of someone are we talking about?"

Eyden shrugged. "A friend?"

"Are you asking if I have friends?"

"You know what I mean."

"I can only be sure if you spell it out," she said, a grin forming on her lips. Lora was enjoying this more than she should.

"You're still insufferable."

She laughed. "I think you enjoy it."

There was a mischievous glint in his eyes. "Maybe." He dipped his head slightly, a few dark locks of hair falling into his eyes. Lora fought against the instinct to sweep them back. "Okay, fine, is someone waiting for you to return? A...lover?"

"No." Lora glanced away. "Are you and Sahalie..."

"Over," Eyden said in a rush as Lora's eyes snapped back to his. She hid her smile.

Eyden brushed his fingers through his hair, his smile fading just a bit. "You don't have to answer right away but...do you think you'd ever come back? Even though Liraen has been pretty awful to you."

This was it. Her chance to bring up the matter of crossing. The lie was dancing on her tongue and somehow, she swallowed it yet again. "Not everything was awful."

His eyes met hers with a newfound intensity. Was it hope she was reading in the warmth shining through the icy blue? Could he see hers reflecting back at him? She wondered if he noticed how her heart sped up. How her skin turned flush as her mind unwillingly went back to last night.

Her phone went off again, interrupting the moment. Lora's eyes darted to the screen as she read Maja's new message. "Just wanted to add, stay careful. Don't do anything I wouldn't do. And do *everything* I would do." Several hearts and smirking emoji were attached. Lora chuckled at the insinuation.

When she looked back up, slipping her phone into her jacket pocket, Eyden's eyes had darkened and his smile had slipped.

"It's my best friend, Maja. She was telling me to...be careful," Lora said, diffusing whatever Eyden had imagined.

He relaxed his shoulders, eyes shining again. "Really? Is that all she said?"

Well, she wasn't going to get into that. "It's the important part."

Eyden didn't seem convinced. "Does she know what you're up to?"

"She's the only one who knows I joined your rescue mission." Maja's questions about her relationship with Eyden were taking over her mind. Lora nervously played with the chain of her necklace. "And she's intrigued about you...and I." Apparently, she was getting into that after all.

Eyden's eyes blazed with intrigue. "What did you tell her about me...*us?*"

"Enough to make her curious." She bit her lip, shutting herself up. Eyden was quietly assessing her. Where was she going with this conversation? This wasn't what they were supposed to be discussing.

A brilliant grin formed on Eyden's face. It was the greatest distraction. "Did you tell her about my dazzling eyes?"

"What?" Confusion took over her. Then mortification. "I— you can't take anything I said in that fight seriously!"

"Oh, I take all compliments very seriously. Weren't you counting compliments?" Lora was saved from replying as Eyden continued on, "Well, so am I. And I think I'm winning."

"I'm going to have to strongly disagree with you. Besides, I said that in a heated moment. I wasn't thinking clearly." Lora could feel her cheeks heat. She wasn't thinking clearly now either. "It doesn't count."

Eyden's lazy smirk increased, turning devious. "Heated, huh? Tell me, what kind of moment are we having now?"

"I..." The logical part of her brain told her they were veering off topic even as her eyes flickered to his lips. "There's still more we should talk about."

"There is, yes." Eyden took a step forward and lowered his head, looking her straight in the eyes. The mix of vulnerability and desire reflected back at her made her breath hitch. His voice turned deep and husky. "But right now, haven't we done enough talking?"

Silent seconds ticked by. Lora's brain felt fried, trying hard to stay on track. It was true that they still needed to talk—and soon. But wasn't there time later?

She could tell him after the rescue mission. When there was no danger lurking before them in the morning. Lora dimly realised she was making excuses, but she too had had enough of talking. Thinking clearly was overrated.

"Maybe." A smirk lit up her face as she casually leaned against the tree behind her. Waiting, her stomach fluttering. Her smile was a silent invitation and Eyden didn't hesitate.

Wordlessly, he took a slow, deliberate step towards her. Sparks of electricity hung between them, heating her skin. Their breaths mingled. Their eyes locked. Trapped in the pale, stormy ocean of his eyes, Lora wanted to get swept up in the waves. In this crazy connection that stretched between them, pulling them together against all odds.

Eyden reached out first, gently tucking a strand of hair behind her ear. His hand lingered for a moment, brushing her cheek. Her breath caught as he drew closer, lightly kissing the corner of her mouth. Eyden's lips felt like soft velvet on her skin. She couldn't help but wonder what they would feel like elsewhere. The anticipation might kill her. Did he feel as dazed, as desperate, as she did?

His eyes were half-closed, shielded by dark lashes. The last sunrays shining through the trees bathed his hair in warm light. Lora let her eyes drift shut, breathing him in as he cupped her cheek more firmly, his lips trailing a lazy path to her mouth.

Fiery sparks danced on her skin when his mouth finally captured hers. The kiss felt soft, restrained at first. Like a secret waiting to be uncovered. She couldn't quite explain it, but she knew she wanted this. Wanted *him*. In this forgotten kingdom, Lora had found something that she would never want to erase.

She grabbed his shirt, pulling him closer. Eyden followed her encouragement, deepening the kiss. His tongue slipping in, dancing with her own. The taste of him overwhelmed her senses. Lora gently tugged on his bottom lip, evoking a groan as Eyden lowered his free hand to her hip.

Her hand, trapped between them, travelled up to his shoulder. Sensing the empty space between them, Eyden leaned in further, trapping her against the tree behind her. The contact made her shiver, yearn for more.

For a moment, their mouths pulled apart. Heads still within kissing distance, their eyes met. His were hooded, loaded with a fire that hadn't been fully unleashed. Lora found it irresistible. A wave of desire went through her stronger than she'd ever experienced. She wanted to set it all aflame, to let the passion brewing between them run wild. Her lips curved up and the answering spark flashing in his eyes was so incredible, it stole her breath even before his mouth crushed hers.

While the previous kiss was sweet and careful, this one was all fire and haste. Teeth clashing, his lips branded hers, his tongue sweeping in fast and determined. The hand on her cheek moved down her neck to her shoulder and under her jacket, slipping it off. Lora pulled on the other sleeve and the jacket landed on the ground, forgotten.

Without hesitating, Lora tugged on Eyden's jacket and he listened, removing it without breaking their kiss. Her hands roamed over his chest, feeling the tight muscles under his thin shirt, before her arms wrapped around his neck. She pushed herself off the tree, closing the remaining space between them. Eyden groaned into her mouth as her breasts pressed against his chest, his hands squeezing her hips.

In one swoop, he lifted her up. One hand grabbed her ass as the other one steadied them against the tree, making sure their position was secure. Lora instinctively wrapped her legs around his waist. The sound Eyden made in the back of his throat filled Lora with wicked ideas.

His hand moved from the tree to brush her thigh, dangerously close to where she craved it the most. She gasped as he pressed his hips against hers. The moan leaving her lips didn't sound like herself. It was wildfire, free and untameable. Judging from the hardness pushing against the sensitive spot between her legs, Eyden was enjoying this just as much. The satisfaction of that knowledge drove her wild with lust.

His lips left hers only to leave a hot trail of kisses down her neck. His tongue flicking over the sensitive spot of her pulse caused her to inhale sharply. Lora's fingers tangled in his hair, holding him close as her hips moved against his on instinct. She felt him groaning against her skin before he stilled her hips with one hand.

"Later," he whispered, voice thick with desire. His warm breath teased her skin.

Eyden's mouth travelled to her collarbone, brushing the chain of her necklace. The fog surrounding Lora's mind lifted for a second and she moved her pendant to the side. Eyden saw it as an invitation, his lips tracing the wide collar of her shirt. His fingertips followed the path he set, stopping as he brushed fabric. His gaze dropped to her chest then up again. A silent question. His eyes were lit with desire. Lora decided right then there was nothing sexier than the look in his eyes, his own wicked thoughts transparent, laid bare before her.

Lora leaned her head back against the tree, staring at him with heavy eyes. Her whole body screamed yes. She wasn't used to her own reaction, to wanting to speed things up this fast. To craving more and more with every whisper of a touch. The pent-up need stole her breath. She nodded, fingers twisting in his hair.

Eyden didn't waste a second. While one hand was still

squeezing her hip, the other drifted from her collar down the swell of her breast. Even through the fabric separating them, his touch felt like delicious fire grazing her skin. She wanted more.

His hand moved further down, catching the hem of her shirt and slipping under. Eyden's fingers drew circles on her stomach, teasing her. She sighed in frustration and Eyden chuckled softly before his hand strayed higher.

Lora's eyes fluttered shut as his skilled hand cupped her breast, her bra not leaving much barrier. She arched her back, leaning into his touch with shocking desperation. His fingers found their way under her bra, pushing the fabric to the side as his thumb brushed over her peaked nipple, drawing a cry of pleasure from her.

Her hips bucked, pressing into him. His growl of approval felt like music to her ears. Eyden's head dropped to her shoulder as his fingers continued to play their magic, moving to her other breast. She clutched his shoulders, breathing in the scent of him.

Cool air brushed over her sensitive skin as his hand left her chest. Everything felt hazy, frantic. Eyden's hand moved to grasp her thigh, steadying her, before sliding up to her hips and back. The repeated movement drove her crazy.

Every other thought had left her. There was nothing but Eyden. His mouth. His hands. The lower part of him pressing against hers, sending a bolt of pleasure through her with each shift. Combined with the heat of his tongue traveling up her neck and stopping to nibble her earlobe, Lora's senses were in overdrive, her breathing coming in fast. Her heart threatened to jump out of her chest as her core tightened deliciously and the tension between her legs built.

Lora's hands travelled up his arms, clasping his biceps, admiring the strength before moving to the band of his trousers. Her greedy fingers slipped under his shirt. She heard Eyden gasp before his lips found hers again, their tongues intertwining.

His stomach was all muscles. She moved her hand over the hard stretch of skin above his trousers, teasing him, fingers moving up and then dangerously low. She marveled as his breathing sped up. Her fingers trailed playfully along his lower stomach until she hit a firm object. Freezing, she drew back from him enough to catch a glimpse.

"Is that a knife?" Her voice was breathy. Barely recognizable.

"Mhm...what else did you think it was?" Eyden answered, planting kisses across her jaw, down her throat.

"Well..."

Eyden chuckled against her skin, the vibration further sparking the fire building within her. "I think you already know *that* happened way before your nifty hands found that knife," he whispered in her ear, pressing against the softness between her legs unapologetically. He swallowed her moan with a kiss. "I could hear that all day and never get tired of it."

She smiled against his lips. Her hand continued its exploration, gracing the knife again.

"You can remove it if you'd like." He drew back, finding her gaze. "Or anything else you want."

The heavy insinuation made her heart skip a beat. She hadn't actually thought this through. How far was she willing to go here? There was no denying she yearned for this. Craved it. She wanted to strip all the layers away until there was nothing separating them.

But here? And now? She'd only had sex with one person and that was in a long-term relationship. Lora had never seen herself as the type to lose herself in someone she hadn't seriously dated. But she'd also never felt like this. Like a fire wanting to be lit by Eyden's touch.

A creaking sound broke through the silence, breaking Lora's spiral of thoughts. Eyden pulled back, alarmed, setting her feet back on the ground before he twisted around. He drew his knife and stepped in front of her, shielding her while his free hand tugged his shirt back down.

Lora glanced at her own shirt, half ridden up, exposing more than her stomach. She adjusted it quickly as her eyes scanned their surroundings. Not finding anything out of the ordinary, she quickly grabbed her jacket off the ground. Her fingers grasped her phone. She couldn't believe she'd dropped it and was thankful the jacket protected it.

Eyden moved forward, seemingly relaxing. "Would you look at that? It's a rabbit." He turned to Lora before pointing to a chestnut brown animal crouching next to a bush.

The animal turned its small head towards her. Its bright green eyes bored into hers as if telling her they had needed its interruption.

Eyden turned to her fully and for a moment neither knew what to say. As much as Lora wanted to pick up where they'd left off, the feeling of guilt took precedence again.

Could she go there with him when he didn't know her most well-hidden secrets? They needed to have that conversation she'd been putting off. After their mission tomorrow, she would tell him. She had to.

She cleared her throat. "I suppose we should head back. Continue this some other time?"

Eyden moved his head in agreement. He glanced at his jacket, still lying forgotten next to the tree where Lora stood frozen in place. Drawing closer, he picked it up. She could still feel the heat of him on her skin. The sexy smile plastered on his face made her heart flutter. Neither of them walked away.

Sighing, Eyden reluctantly turned, but Lora grabbed his arm, pulling him back. "What about the firewood?"

"The what?" His darkened eyes focused on where her hand touched his darker skin.

A smile tugged at her lips. "Firewood? The reason we came out here?"

"Right. Yes. That's definitely the only reason we came here." His eyes drifted to her face, lingering on her mouth.

Before she registered his movement, Eyden's lips captured hers, drawing her in again. He ran his tongue along her bottom lip, making her shudder as the fire inside her rekindled.

They pulled apart too quickly and only as far as they had to, their foreheads touching. "To be continued? *Maybe?*" Lora asked, breathless, her eyes seeking his. The fire was still brewing beneath her skin, awaiting Eyden's touch.

A half-grin stretched his lip upwards. "I'm counting on it."

CHAPTER 46

AMIRA

Amira nearly knocked out an old fae carrying multiple scrolls as she barrelled down the corridors. She barely stopped to apologise and carried on with her run. Nalani's words from the early morning hour echoed through her mind. *They'll be executed.*

That's not what she wanted. She was fine with the two fae being thrown in jail for a while. They should learn their lesson. But *death?* It was awfully permanent, and she couldn't be the one responsible for such a fate. Not again.

Outside the throne room, Amira took a few minutes to collect herself. The afternoon sun was streaming in through the high windows on either side of the heavy door. She tucked a strand of hair behind her ear and calmed her breathing. Satisfied, she opened the door and entered the room.

For the first time since Amira's arrival, the throne room was completely silent. Wooden benches were placed on each side of the throne and members of the court already occupied most of them.

Amira sighed in relief. If other fae were involved in the judgement, maybe the sentence would not be as terrible. Right next to the throne, in a comfortable armchair, Rhay was dozing off.

Everyone watched as Amira walked up to the throne. Unable to decide where she should sit, she was relieved when Nouis indicated a spot right next to Rhay. When she sat, he woke up and almost jumped out of the chair.

"What's happening?" Rhay panicked.

"Everything's fine, Rhay. You're in the throne room," Amira said, trying to calm her friend. She put her hand on Rhay's, but she caught him tensing up and immediately removed it. "I'm sorry, I didn't mean to hurt you."

Rhay waved it off. "It's nothing. Don't worry."

Amira noticed that he himself was definitely not calm. His eyes kept looking at the large door on the other side of the room. "Are you worried about the judgement?" she asked.

He didn't seem to have heard her. She wondered if she should repeat the question, but before she could make a decision, the doors opened. Even though he had been monitoring the entrance, Rhay still twitched when Karwyn stepped into the room.

Everyone except Rhay stood up to welcome the interim high king. Amira noticed that Karwyn kept his gaze on Rhay the whole way to the throne. When he reached him, he squeezed his friend's shoulder in an affectionate gesture. Rhay's face stayed completely blank. The absence of any reaction from Rhay only seemed to fuel Karwyn's vengeful spirit.

"Bring them in," he roared before taking his place on the throne.

Four guards dragged the two defendants into the room. Their

hands were bound behind their backs and Amira had trouble hiding her disgust at the sight of their bloodied faces. It was clear that the guards had abused their authority. Or maybe they had just followed their orders, Amira thought, when she saw Karwyn's pleased smile.

The guards threw the two fae on the ground where they stayed motionless. The man eventually dared to look up. Amira could see that he had sobered up. In his eyes, she read fear instead of malicious intent. Sobs shook the woman next to him. She kept her face buried in her lap.

Nouis stood up and read from a scroll, "Sydna Elned and Mylner Elned, you have been charged with participation in an illegal duel, assault, and attempted murder. Based on the account of multiple witnesses, you, Mylner Elned, threatened the victim, Rhay Messler, into a duel. During this duel, your sister, Sydna, used her powers to help you injure Rhay Messler. You then proceeded to stab Rhay Messler in the hand and in the chest with an almandine knife. Luckily, the guards arrived before you could finish what you started. Mylner and Sydna, how do you plead?"

Amira couldn't believe that they were brother and sister. It made sense, but Amira couldn't envision Wryen risking his life for her if she was ever in danger.

Mylner stood up with difficulty. "We plead not guilty to the attempted murder, Your Majesty," he said, his eyes defying Karwyn's.

The interim high king raised his chin. "Not guilty, you say? And on what grounds?"

"It was an honest mistake. I was just trying to win the duel, not kill the guy."

"You cheated. What kind of man wants to win a duel by cheating?" Karwyn stared at Mylner in disgust.

The fae shrugged as much as he could with his bound hands. "The kind that is drunk and wants to save face."

"You have no honour," hissed Karwyn.

"Maybe, but I am no murderer."

Karwyn shook his head and stood up. "I order the death penalty for both of you." No one except Amira and the two defendants seemed surprised by Karwyn's reaction.

"What? But the victim is fine," Sydna shouted, tears running down her face.

Rhay grabbed Karwyn's sleeve to get his attention. The interim high king lowered himself and his friend furiously whispered into his ear. "I do not care, they hurt *you*," Amira heard Karwyn say.

"I took the wrong blade—that was my mistake—but I didn't aim for his heart. He wouldn't have died," pleaded Mylner.

"You have injured a member of the palace. It is not only an attack on him, it's also an attack on your king. And sources have confirmed that the reason the duel took place was because you assaulted my fiancée, Princess Amira Rosston."

The defendants looked utterly shocked. Amira saw their faces sink as they understood the severity of their actions. Amira's head started spinning. She hadn't expected to be dragged into this mess, as it was clear to her that the only thing that mattered to Karwyn were Rhay's injuries.

Karwyn turned his head to her. "Princess Amira, do you confirm that the defendant grabbed you by the waist and tried to prevent you from exiting the room, leaving Rhay no other choice but to defend your honour?"

She felt her whole body burning as everyone turned their eyes on her. What should she say? Would the truth be the downfall of the siblings? But what lie could she invent to justify the duel?

"Princess Amira?" Karwyn pressured her.

She looked at the two fae and saw their pleading eyes. Well, at least Sydna's eyes were pleading. Mylner was too stubborn to implore her. Amira took a deep breath.

"Are you suggesting Rhay did not defend you? That he started this duel because he was looking for trouble?" Karwyn slyly implied.

Amira's head was about to explode. He had trapped her. "No, Rhay did defend my honour last night. But—"

Karwyn cut off her plea. "Given all the overwhelming evidence, it appears quite clear that Mylner and Sydna Elned are deviant members of our kingdom. They tried to hurt not one, but two people close to the king. Therefore, I can only see one possible outcome to protect my kingdom. I sentence you to death by sword. You will be executed tomorrow at dawn." He lifted his chin to the guards. "Take them back to their cell."

The guards grabbed the two fae and dragged them out of the room. Sydna tried to escape their grasp. "What kind of justice is this?" Her scream echoed through the room long after she was gone. Amira couldn't believe what had just happened.

"Karwyn, please, reconsider—" she tried to say.

He cut her sentence short again. "Do not question your king, Amira."

Amira wracked her brain for any reason, any excuse, for

Karwyn to change his mind, but the creaking of the double doors halted her.

The doors burst open on two young boys accompanied by guards. The oldest one was barely thirteen, his face still soft and round.

"What is the meaning of this?" Karwyn asked.

One of the guards sheepishly replied, "They wouldn't leave the gate, Your Majesty. A word from the king will set them straight."

Karwyn watched with curious eyes as the two children dropped to their knees. "Please, Your Majesty, we beg for the lives of our father and aunt. They are our sole providers," the boy said. Amira's heart tightened in her chest. They were both so young and yet she could see the shadow of death in their eyes. Because of *her*, they were going to lose their parent.

The youngest burst into tears as Karwyn stood up. "Your father and your aunt made their choice when they decided to attack members of *my* court. They did not consider you then. It is too late now. The king's word is law, remember that as you grow older if you wish to avoid the same fate as your father."

Amira saw the light leaving the two boys' eyes. The youngest started crying uncontrollably. His older brother gave Karwyn a hateful look before taking his sibling's hand, pulling him out of the room.

Tears invaded Amira's eyes. She turned to Karwyn, wanting to scream her hatred at him, but he started for the door, turning his back to her. Nouis and the other members of the court trailed behind him.

Amira and Rhay looked at each other and she was relieved to see that her friend was also upset by the events of the trial.

Before she could say anything, Karwyn's commanding voice halted her. "Princess Amira, please return to your room before I am forced to have you escorted," he said.

Amira's furious eyes met Karwyn's. The king stood by the door, guards on either side, ready to intervene. With one last look at Rhay, she got up and moved to the door.

She intended to walk right past the king but something made her stop next to him. "You know you're taking this too far," she said, searching his eyes.

Karwyn leaned closer. "You have not seen how far I am willing to go, Amira. Pray you do not find out the hard way." His voice turned dead quiet. "*Again.*"

Amira had been mulling over the sentencing for hours now. Nalani had stayed with her, trying to distract her with a card game, when a knock on the door stopped their conversation.

Nalani got up from the chair, smoothed her uniform, and opened the door.

Rhay peeked his head inside, his gaze landing on Amira before returning to Nalani. "May I talk to the princess? Alone?"

Amira stood up to stand beside her maid.

"I don't think that is wise," Nalani said, turning to Amira. "His Majesty has ordered me to keep you company and not let anyone else in."

"Please, Nalani," Amira pleaded, "it will only take a few minutes. We haven't had a chance to talk after the fight."

Nalani must have seen the urgency in Amira's eyes because she nodded slowly, stepping aside to let Rhay into the room. She stepped into the hallway and closed the door.

"What can we do?" Amira whispered, dragging Rhay further into the room, away from the door.

"I don't know." Even in his hushed tone, she could hear his distress.

She grabbed his uninjured hand. "Can you convince Karwyn to change his mind?"

Rhay avoided looking at her when he replied. "Karwyn is quite...stubborn. I've tried in the past to persuade him to be more lenient. It has never worked, not even once."

Amira's face dropped. She'd had the tiniest hope that Rhay's friendship with Karwyn would prove useful.

"I can always try," Rhay said with doubt in his voice.

Amira put her head in her hands as she tried to trigger ideas to save Sydna and Mylner. There was one lurking in her mind. She feared the consequences of acting on it, but she was out of options.

"We should help them escape." The words barely left her lips, but to Amira it sounded as if she had shouted them.

Clearly shocked, Rhay grabbed her shoulders. "Are you out of your mind, Amira? We could get in serious trouble. *You* could get in serious trouble."

Amira knew that Karwyn would never hurt Rhay, his love for him was too deep. On the other hand, she would face a darker fate. But her whole life seemed terrible, doomed, so if risking it meant saving the life of two fae and protecting two innocent children, it was a risk she was willing to take. She couldn't live with herself knowing she might have been able to save them.

Pacing in her room, she explained her idea to Rhay, "You showed me the tunnels last night. We could use them to take Sydna and Mylner out of the palace. Then they will have to get the children and fend for themselves. We could give them some silver to help them start over. I'm sure you have more than enough stashed away."

Amira's idea seemed to make its way to Rhay's brain, yet he remained defiant. "What if they catch us? What if they link the silver back to me? And what about the guard down in the prison cell? How are you suggesting we deal with him?"

She stopped pacing around and turned to her friend. "Fine, I'll take care of the silver. We'll be careful. We won't get caught." Her voice was strong, unwavering. She almost convinced herself of her confidence. "How strong are your powers?"

"Very strong," Rhay boasted.

"Strong enough to make someone so tired that they fall asleep?"

"Of course," he said. He sounded offended by her question, but then he added, "Well, I've never actually tried it, but I'm sure it'll be fine." Amira wasn't sure she shared his confidence. She had to depend on luck. How fitting for Turosian.

Amira nodded. "You can put the guard to sleep and then pretend whoever freed the prisoners got us too." This was going to work. It had to. She would be useful. "Should we wait for tonight?"

Rhay shifted uncomfortably. "I'm still not sure about this,

Amira. Think of all the risks. Do you really want to risk *your* life for a guy who assaulted you?"

"I would have preferred another option, one in which they both stay in jail for a long time. But I don't think they deserve to die for what they did. And I'm sure you don't think that either." She sought out his muted blue eyes. "Do you really want to be responsible for the death of two fae? For two children losing their parent? We both know what that kind of loss feels like and we didn't have the added consequence of homelessness."

Rhay looked at his injured hand. "You're right."

"I'll be waiting for you tonight. If I don't see you, I'll just have to do it on my own." Amira couldn't help but tug on a strand of her dark hair. She wasn't sure she would be able to accomplish her plan without Rhay, but she couldn't stand by and do nothing. She couldn't add two more names to the list of lives that were lost because of her.

CHAPTER 47

AMIRA

Midnight bells rang in the distance. Dressed in all black with her shoes tucked under her arm, Amira snuck out of her bedroom. She had spent the rest of the day thinking about her plan, growing more anxious with each passing minute. There were definitely some loopholes in her idea. What would Karwyn do if he found out? Or worse, Wryen? Shaking her head, Amira banished her panic, focusing her fear on the lives of the prisoners.

Amira had been worried Nalani would question her when Amira had dismissed her to the servant's room for the night. But the maid had said nothing and left quickly with some laundry. To Amira's relief, Karwyn hadn't sent anyone else to watch over her.

Rhay had disappeared after their discussion, vaguely mumbling something about going to town. She hoped he hadn't gone to a bar—or worse, to see Karwyn—and was relieved when she saw him at the end of the hallway wearing a shimmery, skin-tight jumpsuit. A very Rhay choice of outfit. He didn't seem to be intoxicated, which was the first win for Amira's plan.

In silence, they descended to the ground floor, stopping each time they heard any noise. They had a few scares as guards were doing their rounds. They managed to hide thanks to Rhay's knowledge of the palace layout.

As they approached the small staircase leading to the prison cells, Rhay took Amira's hand. "You should stay behind me and hide until I get the guard to fall asleep. This way, if things turn awry, you won't be involved in the aftermath."

Amira nodded reluctantly. She wouldn't be of much use anyway given her lack of powers. She would have to help in another way.

They carefully walked down the stairs. At the bottom, they saw a dark corridor stretching out of their sight. Amira had been really surprised when Rhay had mentioned that there would only be one guard. Apparently, Karwyn didn't keep a lot of prisoners down there—at least not for long. Amira shuddered at the thought.

She followed Rhay, making sure that there was enough distance between them to be able to run away. If she had to escape, she wasn't sure she would do it. Leaving Rhay behind to face all the consequences would definitely feel wrong. After all, she was the one with the plan.

Rhay turned around and put a finger to his lips. They had arrived. Amira stopped walking and let her friend take the lead. He disappeared at the end of the hallway.

"Who's there?" she heard a husky voice say.

"Hey there, my friend. Karwyn has sent me to check on the prisoners."

Amira could hear the defiance in the guard's voice. "Has he now? Well, they're fine. The girl stopped crying an hour ago."

"That must be really tiring, to keep guard when nothing is happening," Rhay said.

"I'm not complaining." The guard seemed eager to do his job. Amira felt sorry for him. He would most definitely be fired for failing to guard the prisoners. An added level of guilt took a hold of her. But this was life and death. Better one fae loses his job than two dying.

"Maybe you need some rest," Rhay said in a honey-coated voice.

Amira heard the sound of rustling fabrics. "I...I don't feel so well," the guard said.

"It's okay. Take it easy." Rhay's intonation reminded Amira of the sweet lullaby her mother used to sing to her.

She heard a loud thump and rushed out into the open. The guard was lying on the ground, a peaceful smile on his face. At least he would get some rest before the inevitable backlash. Rhay was busy frisking the guard to look for the keys. Amira looked around at the cells. The whole space was coated with a reddish tint.

"It's almandine," said Rhay as if he was reading her mind.

Amira moved closer to the cell and saw two bodies curled up in one of the corners. The sound of the key turning in the lock didn't even make them flinch. Were they too late? Rhay opened the door and Amira ran up to them. When she was closer, she realised that they were still breathing. But their respiration was weak and uneven.

"Help me drag them out, Rhay," she whispered.

She took Sydna's body and dragged it out of the cell. Rhay did the same with Mylner. Amira could feel sweat glistening on her forehead and the back of her blouse was damp. Shortly after they left the cell, Sydna opened her eyes. The young fae immediately tried to escape Amira's grip.

"Let me go," she faintly said.

"We're trying to help you," Amira said as Rhay finally dragged Mylner's body out and away from the cell. She could see that her friend was suffering from the excessive use of his powers mixed with the almandine's influence.

"Are you okay?" she mouthed to him. He nodded slowly, a paleness taking over his usually glowing brown skin.

Sydna stood up with difficulty. "You weren't really helpful this morning," she spat. Amira noticed that she had two deep cuts on her hand that were not healing. Amira's vision blurred at the sight of the unclean wounds.

"We're saving you from execution, so cool it with the guilt trip," Rhay replied.

"How? By killing us yourselves?" Sydna laughed hoarsely.

Rhay met the fae's gaze. "Of course not. We're helping you escape, can't you see?" He gestured to the guard still fast asleep on the ground.

"Is he dead?" Mylner asked with difficulty as he opened his eyes.

"By Caelo, I hope not," Rhay said with a concerned glance at the guard's body which was now agitated by heavy snores.

"Let's go, we don't have much time." Amira was worried the guard would wake up too quickly. Rhay didn't have practice with putting people to sleep and they needed to be back here before the guard woke up to pretend to have been knocked out too.

She put her arm around Sydna's frail body and Rhay did the same with the much heavier Mylner. Amira let Rhay take the lead since he was the one familiar with the tunnels. They escaped through another long, pitch dark corridor. Using their hands, they made sure not to stray away from the walls. The path led them through winded corridors. As they walked away from the cells, Amira felt Sydna growing stronger.

"Thank you," the young woman whispered to her. "You had no reason to help us after my brother's brutish behaviour." Amira tried to catch her gaze in the low light. She gave her a meaningful look. "And after I stupidly involved myself, of course," Sydna added.

"You made a mistake," Amira said. "I want you to learn from it, not die from it. And I saw your nephews, I wouldn't wish for them to be left alone."

Sydna's serious eyes sought out Amira's. "You have a good heart, princess. A reckless one, but good intentions still. I know I could learn from you."

Amira smiled faintly. Eventually, the dark passage led them to an opening. The hallway was dimly lit by spelled torches. Amira and Sydna looked around, confused by the multiple doors.

"This way," Rhay said while gesturing to a small stone archway.

Just as they were about to leave, one of the doors opened on a confused guard. Amira remembered him from the riot during Falea Night. Layken, that was his name.

"What in Caleo's name is going on here?" Layken said. His lazuli eyes drifted from Amira to Rhay, and finally to the two prisoners.

The four runaways froze. Amira was completely panicked. They needed to stop the guard before he could call for backup. But one look at Rhay and she knew he was drained and the two siblings were looking worse for wear. That only left her to act quickly.

"It's not what it seems," she said. A really great start to attract even more suspicion. Amira had to stop herself from hitting her face. *Useless.*

Layken crossed his arms. "Really? Because it seems to me the king's fiancée and his best friend are helping two dangerous criminals escape." They really were in so much trouble.

Layken moved in Amira's direction, but before he could lay a hand on Sydna's shoulder, Mylner jumped in and punched the guard's face. Amira saw his brow bone split open. They all looked utterly shocked at Mylner and the guard collapsed to the ground.

"Run," Mylner shouted.

"Sorry, Layken," Rhay said, an awkward smile directed at the knocked-out guard.

Following Rhay, they hurried down the new passage, scratching their bodies against the sharp stone walls. Amira had to almost drag Sydna behind her as the young woman was out of stamina. Mylner stopped running to put his arm around his sister.

"Keep running. I've got her," he said to Amira.

Suddenly, Amira felt a gush of fresh air. She rushed to the

door Rhay had opened right ahead of her. For the first time since the beginning of the day, she took a deep breath.

They looked at the dark woods looming before them. "Did we really do it?" she softly asked him, doubt creeping into her voice.

Rhay's lips stretched into a grin as he nodded. "They'll have to go on without us now." His smile slipped. "And get to the kids as soon as possible before Karwyn sends guards after them."

Amira was glad to be reminded of why they were doing this. Why they were risking it all. For the sake of the children. With Layken's interruption, their alibi was gone. They couldn't lie and say they were knocked out like the guard at the cell. They were in it now. No backing out.

Mylner and his sister reached them. Before they went any further, Amira unfastened her silver bracelet and quickly put it in Mylner's hand. "Here. You'll need this," she said.

She could feel Rhay's eyes on her. He probably hadn't been expecting her to give away the piece of jewellery Karwyn had gifted her, but it felt fitting to her. Something Karwyn had given her was now being used for good.

Mylner avoided Amira's eyes when he replied, "Thank you. And...I'm sorry about my behaviour the other day. I will make good use of the second chance you've given me and my family."

Amira wasn't sure she believed him. She hoped that his brush with death would indeed make him a better man.

The four of them walked out into the open and the door closed behind them. Amira looked up at the starry sky. She knew she was going to be punished by Karwyn or her brother—probably both. The terrifying thought was crawling back into her head, trying to sound the alarm.

But it was too late now, she had made her choice. Amira had finally saved someone. She couldn't regret her decision. If it wasn't for her mother, she would run away with them. Instead, she'd have to face the consequences.

She closed her eyes, trying to take a deep breath. What mattered right now was that Mylner and Sydna were safe. Maybe that would be her purpose, saving the ones Karwyn had wronged.

But just as the happy thought landed, four guards came out of the woods, quickly surrounding them. Layken must have managed to sound the alarm after all.

The guards were drawing closer. Like an enraged bull, Mylner launched himself at the two closest guards while screaming, "Run, Sydna!" He managed to throw a few punches, but he was soon overpowered by two guards.

Instead of running away, Sydna joined the fight with her brother and tried to stop the guards from beating him senseless. Her powers were still hindered by her exposure to almandine and she merely managed to get hit in the face. She fell to the ground, unconscious.

Amira looked at Rhay. His feet were buried in the ground like hers, incapable of movement. She thought he would have been stronger than her, but he was just as shocked and helpless. Deep in her heart, she resented him for it. Maybe it was because he reminded her too much of her own weakness. But unlike her, he had training and power on his side. Why wasn't he helping them?

She stepped between the two other guards and the siblings,

not sure what her next move would be. Her experience in fighting was non-existent and she had no power to fall back on.

"Move aside, princess," said one of the guards.

She leaned over and picked a handful of stones off the ground.

The two guards raised their almandine swords. "Don't make us use these on you," one of them said.

"You wouldn't dare," she replied, trying to stop her voice from shaking.

The two guards looked at each other. Before they could decide on an action, Amira threw one stone after another. The guards seemed more annoyed than anything else. Their indifference increased Amira's anger. She threw harder, putting all her strength into it.

The stone hit a guard's nose even as he tried to deflect it with his sword. He cursed and Amira immediately bent to pick up more, but her triumph was short-lived. The youngest of the two waved his hand and suddenly vines tied themselves around Amira. Unbalanced, she dropped the stones and tried to tear the vines away from her body, but they kept growing. She could feel them wrapping around her throat. Amira couldn't help the whimper that escaped her.

"Stop," Rhay demanded, finally moving forward.

The guard didn't give in as he turned his head. "You better stop right there, Messler, or I'll have to tie you up too. I can't hurt you, but I can stop you myself if I have to. I'm sure the king will not be amused by your interference."

Rhay froze, his eyes darting to Amira. She could see he was battling with a decision, yet he chose to do nothing. Anger bubbled in Amira's throat. Completely stuck, she barely managed to turn her head to witness the rest of the fight.

Mylner's efforts had been in vain and he went limp when the guards slashed him with their almandine swords. Sydna was still on the ground with a split lip and a black eye. She watched helplessly as the two guards smashed Mylner's face with their hardened fists. The young fae let out a desperate cry that would haunt Amira for the rest of her life.

The rest of the night was a blur for her. The four of them were seized by the guards and taken back to the palace. She almost expected them to throw Rhay and herself in a cell too. But it seemed like Karwyn hadn't ordered them to take it that far. She got separated from the rest of the group and was accompanied back to her room by a guard.

He pushed her inside the room and said, "I'll be guarding your room for the night. King's orders. He will come to get you tomorrow morning to see the execution." He slammed the door in her face before letting her reply. As she heard the key turn in the lock, Amira collapsed on the ground, flashing memories haunting her mind.

Her brother had done that countless times, locking her away in her room, restraining her freedom so that she would bend to his will more easily. Her skin was burning up and she had trouble breathing evenly as an inescapable boulder started slowly crushing her lungs.

Once again, she had failed to save anyone. She deserved to be overpowered by everyone around her. *A broken doll*, Karwyn had said. Well, now she truly felt like one, with each of her limbs scattered and lost forever.

CHAPTER 48

LORA

The sun was as unrelenting as ever when they exited the cave the following morning. Lora's eyes drifted to Eyden, the vivid memory of their time together in the woods washing over her. It was a welcome distraction, yet she knew she'd have to get it out of her mind for the sake of their mission.

Lora focused on the map in her hand. They were close. Whatever they were walking into, there was no going back now.

"I think that's it," Elyssa said, pointing to fenced-in buildings at the bottom of the small hill they were currently walking on.

As they drew closer to the edge of the hill, Lora could see the distant shapes of people milling around. She was relieved the tracker appeared to have brought them to the right place. At least this mission wasn't a waste of time.

"Let's go this way," Eyden suggested. They moved into the cover of trees, overlooking the scene before them.

Lora was breathless, not from the walk, but the fear that was slowly creeping into the forefront of her mind. Suddenly, the sun didn't feel warm anymore. All she felt was the icy feeling of worry touching her skin, her heart.

Eyden stopped, taking in the scenery below more closely behind the coverage of a tree. Lora knew this look too well. He was assessing their situation, trying to figure out how to proceed. She envied his ability to stay calm. Then again, he must be used to this. Her heart sank thinking of what Eyden had to live through growing up. She wished she could help them find the future they'd craved all their life. But all Lora could do was help them now, here.

"I think the main entrance is on the left. We should go there," Eyden said to Lora before turning to his sister. He caught Elyssa's gaze, eyes shining with determination. "El, take Jaspen and try to find a good vantage point up here. Once we have your friends and we're close enough, come help us. If anything goes wrong, run. Don't rush in to help. I got this, okay? We'll meet you back at the cave to regroup if we split up."

Elyssa quietly stared at her brother. Lora could tell she was itching to tell him off. Probably to yell at him for suggesting to leave them behind.

Jaspen broke the silence. The leader of the rebel camp looked even more annoyed than usual. "If there's a chance to save the witch, we'll take it. I'm not taking orders from you, fae."

Eyden sighed. "You want my help? That's how I'm willing to help."

Sensing another fight, Elyssa stepped between them. "Let's play it by ear, okay?"

"Promise me you'll stay out of this if it gets too dangerous," Eyden said.

Elyssa considered his words, eyes drifting between her brother and Jaspen. "I'm not going to sit by, that's against my nature, but I'll try my best."

Eyden was quiet for a moment. Then he moved forward, pulling Elyssa into a hug. The gesture surprised Lora. She wasn't used to this Eyden, this affectionate side of him. Before she could dwell on it, Eyden stepped away, took off his backpack, and handed it to a less-than-pleased Jaspen.

Turning to Lora, he asked, "Ready?"

Lora gave Elyssa her own backpack and smoothed down her white strappy shirt. She had changed before taking off this morning. Eyden had told her they needed to look like they could afford to buy what they came for, so he had gotten them new clothes before they'd taken off for Rubien. Over the soft material of her shirt, she wore an elegant royal blue jacket, the same colour as her trousers. She still wore her black ankle boots even in the heat. It gave her some solace, knowing she'd be able to run.

"Ready as I'll ever be," Lora replied. She met Elyssa's hazel eyes that were filled with quiet encouragement. Lora forced a small smile. With a final nod, Elyssa turned her back on them and walked off, Jaspen in tow. Lora felt a weight settle on her shoulders. This was all up to her and Eyden. Lora barely knew how to fit in with the fae. If anyone was going to mess up this mission, it'd be her.

"Hey," Eyden said, his voice soothing. He had moved closer and was searching her eyes. "It's going to be okay." He smiled and it lit up his eyes. *Maybe.* His grin could outshine the sun, even the insanely bright one in Rubien.

Lora couldn't help but smile back, but it didn't quite reach her own eyes. She could tell Eyden noticed, but she turned to the buildings below. "Let's do this. No point in waiting."

She took a step forward but Eyden lightly touched her arm, making her twist around. He bent down, retrieving a small, sheathed knife from his boot. "Take this. Just in case." Eyden held the blade out to her.

She stared at the weapon. Fear told her to take it, but common sense made her say, "I wouldn't even know how to use it. You can do more damage with it."

"I have two more. Take it. *Please?*"

The plea got under skin, forcing her to seek out his eyes. As confident as he acted, she could see a shimmer of fear. Lora grabbed the knife, then glanced at herself, unsure where she should hide it.

"Hide it under your shirt," Eyden said.

Lora lifted the white fabric and slipped the knife under the band of her trousers. The leather sheath felt cold against her skin.

"A little further down so you won't lose it." Eyden's hand moved forward, stopping an inch from her skin as if he realised he couldn't presume to touch her.

When Lora didn't object, he reached forward. The back of his hand brushed her lower stomach, sending shivers through her. He only adjusted the knife, but Lora's thoughts had gone blank. Her breath caught as his fingers slipped under her trousers, stilling for a few seconds before pulling the fabric up an inch, trapping the knife.

His hand left her skin, leaving her colder than before.

Yanking her shirt in place, she cleared her throat. "I hope I won't stab myself."

"Most likely you won't even need it. But I could teach you sometime if you'd like."

"Did you teach Elyssa?"

"Yes. I got her weapons from the black market. It was her favourite thing to do when she lived with me." A faint smile broke across Eyden's face. "She wanted to learn it all. Knives, bow and arrow, sword. In the end, she'd rather throw a good punch, though."

Remembering her brass knuckles and how confident she went at the fae by the carriage, Lora could definitely see that.

"Maybe someday," Lora said, answering his question. The knife, if nothing else, gave her an added sense of security. More so than the small pocket knife that was still hidden in her jacket. "Let's get this over with."

Pushing the fear aside as best as she could, Lora clasped her pendant, reminding herself why she had to get through this. To get back to her own goal. To get back home. She might have been wrong to assume all fae were bad, but she still knew where she belonged. Who she was. Her family was waiting for her and she couldn't let them down. There were more people relying on her than she wished.

They walked through a wide, sand-coloured archway into the heart of the Void as if they had every business being there. Lora forced her face to remain stoic as her eyes took in her new surroundings. The booths, unknown objects, and fae wandering around reminded her of the black market in Chrysa. Except this one was above ground. Out in the open. No one seemed to care to hide anything here, and why would they when there were no guards around to enforce laws?

Lora was scared someone would stop them and ask how they had found this place, but it was quite the opposite. Every time they walked by a booth, the fae would rattle off prices or special offers. They must think they had silver to burn and everyone wanted a piece.

"Fortae. Buy 10, get two for free," a fae shouted to their left, trying to draw their attention. Lora took in the small pills, flashing silver and red in the sun. This was why they'd taken her, why they'd put her in a cage. All for this drug, for the amusement of fae. She twisted her fingers into a fist.

An arm brushed hers and Lora tore her eyes away from the fae's disgusting products. Her eyes found the calming blue of Eyden's. The warning in them made her come to her senses. She must have shown her discomfort more than she realised.

Eyden picked up his pace as they passed this particular booth. Lora trained her eyes straight forward, matching his steps.

After walking through what seemed to be the main market area of this place, Lora could tell Eyden was getting restless. She imagined it was more than the fear of not finding the captives, but knowing that Elyssa was waiting for them to return.

They had slowed down, taking in the stone alleyways leading away from the busy market area. Eyden seemed to consider exploring the less populated pathways. But the Void wasn't a small place. How long until someone questioned what they were looking for?

"We should ask," Lora whispered, drawing Eyden's gaze to hers. "We're rich buyers, right? Why not ask where we can find what we're willing to pay for?"

Eyden stopped in a corner. His eyes travelled around the market before he met Lora's gaze. "It's worth a shot. Who should we ask?"

Lora didn't expect the question, thinking he'd already made a mental list of everyone here. She turned to size up the fae nearby while trying to appear disinterested. Every seller had the same hungry look in their eyes. And the buyers would most likely not know—or worse, would question them.

Her eyes landed on a man in worn-out clothing, sweeping dirt mixed with sand to the side. He was working by himself, not bothering to look at anyone. It seemed like senseless work to Lora. The wind would keep blowing in more sand over the stone wall no matter how hard he worked.

"Him," Lora said, keeping her voice a bare whisper.

"Agreed." Eyden started walking towards him.

The fae didn't look up as they stopped a short distance away. Eyden cleared his throat quietly. "Apologies for troubling you, but would you be inclined to give us some directions?"

The fae's hand stilled on the broom. "I don't sell nothing." He resumed his work. His shaggy blonde hair hid most of his face.

"You know this place well, don't you?" Eyden asked. "Would some silver help our case?"

The fae's movement stopped abruptly. "Nothing. I don't want *nothing*. No silver." He turned his head. Lora almost gasped out loud. There was something behind his misty gaze, a forgotten power shining through. She didn't know much about fae powers, but somehow, she knew this fae held a high level even though his appearance said something else entirely.

"We didn't mean any offense," she heard herself say. The fae's eyes met hers. There was intrigue there. She had his attention. "We're looking for someone who provides human blood. Who sells...them."

"You're one of those, huh? I don't want no part of that. And if you were smart, girl, you'd stay away too. It's no good. Nothing is."

"Unfortunately, that's not an option." Her eyes stayed on the fae's. She could feel Eyden drawing closer, maybe to stop her. "Please, tell us."

There was a subtle shift in his eyes, as if a fog lifted and he could read her true intention. The fae exhaled slowly, his gaze flickering to an alley close to them. "Follow that path, turn left at the end. There's a door close by, red like blood."

"Thank you." She turned to Eyden and he nodded. After giving the fae one last grateful glance, she set her eyes on the path before them.

Before she could take more than a couple of steps, the fae's faint voice followed them. "Be warned: Nothing good is here. Nothing escapes."

Lora and Eyden didn't turn back. They both knew they were walking right into danger, but there was no other path for them.

They followed the fae's directions until they could spot the blood red door. Two fae were guarding it.

"Let me do the talking," Eyden said under his breath as they approached the fae.

Both of them saw them coming. One of the fae went so far as to draw a knife. "What's your business here?" she asked.

Eyden didn't show any indication that her weapon threatened him. He kept walking, only stopping once he was dangerously close to the armed fae.

"We're buyers. Here for a special kind of fortae ingredient. You have some live ones, don't you? I'm willing to make an offer."

The fae looked at each other. In agreement, the one with the knife spoke up again. "I've never seen you here before. What's your name?"

"Eyden Kellen. I usually only stop by to buy blood bags, but my boss has recently decided to upgrade his business."

"Who's she?" the other fae asked, looking her up and down. Lora refused to cower from his stare.

"My business partner," Eyden answered smoothly.

"Does she talk for herself?"

Lora briefly met his eyes. "I sure do. Can we get down to business now or what?"

"Mhm, I'd rather get down to something else." The suggestive grin set the anger in her veins aflame. Yet Lora managed to drop her gaze, pressing her lips together to keep her remarks to herself.

"Do you have what we seek or not?" Eyden asked, his voice underlined with barely contained aggression.

The fae's eyes left Lora. "Depends. Who's your boss?"

Lora's heart sped up. Would they already fail before they even found the prisoners? How did they ever think this would work?

"Rahmur Piers," Eyden answered, not missing a beat.

The fae seemed pleased with the answer. "In that case, we currently have three products. How many do you want?"

Lora relaxed slightly. They were buying their cover. Eyden was more connected than she'd realised. Did he have the trader's name written in one of his many notebooks? Was he planning on taking him down if the chance presented itself?

Eyden removed a bag of silver notes from his pocket. "All of them." The fae drew closer as if to take the money, but Eyden pulled back swiftly. "First, let us see if the products are worth it."

"Tell Kelvion we have buyers," the fae with the knife said to the other one. The latter disappeared behind the red door.

Lora began to feel hopeful against her better judgement. Could it be this easy?

The sound of clashing chains made her focus on the door in front of them. The noise steadily increased and soon enough a young man limped outside. His hands were bound in front of him. The shadows under his eyes and bruises on his face told the story of a painful capture. His right eye was almost completely swollen shut. The man had noticed Lora first, but his good eye lingered on Eyden.

Behind him, a middle-aged man and a woman who couldn't have been older than thirty followed, dragging their tired feet forward as the fae ordered them to keep walking. Their eyes were wide with fear, unaware of what awaited them next.

"As you can see, they're all just alive enough. They won't give you any trouble," the fae said, twirling the knife in her hand.

Eyden observed the captives. "6,000 silver. That's my offer."

"They're worth 8,000."

Lora wanted to speak up, to tell them they agreed to the

price, but Eyden cut her a warning glance. This was trade business. He was playing a part.

"They're weak. They won't last long. 7,000 silver," Eyden countered.

The fae sighed. "Fine."

Eyden pulled the silver notes out of the bag, counting it in front of them before handing it over. Once the money left his hand, he gestured to the three humans. "Follow me if you want to see another day." He moved to take the alley they'd come from.

"Not so fast. I'm always keen on meeting Rahmur's traders," a strangely familiar voice said.

Lora met Eyden's alarmed eyes. The fear in his gaze sent a shiver down her spine. His eyes pleaded with her to get ready to run even as his own feet stayed rooted in place.

The full meaning of his fear was lost on her until she twisted around and was met with the cold gaze of a fae.

A fae she'd encountered before, in the diner on the way to Ilario's house.

"Well, well, look who we have here," the fae said, taking in the both of them.

Lora thought she'd never have to see his face again, his twisted smile. He definitely hadn't forgotten about them either. She'd imagined many ways of how their mission could go wrong, but none of them had included him.

"You know them, Kelvion?" the fae who had taken their silver asked.

"We've crossed paths."

Eyden glanced at the prisoners, still very close to the fae, then back to Kelvion. "We're here for business. We paid and now we'll be on our way. You won't have to deal with us anymore."

Kelvion crossed his arms, leaning against the wall next to the door. He was dressed well in maroon attire. "What if I want to deal with you?"

"A deal is a deal, remember? You have our silver. Now we're taking what's ours." Eyden caught Lora's gaze, telling her to retreat as he moved away slowly.

Kelvion stepped forward. "A deal is a deal once I say so. Kayai, let me take a look at that silver." He held out his gloved hand, the shiny maroon leather reflecting in the sun, and the other fae, Kayai, followed his order, placing Eyden's silver in the palm of his hand. "Let's see if your intention is true. I'll test your silver. That won't be an issue, will it?"

"Of course not. Go ahead." If Eyden was surprised, he didn't show it. His face remained blank and Lora tried hard to imitate his calmness even as her body froze over with anxiety.

Kelvion slipped his hand into his pocket, retrieving a scanner of sorts. He held the magic device over the top silver note. Lora held her breath as everyone observed quietly. A few seconds later, it flashed green. Lora's breathing steadied.

"Pleasure doing business with you," Eyden said, inclining his head to the human prisoners. They limped forward. Lora took a careful step backwards.

"One more." Kelvion's voice was laced with threat. He was clearly itching for a fight. As he grabbed a silver note from the middle of the pile, Lora thought she saw Eyden tense slightly.

Her eyes drifted to the alley. Could they escape? With three prisoners who could barely walk? It seemed impossible. They had to come to an agreement with the fae.

But the scanner flashed red, erasing that possibility. The vile grin stretching across Kelvion's face was pure evil. His eyes stayed locked on Eyden as he addressed his fellow fae. "Kill them both."

CHAPTER 49

LORA

"Are we really doing this again?" Eyden asked, stepping forward into the crossfire that was surely looming before them. "It won't end well for you."

Kelvion drew a large dagger from his side. "We'll see about that. Take him." His voice was vicious. "The girl's my kill."

Eyden tensed, much to Kelvion's enjoyment. "Run," Eyden said to her before taking on his opponents.

Kayai unsheathed her sword, twisting it as it caught the light. The top edge was darker, the red tint promising pain. But it was the other fae who moved first, pulling out a knife as he advanced on Eyden. He barely made it one step before one of Eyden's knives was embedded in his chest. His dumbfounded expression almost made Lora smile, but Kelvion drew Lora's attention. He was moving towards her in slow, predatory steps.

Lora glanced at Eyden, but he was focused on the other two fae. She was on her own. *Run,* a voice in her mind screamed. But if she ran, what would happen to Eyden, to the humans they were supposed to rescue? Eyden couldn't take them all on at once. Maybe she could distract Kelvion long enough for Eyden to take care of the other two fae.

Kayai let out a curse as she lifted her sword, ready to strike. Eyden remained calm, prepared, another blade about to leave his palm. To her surprise, Kayai plunged her sword into the dry ground. The earth shook and Eyden's knife clattered to the floor harmlessly. One of the humans fell as he had trouble steadying himself with his bound hands. The other two lifted him up as they scrambled back on unsteady feet, away from the unavoidable fight.

Lora tried to balance herself as she took in their situation. Kayai must possess earth magic. It was an unfair fight. Lora was reminded again that she wasn't any help in this fight and neither were the humans. But she couldn't run. With trembling fingers, she reached for Eyden's knife under her shirt, unsheathing it and gripping it tightly as she guarded herself.

Kelvion laughed at the sight. "You think you can take me? Let's play then, little girl. I've been waiting for this." His steps were sure, his dagger unwavering in his hand. This was not the same drunk man she'd met before, it was the clear-minded version. He was just as evil, but more calculated in his attacks.

Kayai advanced on Eyden, swinging her sword as the ground ceased shaking. Eyden dodged her move, slipping to the side faster than Lora's eyes could track. He had another knife, but it was no match for her sword. Yet Eyden danced around her attack in graceful strides. The other fae had removed Eyden's knife, revenge turning his features sinister as he slowly rose.

Kelvion stopped in front of Lora, just out of arm's reach.

She wasn't sure if she was still breathing. Was he waiting for her to attack first? She'd rather draw out the fight. She knew she couldn't win this unless she got lucky. Her eyes kept darting back to Eyden.

A slash of pain made Lora take a hurried step back. The dagger had grazed her stomach, drawing blood before she had fully registered his movement. The sight of her blood seeping her white shirt seemed to please Kelvion immensely. He slashed again, but this time Lora jumped out of reach. If she could avoid him long enough...

Pain laced her arm before his fist caught her nose. Once. Twice. He knocked the knife out of her hand. The metallic taste of blood filled her mouth. It was running down her face, further splashing her once pristine shirt.

She tried to turn, to run, but Kelvion grabbed her arm, pulling her closer. His head was mere inches from her face. With her free hand, Lora struggled to grasp her pocket knife. Before Kelvion noticed, she swung it at his face. He lifted his hand just in time; the blade didn't even draw blood as it went into the leather of his glove.

He laughed in her face as he drew closer, removing the knife with ease. The smile plastered on his face was as disturbing as ever. She tried to take a step back, but Kelvion's dagger pressed against the sensitive skin on her neck, barely drawing blood. Taunting her. The slightest move and her throat would be cut open.

The clashing of knives in the distance turned into white noise. Lora closed her eyes, not wanting to have Kelvion's face be the last thing she saw.

But instead of the sharp edge of the blade, Lora felt a rush of movement and suddenly the pressure eased off her completely. Her eyes opened in surprise to find one of the humans, the young one, had found her fallen knife and stabbed Kelvion in the back. He tried to hold the knife in place, but Kelvion pushed him off, enraged.

The human woman attempted to drag the fallen man out of the crossfire, but Kelvion's dagger caught her side before they could move out of the way.

Lora ran forward as she took in the two barely conscious prisoners.

At the same moment, shackled hands came over Kelvion's head from behind, pulling tight against his throat. The third human was strangling him. Taken by surprise, Kelvion lost his grip on the dagger.

Lora risked a quick sideways glance. Eyden was still fighting Kayai, who was using her magic to trip him up. The other fae was lying dead at their feet. A small victory, at least.

"Hurry," the human man said, his face coated in sweat from the effort of holding Kelvion in place. Lora knew she had to intervene. Fae weren't easy to kill. She wasn't sure if they could be strangled.

Her gaze flew over the ground until she spotted the dagger at their feet. She rushed forward, ignoring the pain searing her skin. Lora grasped the dagger, her eyes fixing on Kelvion. His hands clutched at the human's. The skin around his shackles was scratched up and bloodied.

She pointed her weapon, his dagger, at his heart. Her hand shook. Her mind raced. She had to finish him off. She knew she had to. But could she actually do it? Kill him? It was a line she could never uncross.

"Do it, dammit," the human shouted at her, his face constrained in pain. Kelvion grunted as he struggled against the human's grip.

Lora tried to shut off her brain, focusing on the feeling of the dagger in her hand. It was all on her now. Her grasp on the dagger tightened in preparation.

Then the human burst into flames.

Fiery heat blew in her face. Lora stared in horror as the man's back caught fire. Kelvion immediately used it to his advantage, throwing the screaming man's arms off him before the flames could take him too.

Lora took her chance. Kelvion's shocked eyes met hers just as the dagger plunged into his chest. She watched as the blood drenched his sweater, turning her fingers red. Her hand was shaking badly as she pulled it back, leaving the dagger in his chest. She never thought she'd discover what it felt like to plunge a dagger into blood and bones.

Painful screams tore her back to the present. Lora kicked at Kelvion's shin with as much force as she could muster. She didn't even wait to see Kelvion fall before she rushed to the burning man's side.

Almost his entire body was on fire now. He had dropped to the ground, twisting around to extinguish the flames tearing at his flesh. Lora tore off her jacket, quickly removing her phone and WiFi cube and half jamming them under the band of her trousers. She waved the piece of clothing over the man, trying to cover the flames. The smell of burned flesh assaulted her nose. She couldn't stop it.

Her gaze travelled around, catching sight of a group of fae drawing close. One of them must have fire magic. This is what they did, the fae. This is how they chose to use their powers. What her mother had warned her about all her life. As she knelt at the dying man's side, trying and failing to kill the flames, all hope seemed lost. More fae were coming. Even taking Kelvion out wouldn't save them.

A scream tore out of her as someone grabbed a fistful of her hair, snapping her head back. She let go off her jacket as she was shoved to the ground. Twisting around, Lora met Kelvion's furious face. Blood covered his chest, but the dagger was gone. She must have missed his heart or the dagger wasn't almandine. Lora had been right the first time. She was completely useless in a fight.

Helpless, she tried to kick out, but the fae lowered himself on top of her, pinning her legs. Her hands reached out, blindly throwing punches, clawing at Kelvion. She brushed his open wound and Kelvion yelled out in rage. His fist hit her cheek with so much force her vision went blurry. He threw her back against the ground. The impact stole her breath and pain exploded up and down her body. Her struggle ceased. Her arms fell useless to her sides.

It took all her effort to keep her eyes open. She saw Kelvion's gaze flicker to her necklace. A bloodied glove clasped her pendant, forcing her upper body up as he pulled. "What do we have here? This is worth more than your pathetic life." His other hand held the dagger, the edge grazing her stomach. One final strike and she'd be done.

Lora's eyes slid to the humans. The sight of the burned corpse almost made her gag. The others were still immobile. The group of fae had almost reached Eyden, who was still fighting off Kayai. They circled him. Was this the end for both of them?

A yell drew her attention to another alleyway. Elyssa and Jaspen emerged out of the shadows. The redhead stormed forward, a throwing star hitting the closest fae before he could even turn around. Jaspen had a long knife ready but moved forward carefully, dodging a fire attack.

A sharp pain pulled Lora's gaze back to Kelvion. The blade had nicked her skin. "They can't save you now, girl. You're mine." The blade started to push into her flesh and a strangled scream escaped her.

It was true, they were too far away still. Eyden was the closest. His gaze caught hers as he yelled her name. The pain in his eyes must have been mirrored in her own. There was no way out of this, was there?

Eyden was about to move, maybe to rush to her, when Kayai stood up behind him. Lora tried to shout his name but it was too late. The sword went through his back. Eyden's eyes widened as he took in the blade sticking out of his chest. He dropped to his knees, blood dripping from the blade.

The scream piercing the air might have been hers. Did Kayai get his heart? Would she stay alive long enough to find out?

She felt the cold chain of her necklace digging into her neck, still holding her up. She'd never taken it off since her mother had given it to her. She'd promised she *never* would. But what good was it to be careful, to be *human*, when everything was lost around her? What was the point of holding back when the alternative was death? This was a risk she'd regret not taking.

Her eyes met Kelvion's bloodthirsty ones. "Your turn, bitch," he snarled, the blade slowly digging in further.

He couldn't win. He wouldn't. She'd rather risk it all, go against her every instinct, than see him take them out. *No more holding back.*

Lora drew in a strangled breath, gritting her teeth as she threw her body backwards with the last of her strength. Her head hit the ground, but she barely registered the pain.

The chain broke, leaving her skin. A rush of something indescribable spread through her.

Adrenaline.

Strength.

Power.

Fire was flowing through her veins, heating her blood, energizing her. She was bursting with it. Her body contained a living flame and it craved an outlet.

The dagger was still in Kelvion's hand, the edge bathed in her blood. His other hand held the broken necklace. When his eyes locked with hers, his twisted smile turned into surprised fear.

Lora smirked as she lifted her hands. "Go to hell," she snarled. With a scream, fire exploded from her. The force of it threw Kelvion back. The flames clawed at him, not letting him go.

Her heart was singing as the constant fire brewing beneath her skin had finally found its escape. The magic of her fae side fuelled her. Healed her. The fire inside her felt endless. Lora encouraged it, stretching it from Kelvion to another fae who had drawn closer. He might have tried to counter her magic with his own fire, but hers was unstoppable. She was unstoppable.

Lora got to her feet as her eyes searched for Eyden. Relieved, she found the sword was no longer impaling him. His knife dug deep into Kayai, but his eyes were locked on Lora. Astonishment flashed over his face. Maybe something like anger too.

Lora tore her eyes away, searching for her next target. Elyssa was locked in a fight. She had the upper hand. But then Lora noticed another fae sneaking up behind the girl. She channelled her fire, but could she aim that far without hurting Elyssa?

"Elyssa!" Eyden screamed, his tone warning. Yet his sister didn't react.

Lora rushed forward, her eyes flickering between the many dangers surrounding them. Her eyes fixed on Eyden for barely half a second before he vanished. Lora stopped in her tracks, turning her head in confusion until she spotted Eyden next to Elyssa. How in the world?

He reached out just as Elyssa turned, delivering what would be a fatal blow to the fae sneaking up on her, but her knife never connected. The moment Eyden's hand touched her shoulder, both he and Elyssa disappeared into thin air.

They were gone. Eyden had removed them from the fight. He had vanished. Teleported away. No level one could do that. Even for a high-level fae, it was a rare power to have. Lora was sure of that.

Just as sure as she was of the fact that Eyden had kept her in the dark on purpose. He'd never told her, never used his power in front of her until his sister's life was in danger.

"Lora." It was Jaspen's voice that drew her eyes away from the now empty spot. "Take them out!" The remaining fae were overpowering him. Jaspen slashed out with his blade then ran in her direction, towards the humans.

Lora focused her energy. She threw her fire outwards, but her intended target dodged it easily. She wasn't used to any of this. She couldn't pinpoint her flames. It was like wildfire was coming out of her, powerful but uncontrollable. She couldn't keep it in but couldn't focus it either.

An idea formed in her mind and she threw fire between the fae and herself as Jaspen passed her. One of them snickered as she missed. Yet she didn't.

Lora spread her arms, willing the fire to follow her command. A wall built, rising high and stretching out between the sand-coloured buildings. She felt it draining her, but she pushed on nevertheless. A shrill yell escaped her as she forced the fire to burn brighter, more intensely.

One of the fae jumped through the wall and screamed as the fire tore at him.

In the corner of her eye, she saw Jaspen reach the humans. The young man, now awake, was trying to lift the almost-unconscious woman. Jaspen rushed to her side and the two of them dragged the woman forward.

The young man's eyes met Lora's. "Go, I'll be right behind you," Lora said. With a nod, he turned to the alley closest to them. Lora's gaze travelled back to the flames, fixating on them. She had to hold on long enough for them to disappear. Just a little longer.

Her skin felt scorching hot, her veins carrying lava. She was getting lost in her flames. It was merely her and the fire now. Everything else faded away.

"Lora, we need to go." Was that Eyden's voice? No, he was gone. There was nothing but the endless smoke of her creation. Engulfing her. Trapping her in place.

"Fucking hell. *Lora,* come on." The voice drew closer. In her peripheral vision, a blurry Eyden stepped towards her. "We need to go now!"

But Lora couldn't move. She was locked in her own fire. Her hands were still outstretched, her feet rooted in place. She could feel her energy leaving her, yet stopping it seemed impossible. Would she keep the fire up until she burned herself out too?

There was nothing but fire and smoke, the soot coating her skin, the smoke filling her lungs. Lora couldn't shut it off any more than she could her brain. She was entranced, anchored into this moment. Was this the price for unleashing her fae side?

Eyden hissed as his fingers brushed her skin. His touch electrified her system, shocking her back to reality. Lora compelled her arms to drop, now feeling the source of her fire and snapping it shut, forcefully breaking the stream of power.

But she didn't anticipate the chain reaction. As her fire faded, her body shut down with it. She dimly realised her wall had ceased burning before her eyes glossed over and she fell into mist and smoke.

CHAPTER 50

AMIRA

The sound of a key turning in the door to Amira's antechamber startled her. Amira turned from her bright window and was greeted by Karwyn's fake smile. The grin briefly chased away her fears, replacing them with fury. She desired nothing more than to slam the door in his face. He looked her up and down, obviously displeased at her attempt to honour Sydna and Mylner's imminent death with a long black dress.

She'd had to dress herself this morning as Nalani was nowhere to be found. Maybe the guard at the door had prevented her from coming in. The alone time had given her the dreadful opportunity to think about all the horrible things that were bound to happen. She would either marry Karwyn, a tyrant in training, or the marriage would be called off and she'd have to go back to her brother, her long-time abuser. A frightening numbness spread through her. Was there any point left in hoping for a better life?

Karwyn extended his hand. "Come, we would not want to

miss the show, would we?" When she made no move, he grabbed her arm forcefully and pulled her out of the room.

On their way to the palace's gates, Karwyn leaned towards her and whispered in her ear, "I am truly sorry, but I have had to mention your little rebellion to your brother. He is coming to the portrait reveal in a couple of days. You do not deserve to attend, but I am sure he will find the time to come talk with you."

The threat made Amira's blood run cold. So he wasn't calling off the engagement, but he was still throwing her to the wolves.

"And I am sure you will be glad to know that your little attempt yesterday has added a new name to the executioner's list," Karwyn said with a cold smile.

Amira's eyes widened. Who was the other victim she had condemned to death? Rhay? No, Karwyn would never. *Me?*

"Who?" she finally asked in a shaky voice.

"The guard who was supposed to keep them in their cage. He failed at a very simple task and then had the audacity to pretend that he rang the alarm when I know for a fact that Layken did. He deserves to perish just for the lie."

Karwyn squeezed her shaking hand, anchoring her guilt deep inside her. Three fae were going to die because of her. Once again, instead of helping, she was the burning flame destroying everything in its path.

"Have you seen your maid recently?" Karwyn asked. His lips pulled into a sly grin as he caught her questioning gaze. "I would not hold my breath for her return. She has no interest in serving such an ungrateful brat."

Amira tensed up. Like Wryen, Karwyn was truly removing

everyone she cared about from her life. Or was Nalani relieved to be taken from her service?

During the rest of the walk, Karwyn remained silent. His grip on her arm was strong, but he didn't bother trying to read her thoughts. After all, he could see all of them painted on her face.

Karwyn dragged her to the open front door. Amira let herself be handled like a capricious child. At the bottom of the stairs, a wooden platform had been built. A chill ran down her spine when she caught sight of the executioner with his shiny almandine sword.

Grandstands had been put up in front of the platform and most of them were already filled with an excited crowd. Amira recognised a few faces from the palace, but she noticed that a lot of the fae were just regular folks who had been drawn in by the prospect of seeing blood. The absence of war had given people a taste for violence. It was like they were longing for it, Amira could see it on their faces. She had never understood how the fae still had an appetite for bloodshed after the war against the Dark King.

The closer she came to the platform, the stranger she felt. Her whole body was pulsating with dread and she wasn't even aware of what was happening around her. She could see herself walking but it didn't feel like she was moving. Everything turned dark and she squeezed her eyes shut.

When she opened them again, she was sitting next to Karwyn in the centre of the main grandstand. She looked around but couldn't see Rhay anywhere. Even if Karwyn's face showed no emotion, Amira knew that he must be upset by his absence.

Karwyn stood up and nodded at a guard. Sydna, Mylner, and

the young guard were brought onto the platform, gagged and bound. No chance to escape, no chance to scream. Amira could see Sydna's desperate eyes looking for her in the crowd. She wanted to avoid them, but her head wouldn't move away, as if she was looking for punishment in her once trustful eyes.

People were shouting insults at the three fae. Amira hummed to fill her head with a buzzing sound instead of the angry voices surrounding her. Her body turned cold and pain shot through her body so intensely, she had to dig her fingernails into her palm to stop herself from screaming.

She saw herself six years ago, strands coming out of her perfect bun, trapped on a balcony overlooking another execution. She couldn't do anything, couldn't even move. She had tried to catch the victim's eyes. Amira had pleaded in her head for the crowd to move so that *she* could see Amira right before being executed, burned alive at Wryen's hand. But Amira had been too far up.

For anyone close by she would have looked like a calm bystander. No one could have seen that Amira's hands had been tied behind her back, no one but the person standing next to her. But he was the one who had tied the ropes. With a grin Amira would never be able to erase, Wryen had sent a spark from the balcony to the waiting pyre, setting it on fire, and her life with it.

Four screams echoed through her head, the present and the past blending together. Amira felt a warm breath on her cheek. "It's all your fault," whispered a man's voice. *It's all my fault,* she repeated in her head as her heart broke into a million pieces.

She watched in horror as the almandine blade plunged into

the hearts of Sydna, Mylner, and the guard, one after the other going limp, the light in their eyes smothered by death.

A memory of green eyes flashed in her head. So full life until that fateful day. The fire had taken it all. It had clawed at Amira's mind, making her feel utterly alone and trapped as she watched until only ashes remained.

The crowd cheered, forcing Amira back to the present. The bodies of Sydna, Mylner, and the guard lay perfectly still on the platform. A silent cry left Amira's throat. Her own body felt lifeless in that instant. All the smiles around her looked crooked and menacing. Her instinct told her to run. They had died because of *her*.

Amira stood up with no feeling in her legs, ignoring the annoyed look coming from Karwyn and moving away before he could send guards to escort her back. Fae were wanting his attention, trapping him in some conversation. She hoped it was the kind of meaningless chatter he hated.

As if she was sleepwalking, she climbed down the grandstand fast, avoiding the groups of fae talking enthusiastically about the execution.

As she came down, she noticed that four guards were taking the bodies of Mylner and Sydna and dragging them up towards the palace. She would have expected the corpses to be burned quickly after their death so that their souls would be able to reach Caelo. A new wave of uneasiness took over her mind. What were they going to do with the bodies?

Amira couldn't forget Sydna's eyes searching for hers in the crowd. She owed it to her that her soul would at least take to the sky.

CHAPTER 51

LORA

Something stung Lora's arm, bringing her back to consciousness in a disoriented flash. Her eyes focused on an unfamiliar face and she immediately tried to sit up, hissing as her body protested.

"Easy there," the young man said. He was one of the prisoners they'd rescued. His eye was still swollen but his hands were free. Ashes were mixed in his short dark hair.

Lora turned around, her eyes settling on Elyssa and Jaspen tending to the human woman who was crying out in pain.

They weren't out in the open anymore. No longer at the market, at their battlefield. The stone structure around her seemed familiar. Was it the same cave they'd been in before?

A flash of pain drew her attention to her stomach. Her now ash grey, bloody shirt was ripped and revealed a gruesome wound that was covered by some kind of paste. Her face felt badly bruised. The stab wound on her arm either hadn't closed yet or had reopened, slowly dripping blood.

But beneath all that, she felt strange for an entirely different reason. She felt drained, but at the same time wired. There was power coursing beneath her skin, faint but unmistakable. Her hand flew to her neck. Where she'd usually find her pendant, there was nothing now. Nothing but dried blood and dirt.

She had really done it. Removing her almandine necklace had been unimaginable. She'd held onto it practically her whole life, holding onto her humanity while she disregarded her fae side in every way possible. She'd buried her powers so deep that having them felt like a distant memory—a nightmare she never wanted to experience again. She hadn't even allowed herself to think about them, erasing any treacherous thoughts as soon as they sneaked up on her.

Who was she now? What would her family say? Would her mum be able to look beyond her disappointment?

She wondered what Eyden thought of her now. Did he suspect the truth behind their deal? Did their lies cancel each other out? Lora's eyes searched the cave. She needed to talk to him, but there was no sign of him.

"Where's Eyden?" she asked. Her voice was like gravel.

"I think he went to get more water from the stream," the man at her side answered. Lora noticed he held a scrap of cloth that had turned bright red. He had been cleaning her wounds.

The woman cried out again, sobbing uncontrollably. They both turned their heads in her direction. "She woke up to find out her boyfriend's dead," the man said, grief twisting his features.

Lora met his dark eyes. "You mean the man who burned?" She'd wanted to save him. Her hesitation had gotten him killed. "I...I couldn't save him."

His eyes were kind and loaded with sadness. "You did what you could. We wouldn't have escaped with our lives if it wasn't for your fire."

"I'd be dead too if you hadn't intervened," Lora said.

He smiled softly, as if trying to wash the tragedy away. "I'm Farren, by the way. We haven't been formally introduced."

Farren. The witch. She had guessed as much. "How did I get here, Farren?"

"We ran when you told us to. I wanted to turn back but Jaspen insisted we keep moving. When we showed up at the cave, you and Eyden were already there. So was Elyssa."

He'd brought her here? A memory resurfaced. Eyden calling out her name in a web of smoke and fire. Her eyes slid to her hands. They were coated in blood. The red reminded her of fire before the image of burned flesh took precedence. Whose blood was staining her hands? Whose death was she responsible for?

"How many did I kill?" The question wasn't much more than a shaky whisper.

"I'm not sure. It'll depend on how fast they can get to a healer. But even then, the recovery would be slow and painful. You probably took out some of them."

Lora grabbed the piece of cloth from Farren's palm. She scrubbed at the reminder covering her hands. She didn't want to see it. Didn't want to take it all in. She thought burning herself out was the price, but it was this feeling right now that was the real price.

Farren's dark-skinned hand covered hers. "I don't like the violence of it either. But remember, it was self-defence. We would all be dead without you."

Lora's hand stilled. Most of the blood had washed off, but some lingered under her fingernails. It would always linger, wouldn't it? The back of her hand burned where she had roughly scrubbed over a wound. Fresh blood appeared. At least it was her own.

"I feel like someone drained all my energy." She didn't feel like herself anymore. That's what she really wanted to say but couldn't.

"I know the feeling. If they hadn't taken my blood, starved, and beaten me, I could have used my magic to help. I'm not a fighter. Sleeping spells are my specialty, actually."

"How does it work? Your magic?" She'd heard the basics before, but any distraction was welcome.

"It's not as different from the fae as they like to think. The fae see us as rare—well, *unnatural* would be a better description. But witches are just born with a different disposition. Instead of having one or in rare instances two specific powers, we draw on and manipulate energy around us. We can pull from our own too, but that's always risky. Witches often don't even realise their power until something triggers it."

She'd heard similar definitions before. In books, witchcraft was often described as cursed by the fae. But in the end, wasn't it all the same? Some witches even looked like fae. Depending on their eye colour, they could blend in well, much like she could as a half-fae. Lora looked up into Farren's dark brown eyes. She would've assumed he was human if she didn't know better.

"What triggered yours?" Lora asked.

Farren glanced towards Elyssa. "My parents died in front of my eyes when I was fourteen. It unleashed something inside me, but I couldn't save them or anyone else at the camp. I didn't know how to channel my powers properly."

"I'm really sorry." Lora met his saddened eyes. She wondered if there had been other witches at the human camp. Farren had to have had a witch in his bloodline to pass down the witch gene. "Can I ask, were your parents witches too?"

"My parents were both human. Well, my adoptive parents. They found me in the streets when I was a few weeks old and took me in. They assumed I was human. It was probably for the best that my parents didn't know. I think they would've taken me in either way, but they would have worried even more. Witches are hunted even more so than humans. The fae see us as this big threat. They will never let us live in peace."

If humans could accept witches, why couldn't they accept certain fae? It was as hypocritical as fae looking down on witches but still using them for their power, enslaving them with life contracts—if they didn't outright kill them.

"I don't see why the fae think they're so different," Lora said.

"You say that like you're not one of them," Farren said curiously.

"I..." She caught sight of Eyden instinctively as he re-entered the cave. He was carrying a bucket and dropping it off next to Elyssa, whispering something she couldn't make out. His shirt had holes and was drenched in blood where the sword had cut through flesh. His hand moved to cover his chest as he seemed to catch his breath.

Eyden's gaze met hers when he looked up. She tried to read him, but there was a wall of ice veiling his eyes.

And just like that he dropped his hand and walked out.

Lora started to rise even as her body hated her for it.

"I don't think you should get up yet," Farren said.

Lora didn't listen. Her legs felt unsteady, but she managed to get up. "For what it's worth, I don't think we're all that different," Lora said, pausing long enough to meet the witch's gaze. Farren's smile was faint as he tilted his head, telling her to go.

She saw Eyden's shadowed figure in the distance as soon as she left the cave. "Eyden." He kept moving forward, but she caught the hesitation in his step. "Can you wait a second?" Lora realised she was panting, out of breath already. "*Please.*"

This time, Eyden did halt. He turned around but made no indication of moving. Lora walked forward on shaky legs. She stopped some distance away, taking him in, peering into those eyes that had turned stone cold. She could read the exhaustion in his expression. The dark circles under his eyes, the blood and grime sticking to his skin. She could guess the only reason he was still standing was his high power level quickening the healing process.

Lora opened her mouth to explain, to justify her lie, but Eyden spoke first. "You know what I've been wondering about ever since I met you? What is it exactly that makes you so fucking *special?* How come you found a way to cross, just in the nick of time, when so many before you have tried and failed?"

Special. The way he said it now was so different than the last time she'd heard the word leave his lips. Last time it was like wonder and honey, now it was disdain and poison. "You're clearly not human. Not completely," he continued.

He knew, then. Didn't he? There was no point in playing games anymore. She'd long decided the charade needed to end.

"I'm half-fae." She said it quietly, a whispered secret in enemy territory, in a world that wasn't her own yet somehow had always been.

Eyden's face remained blank, void of emotion even as his voice carried a million. "It's how you could cross, isn't it? You knew all along there was nothing you could give me."

All Lora could do was nod, her lips wouldn't move. His words hit her harder than all her physical wounds combined.

Finding her voice, she took a step towards him. "Eyden—"

But he was already turning away, taking any hope that her secret wouldn't ruin whatever had been building between them with him. It was all gone now.

Forever.

CHAPTER 52

AMIRA

At a reasonable distance, Amira followed the guards into the palace. They had no reason to be wary of her given that other fae from the court were also going back inside. No one seemed to care much about the two dead bodies. A few even made jokes about them.

The tricky part started when the guards moved away from the entrance and started taking small corridors. It would appear too suspicious for her to walk right behind them. Amira decided to wait at the start of the corridor while noting their general direction. There was a chance that she would lose their tracks, but she couldn't risk them suspecting anything.

Her plan worked at first, but the palace was a true maze and she lost all sight of them. A few doors lined the walls and Amira wondered if she should just open each one of them. She reached for the first one, but her mind was distracted by a strange pattern on the wood next to the third door. She went to it and leaned down for a closer look.

Blood. The viscous dark red matter was unmistakably blood. Standing up, she looked at the door more carefully. The wood was dark grey making it less discernible on the stone wall. Slowly, she pushed the door open. On the other side of it, a flight of stairs descended into darkness. She took a deep breath before starting her descent. The pungent smell of blood filled her nostrils. The bodies were probably very close. Completely in the dark, she followed the smell and the faint light at the end of the corridor.

Amira found an empty room at the end of the path. The dampened stone walls were left bare and no furniture filled the large empty space, just a dark alcove in one corner and nothing else. Thinking she had made a mistake, Amira was about to turn back when she heard a voice coming from behind the wall facing her. She moved closer and pressed her ear against the cold stone.

"Where should we put them?" said an almost boyish voice.

"Lay them on the table. His Majesty should be here soon." This voice, on the contrary, seemed older than the palace itself. Amira couldn't even decide if it was coming from a man or a woman. "You should leave now," continued the ancient voice.

Amira almost took the order for herself, but the sounds of swords clinking indicated that the voice was referring to the guards' presence. She heard them coming closer to the wall. Quickly, she tried to find a hiding spot. The decision was easy to make, given the emptiness of the room. Just before they opened the wall, she rushed to the alcove, hoping that the darkness would hide her away.

The stone on the back wall started moving and soon, a space large enough to fit a tall man appeared in front of Amira's amazed eyes. The four guards she had seen earlier came out of the hole and made their way back to the exit without even glancing in her direction. As soon as she heard their voices fading away, she rushed to the hole in the wall while trying to make the least amount of noise possible.

Peering through the opening, she realised that the room it was leading to was split in two parts, separated by a heavy dark blue curtain. Hearing the stones beginning to move around her, she made her choice. She snuck into the new room. There, she found that the walls curled into two symmetrical alcoves right next to the curtain. She went there to hide. From her spot, she could move the curtain just enough to see what was happening on the other side of the room.

What she saw made her stomach turn. Illuminated by torches hanging on the wall, a large stone table was the first thing she noticed. The two bodies had been laid there and a woman was busy undressing them while muttering to herself. Amira noticed that the woman was limping around the table. She had her back turned to Amira, hiding her face. All that was visible was her grey hair curled into a flat, low bun.

Amira took note of the numerous shelves on the walls stocked with strange-looking jars and pots filled to the brim with what appeared to be magical ingredients.

Next to the two bodies, multiple sharp instruments were arranged on a small table. To Amira, they looked like torture instruments. She hoped she was mistaken. But the most dreadful part of the room was the floor, soaked in so much blood that it had turned the stones a deep burgundy. The weathered aspect showed that someone had tried very hard to clean the blood, but it had infiltrated every little crevasse of the stones.

Amira closed her eyes, trying to avoid the dark spectacle of the red floor. She opened them immediately when she heard the stone wall opening again. Hiding in her corner, she saw Karwyn and Saydren, the royal healer, open the curtain and enter on the other side of the room.

The woman had finished undressing the two fae and she turned around to face Karwyn. Just before she plunged into a deep bow, Amira had time to see her face. Her dark brown skin was marked by fatigue and sadness and her almost black eyes indicated that she was not fae. Her eyes lacked the vibrant, glowing light of the fae. She raised her head again and Amira saw her hollow cheeks and fragile neck. She didn't appear that old, just completely drained.

Yet she smiled at Karwyn with forced joy. "The spell worked as usual, Your Majesty. They still have their magic," she said.

"Good. You know how angry I would have been otherwise," Karwyn replied.

Amira could see the woman shiver as a shadow passed over her eyes. She had to be Karwyn's personal witch.

She took a step back to let Karwyn and Saydren approach the corpses. Karwyn walked around them, deep in his thoughts, while Saydren and the witch remained silent.

Karwyn pointed at Mylner. "Toss this one aside. He is merely a level one, useless."

"Should I dump him with the others?" Saydren asked.

"I do not care. Get rid of him however you wish. Bury him for all I care."

Amira stopped herself from gasping. Karwyn knew very well that a buried fae would never find peace in the sky.

The bodies needed to be burned and the ashes turned to the wind in order for them to reach Caelo in the sky, otherwise their souls were going to be trapped here forever. They would be cursed to forever haunt Liraen, waiting for salvation that would never come. Burying the bodies meant Karwyn would further punish them even in death, forcing them to never move on. Even if she wasn't the most religious, Amira still believed in heaven. It was the worst possible fate to be denied entrance.

Amira could sense Karwyn's agitation. A veil of sweat highlighted his tense forehead and his eyes kept looking away from the bodies. She stared in horror as Saydren grabbed Mylner's corpse and swung it across his shoulder, showing a surprising strength for his frame. Without saying a word, he walked away with the body, leaving Karwyn alone with the witch. The king stared at the woman, who expectantly looked back at him.

"Well, Cirny, do not just stand there," Karwyn said. "Get to work."

"Of course, my king. Right away." There was no sarcasm in the woman's tone, only a painstakingly obvious desire to please.

She ran to the shelves to grab a few weird-looking jars and took out their contents right next to Sydna's exposed corpse, revealing a dark red crystal and some herbs. Cirny waved her hands above the three elements, her eyes fluttered closed in concentration.

Amira had never seen a real witch at work, but her brother had told her many tales about these cursed beings. He revelled in relating the most gruesome details and Amira had spent a lot of sleepless nights as a child thinking back on the twisted stories. When she saw Cirny's eyes turn even darker, she couldn't help but feel sick. Her insides turned upside down and she fought back a scream. This truly looked like the work of a cursed being.

Amira understood why some fae, upon learning that they had some witch ancestry, decided to never have children in fear of passing on the curse even if it had jumped their own generation. Who would wish to bring more cursed beings into this world? She was actually glad Wryen had always insisted on not keeping any witches in Amryne's palace. Unlike Karwyn, he didn't rely on witches and cursed spells to do his bidding.

Next, Cirny took a large jar and a long knife and carved open Sydna's body. As if she was still alive, the dead fae's blood spurted out of the wound, splashing Cirny's face and Karwyn's outfit.

Amira felt her own blood rush from her face. Her vision swam and her cheeks tingled. *By Caelo...* The smell of it was bad enough, but she couldn't stand the sight of blood. She was going to faint. She braced herself against the wall.

"Be careful, you halfwit," Karwyn said as he wiped at the blood on his jacket.

"I am deeply sorry, my king." Cirny pressed the jar she was holding next to the cut and let the blood fill it. Amira's stomach started to turn as the metallic smell of blood in the air increased. She repressed a few gags, but it was too much. If she stayed here any longer, it would be the end of her. She would pass out and someone would surely discover her then.

Carefully, she put the curtain back in place and snuck back to the stone wall. She had to act fast. Saydren could come back any moment. Her hand searched for a switch, but she couldn't find any strange asperities in the wall.

For a second, she panicked. What if the wall was spelled and she needed a password to open it? But then her finger came in contact with a smooth stone and the wall opened in front of her. The noise of the mechanism echoed in her ears.

"Saydren? Is that you?" Karwyn called out.

She ran out of the room and almost twisted her ankle on the way out. Her mind kept going back to what she had witnessed as she made her way out of the underground. What was Karwyn doing with fae's blood?

Amira ran all the way back to her room, barely controlling her erratic breathing. In her haste, she bumped into someone walking in the opposite direction. She was almost back to her room. Just a few more steps—

"You in a rush?" the fae she ran into said with a teasing tone.

It took her a few seconds to recognise him. Thyl's sleek black hair was pushed away from his face, revealing his dark emerald eyes. He had the same cheeky smile as the night she had met him.

"I'm sorry." Amira's eyes searched for her bedroom door. She was so close. She took a step forward but Thyl moved in front of her, blocking her way to the door.

"Wait, I might have something to help you." Reaching into his pocket, he took out the same shiny silver and red pill. "Here. It will take your mind off things."

"I don't want it," said Amira, remembering Tarnan's words.

He grabbed her hand and placed the pill in her palm. "I really think you should take it. Who knows, you might need it someday," he said as his eyes searched hers. And before she could reply, he disappeared around the corner.

Back in her room, Amira looked at the tiny pill, wondering what it would feel like to just swallow it. She had never taken any sort of drugs. Hell, she hadn't even known about fortae until a few days ago. Would it be so wrong to feel good, worry-free for only a moment?

She closed her eyes, imagining an hour of pure bliss where nothing could touch her. Where she could forget about all the pain in her life, all the pain she had caused and witnessed.

Tarnan's voice growled at her ear, "You're better than that, Amira."

She didn't want to disappoint him. And she couldn't let herself forget what she had just witnessed in the underground.

Karwyn's behavior reminded her of the Dark King. Using fae blood could mean his witch was playing with dark magic. Everyone knew where that path led. To destruction. The Dark King had paid a high price for his involvement with dark magic. It had twisted his very being, made him dependent on feeding on other fae's life sources.

Amira didn't know Karwyn's intention, but she was sure it wasn't good.

If she told the foreign advisors, they could discredit him as a viable option for the contest. That would mean that the blood contract between Karwyn and her would be terminated. It wouldn't free her of her brother, but it might very well be her way out of this particular nightmare.

CHAPTER 53

LORA

The journey back to camp was less than pleasant. They didn't dare stop for too long, but none of them could walk very far with their injuries. They took multiple breaks that lasted for short stretches of time, and even at night they never rested for long. Whenever they stopped, Lora would pass out from exhaustion until it was time to make it through another brutal section of the desert of Rubien. When she was awake, her mind raced restlessly, fearing someone had followed them even though they had no indication of being trailed.

Lora was still highly aware of her injuries. Every step she took felt exhausting. The wound in her stomach pulsated if she only slightly moved the wrong way. At least her head wasn't screaming in pain. She assumed it was her fae side healing the concussion she must have gotten. The wound on her stomach took the longest to heal.

But she didn't have it as bad as the human woman, who was still in critical condition. They carried her on an improvised stretcher. They didn't have the tools or enough healing items to fix her up completely right then and there. Fae healing items worked much better on fae. Farren had stitched the woman up as well as he could at the cave, but he needed to take a closer look at home and make sure the wound didn't get infected.

Home. If everything went right for once, Lora would be home in a matter of days. She didn't think she could count on Eyden's help anymore, but she'd figure it out. She didn't survive all this to give up now.

She had glanced at her phone during one of their breaks. Her family had been worried by her radio silence the past days. But it was her brother's private message that had twisted her heart.

"Mum doesn't want me to tell you, but she's getting worse fast. If you can't get a cure, please come home. I need you here. We all do," he had written this morning. The words became blurry on the screen as a sinking feeling turned her insides.

She tried to catch Eyden's eye, but he avoided her gaze at every turn and kept as far away as possible, talking to Elyssa and Farren most of the time without uttering a single syllable to Lora. She had tried to get to him, but refrained from talking to him in front of the others. Elyssa might already know what Lora's awakened powers meant, but the others would assume Lora was fae. They wouldn't guess she was half-fae, not knowing she'd crossed over from Earth, and she'd rather keep it that way.

Even if he chose to avoid her forever, did it really matter in the end? Maybe she'd put too much thought into their relationship. Maybe it was nothing at all. After all, they had both lied. They had both been holding back. It seemed like that would never change. They had known each other for just over a week.

It had been stupid to explore a meaningless crush when she had known from the beginning that she would be gone soon. That she wouldn't—*shouldn't*—ever return.

Her gut twisted as she thought about how she'd been led astray from her mission. No more distractions. She'd find her way home tomorrow no matter the cost.

They were nearing the camp now, making their way through the woods. It was starting to get dark again. Lora felt the fatigue deep in her bones even as a shimmer of power seemed to continuously simmer under her skin, making her jittery. It felt like she was a bomb recharging, waiting to go off again. The thought sent shivers through to her very soul.

Lora had wondered why Eyden wasn't using his teleporting powers now that it was out in the open. But she noticed he put his hand on his chest several times, covering his wound. He wasn't invincible either. Eyden, much like everyone else, was walking at a slow, tired pace.

From the few pieces of conversation Lora had overheard, Elyssa was less than thrilled about Eyden's actions during the fight, mainly removing Elyssa from the situation entirely. She hadn't started a fight—not yet, at least. Lora hadn't failed to take notice of the restrained rage in Elyssa's eyes.

Elyssa had been quiet in Lora's presence as well, only talking to her about injuries or her tracker. She could tell the other girl wanted to say more but decided to stay silent. At the very least, Elyssa and Farren didn't give her the same look Jaspen gave her anytime their eyes met. The suspicion made Lora's skin crawl. He must regret letting Lora into their camp so easily after seeing her fae powers. Even though he'd asked for her help during the fight.

Thankfully, Jaspen didn't utter any objections when the group, including Eyden and Lora, entered the rebel camp. The spell had held, everyone was safe and running towards them as soon as they broke through the trees. There were cheers and howls of sorrow. Chaotic reunions.

Lora found herself on the outskirts, lost. Her eyes searched for Eyden unwillingly. He was walking back into the woods, disappearing into the night as he'd done many times before. She took a step in his direction. Even if there was no point in an impossible reconciliation, she needed to have at least one final conversation. Not only to discuss the cure.

A hand touched her arm and Lora froze. She turned to find Elyssa looking at her.

"You should let him go. I'm sure he'll be back by morning."

Back for his sister, not for her. Would he even stop by before she left to find Saydren? Would she have to ask Ilario to take her back to the market instead?

Elyssa's face was free of spite, yet Lora couldn't help but wonder. "Do you hate me too?" she asked, the question spilling out of her before she could stop herself.

Elyssa sighed. "Hate? No. Am I thrilled you kept a secret that could've been pretty goddamn useful to know? Again, no. But you did come through in the end. There would've been more death if it wasn't for you, so I can't be too mad. And if you're worried about your mission, don't be. I'll still help you get to Saydren. I won't abandon you now. It's not my style."

The ache in Lora's chest healed a fraction. She hadn't known how much she needed to hear that, to know there was still someone in her corner. But did Elyssa know everything?

Even though she hated the thought of further risking their friendship, Lora knew she wanted her friend to make up her mind with all the facts laid out in front of them. "You know what this means, right? About crossing the border?" Lora asked, biting her lip.

A tired smile grazed Elyssa's lips. "I never wanted to cross anyway. I belong here. More so than you in some ways, I think." Lora wasn't sure if that was meant to be a compliment or an insult. Maybe it was neither. It was just the truth. "I'm only disappointed you didn't have more faith in Eyden and me. I mean, come on. I know it was never strictly business with you two. I'm not blind. I knew from the moment Eyden told me about you on Falea Night that there was something there. You two are too goddamn stubborn to trust each other. But after I told you everything he did to get you back, I thought..." She shook her head, her gaze darting around the camp. "Never mind. It doesn't matter now. What's done is done."

Lora tried to wrap her mind around Elyssa's words. Falea Night. Eyden had talked to his sister that night. About *her*. He must have teleported away in the woods. Her heart squeezed, but she instantly shut down the feeling and refocused her anger.

"Eyden has barely talked to me since, so I guess I was right to have my doubts." Her tone came out more bitter than she intended. "I am sorry, though. It might not mean much now, but I do wish things had gone differently."

Elyssa met her eyes, taking them in with curiosity. "How did you do it? How did you hide it so well?"

Lora's gaze shifted around them. There was no one within hearing distance anymore, but she moved closer to Elyssa nonetheless as she lowered her voice. "My necklace. I was wearing almandine." Elyssa's eyes travelled to her collarbone. "I don't have it anymore." Her hand instinctively went to the bare spot. It felt like a part of her was gone. Part of her humanity had broken off with the physical trinket she'd loved wearing.

If you carried something with you for such a long time, would it not become a part of you in some way? The necklace was more than a power dampener. It had been a gift from her mother and a reminder of home. The image of her mum almost brought tears to her eyes.

"You were wearing almandine every day? For how long?" Elyssa asked.

"16 years, more or less."

Elyssa's shocked expression made Lora feel uneasy. "That's nuts. No wonder your fire was that intense. It'd been building up for such a long time. I'm surprised not using your power didn't drive you absolutely batshit crazy. I guess your...kind is not quite the same as most fae."

"I wouldn't know." There wasn't much she could find out through her research. Half-fae were impossible according to every history book, every article. Clearly, that was incorrect.

"I wonder how you survived when, as far as we know, there's no one else like you—alive, at least. You're a mystery, Lora."

A mystery. Yes, in some way she was, even to herself. "I don't mean to be. Not anymore." Lora wished she had all the answers, but she suspected she'd never get them.

A scream pierced the night air. Lora tensed out of reflex, scanning the camp. There was no movement. The cry came from one of the tents. Were they treating the wounded woman?

"Was that a scream?" Elyssa's face was anxious, pained as if she was the one hurt. When Lora nodded, Elyssa continued on, "I should go help, but I do wanna talk more. Tomorrow. Once we both got some sleep, okay?"

"What about Saydren? I was texting my brother earlier...my mum's condition is critical. I need to go home tomorrow no matter what."

"I'm sorry. For what it's worth, I think you and Eyden are all set for tomorrow. He stored some silver in my room." At Lora's questioning expression, Elyssa added, "Real silver. He'll know the way to River's Point. Saydren will be the nicely dressed man with short black hair. He's usually there doing all kinds of business in the late afternoon or evenings."

Why Elyssa assumed Eyden would still go with Lora was beyond her. Lora could probably find her own way to River's Point. She'd been there before and she was now more familiar with the map of Liraen on her phone. Most importantly, no one would question her now that she had fire at her disposal, would they? Lora might have no idea how to control her powers, but if need be, she'd simply have to figure it out.

She could pull this off on her own. She *would*.

"Thanks," Lora said, trying to sound untroubled.

Elyssa stepped closer, putting an arm on her shoulder. "Even if Saydren needs a bit of time to mix a cure, you will go home tomorrow. We can get it to you once it's done. *I'll* make damn sure of it."

Lora was out of words. She didn't feel like she deserved Elyssa's kindness, but she was grateful nonetheless.

"Now go get some rest, okay?" Elyssa said, dropping her arm.

"No offense again, but you look worse than the last time you were beaten up."

Lora smiled. The movement still hurt a bit. Half of her face felt bruised.

"There's a med kit by the showers. If you need anything else, come find me. I'll be with Farren and the others."

Another scream pulled Lora's focus away and Elyssa's gaze followed.

They all wore scars from that fight. Lora could still feel her own. Some were invisible but etched deeply in her soul.

The eyes staring back at Lora didn't look like her own. They didn't look natural, *human*. It was as if there was a storm brewing behind them, making them more vibrant, untamed. The blue-green had turned a vivid shade of turquoise.

Did everyone notice? Would she be unable to hide her fae side from now on?

The shimmer of power brightening her eyes in her reflection was unmistakable. Lora didn't know how to dim it. As much as she tried, every time she forcefully shut her eyes, she reopened them only to find the same telling shade reflected back at her in the bathroom mirror.

Eyden could dampen it. His eyes looked fae, but she'd never seen his true level of power staring back at her.

Standing there, blood and dirt washed away, Lora took note of her injuries. Her nose had healed but there was a faint bruise on her left cheek and a cut that hadn't quite healed yet. Her face appeared dull. Her usually tan skin was washed out by exhaustion.

The slash on her arm had closed but was still faintly visible. The most gruesome was the stab wound on her stomach. It had closed but was still an angry shade of red. Lora had cleaned it again the best she could and added a bandage, not wanting to see the reminder of Kelvion's attack. Kelvion, who was now dead. He had deserved it, but that fact alone didn't erase the guilt of being the one responsible.

Lora gripped the counter of the makeshift sink that she had filled with a bucket of fresh water. All of this, her injuries and scars—physical and mental—in some way had all been for Eyden. To return the favour, to fight with these people that deserved more than what life had treated them with. Most were grateful, she knew that.

But the person she cared most about in this not-so-foreign world wouldn't even talk to her. She'd thought they'd broken through a barrier, built a bridge of understanding and shared empathy. Yet he didn't understand now. He wouldn't even let her explain herself even though he'd carried his own lies.

And as much as she'd liked to avoid the thought, Lora needed him now. Her parents' lives were hanging in the balance more than ever and the one person she wanted to confide in was avoiding her. It was a cruel world. Just when she thought she'd made a connection, built the outline of trust, it was all torn down, leaving her in shambles.

Lora's skin felt on fire, her body overheating as the anger and despair filled her to the brim. She dunked her hands in the cold water and a hissing sound startled her. The water was boiling under her touch. Lora quickly pulled her hands back as the water steamed from the heat of her.

Was that another price she had to pay? Her fae side was untrained, unpredictable. Lora was way over her head.

She remembered the first and only other time the fire had overwhelmed her. She had barely been eight years old. Her parents had been arguing; she couldn't remember the reason. All she could picture was her own tears and her small voice trying to break up the argument. The two of them had been too engrossed in their fight to stop and acknowledge Lora's presence.

Finally, she had screamed and stomped her foot, demanding their attention. They had paused then, but not to look at her. No, they had been staring at the fire stretching across the living room. Her dad had frantically tried to put it out while her mum had screamed at her to stay back before running off to make sure her baby brother was safe.

Although her mum had told her she wasn't mad at her, Lora would never forget the look of fear and panic in her dark eyes. It haunted her to this day. The necklace hadn't just saved her from accidentally starting another fire, it had saved her relationship with her mother.

An angry tear ran down Lora's cheek, over the bruised skin. She wiped it off and forced her mind to clear. Once she was home, she'd get another almandine necklace. Her mum never had to know she'd let the fire out. Her fae side would be a secret again and she'd lock away every single painful moment she'd experienced in Liraen as if it never existed.

Lora's head felt heavy as she made her way back to her tent. She was craving a good night's sleep. She needed to rest for the mission still looming before her.

But every thought of tomorrow's struggles left her when she spotted Eyden at her door, pulling the fabric back into place. He had changed too. No one would be able to tell he had been in a gruesome fight or had been walking through the desert for over a day. But Lora could see it in the shadows underneath his eyes.

As he turned to walk away, their eyes met. Neither of them spoke. The silence was unbearable. An eternity passed in a few seconds.

Eyden shifted on his feet as he dropped his hand and the fabric of the door with it. "I thought Elyssa might be here." His voice was all business, no hint of what was brewing beneath his concealment.

"She's probably with Farren," Lora replied, uncertain of how to act now. She hadn't expected to find him here tonight.

Eyden was still holding her gaze. It was the longest he'd looked at her since their conversation outside the cave. Part of her wanted to take this opportunity to spill everything she needed to say before her chance ran out, but the words were stuck in her throat.

He turned his back on her, ready to leave her yet again. Just like that. As if she didn't matter anymore.

"You really won't even talk to me anymore?"

Eyden stopped, waited a few seconds, then turned back to her. His pale eyes were haunting. "Are there any more lies you'd like to tell? Let's hear them, then."

He disappeared inside her tent.

Lora steeled herself and followed quickly. She hadn't expected him to let her talk and she was glad not to have this confrontation out in the open.

Eyden stared at her as she entered, right down to her soul. "Here's your fucking chance."

Words flew through her head way too fast to grasp them properly. "I didn't lie. I told you I'd tell you how I crossed and I would've." She never said he'd be able to cross too. Lora could hear the hypocrisy and although she didn't say it, Eyden picked up on her unspoken words.

"How very *fae* of you." The comment stung and he knew it, looking pleased as hurt crossed her face.

"Coming from the fae who lied or withheld information more often than I did," she spat out.

Eyden ceased to rein in his anger. It showed in a storm of furious waves flashing behind his eyes. "Does my fae ability change our deal in any way?"

Lora remained silent, lips pressed in a tight line.

"No? I thought so. Any other pointless arguments you'd like to bring up now?" He pulled the vial of her mother's blood out of his pocket. "Here, take this. It's all you care about anyway."

Lora took the vial and set it on the surface closest to her. Although she was relieved to have it back in her possession, her thoughts lingered elsewhere.

She pushed her damp hair over her shoulder. Drops of water coated the top of her shirt. Lora didn't know if the cold setting into her bones was from her wet hair or the intensity of this conversation. Her voice became quiet. "You know why I didn't tell you right away. You would've never helped me."

He didn't deny it, dropping his gaze. When he looked up again, his eyes were strikingly vulnerable. "And later on? Did you think I'd leave you stranded after we kissed? After what happened in Rubien?"

His words startled her. Hearing him say it aloud somehow made it all the more real.

"I don't know, Eyden. I never know with you. I was planning on telling you, but the fear you'd walk away, disregard our deal—all promises, every *maybe*—was still there. Telling you the truth felt like a big risk and you can't blame me for feeling that way after you did just that. You walked away."

Now he was the one with the hurt look on his face. "Truths can be dangerous. They're always a risk. It's why I didn't tell you everything even though I wanted to. But I didn't keep anything to myself that directly affects you."

"But it *does* affect me. Keeping secrets...it gave me more than one reason to mistrust you."

"I told you about Elyssa. About all of this." He stretched out his arms, pointing to what lay outside her door. "Does that mean *nothing?*"

"That's just it. You never did, not really. I found out because you needed their help to save me. And I'm glad you did. But you never would've told me otherwise, would you? Be honest." She already knew the answer. She was waiting to see if he'd admit as much.

"I might have. If it had come up. It doesn't change the fact that I never did lie when it mattered. Some truths are better left unsaid. Some lies are ruin. They betray and burn everything down with them."

"Burn everything down." The laugh coming out of her was near the edge of insanity. "I know *all* about that now, don't I? You know, I never planned on unleashing my fae side."

"You would've died if you didn't. I tried to get to you, but I couldn't use my powers in time." Was that regret flashing behind the anger?

"I was saving my own life, yes. But I didn't decide to risk it until I saw *you* fall," Lora admitted.

Eyden was quiet. His eyes widened before he broke their staring match. Shifting his weight, he looked anywhere but at her. "Whatever the reason, it was necessary that you did. I know you dislike the fae, but you can't deny forever that you're one of us."

"I'm human too. That part of me will always win out." She had to hold on to that.

Startling eyes met hers again. "Of course," he replied, a bitter laugh chasing his words.

"What's so funny?"

"I've risked my life several times for you, Lora. I went along with your mission. I could've saved myself a lot of trouble if I never agreed to help you. Yet you still see all fae as less than human. You still put us all in one box. The only exception is *you*."

Did she? No, Eyden, even with all the secrets, defied the picture of the fae she'd painted all her life.

"That's not true," she whispered.

"Are you sure? Because I'm not convinced. Which is funny, because you know damn well I drew the short end of this deal. You're going to get exactly what you want because *I* don't break my promises. I'll get you that cure. But me? After every fucking risk I took, I won't get anything. What is it you said back at Halie's? I gave you hope and it's drowning you? How am I supposed to feel now? I might have walked away yesterday, but you're the one who's going to disappear in the end."

His words vibrated through her, making her shudder inwardly. He was not wrong.

Lora couldn't disagree, but at the same time, she couldn't help but argue nonetheless. "Then why did you agree if it's such a risk? You knew Elyssa would be impossible to convince to leave. It was already hopeless. Did it really have nothing to do with your trade business?"

She saw the moment Eyden lost the last of his restraint. His eyes darkened. He ran his fingers through his hair as he let out a curse, then another. "By Caelo, you really think that low of me, don't you? After all this time. Fuck it, I can never win with you."

"Why, then? What made you agree to help me?" She couldn't let up now. She was too far in it to give up on her argument as guilty as she felt for bringing it up.

"If you must know, I owed Marcel a favour."

Cryptic as usual. It wasn't enough of an answer. It never was. "*Why?*"

"It doesn't matter," he insisted.

"There it is again! The exact reason why I can never fully trust you," Lora shot back, raising her voice.

"It doesn't affect you! It doesn't change anything," Eyden yelled back.

It was infuriating. He was infuriating. The flames beneath her skin heightened. "For you! For me, it does. It fucking *matters.*" She took a step closer, not backing down from his riled-up eyes.

"Every single goddamn thing does, Eyden. I can never trust you if you can't trust me, if you shut me out again and again."

"I guess we're at a stalemate, then." Their eyes were locked. Heated anger travelled between them, a stream of emotions.

Lora tilted her head up, taking in his molten eyes. "We are."

"You'll leave tomorrow. For good."

"I definitely will." She would leave Liraen forever. Never see his face again. Never deal with his insufferable arguments.

"That's it, then," he said even as he took a step towards her.

Lora's feet moved forward without her command. She was close enough to feel the heat of his skin. Tingles ran up her arms.

"It was foolish to think we could ever find common ground," she said. They had nothing in common. Nothing but *lies*.

Eyden's eyes blazed. "Agreed."

"Brilliant. We finally agree on something." Lora's voice didn't sound like herself. Her throat felt tight. Eyden's gaze travelled down, lingering on her lips. She could taste him. The last time they'd kissed. Heat blossomed in the pit of her stomach.

He looked her up and down and she knew he was remembering the same thing. "There's nothing good between us," he said. His voice had turned husky and Lora's thoughts emptied as the fire inside her took over.

"Nothing but insanity," she breathed.

"Nothing but ruin." He said it like a dare.

Their eyes met again. The furious heat stretching between them had transformed into something else. This time, Lora welcomed the flames dancing on her skin, the lingering fire inside her begging her to get closer to him.

"Burn it all down," she whispered.

Their lips clashed together.

CHAPTER 54

◊
LORA

Lora didn't know who had moved first but somehow, they were kissing. If she thought their kiss in Rubien was all fire, she'd been wrong. This was.

Eyden's tongue was claiming hers, his lips almost bruising as if he was punishing her with a kiss. If this was the feeling of penalty, she'd go to hell willingly.

She felt it all the way to her toes. Fire shooting down her body, settling in interesting places. She clutched his shoulders, holding on to him. She wasn't ready to let him go just yet and he seemed to reciprocate the feeling.

His hand found her cheek, fingers softly dancing over her bruise before brushing a few tangled, dark blonde strands behind her ear. The same hand moved down her neck, fingers damp from the water that still clung to her hair. His cool fingers did nothing to weaken the fire in her veins.

Lora had no illusions about this. This wasn't a new beginning. It was a goodbye. They were no match. Coming from different worlds, both carrying a baggage of secrets, there was no hope left for them, only this stolen moment. They both knew it.

And if this was all they had left, why not give in to temptation? What did they have left to lose?

Her hands trailed down, tearing at the hem of his sweater. Eyden's hand followed her path, sensing her silent demand. He broke their kiss to pull the piece of clothing over his head. Lora let her gaze roam over the hard muscles of his stomach, rippling in the dim light as he moved to close the distance between them.

She raised her hand, placing it on his chest as her eyes settled on the wound a few inches from his heart. Her fingers halted underneath the swollen cut, no longer bleeding but far from healed. It could've been fatal.

Eyden's hands splayed over hers, dragging her gaze up to his again. "It's okay." His voice had lost part of the anger fuelling this moment.

She needed it back, needed to get lost in nothing but his searing touch.

"Good," she said, letting her hand slip further down, banishing everything but the desire in her blood. She roughly pulled him closer by the band of his trousers. Eyden followed all too eagerly. His hand tangled in her hair as the other burned through the fabric around her waist. Lora brushed her tongue against his parted mouth, turning the kiss feverish.

He walked backwards, gripping her hip and moving her with him. She followed him as if in a trance, her blood boiling. The back of his legs hit the bed frame and he pulled her with him as he lowered himself onto the mattress. Lora straddled him and his hand moved up, fidgeting with the hem of her shirt. Lora lifted her hands with no hesitation. Eyden didn't waste any time and the shirt landed somewhere out of sight.

Lora slipped her phone and WiFi cube out of the waistband of her trousers, putting them out of harm's way. When her eyes sought his again, Eyden's gaze was set on the bandage on her stomach. Setting a finger under his chin, she tilted his head back up at her.

"It's fine," she whispered against his mouth, hot breath mingling with his. She nipped at his bottom lip and sighed as he groaned against her skin.

His finger slipped under her bra strap, slowly sliding it over her shoulder, giving her every chance to stop it. Lora let her other strap fall, catching his provocative stare. Eyden's hand travelled from her shoulder to her back in search of the clasp. As his clever fingers found their goal, he searched her gaze before undoing it, sliding it off her arms completely.

He looked his fill, taking her in. The raw desire in his eyes burned her with torturous anticipation. His lips found her neck, teeth gently scraping against the sensitive skin. Lora's eyes fell shut as the flutter in her chest increased, moving lower, tightening. His mouth skated down as his hand trailed up, his thumb brushing against the skin beneath her breast.

Every touch burned hotter than whatever argument had brewed between them.

When his lips touched the swell of her breast, she glided forward, pressing down on the hardness of him. He let out a growl of approval as his tongue drew a circle around her nipple, teasing her senseless. She cried out as his thumb grazed her bare breast and his tongue swept over the other. Arching her back, she leaned into his touch. His movements were determined, torturing her in the best way.

She didn't know if the fire was in her or if she was the fire.

Eyden's lips found hers again, sucking on her lip as if he couldn't get enough either. His hands strayed over bare skin, leaving fireworks everywhere in its wake.

"You're hot," he mumbled against her mouth.

The comment made her chuckle. A snarky remark was on the tip of her tongue, but Eyden pulled back enough to meet her hooded gaze. "No—I mean, you're beautiful, especially beautiful —but your skin is hot to the touch. Feverish."

So it wasn't just her imagination. She was literally burning up, more so than ever. More than humanly possible. "Does it bother you?" she asked, voice husky, barely recognizable.

"Not if it doesn't bother you." The question was laced with subtext.

Lora tried not to overthink for once. Not now. Not when this would be the last time they'd be this close.

All her senses felt heightened, overwhelming but exhilarating. It was as if a fire had been lit in the dark, bringing the light she had unknowingly been missing all her life. The thought should scare her, but it didn't. The fire burning inside of her, unfamiliar yet not, was part of her, at least for this moment.

"It doesn't," she replied.

Her answer seemed to please him. A slow grin stretched his lips before they captured hers again. His hands tightened on her waist and in one fluid movement, she was on her back. Eyden leaned over her, soft lips brushing her collarbone before trailing a path down her chest, her stomach.

His head lifted, fingers playing with the button on her trousers. Lora lifted her hips in agreement. He removed them in a heartbeat. Eyden's hands travelled up her bare legs, sending sparks all through her.

She pushed against the band of his trousers, demanding them gone. Faster than she thought possible, the only thing separating them were thin scraps of underwear. As his weight settled over her, it didn't feel like a barrier at all. Yet she still craved more.

Hooking her legs around his waist, she pulled him closer. Heightened tension built between her legs as he moved against her, rolling his hips. His bare chest touched hers, like fire touching fire.

She nuzzled his neck, breathing in his scent. His hand moved from her hip to grasp her thigh and the friction between them increased, erasing everything but this very moment. It was as if the world shrank.

There was just him and her. Nothing but their frenzied moves and sighs of pleasure.

His scorching breath teased her neck then her ear. "I want to see all of you," he said, voice a low rumble.

Words were beyond her, but Lora found herself nodding. The weight between her legs lifted as he pulled back to go lower. Fingers slipping under her underwear as he dragged it down her bare legs. She wanted him to hurry but he took his time, his hands leaving a hot trail as the last piece of clothing left her.

Eyden kissed a path up to her inner thigh, his tongue burning her, getting so close to where she ached the most. But his head moved up, past that sensitive spot. Eyden's hand still branded her thigh as his lips claimed her mouth once more, parting her lips as his fingers inched closer, teasing the inside of her upper thigh.

"What do you want?" he asked, lips moving to her ear as he drew a circle on her skin.

Lora opened her eyes to heated, liquid blue. "What do you think?" she answered, breathless as his fingers hitched up.

"I think I can't know unless you spell it out."

The use of her own words made her heart flutter against her will. She should be frustrated, but a daring smile split across her face. "If you move up an inch, you'll find out pretty quickly."

Eyden's eyes widened a fraction. She opened her mouth to speak, but when his fingers brushed over that aching spot, her words became incoherent, drowned out by a cry of pleasure as her eyes squeezed shut. A satisfied groan vibrated on her skin as Eyden felt the evidence of how much she wanted this.

His hand pressed down on the bundle of nerves, moving up and down the centre of her. The moans leaving her lips were untamed, carefree, filling the room.

"I see what you mean now," Eyden said, chuckling against her neck. His tongue branded her while his hand became relentless.

A finger slipped in and her hips flew off the bed as she shamelessly moved against him. Lightning ran through her. Lora pulled his lips back to hers. Her tongue mixed with his before her teeth caught his mouth, tugging on his bottom lip. Eyden made a sound she was becoming all too familiar with.

He pulled back barely, his mouth a feather-light touch on hers as his hand stilled and then moved to her hip, much to her disappointment. Eyden caught her sigh of protest, laughing softly, his breath dancing over her lips.

He lifted up on his elbows. Mischievous eyes caught hers as he started sliding down her body. "I'm thinking, I should find out if you want this even more. Find out just how much I can make you scream." His tone was sinful, filthy, and she wanted to bottle it up to replay in her mind forever.

His head settled between her legs. The image would make her blush if she wasn't already completely set alight. At the first brush of his tongue, a breathless scream left her lips. Her hips bucked, only steadied by Eyden's hand. The hand around her thigh parted her legs as he dove deeper.

Her imagination hadn't done him justice. The way he worked her was better than her steamiest dream.

She threaded her fingers into his hair. The pulsating heat in her core tightened more and more. Her breaths became faster, her skin burned like the brightest explosion. Her free hand clutched the duvet under her. Every muscle became tense.

And then her body turned into liquid lava as the intensity overwhelmed her, reaching its peak as she came. She might have screamed his name, but it got lost in the feeling of pleasure spreading through her.

Moving up, Eyden fell on his back next to her, breathing fast. Her body felt boneless, spent. Lora turned her head, placing her hand on his chest. She thought about moving her hand lower, but Eyden's eyes drifted shut before Lora could do or say anything. Was there anything left to say? Anything that wouldn't break this peaceful illusion they'd created tonight?

For once, Lora wasn't plagued by thoughts of what tomorrow would bring. Blissful exhaustion took her mind as she lay beside him, listening to the gentle cadence of his breaths until she fell into a dreamless sleep.

CHAPTER 55

LORA

Sunlight bathed the tent in yellow light. It was the first thing Lora noticed when she opened her eyes. The second thing was Eyden lying next to her, one arm thrown over her midriff, their legs tangled together.

Lora moved his arm slowly off her as she detangled herself. Scooting back on the bed, she searched for her phone and found it on the floor next to her shirt. Peeking at a sleeping Eyden, she quietly got out of bed, picking up clothes as she hurriedly dressed herself.

She almost cursed out loud when she unlocked her phone and saw the time. It was already late afternoon. They'd slept half the day away. She must have needed the rest, but she shouldn't have been this careless. This was the day she'd return home.

Her gaze travelled to Eyden again. Daylight warmed his brown skin. The sheet hung low, revealing his bare back. Sleeping, he looked so peaceful, untroubled, so different from the furious version she'd seen yesterday. Or the teasing, wicked version she'd seen resurface later that night. She'd never see him like that again. He wasn't hers to have. He never had been.

Part of her wished she didn't have to see him again after what they'd shared. Whatever spoken goodbye they'd have later, it wouldn't compare to their goodbye from last night. But Eyden was her easiest way back to the market, to home. She needed him, but she wouldn't let him take any more risks than necessary.

His words still felt like a slap in her face. He *had* risked his life for her more than once and there was absolutely nothing in it for him. Lora had nothing left to give.

She would disappear, putting her focus on her world while Eyden would remain here, likely fighting more battles soon enough. This time, she'd take the risk alone.

With one final, lingering glance, she exited her tent. Her phone, the WiFi cube, and the vial of blood took their usual spots in her pocket. Lora had found another jacket in her wardrobe. She didn't have a knife, but last time she'd been the only weapon she needed. Lora hoped that even though she'd had no time to control her ability, if she was in danger, instinct would take over again. Once she was home, she wouldn't use her powers again, but she would do whatever was necessary to get home as fast as possible.

After a quick pit stop at the bathroom, Lora reached Elyssa's room. She knocked several times and even called out her name, but there was no sound of movement. Careful, Lora lifted the door a tiny sliver, peeking in to find the room empty.

As soon as she walked in, her eyes searched for the promised silver. It was the last thing she needed before she could go. She wanted to leave as soon as possible before Eyden woke up and went looking to pick another fight with her.

Lora twirled around as the flap of the tent lifted, the noise startling her. She found herself face to face with Elyssa.

Surprise flickered over the other girl's face, but then an easy grin relaxed her features. "You're up. I thought I'd have to start clanging pots together in front of your tent or something to get you two to wake up."

Her lip curved up in an apology. "Sorry, I—wait, did you say *you two?*"

Elyssa gave her a look as if Lora should know the answer already. "Eyden stayed with you, didn't he?" she said, nonchalant.

"Why would you think that?" Lora asked, trying to keep her voice even.

"It sure sounded like it last night when I went to check in on you." Auburn brows lifted, hazel eyes glinting teasingly.

Lora buried her face in her hands. "Oh, God."

Elyssa grinned, clearly enjoying watching Lora squirm. "Don't worry, Farren pulled me away before we even got that close to the tent. Said I'd be scarred forever if I went in."

Lora could feel her face heating. She hadn't even considered the fact that all that separated them from the outside were heavy scraps of fabric. Definitely not soundproof.

"Judging from your face, he was right. About freaking time." Elyssa bit back a laugh. "Don't sweat it. Trust me, it happens all the time. Thin walls never stopped nobody."

Lora was pretty sure it had, in fact, stopped some people. People with functioning brain cells.

She smoothed down her hair as her eyes fixed on anything

but Elyssa. "Let's drop it. Forever." Lora forced herself to meet the other girl's gaze. "I came to get the silver. I'm leaving now."

"Ah, of course." Elyssa squatted as she reached for a bag under her bed. She removed a small satchel and handed it over to Lora. "Here you go. You think it's safe for me to go meet Eyden with you?" Elyssa teased.

"Eyden's not coming."

The smile vanished from Elyssa's face. "What? That son of a bitch. I'll kick his ass—"

"I didn't ask him to go with me. He doesn't know and I'd like to keep it that way," Lora explained as she weighed the satchel in her hand. It wasn't heavy. It had to be mostly silver notes, which were worth more than coins.

"Why? Frankly, if you can avoid it, it's pretty fucking stupid to go alone." Her tone was light, yet Lora still took offence.

"Thanks for the vote of confidence," she muttered.

Elyssa quickly realised her mistake. She uncrossed her arms. "Look, it's not that I don't think you can do it. Obviously, if you had stayed behind and went while we were all in Rubien, you would've gone alone anyway. Still, *now* you don't have to do this alone. Eyden will keep his promise even if he's mad at you. And clearly he can't be *that* mad."

"He's already done enough. I wouldn't have gotten this far without him. But this, this I *can* do alone. I can find River's Point, I have payment, I look fae. I'll be fine. Depending on how the meeting goes, I might need both of your help again, so let's save it for when I can't avoid it. Worst case, Saydren won't help me on the spot. Either way, I'll be back here to be escorted back to the black market."

Elyssa's forehead creased as she considered her words. "All right. Then I'm coming with you."

"That's a bad idea." The last thing Lora needed was to put Eyden's sister in danger.

"It's a marvellous idea," Elyssa countered, nodding as loose curls escaped her messy ponytail. "This is great timing. Gives me an excuse to avoid Jaspen. I know he's itching to tell me off. I'm surprised he hasn't hunted me down yet." Elyssa sighed. "I'm so sick of his pointless alpha male monologues."

"You won't pass as fae," Lora reasoned. "And anyway, I know you can stand your ground against Jaspen. I've seen it."

A smirk appeared on Elyssa's face before she said, "I don't need to look fae. It'll be dark by the time we get out of the woods. I'll keep my face hidden and I won't enter the bar. I'll be the lookout while you do your thing. It's nothing I haven't done a million times before." Noting Lora's scepticism, Elyssa added, "Eyden wouldn't want you to go alone."

"I highly doubt he'd approve of you going with me either," she countered.

"It'll teach him a much-needed lesson," Elyssa said, grinning. Somehow, Lora found herself smiling as well. "It's settled, then." She pivoted and opened her closet, pulling out a bow and arrows. "This works better for stakeouts. And sadly, most of my throwing stars are lost in Rubien. RIP."

Lora took in her weapons. "A truly tragic loss."

"It's pretty damn hard getting your hands on almandine weapons. So in that regard, it is." Elyssa reached for a dark cloak, wrapping it around her, hood up. It reminded Lora of her first day in Liraen when she'd exited the market completely draped in black. Elyssa's cloak was similar, but much more worn out judging by the rips in the fabric. "I don't know how Eyden has managed to get as much as he did. No one really knows where almandine is being grown, but somehow small amounts find themselves at the black market, much to my joy. Best birthday present ever." Elyssa's teeth flashed as she gave her a vicious smile.

Weapons for birthday gifts. A strange concept, but so fitting when it came to Elyssa.

Lora stored the silver in her pocket, buttoning it up before she moved to the door.

Elyssa followed her lead, stepping forward.

Just as Lora was about to lift the flap, Elyssa's voice drew her attention back to her. "Before we go, I need to ask. Leaving Eyden behind, is it really to keep him safe, or are you punishing him?"

"Why would I punish him?" She hadn't expected the question and wasn't sure what prompted it.

"He did lie, didn't he? You can't be thrilled he never told you about his power," Elyssa reasoned.

Could there be another reason hidden behind her motive? A nagging feeling was clawing at her heart. Was this a selfless act or revenge? A mix of both? She wondered how Elyssa could read her better than she could read herself.

"I'm not sure," Lora admitted, conflicting thoughts racing in her mind. "I just know I need to do this by myself."

Elyssa's gaze softened. "I'm the first person to tell you that Eyden can be a tight-lipped fool, but he has his reasons. He always does. Sometimes they're more justifiable than others. But it's never to hurt the people he cares about. If someone saw his power and told even one guard, he'd be hunted. That's why he never drifts if anyone's even looking in his direction unless he absolutely has to. If anyone saw, they can't be left alive to tell the tale."

Lora sucked in a breath. "What if someone survived?" Farren had said they couldn't be sure who lived on to haunt them.

"Let's hope they all get crispy in hell. But even if they survived, I have a feeling they'd be hunting us down to kill us, not to rat us out to the guards."

"They do seem like the vengeful type."

"Aren't they all." She said it like a fact, not a question.

"The fae?" Lora asked. She had definitely met more than one fae who had murder written all over them. Her gaze connected with Elyssa's and Lora thought she caught a hint of sadness in those fierce hazel eyes.

"People. *Everyone*," Elyssa said before stepping past Lora and disappearing through the door.

CHAPTER 56

AMIRA

The execution was still playing through Amira's head two days later. On a loop, one scream after another echoed through her, each more desperate than the last. Day and night, a guard was standing in front of her door, preventing her from escaping her golden cage. She had spent her time stuck in her room trying to come up with ideas on how to talk with the royal advisors of the other kingdoms. She wasn't convinced the advisors of the Turosian court would go against Karwyn.

Asking Rhay was impossible; he had made his choice. She hadn't heard from him since their failed attempt at liberating the prisoners. Of course, she wasn't expecting him to waltz into her guarded room, yet she couldn't help the sour taste in her mouth when she thought back on the last time she had seen him, refusing to fight. Choosing to stand by once again.

Sending a letter was also out of the question; no one would allow her to contact the advisors. Maybe if Nalani hadn't left, she could have smuggled Amira's letter out of the palace. But the maid hadn't returned.

Her door opened and a guard walked in, carrying a tray with some food. Not just any guard, Amira noted.

"It's *you*," she said, the accusation in her voice clearly audible. Layken dropped the tray on her desk and turned back towards her door. "You have nothing to say now? Seems to me you had a lot to say a few days ago."

If it hadn't been for Layken, they could have escaped. Her plan could have worked. It was supposed to have worked.

"Seems to me, *princess*, I was the one who got knocked out that day, so you really shouldn't be accusing me of anything." Layken met her eyes and there was something in his gaze that made her feel unsettled.

Before she could swing another verbal attack at him, he stepped outside her room. It was just as well. She wanted to blame him but really, she only had herself to blame.

A few hours later, Amira's bedroom door swung open just as she considered finally taking a bite of the food. Annoyed at another reminder of her mistake, she turned around expecting Layken. Instead, her brother stood in the doorway. She'd feared his return, dreading what cruel punishments he had come up with.

"Hello, little sister. I just attended the portrait reveal and couldn't leave without saying goodbye. Such a shame you couldn't join us," he said with a devilish grin. "In all honesty, I think it's better you weren't there. I saw the painter overtly flirting with another girl. No decency. I wouldn't want you to get any ideas."

Amira curled up as Wryen sat on her bed. *Ideas.* Her idea right now would be to push Wryen out of her window, but she'd never succeed. She wanted to be as far away from him as possible, but the room felt like it had shrunk. Her body shivered, expecting Wryen's torment. How much did he know? What had Karwyn whispered into his ear?

"You know, I've heard you had a great bonding experience with Karwyn recently," Wryen continued.

She took the bait. "What are you talking about?"

He grabbed a strand of her hair and played with it. "The execution. You've always been so fond of them. Such a shame you haven't been to one in, what, six years? It was time." He stared right at her, his lilac eyes shimmering with sadistic pleasure.

"Yes, six years," Amira said, her low voice floating in the room like a haunted whisper.

With no warning, Wryen yanked at a piece of Amira's hair. Sharp pain shot through her skull, but she wasn't surprised. She watched, motionless, as Wryen burned the ripped-out hair, turning her dark lock into ashes.

Amira braced for another attack, but Wryen stood up and paced around the room. She knew that as long as he was moving, she'd be fine. A stationary Wryen meant that he had settled on his next attack.

"I've been very disappointed by you, Amira. I gave you a simple task and you keep messing up. Your latest antic could have been the end. Fortunately for you, Karwyn hasn't yet decided to break off the engagement. Unfortunately for you, I believe you deserve to be properly punished for your crime."

Amira rose up from her bed. "Karwyn has already punished me."

Wryen's grin widened. "Oh, but there's nothing like family law. Speaking of family, look what I've taken from your mother's place." He took out a bunch of letters from his pocket. Amira immediately recognised her mother's handwriting. Her breath got stuck in her throat.

"What did you do?" Amira screamed, reaching for the letters.

Wryen chuckled, keeping them out of reach. "Nothing...*yet*. I'm banning you from any communication with her. And if you disappoint me again...well, there's no limit as to how far your punishment could go. I could invite your dear mother to the palace for a private show of my power." He lit up his hand, the fire reflecting in his insane eyes.

Amira froze, fighting back tears. She couldn't lose her mother, the one person who loved her unconditionally. But she couldn't see a future where she played along with Karwyn's games, turning a blind eye to his cruelty. An idea lit up her eyes. What if she told Wryen about Karwyn's secret experimentations? She couldn't reach the advisors on her own, but he could.

The information would give Wryen an advantage, something to show how important he was to Liraen. It would make him stand out in the eyes of the royal advisors.

She was certain now that Karwyn didn't belong on the throne. He needed to be stopped. If Wryen was her way to stop him, she'd have to take it. And Wryen would surely decide Amira shouldn't marry Karwyn once he knew. If Karwyn was ruined and she was married to him, she'd be ruined too, and by extension, the whole Rosston line.

"Karwyn is experimenting on dead fae with the help of his witch," she blurted out.

Wryen stared at her with an incredulous face. And then he let out a roaring laugh. "My, oh my, Amira, I didn't know you had such a vivid imagination. You should get out more." He chuckled to himself. "Oh yes, that's right, you *can't*."

Amira walked up to him. "It's true. I've *seen* it."

Wryen raised the letters in front of him. He lit up his free hand and let the letters catch fire. Amira didn't even blink before they were nothing but ashes. Her eyes couldn't move from the leftovers in Wryen's hand. She would never know what they had said.

"Stop being such a lunatic, or the next thing I'll burn won't be your mother's silly letters," Wryen said. He blew the ashes right in Amira's face, provoking a coughing fit. Laughing, Wryen opened her door.

"I'll bring you proof," Amira said in between coughs.

"Sure you will," Wryen said as he left the room. Amira caught the confused eyes of a guard she didn't know before Wryen slammed the door in her face.

Amira took a deep breath to calm herself. If she could bring proof of Karwyn's experiments, her half-brother would have to believe her. But so much was at stake—her mother's life, her own safety.

She stared at the closed door in front of her. This was to be her life, locked up in her room until she was taken out to look pretty next to Karwyn. And to think of all the fae he would hurt while she was forced to stand by. He wasn't even high king yet. How much worse would it get? She had to stop him.

A small voice in her head told her that Wryen would not hurt her mother yet. He needed her as blackmail material. It was probably the only reason he had kept her alive these last eight years since their father's death.

With new determination, Amira looked around the room for a means to escape. The door was hopeless, she wouldn't put one foot outside before her guard would toss her back in. No, the only way was through the window. Amira opened it and looked down. Her room was only on the second floor, not that high, and she would arrive in the always empty indoor garden.

She opened her wardrobe and took out all her expensive dresses. Tying them all together, she created a rainbow rope that she secured around her desk before throwing it out of the window. She quickly put on a cloak and then started her descent. Her way down was quick and painless. She had to leave the makeshift rope hanging out of the window, so she hurried down the corridors, back to the grey door.

Amira knew that more suffering awaited her on the other side, but it was her only hope. To win freedom for herself and her mother, to put an end to Karwyn's rule, and to give Sydna's soul peace, she had to do this.

Amira knew all the steps, each one throwing her back into her memories. A faint scent of blood lingered in the air, reminding her of the terrifying scene she had witnessed. As she was about to exit the staircase, she heard a noise on her right. Stopping in her tracks, she held her breath, fearing the monsters that could be lurking in the dark. A shadow moved along the wall next to her and she retreated back on the stairs.

One of the torches shined on Saydren's face. The royal healer was well-dressed and obviously not bothered by the dreadful atmosphere. Without any hesitation, he made his way towards a winding corridor. Amira thought about going to the experimentation room and ignoring Saydren's suspicious behaviour, but she remembered that he had been the one dealing with Mylner's corpse. Maybe he would lead her to Mylner and Sydna's bodies. If she had proof of Karwyn and Saydren's wrongdoings, her brother would be forced to listen. And she would also be able to offer the dead the chance to go to heaven, to join Caelo.

Her steps were as light as a feather and her eyes quickly grew accustomed to the dark. She trailed her mark while allowing some space between them. The cloak and the long dress she was still wearing quickly proved to be a problem. They kept getting caught up on the uneven stone walls. Not wanting to lose her target, Amira ripped out a large quantity of fabric at the bottom of the skirt. A strange feeling of satisfaction ran through her at the tiny act of rebellion.

The path underground was longer than she had expected. It must be taking her further than the one she had taken with Rhay. In the distance, she heard a door open, pulling her back to her current situation. Amira waited a few seconds before continuing her way. She found a door similar to the one Rhay had showed her. She pushed against the ancient door and, surprisingly, it opened to the courtyard of what looked like an abandoned house. Amira looked around but saw no sign of Saydren. Had she lost him already? She searched around and saw a door left ajar on the opposite side of the secret passage. She ran to it. It opened onto a city street.

Chrysa.

She caught a glimpse of Saydren turning onto an adjacent street and hurried out onto the cobblestones. Seeing the city in the late afternoon sun didn't stop the pit of despair in her stomach from consuming her. Three days ago, she was here with Rhay, having fun. And then everything turned even worse than before.

Shaking her head to keep the bad memories at bay, Amira focused on tracking Saydren.

Most fae around her were carrying on with their usual business and leisure. She saw street merchants fighting for attention and couples strolling along, stopping from time to time to look at a shop. A few kids were running wild and almost made Amira trip. A completely normal end of day for most fae, but definitely a strange one for Amira.

The shining uniform of a guard caught her eyes and she immediately froze. Had he seen her? Should she hide? Thinking fast, she pretended to browse the stalls of a fae selling delicious, golden buns. In the corner of her eyes, she saw the guard joining Saydren. They barely exchanged more than a few words before continuing their walk, oblivious to her presence.

"Are you going to buy anything?" said a shrill voice.

"Oh, no, I don't have any silver," Amira was forced to say.

The fae slapped Amira's hand away from the food. "Then don't touch my buns," she yelled.

Fae were starting to watch. "I'm so sorry," said Amira before walking away.

In order to stay undetected, she pulled the hood of her cloak over her head. Saydren and the guard were not that far and she had no trouble following them. They entered a bar called River's Point together and after some consideration, Amira decided that it would be better for her to watch them from outside. She could see through the window around the corner of an alleyway, so she stayed there and watched.

Saydren sat at a table and was quickly joined by a young woman with two dark braids. She slid a bunch of silver notes on the table and waited anxiously for the healer's reaction. He took his time, carefully counting each note with an almost sadistic slowness.

Finally, Saydren spoke. Amira had never been good at reading lips, but she figured that whatever the healer said was the answer the woman was expecting. A large smile curled the fae's lips upwards and she welcomed the tiny vial Saydren gave her with visible excitement.

As soon as the woman left, a man took her place in front of the table. Amira had noticed him earlier as he had been lurking around a pillar, obviously waiting for the spot to free up. His face was almost completely hidden by a hood. She only saw a strand of dark hair escape the hood for a moment before the man quickly adjusted his cloak.

Saydren looked intrigued by his new customer and his interest only seemed to grow as the man spoke. A devilish light appeared in the healer's eyes. He waited a few seconds before nodding. Amira wished she could see the face of the hooded figure to see his reaction.

This time, instead of exchanging silver, the men exchanged a nod heavy with promises. Amira shuddered as she watched Saydren's face. To her it seemed like the hooded fae had just made a deal with the devil.

The hooded man left, but Amira wasn't able to see his face as he quickly passed by her. She caught a strong scent of pine trees when he brushed against her.

After his departure, Saydren called up the guard who had been standing at the bar drinking ale. The healer whispered into the fae's ear. Following his new orders, the guard ran out of the bar. Amira panicked and ducked further around the corner to hide, but when she found the courage to look back across the street, she found her fear was once again misguided. The guard quickly disappeared from Amira's field of vision.

After this interesting exchange, Saydren seemed to be going back to his usual business. A few customers came and went to his table. Amira stayed to watch even as the sun started to sink. She was waiting for him to leave and lead her back to Sydna and Mylner's bodies. He was her best shot at finding compromising evidence on Karwyn, but time was running out. Amira thought back on the makeshift rope hanging from her window. It couldn't have been for nothing.

She was starting to grow tired of her stakeout until she noticed a young woman approach the bar. Her dark blonde hair was floating freely and she sported a casual jacket. Although she had been walking with determination, she stopped in front of the door. For a few seconds, the fae's apparent confidence seemed to crumble. The young fae turned around and looked up to the roof on the other side of the street. Amira looked too, but saw nothing. Yet the young fae walked into the bar with her mask of confidence back on.

Amira looked back at Saydren through the window. He was watching the entrance, a frightening smile on his tight lips. Amira's blood curdled in her veins. What was he planning? Was she going to get closer to the proof she needed? The one thing she was sure of was that nothing good could ever come of such a smile.

CHAPTER 57

LORA

Lora had a strange feeling when she entered River's Point alone, like a presence was missing from her side. She'd grown used to Eyden keeping close to her, always ready to pull her out of danger. She reminded herself that Elyssa was keeping watch on the roof of the opposite building. Lora wasn't completely alone, but she could do this part on her own. She couldn't rely on Eyden anymore. She had already said her goodbyes.

The bar was relatively full, probably not surprising for this time of day. The sun had almost completely set, bathing the town in a dark orange light. The room wasn't well lit, but Lora had no issue finding Saydren. The elegantly dressed fae was sitting at a round table for two, handing over an item Lora couldn't name to the fae opposite him. The other fae slid a few silver notes across the table before walking off, a relieved smile plastered on his face.

Recognising her opening, Lora hurried forward, taking the now empty seat across Saydren. Iron grey eyes met hers as the healer lifted his head while lazily pocketing the money he had received.

"I didn't realise I had another appointment scheduled. What brings you to my table?" Saydren asked, sounding absolutely neutral. Lora couldn't tell if he was annoyed or glad to have more customers. He had an old soul presence about him, even though he didn't look older than thirty.

"I was hoping to catch you here. There's a special healing case I need help with." Worrying about not having an appointment, Lora hurriedly added, "And I have enough silver to make it worth your while."

Saydren looked utterly unimpressed. "You do know I'm the king's healer? Nothing I earn here in Chrysa is ever worth my while unless I'm intrigued enough by one's proposal."

"I'm sure you've never had a case quite like mine."

Saydren crossed his arms on the table. "Go on, then. What is it you're so eager to spend all your silver on?"

Lora took a deep breath. This was what she had come for, her last hope. "There's a virus in the human world and I want to find a cure for it."

Saydren let out an amused laugh. "Why in Caelo's name would you want to do that?"

Channelling Eyden's cool attitude, Lora remained composed. "Profit. We all got to make our living, don't we?" She could clearly imagine Eyden saying these exact words, his voice whispering through her mind.

"Interesting." Saydren leaned back in his chair. His gaze darted around the room.

"You haven't heard the king talk about providing a cure, have you? I'm sure the humans would pay good money for it," Lora said, drawing his attention back to her.

"The king has more important issues to entertain than some human virus."

"Of course," she answered. Underneath the table, she squeezed her hand into a fist. "But you seem like an opportunist. Are you not intrigued by the chance of being the *one* fae to come up with a cure?"

She caught a spark of intrigue in his eyes. "Indeed, it does seem worth my time. But alas, not even I can create something out of nothing. Unless you managed to get an infected human over the impenetrable border, I'm afraid you have wasted my time."

Lora scanned the room, making sure no one was paying them any attention before she pulled the vial of blood out of her pocket.

Saydren leaned forward as he regarded the glass vial in her hand. "Blood?"

"Not just any. It's the blood of an infected human."

A half-smile lightened his serious face. "Your case is getting more interesting by the minute."

A spark of hope made Lora's heart beat faster. "You can help me, then?"

His eyes drifted from hers. She was so close, she could feel it.

Saydren met her gaze once more, still faintly smiling. "Oh, I'm sure I can." Relief flooded through her in a way she hadn't dared dream of. "But not here. I'll need my healing station. How about you and your blood sample come with me to the palace?"

Lora's heart sank and a shock zapped through her. She tight-ened her grip on the vial. "How about I wait here while you get your supplies?" Nerves electrified her system. Going to the palace sounded like a one-way ticket to hell. It wasn't part of the plan, nor would it ever be. Lora could feel the fire inside her waking up, flowing through her. It did nothing to calm her mind.

Saydren moved his head and this time Lora followed his line of sight. Right to a guard. Sword sheathed at his side, he was watching them from the entrance. Two more walked in as Saydren said, "I'm afraid that's not possible." His cold eyes sought out hers. He looked more ancient, more powerful than she had first given him credit for. "You see, your case is so intriguing that I know the king would like nothing more than to have you in his grasp."

Lora's breath caught. She thought she'd mapped out all the paths this conversation could go, but she was once again proven wrong. Had he been stalling for time until the guards arrived?

"You just said the king has no interest in a cure for humans," she said as her gaze flicked around the room, trying to find an exit strategy. The guards were blocking the only visible door. What if she ran to the kitchen? No, another guard had already taken up post. Was there another way out she couldn't see now? Eyden would know. He would have already let one of his almandine knives fly as he disappeared.

"He couldn't care less. But you, *you* he'd be interested in," Saydren said, his tone suggesting he was about to get exactly what he wanted.

His words drew her eyes back to him. "Why me? I'm no one." Without breaking eye contact, Lora carefully slipped the vial back in her pocket.

"You clearly don't give yourself enough credit. A half-fae crossing the border? Incredible."

Lora forced her face to remain unchanged even as her heart threatened to jump out of her chest. How in the hell did he know? A panicked feeling took over her body. Her palms started sweating even as goosebumps settled over her skin. It made it harder for her to feel the slumbering fire inside her.

A fake laugh bubbled up her throat. "By Caelo, you're insane. I'm just a fae trying to make some silver."

"You can deny it all you want. Your friend already assured me you are not who you say you are, and after seeing you in person, I am sure he's not mistaken."

"My friend?" There was an unsettling buzzing in her ears.

Saydren smiled as if he knew her every secret. "Everyone can be bought."

"Nothing you're saying makes any sense."

"We both know it does, *Lora*. He wanted to remain anonymous, but I think you have a right to know. Let's see, how to describe him...? Tall, dark, curly hair, haunting blue eyes...ring a bell?" Lora couldn't help the shock crossing over her face as her head spun. "So you do know him. Betrayal hurts, doesn't it? Who was he to you? A friend? Business partner?"

Lora met his eyes. A storm was brewing inside her. "Even if I did know whoever you're talking about, he lied. I'm no one special."

With a grin on his face, Saydren waved a hand as if her insistence was ridiculous. "None of the above, then? A lover's quarrel?"

Lora shot to her feet. "I'm done here."

Eyden couldn't have done this. He *wouldn't*. But who else could have given Saydren her name? Eyden was the only one who knew she was coming here besides Elyssa.

The guards drew closer. The unknowing fae around them were taking notice now. Lora took a step back as she willed the fire in her to respond. She could feel her skin burning, but it was like an ember trying desperately to catch fire. Her panic was smothering the flames.

"I wasn't aware I gave you an option. You're coming to the palace, Lora. Willingly or not," Saydren said, pushing back his chair as he nodded at the guards approaching them.

Lora sped through her options. There were three guards in front of her and one somewhere in the back. She was more than outnumbered. If they took her, would she become another name in Eyden's notebook? Would she merely be another person who vanished in this town? Would her family ever know what happened to her?

Riding the adrenaline pumping in her veins, Lora turned to run. She barely made it one step before air magic dragged her feet backwards and then a firm hand squeezed her arm. She looked up into the violent eyes of the guard.

Anger won over fear and suddenly the fire in her veins took form. In a matter of seconds, flames travelled up the guard's arm. As his hold broke, Lora scrambled back quickly, almost tripping over her own feet. She blindly threw fire behind her as she ran to the kitchen door. Fae were screaming around her. Lora ignored their surprised faces as she forced her way through the crowd. The wound on her stomach strained, but she pushed on anyway.

The kitchen door was unguarded now. Behind her, the sound

of chaos followed on her heels. Lora looked over her shoulder, prepared to throw more fire, but the guards were still trying to get through the flames. She didn't have much time, but enough to get out of here.

Relieved, Lora turned back to the door and stopped cold as she came face to face with the sharp end of a sword. The guard holding the weapon moved forward and his blade grazed her throat. "I wouldn't move if I were you," he said.

Something about him was familiar, but Lora couldn't think much about it. All she could focus on was the cold, sharp steel against her skin. She needed to get the hell out of here. But could she act fast enough without getting her throat cut? The pressure of the blade spread through her, keeping at bay the fire that had been longing to come out only a second ago.

"Good job, Layken," another guard said as he drew closer. Lora was still frozen in place, quietly panicking. The guard grabbed her arms and shackled her hands in front of her quicker than she could track. Only then did Layken lower his sword.

The constant simmer of power under her skin vanished almost completely, making it hard for her to breathe. She knew it was there, but it felt as if it was buried too deep to access. Lora took in the red glint of the silver shackles binding her. *Almandine*. This is what it felt like to have her power taken from her by force. Like a part of her was hollow, missing. She'd lived without it for most her life, yet the loss hit her surprisingly hard.

Lora had lost so much already. She didn't face the fae world and unleash her own powers just to end up a forgotten face in history who accomplished nothing. This couldn't be the end. Her family was still counting on her. She refused to let the fae win—let whoever had set her up win.

Maybe Elyssa was right again. Maybe vengeance was burnt into everyone. And maybe it served its purpose now, keeping Lora from falling apart.

"Well, that was quite a show," Saydren said. "I'm sure Karwyn will be thrilled to hear about your talents."

Lora met his gaze as the guards pushed her forward to the front door. All the anger and fire she couldn't let out gathered in her eyes. When Saydren looked away, seeming unsettled by what he saw in her gaze, she almost smiled.

They might have captured her, but she refused to be another forgotten victim of the king.

CHAPTER 58

❦
ELYSSA

Perched on the flat roof across the street from the bar, Elyssa kept her eyes on the entrance. Guards had followed Lora into the bar and Elyssa was on edge. But there could be many reasons for their presence. Elyssa didn't want to make a scene and draw unnecessary attention. Her hand opened and closed around an arrow. Her bow was ready to strike. It took all her willpower to observe silently from afar.

She scanned her surroundings, making sure no other guards were approaching. It was getting darker, making it harder to see the street. Thankfully, the street lamps provided enough light to illuminate the entrance area of the bar. She couldn't really see into the bar as she was too high up. There were few things Elyssa hated more than not being able to see. She relied heavily on sight since her hearing wasn't strong.

She looked to the alley next to the building and her eyes landed on a cloaked figure. The person stood pressed against the wall, keeping to the shadows while peeking through the window on the side. Somehow, they had managed to stay out of Elyssa's line of sight until now. Elyssa couldn't see their face, as it was hidden by the hood of their cloak, but they seemed invested in whatever was happening inside.

Elyssa drew an arrow and pointed it straight at the person. Interest could be dangerous. If they showed their hands and appeared to be a danger to her friend, Elyssa would be ready.

Suddenly, the figure shifted from the window. The hurried step made her hood slip half from her head. Long dark locks of hair spilled out from her cloak. Her face appeared shocked, angered, yet it did nothing to diminish her beauty. The mystery girl moved forward, glancing around the alley. It was hard to tell from her place on the roof, but Elyssa could swear she saw fear take over the girl's face.

Alarmed, Elyssa turned from the intriguing girl. A carriage was heading in their direction, steered by a fae dressed in a guard's uniform. She could hear it now, the noise of the wheels against the ground as they neared the bar. She wouldn't have been able to tell where the sound originated from if she didn't have a clear view of the scene.

The carriage stopped in front of the bar and Elyssa held her breath. This was a very bad sign. First the guards and now this. She'd never seen Saydren take a carriage back to the palace. Why the hell was it here?

Before she could act, the door to the bar opened and two guards led Lora outside. She was shackled. A bag covered her face, but Elyssa recognised her friend. Saydren followed behind, commanding the guards. What in Liraen was going on?

Elyssa noticed the jacket of one of the guards was singed.

If Lora had shown her fire power by accident, they could have falsely assumed she was a higher level than she probably was. But even then, there were too many guards. She'd never seen so many at once. Three left the bar. Two more came with the carriage. If they drove off, that would be it.

Elyssa didn't think twice and let her arrows fly. She hit the guards on either side of Lora first. She imagined they were cursing her from below. They let go of Lora and she tried to run away blindly, but another one forced her to her knees.

Elyssa lost count of how many arrows she let loose. The fae were taking cover behind the carriage until one of them pointed to her position on the roof. He might have yelled a warning or a threat; Elyssa tuned it all out. The chatter was unrecognisable to her anyway. She'd long since stopped relying on her hearing to help her in a fight. Her laser-sharp focus was all she needed.

She ducked just in time to avoid an arrow flying over her head. The wind whipped against her dark hood.

Drawing another arrow, she took a deep breath, rolled to the side, and peeked over the ledge enough to shoot another round. She was met with open fire, forcing her to lower herself behind the stone barrier of the roof once again. Under cover, Elyssa moved on the roof, trying to surprise them from another angle.

She peered down the street. Two of the guards were running to the door of her building. Elyssa reached for her arrows. There was only one left, not nearly enough.

Lora had pulled her hood up with her bound hands. She met Elyssa's gaze over the rooftop and shook her head in defeat. Giving up was always the last possible resort and not something Elyssa liked to even consider. *If one considers defeat, one has already been defeated.* It was something her mother used to say. She had always told her to be smart but brave, to keep fighting for what she believed in even if defeat seemed the more likely outcome.

A loud noise drew Elyssa's attention. She quickly scanned her surroundings. The door handle to the roof entrance rattled. The guards had reached her. She didn't have enough arrows left. She could defend herself with her small knife, but even if she managed to fight them off, they would keep her from saving Lora. It was a lose-lose situation. There were too many for her, as much as she hated to admit those odds.

Elyssa glanced back at Lora. Her friend's lips moved. Elyssa immediately understood. Lora was telling her to go, to leave her. A guard shoved the bag back over Lora's head at the same time as an arrow flew past Elyssa's head, snapping her back into action. Elyssa sprang to her feet, firing her last arrow. The guards ducked.

Her arrow hit its true mark. She couldn't distinguish the yell of pain Saydren had surely let out, but she'd hit him. It drew the guards' attention away from Elyssa as she ran across the roof. She climbed onto the ledge. The door on the rooftop smashed open just as Elyssa jumped, bracing herself for a rough landing on the balcony below. Her legs screamed as she hit the floor, but she ignored the pain and rushed down the ladder. She had almost made it to the street when two fae faces appeared over the ledge.

Elyssa pushed herself off the ladder, barely avoiding an arrow as she dashed from the scene, running as fast she could. Air rushed in her ears. Her pulse was so loud she couldn't hear anything else as she raced to the nearest alley.

She whipped her head around several times. She could make out the two guards in the distance. Her bow hit her back with each step. Elyssa drew her hood tighter as she ran past unassuming fae on the street. Usually, she would walk carefully, keeping to unpopulated areas, but with the guards chasing her, she didn't have that luxury.

Her vision was partly obscured by her black hood, but she knew where she was going. Elyssa had spent years mapping out Chrysa, taking note of places to hide out from any dangerous fae. Taking a sharp right, she took a narrow path between two buildings and disappeared through the hidden back door of a storage room.

Closing the door quickly, Elyssa turned in the dark space and almost cursed out loud when she found herself looking into the wide eyes of the girl from outside the bar. Her hood was now completely drawn back, revealing her shocked face.

The girl opened her mouth and Elyssa rushed forward, silencing her with one hand as she strained her ears to listen for movement outside. She couldn't tell if what she heard were footsteps or how close they were, but she wasn't about to take the risk.

The brunette didn't struggle against her hold. Standing this close, Elyssa saw surprise in her unique eyes. They were the colour of an amethyst, speckled with shining brown spots that even the dim light could not erase.

After a minute, the girl put her hand over Elyssa's. Her touch was soft, gentle. Elyssa sensed no danger. She let the girl remove her hand with no struggle, but Elyssa's suspicious eyes never left the girl's.

"Do you hear anything?" Elyssa asked in a low voice, taking a step back.

The girl shook her head. Her cloak had parted, revealing the sort of fine clothing only rich fae had. Her jewellery alone promised money. What a girl like that was doing out on her own —hiding from guards, no less—was more than intriguing, but Elyssa had no time to play interrogation. The less this girl knew about her, the better.

Elyssa moved to the door on silent feet. "You never saw me," she said, before stepping outside. There was no sign of the guards. She looked over her shoulder, meaning to close the door, but the girl had drawn closer too, blocking the entryway.

Elyssa looked her up and down from her styled hair that had come undone to the rip on the bottom of her dress. She tried to keep the imminent smile off her face. "Piece of advice, next time you spy, keep your hood up."

"Piece of advice, next time, don't run out of arrows," the girl shot back.

Stunned, Elyssa's smile broke free. "Touché." She didn't wait for the girl's reaction as she turned her back and took off.

Elyssa ran most of the way back to camp. Her breaths came hard and fast and she had a dull ache in her knees from jumping off the rooftop. Her legs felt as if they might give out at any point, but she did her best to ignore the pain. There was something coming her way that would hurt even more—a discussion with her brother she'd rather not have.

She spotted Eyden the moment she arrived at the camp. She

didn't have time to catch her breath. His face was twisted in anger, his brows furrowed as he stormed forward. "What the hell, El? You and Lora left without me?"

As he got closer, his eyes wandered over her face. She knew what he saw. They had always been able to read each other. Concern took over his features.

"What happened?" He looked behind her, scanning the woods. "Is Lora still with Saydren?"

Elyssa turned her head, not meeting his gaze. "I'm sorry."

He took a step back as if her words had physically struck him. "Where's Lora?" His voice shook as he dragged his feet over the grass. Eyden moved closer again, searching her eyes. "She left, didn't she? She crossed without me." His bitter laugh rang in the air.

Elyssa sought out his eyes. "She didn't leave. They took her. The goddamn guards did."

"What? No. No, that makes no sense."

It didn't. And yet it did. "I thought it was because of her fire power, but now I'm not so sure. I think Saydren was behind her capture. Maybe he could somehow feel she isn't from here, then put two and two together when she asked for help."

Eyden pushed a hand through his hair, messing it up as he often did. "She's gone, then. Whatever the reason, she's gone either way and she's not coming back. It's over."

Elyssa punched his shoulder with force, drawing a curse from her brother.

"What the fuck was that for?"

"You deserved it. Snap out of it, Eyden. It's only over if you give up." She might have chosen to play it smart by leaving, but she had no intention of giving up. It wasn't in her DNA. And she was pretty goddamn happy about that.

Eyden's voice turned quiet, razor sharp. "You know what happens when fae get taken. They *never* make it back. I've lived it. You know better than to suggest I can do anything about it."

She did know. But she also knew that deep down, hidden under the fear and the past, Eyden was sick of standing by as much as she was.

Elyssa was about to respond when she noticed Eyden turning around. She followed his gaze. Out of all people, it had to be Jaspen who was approaching them.

"There you are," he said, looking from Elyssa to Eyden.

"This isn't a good time, Jaspen. I need to have a talk with my sister." Eyden took a step back, giving Elyssa room to move so that Jaspen wasn't standing to her left side, making it harder for her to catch every word. The asshole never bothered to consider her hearing.

Jaspen's face was set in stone. "Go ahead and do that elsewhere, then. It's time for you to go. You're not welcome here anymore."

Elyssa advanced on Jaspen, turning her back to Eyden. "Are you fucking kidding me? You're kicking him out? After he saved our asses?"

"We can't trust the fae. Or anyone who picks them over us." He stared right at her, unflinching.

"What are you trying to say?" she asked, crossing her arms.

Jaspen's eyes travelled over her head to her brother. "I'm saying he needs to leave." His gaze returned to her. "And so do *you.*"

She sucked in a breath. "*Excuse me?* Do you need another god-damn lesson about why you need me?"

"Not only did you let *two* fae into our camp, you've been lying to us for years. You never broke contact with Eyden and you told him, a *fae*, how to access our camp. You might be a good fighter, but you're not irreplaceable, Elyssa. You betrayed us. I have no choice but to remove you from my camp."

"Yes, you do. Without me and Eyden, you'd be dead," she said, her voice rising.

"That's merely speculative."

Elyssa rolled her eyes, holding in a laugh. "Speculative, my ass. You'd be burned to a crisp by now." Jaspen's lips were pressed in a tight line. She wondered what ridiculous argument he would bring up next. She had more important things to do than dealing with Jaspen's stubbornness yet again.

"What's... here?" Farren asked as he jogged towards them, his words getting slightly lost in the wind. His concerned eyes took her in.

Elyssa breathed a sigh of relief. Farren was way better at keeping a cool head than her. "Jaspen is kicking us out—trying to, at least."

"It's *my* camp, Elyssa," Jaspen said before turning to Farren. "What I say goes. And I say, anyone who's picking fae over us is a liability."

"Then I'm going too," Farren said. Elyssa's gaze cut to him. His eyes reassured her. He'd always had her back and he was willing to continue to do so. He knew exactly what he was doing. She might be replaceable in Jaspen's eyes, but Farren wasn't.

"You would put the whole camp in jeopardy? I don't believe

you." Jaspen knew him well enough to know Farren wouldn't hurt a fly if his hand wasn't forced.

"I'll keep the spell hiding the camp up. But anything else you need, I won't be here to assist with."

Elyssa felt her lips turn up in a smug smile. She looked to her friend in gratitude before addressing Jaspen. "I don't think people will be too happy about having to risk their lives even more—to get stuff without spells helping them out—just because you were acting like a closed-minded jackass. Don't you agree?"

"I don't like being threatened," Jaspen bit out. He looked around as if searching for backup. She was surprised Ian wasn't lurking close by. He was always so eager to jump at Jaspen's command.

"Well, I don't like being removed from my home," Elyssa shot back.

Jaspen glanced between her and Farren, fury turning his eyes into a dark storm. "Fine. You can stay for now, but Eyden leaves. He better be gone by dinner." With one last disappointed look, he walked away. Elyssa needed to have another conversation with Jaspen later. But right now, her priorities lay elsewhere.

Once he was out of earshot, Eyden caught her gaze. "Are you really going to stay here? With that asshole?"

Elyssa shifted her head, taking in the tents set up some distance away. Her home. One day, she'd make everyone see the good in Eyden. Everyone but Jaspen. "For now. Dickhead and I still have the same goal. We need allies. We need all the support we can get for what's to come."

"You think it's time?" Farren asked.

They've had plenty of discussions about the future. About

risks and rewards, about banishing the thought of total defeat. Farren had reasoned with her more often than not, but he knew it was only a matter of time.

Eyden shifted his feet. "Time for what?"

"To finally take action," Elyssa replied, meeting his eyes.

Eyden nodded. "I'll do more of my shifts, see if any of the guards can be persuaded to our side to get info on the disappearances."

Elyssa shook her head. "That's not enough, not anymore. They took *Lora*, Eyden. How many more people are we letting them take? How many more humans have to die before we intervene?"

"We're not *letting* them take anyone," Eyden said through gritted teeth.

"I wasn't trying to blame you. But what are we really doing? Waiting around for the perfect opportunity to step up our game? There's no such thing. But right now, there's a window. There's no almighty high king, not really. The contestants haven't even been selected, as far as I know. This is the best goddamn chance we'll get to turn things around in our lifetime. Mine, at least."

"We *are* trying, El."

She hated seeing the pain in his eyes, but she needed to let this out. She had to spell out the hard truth, it was what her brother responded to. "But *trying* isn't enough. We need to *do*." Suddenly, her cloak was suffocating her as anger fuelled her. Elyssa all but ripped it off her, letting it fall to the ground with her bow while her eyes stayed trained on Eyden.

"I can't spend my whole life on the sidelines. I'm so fucking sick of it. The Adelways can't take our lives like this. I won't stand for it. No more. This is it, Eyden. I won't watch him take everyone from us while I grow old and you wait for the next power change, the next king. Probably Karwyn's son, who'll step right into his footsteps. Aren't you *done* with this fucking bullshit?"

"Of course, I am. But what else would you have us do? Storm the palace? That's suicide."

"I'm not saying we go in blind. We come up with a plan." She quickly glanced at Farren as she prepared herself for her brother's unavoidable reaction. "I have a map of the palace."

Eyden's lips parted in shock. "You what? How?"

"I may have snuck into a former guard's home. The map is a bit outdated, but—"

"By Caelo, when were you going to tell me? Are you out of your mind?" Eyden asked, walking in a circle. "Why didn't you let me get it?"

Elyssa searched for words, excuses. Of course, Eyden could have drifted in and out of the house in no time. But she had a suspicion he knew very well why she didn't involve him. His stunt in Rubien proved her point. "It was a spontaneous decision. I didn't know the map was there, but I was hoping I'd find something—anything—useful. It was a risk, but a smart one. I knew I could do it."

"That's insanely risky," he shouted.

"And *that's* exactly why I didn't tell you. You worry too much about me. And you didn't have to. Farren used his sleeping spell." She shrugged. "It was all fine. As expected."

Eyden dragged his fingers through his hair. "And you never mentioned this afterwards because...?"

"Because I knew this is how you'd react! You weren't ready to hear it. And maybe you're not ready now either, but I need you to be. We can't sit by any longer. We can't miss our chance." She drew closer, her words aiming where she knew they'd hit. He needed to hear it. "And I promised Lora I'd have her back. Are you really going to accept she's gone?"

He pulled back from her, averting his eyes. "What are you suggesting?"

"Karwyn needs to go."

"Agreed. But assassinating the king is definitely a suicide mission."

Farren raised his hand, intervening. "I'd like to add that as long as we get him to give up the throne, that will be enough. We might not have to commit murder. Just throwing that out there."

"Sign away his right to the throne? That's never been done before. Why would he?" Eyden asked no one in particular.

"We'll find his weakness and exploit it. Hit him where it really hurts," Farren answered.

Elyssa smirked. "I think I've corrupted you."

"What are friends for, right?" Farren's smile was timid but true.

Eyden remained serious, but Elyssa could tell he held back a smile. His eyes travelled between her and Farren. "Even if we somehow achieve all that without ending up dead or worse—and that's a big if—how do we know whoever takes over the throne after him is any better?"

Elyssa didn't miss a beat. She had thought about this often. "It won't be an Adelway, that's a good sign. Karwyn has no kids. He has no relatives except that uncle who was banished years ago. I heard he's engaged to some princess. But if they're not married, I guess she wouldn't be eligible to take over."

"We need to find someone respectable who can argue for the Turosian throne once Karwyn's out of the picture," Farren stated.

Elyssa tightened her ponytail as she considered the easiest path. "Maybe we can find out more about Karwyn's fiancée. She can't be worse than him, can she?"

Farren squinted in thought. "Just so I'm following, you want to find out if this fiancée is a perfectly nice, humane fae who at the same time would jump at the chance to become a widow?"

Elyssa tucked a curl behind her ear, hiding her grin. She couldn't deny it was a tricky situation. They wouldn't come up with a solid plan as quickly as she'd like to. "I see there might be a flaw in my logic."

"You think?" Farren's voice was light as he grinned.

Eyden let out a loud breath. "The stakes are too high, El. We can't just hope for the best."

"No one said it'd be easy. But we have to try. Otherwise, what's the point? If we do nothing, we can accept defeat right now and go bury ourselves. It's now or never, the way I see it. We have to take bigger risks—gigantic ones, even." She set her hand on her brother's arm, meeting his gaze. "For everyone who's taken to the sky. Everyone who's soon to be lost."

Eyden's eyes were a pool of uncertainty and desperation. "For Lora. For us," he whispered, loud enough for Elyssa to hear at this distance.

"Does that mean you're in?" she asked. She needed her brother by her side more than anyone. Together they could achieve what she'd been dreaming of all her life. With her brother's protective determination and fighting skills, Farren's kindness and spells, and her own badassery, she had to believe they had a fighting chance.

Eyden looked up to the darkened sky. Whatever he saw, it made his eyes shimmer. When he turned his gaze back to her, his pale eyes shone brighter, more determined. Fear wasn't holding him captive in this moment and Elyssa wished he could hold on to that forever.

"No more holding back," he said.

CHAPTER 59

AMIRA

Was she too late? Amira had run faster than she thought she was capable of to get back to the palace after her strange encounter with the human girl. The redhead's face was still imprinted in her head. It was her first time meeting a human and she was scared to admit that the girl had seemed more similar to her than Amira would've liked. Their banter came back to Amira's mind, but she pushed it away, trying to focus on a more important matter. Saving the human girl's friend.

Amira couldn't help but wonder how an apparently powerful fae had become friends with a human girl. To her knowledge, the two kinds never mixed. There were few humans left in Liraen and the fae had no love or respect for them, as far as Amira knew.

It didn't matter who the fae was, this time, Amira was going to save someone. The panicked eyes of the young woman were burned into her. When she had seen the young fae being dragged outside, Amira had made a silent promise that she would help her break free.

She had to act fast. Amira wasn't sure if anyone had noticed her absence yet or had discovered the rope hanging out her window. She tried her hardest not to think of the consequences.

She'd free the young woman and go back to her room. For Amira, a real escape was still impossible while Wryen had control over her mother. As long as no one found out Amira had helped this new prisoner, she'd be able to deal with the repercussions of sneaking out of her room.

Next to the experimentation room, she caught sight of a strange door she hadn't noticed on her way out. Wondering what could be hidden there, she pushed it open.

It appeared to be an office. Ancient books written in a long-forgotten language were splayed across the large wooden table as well as piles of notebooks. Amira suspected they were magic books. A family tree of the Adelway line hung on the wall. Approaching it, she noticed that someone had written on it quite recently, as the ink appeared less old.

Karwyn's uncle, Lozlan, had his name underlined multiple times. It seemed strange to Amira, considering he'd been exiled over a decade ago. Being exiled from Liraen was the worst disgrace one could wish upon their enemy besides burial. Wryen had threatened Amira with a similar fate more than once.

Another thing she noticed was that Karwyn's mother didn't have a maiden name listed and the space dedicated to her family was completely empty.

Just as she was about to open a small notebook, she heard a faint voice coming from another room.

The fae. How could she have wasted time when someone was in danger? Amira rushed out of the room.

She returned to the wall outside the experimentation room. Hastily, Amira pressed all the stones on the wall, trying to open the hidden passage. After her tenth try, the stones started to turn. She didn't even wait for it to be completely open and carefully stepped inside the room.

The experimentation room was unoccupied. Amira looked for clues of the young woman's whereabouts and her gaze settled on the table where a body was covered up with a black cloth. A lifeless, pale hand hanging from the table was the only visible body part. Amira dropped her gaze, but the shiny red floor did nothing to calm her.

Had they already killed her? No, it couldn't be the fae girl. The hand of the body looked as if it had been dead for a while, not less than an hour. It had to be Sydna. The fae girl from the bar might still be alive. Amira fought back the tears that were gathering in her eyes. Where could they have taken her?

"Come on, Amira, think," she muttered.

She knew she had to make sure it was Sydna and not the girl from today, so Amira reluctantly moved to the table. Her fingers gripped the cloth covering the dead. A pair of emerald eyes appeared in her head. Frantic. Pleading. *Punishing.* Her breathing quickened. Her heart sped up. Her hand burned with such intensity, she let go of the cloth and hurriedly stepped back.

In her frantic state, Amira knocked into a shelf and one of the jars fell. It shattered at her feet. A potent-smelling liquid spread on the floor, staining her already dirty shoes.

"Dammit!" She tried to gather the fragments of the jar and

cut herself on a particularly sharp one. Her mind was quickly unravelling and the sight of blood didn't help her stay grounded in reality. The red liquid spurting out of her wound shifted colour in front of her dizzy eyes, turning from burgundy to completely transparent. She put her finger in her mouth and let the red liquid coat her tongue with its silvery notes.

"What are you doing?" a strange voice asked, startling Amira. She turned around, her finger still pressed against her lips.

A face emerged from the darkness. A sickly twisted face. The *witch*.

A wave of panic took over Amira's body. She frantically looked around for a way to escape this dark presence. Cirny took a step forward and Amira noticed her limp. She could outrun her. But what about her powers?

"What are you doing here, girl? This is no place for you."

A list of lies passed through her mind, none convincing enough to evade the witch's watchful eyes. Amira stayed silent, hoping to buy herself some time to come up with an escape plan.

The witch came closer and detailed Amira's face. "Who are you, dear? You look familiar."

"We've never met," replied Amira with more contempt than she had intended.

Cirny smiled sadly. "I know. I'm just a freak to you and everyone else. A cursed being, cast away by the Gods. Someone they share scary stories about." As she spoke, she came closer and closer to Amira. "Yet no stories tell you about the ropes that bind me. The orders I follow, the sanity I slowly lose—" The witch broke off with a scream. For a second, her face lost all colour and she brought her hands to her neck as if to remove the invisible bind that was strangling her.

"No, no, no. I'm sorry," she whispered, completely out of breath.

Amira reached out to her, but before she could grab the witch's arm, Cirny's wide dark pupils locked on Amira. "Your soul, it has been stained like mine. I can feel it..." She extended her hand to touch Amira's face, but Amira didn't let her.

Completely terrified, Amira pushed her away. Only she didn't properly evaluate her strength and Cirny fell against the table. On instinct, Cirny tried to break her fall and grabbed at the table. Her hand tightened around the cloth draped over the body. Amira watched as the cloth came off while Cirny slowly fell.

For a few endless seconds, her brain didn't catch on. She couldn't understand what she was seeing. *Who* she was seeing. It wasn't Sydna. It wasn't the captured fae girl. The almond-shaped face and chin length black hair were all too familiar.

"Nalani," Amira whispered, tears already running down her cheeks. She rushed to her maid's body, but the fae was long gone.

The witch got up. "You're not supposed to be here," she hissed, stepping forward. Acting on reflex, Amira pushed the witch again. This time, Cirny fell on the ground hard, her frail body twisting in a strange angle as she whimpered.

With her mind in shambles, Amira fled.

Amira was surprised to find her makeshift rope untouched.

She couldn't process what had just happened. Who she'd seen. *Nalani.*

She was barely holding on as she climbed the makeshift rope back up to her bedroom. She needed to be alone, to sort her spiralling thoughts, to forget about Nalani's lifeless body. She needed to *breathe.* But when she looked up, Rhay was sitting in her chair.

"Amira, I was so worried," Rhay started, straightening when he saw her. "The guard let me in. He almost saw your emergency exit, but I closed the door quickly. I was worried you'd gotten yourself into trouble again and I didn't wanna make it worse..." He trailed off as he noticed Amira's frantic state.

She violently pulled on a strand of her hair and muttered under her breath, "It's my fault."

Rhay ran up to her and held her arms to still her movements. "Princess, what have you done now?"

She couldn't tell if it was worry or anger filling his voice. Her whole body was shaking uncontrollably even with Rhay holding her. She felt like something was growing underneath her skin, wanting out.

Tears stained her cheeks. "I'm a bad person," she wailed. "Why do I keep hurting everyone I care about?" Her heavy tears burned her face, reminding her of all the pain she had caused. All the death.

Rhay was visibly uncomfortable by the strength of Amira's emotions. He tried to wipe her tears as best as he could, but new ones kept ruining his efforts. He tried to reassure her, "It's okay, princess. Karwyn's going to forgive you. You're going to be queen and you'll be happy. I just know it."

Amira pulled away from him as she whispered to herself, "My brother's right, I ruin *everything*. Why can't I just ignore my feelings? If I don't get attached, they don't get hurt and I don't get hurt." She jumped when she felt Rhay's hand on her shoulder.

"It's all right, Amira. I've got you," he said as he drew her into a warm hug. "I've got you. I promise I'll be there no matter what. We'll find ways to see each other even if Karwyn forbids it. I won't abandon you."

Amira pulled back to stare deep into his eyes, letting the shimmering blue calm her down. If she could focus only on them for just one second, maybe the weight on her chest would be lifted. Hypnotised by his eyes, she didn't notice that his face was inching towards hers until she felt his warm lips on hers.

She closed her eyes on instinct. The fire of Rhay's kiss wasn't strong enough to heat up her lips. A disorienting numbness took over her body. This kiss was nothing like her last one. The pleasing twist in her stomach, the frantic desire to hold the kiss forever, the tingle in her heart, they were all missing. Instead of blossoming her feelings into love, the kiss was filling her with an overwhelming sense of hopelessness.

Rhay's tongue caressed her lips and Amira came fully back to her senses. She pulled her head back and gently pushed Rhay away. A strange irritation replaced her numbness. Her friendship with Rhay seemed meaningless now. Her chest burned with a sense of betrayal. Was this all he was after?

"Why did you have to do that?" she asked, taking a step back.

Rhay looked utterly confused. "I thought that's what you wanted."

"And I thought I'd found a *real* friend. Someone with no

ulterior motives! Why did you have to ruin it, Rhay?" She ran her fingers through her hair, twisting the ends. "Are you trying to anger Karwyn more and damn me in the process? How do you think this will end? Karwyn will end the engagement and I'll just be with you instead? Do you think you're so irresistible that I'd have to fall for you? Or did you think I'm an easy target, an inexperienced and powerless fae?"

She wasn't sure if it was sadness or anger building in his cloudy eyes. Maybe a mix of both.

"Who do you take me for?" Rhay asked. "You gave me signs, Amira. *You* asked me how to make a guy like you. And that evening in the drawing room... I betrayed my best friend for you. I thought you knew how I felt."

"It wasn't about you, none of it was about you!" She was screaming now, with no care for anyone who could overhear her. "I thought you were my friend. Why isn't that enough? Why do you twist my actions to fit your story?" Her voice broke. No, she shouldn't be crying. He wouldn't take her seriously if she was crying.

Rhay brushed a hand through his precisely styled hair. "Shit. Amira, I'm sorry. I shouldn't have kissed you. But you can't deny you've been taking advantage of me ever since you've arrived."

Amira scoffed. "Really? And how would I have done that? I have no power, I have nothing useful to give. Was I taking advantage by asking you to do the right thing and free the prisoners? How dare I, right? How dare I ask you to think of someone other than yourself."

"It's not that simple." Rhay dropped his gaze.

The words left her lips before she had time to think about

them. "Do you know what they've done with the bodies? Because *I* do," she furiously whispered. Her desire to hurt him, to force him to have a reaction, any reaction, was getting stronger. He looked around like a little child caught misbehaving. It only fuelled her anger. "Did Karwyn tell you where he took them? Do you know what happens in the underground?" She plunged the knife deeper, waiting for him to lash out against her, to finally stop being the perfect guy who always tried to even things out.

Rhay finally looked at her and she could see that she had aimed right. Dark stormy clouds had gathered in his usually calm blue eyes. "Amira, you should stop," he warned her.

No. She wanted him to listen. She wanted him to see what kind of monster Karwyn was. "I think you should know who you're friends with." He grabbed her hand and she could feel him trying to fight Amira's anger. She tore her hand from his. "You can't pretend everything is fine all the time, Rhay." The heat of the argument made her raise her voice. "I'm sure you know what happens in the underground. You can't tell me you don't know about Karwyn's sick experiments or whatever he's doing down there."

Rhay looked like the picture of perfect surprise. Pretence, Amira thought. "I don't know what you're talking about," he said. "Whatever you saw, there must be an explanation."

She thought of Nalani, sweet and gentle Nalani. A mother without children. Tears started flooding again, briefly overshadowing her anger. "Why did he have to kill her?" Her voice broke, turning into a whisper. "She was just a maid."

She pulled at a strand of hair. Sadness and anger swirled inside her. She felt like her skin was cracking open, slowly letting out the strange beast that was growing inside of her. A burning sensation radiated from her body, turning her thoughts numb and confused.

"I can't handle this anymore, this twisted place. I want to go home."

"Good luck with that," Rhay said, turning away from her. "Karwyn has just been selected for the High King Contest. The first part is done. He's almost assured to be the new high king and you his queen." Rhay's bitter words were like poison to her mind.

So she had lost. Her fate was sealed. Karwyn would become high king, ruling, playing his twisted games. All the while Amira would have to watch. For a second, Amira saw her whole life spread out in front of her. She saw the misery and pain. A life empty of any pleasure, at the mercy of Karwyn's cruel moods. She had dreamt of escaping her brother's control, but she had only exchanged a demon for the devil.

Who knew how many fae she would see disappear into the underground, never to be seen again? And all this time, she would have to imagine the kind of dreadful torture they would have to live through while she was powerless to change anything.

Rhay's panicked voice reached her ears. "Amira, what are you doing?"

She looked up. The whole room was shaking.

"I...I don't know." Her body was twitching, trying desperately to keep something inside of her. Something dark and menacing. Something that should never escape.

A voice screamed in her head. *Keep it inside! Stop doing that, you freak of nature!* The voice was getting louder and louder.

A sharp pain tore through her face. More pain, all over her body. Invisible hands were furiously hitting her. A scream tore at her ears. Was it hers? But her mouth was shut.

It was a memory, long suppressed. Wild lilac eyes stared at her. His hands were stained with her blood. The pain had been almost unbearable, yet she had welcomed it with relief back then. Now it just felt like she was broken apart, each bone in her body turning to dust. The overpowering odour of freshly drawn blood mixed with the scent of burned flesh.

She coughed up several times in her hands. Droplets of blood coated her skin, yet she seemed to be the only one seeing them. Rhay was more concerned about holding on to her bed's pillars to avoid falling down.

The candles on Amira's dressing table lit up suddenly. In her distorted vision, she saw the flames grow menacingly and spread onto a faceless body as another memory fuelled her vision. A childlike voice screamed, "No, Quynn. Please! Wryen, stop. *Please make it stop.*"

Wryen had taken so much from Amira. But not *her*. Not Quynn. She couldn't live without Quynn.

But she'd had to.

The memory came in flashes. Amira at seventeen, watching Wryen burn her first and only love at the stake. *Treason*, that's how he had justified it. But Amira knew that it was to hurt her. To *punish* her. He had forced Amira to watch Quynn burn. The screams had torn her heart apart, triggering something inside of her that she never knew she possessed.

Witch powers.

Wryen had rushed to move her inside, away from the balcony

and any prying eyes. He had beaten her senseless, commanding her to bury her powers. Her memories had sunk deeper and deeper inside of her with each strike, each slap, each burn.

The flame went out and Amira's room went dark. As if she was outside her own body, Amira saw herself slowly fall to the ground, like she had at seventeen, broken by Wryen's wrath.

Her whole body gave up as she struggled to grasp the past and was swallowed by a cold emptiness.

CHAPTER 60

LORA

This was the second time in a week that Lora found herself in a cell. The cold, stifling air made her think she was underground. They had kept a bag over her head until she got here, but she assumed she was in the palace dungeons.

Her hands were now free, but Lora soon realised the almandine shackles were unnecessary. The whole cell was made from it, including the floor she stood on. The bars and shiny ground all held a tint of dark red. Surrounded by such a high quantity of almandine, Lora found it hard to focus on anything other than the dying buzzing in her veins.

She wondered if she had ever felt like this when she had first started wearing her almandine necklace. Had she been young enough that she simply forgot the hardship of it? Maybe it was only her attitude that had changed. She had wanted to get rid of her powers as a child. She had wanted to make her mother's worries vanish and make her own life easier. But it wasn't and maybe it had never been. All she ever did was play pretend. And you could only hold onto lies for so long.

Trying to escape the almandine, Lora rested her head against the one stone wall but she couldn't escape the floor. She still didn't know how the hell Saydren knew who she was and that she'd crossed over. Elyssa had tried to save her. There was no way she was responsible for her current dire situation. Lora had to believe the other girl managed to escape.

That left Eyden. Saydren hadn't said his name, but the description he gave painted him well enough. Had Saydren spied on them? Had she been doomed to be captured? It was the only explanation that made sense. The alternative was too painful to consider.

She was on her own now. No one would come to the palace to save her. No one could. Lora pictured Eyden sitting in his closet, adding her name to the long list in his notebook. How long would he think of her? Or had he already erased her from his mind? Erased the time they'd spent together? It hadn't even been two weeks, maybe it wouldn't be hard for him to forget.

She forced the image out of her mind. There were more pressing worries. What would the king do to her? Experiment on her to see how she had survived the journey? Goosebumps travelled over her skin, heightening the cold feeling that had settled in her veins and extinguished the flames buried inside her.

They had taken everything from her. The silver, her phone, the WiFi cube, even the vial of her mother's blood. The only thing holding her together was the sliver of hope that she could somehow get Saydren to create a cure in exchange for anything he wanted. Saving her family remained her priority, and she wasn't ready to give up yet.

The cards weren't in her favour, but she was prepared to make sacrifices. There was nothing else she had left to give but her secrets.

The door creaked and a guard, Layken, strode in. His face was exempt from any emotion. He held the door open, not meeting her gaze as he waited. Lora craned her neck to sneak a peek outside without leaving her spot next to the wall.

She didn't have to wait long before another fae walked in, taking his time as he beheld Lora. He was wearing fine clothing, his golden hair brushed back to reveal intense eyes. He looked her up and down and flicked his finger. Layken pulled the door closed as he exited, leaving Lora with the golden-haired fae.

With slow, determined steps the fae strode towards her. He stopped a safe distance from the bars. The corner of his mouth pulled up into a relieved and twisted smile. Lora refused to cower in his presence. She stayed deadly still, angry eyes trained on her captor.

"You know who I am, don't you?" the fae asked, crossing his arms behind his back.

She had a strong suspicion. "Karwyn Adelway. The king." The smug grin spreading across the king's face further enticed her anger. "More importantly, kidnapper. Probably torturer. Nothing to be proud of," she said, lashing out with words. It was the only weapon she had left.

Karwyn didn't move a muscle. "I admit I probably did not make the best impression on you, dragging you here and all. But you see, I have been looking for you for quite some time. And I was not about to let you slip through my fingers."

His words took her off guard. Her mind tried to connect the dots that were swirling around aimlessly. "Why would you look for me?"

"First of all, let us discuss what you want."

Lora pushed herself off the wall, standing up straight. This conversation wasn't what she expected. She couldn't put her finger on where he was going with this.

Karwyn took a small step forward, eyes watching her every move. "You did not cross out of boredom, did you? You are trying to save someone. Whose blood sample have you been carrying around?"

"None of your fucking business." She twisted her hands into fists by her side. She noticed Karwyn's gaze dropping, taking in her reaction.

"And here I thought you would want a cure. Was I mistaken?" he asked, voice almost mocking.

Even if he had a way to create a cure through Saydren, Lora knew well enough he wouldn't give it up for free. He hadn't threatened her out loud yet, but clearly, he wanted something from her.

She was sick of the games, lies, and veiled threats. "Spit it out already. What do you want from me?"

The room was eerily silent until Karwyn said, "Your power." He started pacing in front of her cell.

Of course, fae and their obsession with power levels. Yet Lora had never heard of the possibility of a power exchange. "Isn't that impossible?"

"Oh, I know all about how impossible it is. Fortunately for me, there is always a loophole. You are the living proof of that. I cannot take power from other fae. But I can take it from *you*, a half-fae."

Understanding dawned on her, the dots finally connecting into a twisted puzzle. Everything she'd learned from Eyden came together in her mind. "You've been trying to steal power from high-level fae. What happened to them?"

"That is nothing for you to worry about." Karwyn continued his slow walk.

"You don't care, do you? You're sick. You disgust me," she said, her voice layered with icy repulsion.

This time, she got a reaction. The fae halted in his tracks. Turning to her, Karwyn moved closer to the bars as his eyes settled on her once again. "Come now, that is no way to speak to *family*." He smiled unpleasantly as her mouth dropped open. "Oh, did I not mention we are cousins? If I am sick, the odds are not in your favour. I see you got the Adelway eyes. I wonder how far the similarities run."

"You're lying." Her voice had dropped to a furious whisper.

"You do not wish to be royalty? Or is it the fact that your father is a traitor to the crown that is bothering you?"

Lora's mind was on overload. Too many life-changing facts were being thrown her way. She didn't know where the lies ended and truth took over. "Why are you so certain we're related?" He couldn't be. Her mother would have known if her father was fae royalty, wouldn't she?

"I had my witch do a spell to be sure," Karwyn answered.

"Assuming you're right, where is my father?" Was he here, on the same ground as she was? In the same building? Her hand went to the empty spot on her collarbone, pulling on the invisible chain. What she wouldn't give for her reminder of home right about now.

Karwyn's smile grew vicious. "My father banished his brother after he tried to overthrow and kill him in cold blood. Your dear father is a murderous traitor. Be glad he is gone." His tone suggested he was anything but sorry.

Lora doubted "sorry" was an emotion he ever experienced. If there was one thing she knew about her apparent cousin, it was the fact that he was nothing more than a bloody psychopath.

"Even if that's true, you're no better," she said.

He drew even closer, almost touching the bars. "You should watch your mouth, dear cousin. I hold all the power here, and I am growing impatient."

"Get to the point, then. Take my power. What are you waiting for?"

Karwyn let out a cold laugh. "If only it were that easy. I would have taken it the second I walked into this room. No, the only way this is going to work is if I follow an ancient ritual. A merge of powers only works under specific circumstances. I need a relative of blood with a similar level of power who participates willingly. From what Saydren told me, your power is still uncontrolled, foolishly so. You will need to train. The ritual cannot go wrong. I want you to join this merge with me, willingly. And then resign, giving me all your power."

"Why the hell would I choose to participate in your plan?"

"I can get you that cure you so desperately want."

Her breath caught. "I have no proof you'd even manage to create one."

"I already have it ready," he said with a satisfied grin.

All other thoughts stilled as her mind spiralled. "Why? You clearly had no intention of delivering a cure to my world."

Karwyn's grin grew bigger as if he took notice of her inner turmoil. "Well, the fools have not reached out to me. Their mistake. I was merely waiting for the right time. I knew if they got desperate enough and I offered a cure in exchange for one human, they would not hesitate to find you and hand you over. Survivor's instinct always wins out. I was about to contact them, actually. But you saved me the trouble."

Her mind spun. She was closer connected to the fate of her world than she ever thought possible. There was too much information for her to process in a matter of seconds, but something drifted to the forefront of her mind. "If I give you all my power, what will happen to me? Won't it drain me completely?" Lora asked, remembering how closely tied a fae's power was to their life source.

Karwyn shrugged. "Not my concern."

Lora laughed. It sounded broken, desperate, to her ears. "Right. Why would you care?" She swallowed the tears that threatened to come. Lora couldn't fall apart. She swore she'd fight. She *had to.* Everything depended on her move in this cruel game the king had set up. "If you want me to participate in that bloody ritual, you'll have to distribute the cure to everyone. Hand it over to my family and the government."

Karwyn narrowed his eyes. "I suppose I could play hero. I will fulfil your request after you sign a blood contract."

His last words almost knocked her to her knees. "No," she said louder than intended. The word echoed in her cell, reminding her of how trapped she would be if she were to accept.

"No?" Karwyn tilted his head as he regarded her with menace. "You wish to be the reason your family and a big part of the human race dies?"

"I'll need proof. I don't trust whatever contract you'll pull up. Cure everyone first," Lora rushed to answer. She needed to find a way out of signing a blood contract. An agreement like that was final. She'd never escape it.

"That is not how it works, little cousin."

"Then at least cure my family and let me call them to make sure. Once I know it worked, I'll sign your contract and you'll hand the cure over to the government." If she couldn't get out of signing, she'd make damn sure it wasn't for nothing. She wouldn't hand over all her cards with no insurance.

Karwyn considered her counter offer, fidgeting with the sleeve of his blazer. "How many?"

"Three for my family, four for my friend's family who helped me."

"I will give you one. The contract will state that I am to provide six more cures to speed up the process for your loved ones. And I will contact the human government." He was negotiating as if it wasn't her life he was demanding.

Lora knew time wasn't on her side. Her heart threatened to explode in her chest; her skin felt as cold as the future that lay before her. "Two. And you'll make sure to get them to Marcel, a human trader, with a note from me." They needed to know it came from her.

Karwyn nodded once. "I agree to your terms. Let us shake on it." He extended his hand through the bars. If the almandine affected him, he didn't let on.

Lora was surprised by the human gesture. Against her better judgment, she walked forward. This close, she could see the turquoise in his eyes that had stared back at her in her own reflection. She took his hand, barely putting pressure, but his grasp was firm. She tried to pull back but he held on, staring straight at her. Lora thought she saw surprise flicker in his gaze before he finally let go.

"The guard will get you a piece of paper to write on," Karwyn said, turning his back on her. He looked over his shoulder as his hand stilled on the door handle. "Welcome to the family, little cousin. If only for a short while."

The door closed shut behind him. Lora walked backwards until her back hit the wall. The truth of her situation was a heavy weight and she slid down to the ground, no longer able to keep upright. She was irrevocably connected to the fate of her world. All she could do was make certain the virus was erased.

Her fate, it seemed, had been sealed from the moment Karwyn had somehow found out about her existence. He would have found a way to bring her here no matter what. To trap her in this very cell and force her hand. She could see it in his eyes that were so much like her own. The madness behind them was new. It told her there was no line he wouldn't cross.

She came from a line of psychopaths. How did her mum not know? If her birth father hadn't been banished, would he have been at this year's quarter-century treaty meeting? Would he have hoped to see Karla again, or did he never think about what happened 25 years ago?

If Karwyn hadn't found Lora here, the treaty meeting would have been more eventful than it had been the past couple of times. Karwyn had something the humans needed, something the human government couldn't have passed on.

If they had decided to look for her, to hand her over, Lora couldn't even have blamed them. One human's fate for a cure— an easy call, wasn't it?

The blood contract would bind her life to their agreement. Lora knew death waited at the end of their deal, but she wouldn't go down easy. And if she couldn't win, then maybe, just maybe, she could at least take him down with her.

That was the one promise to herself she intended to keep no matter what came her way. One final promise until the end of her hopeless journey.

CHAPTER 61

§

RHAY

Distraught, Rhay left Amira's room while she was still on the floor. What in Liraen had he just witnessed? Why? *Why* was he repeatedly being put in these positions where he was forced to look past something? He had done it multiple times in the past, but each time had taken a toll on him. Everytime he looked away, a little part of him died, yet he felt like there was nothing he could do.

The guard keeping watch in the corridor cleared his throat. "I was about to come in. Sounded like quite an argument," he said.

Before he could take a look into Amira's room, Rhay quickly closed the door and leaned against it, putting on his well-rehearsed mask. "She's pretty pissed at me. I wouldn't go in there."

The guard nodded. "It's late. My orders are to lock her in for the night."

Rhay took a hesitant step back and let the guard follow his

order. He dropped a few silver notes into the guard's waiting hand once he was done. Satisfied, the guard walked off.

Hands and legs shaking, Rhay let himself slide to the ground against Amira's door. He leaned his head against the wooden door, taking in the empty corridor. At least no one else had witnessed the kind of power the princess held.

The *witch*.

As the word entered his mind, he quickly slipped his hand underneath his jacket, grasping his flask. He always had one with him. One could never know when alcohol was needed. And if there ever was an occasion, it was now.

Rhay took a few deep sips to refocus his mind. He tried to grasp a single coherent thought, but everything was tangled in his brain. The feeling was stifling, so he drained the last of the liquid swirling in his shiny flask.

As he put the flask back in its hiding spot, Rhay steadied himself against the door and stood up. He took off, away from Amira's room. He was glad that the few fae he passed by didn't pay him any attention. Everyone was too excited about Kawyn's nomination.

Rhay slapped his forehead. "Fuck," he said way too loudly. He glanced around the corridor, but no one was around to notice his outburst. What should he tell Karwyn?

Curses went through his head like a mantra. Why did he have this overwhelming desire to save broken people? First Karwyn, now Amira. He couldn't believe he hadn't seen the signs before. The princess was probably a very powerful witch. She'd have to be in order to hide her condition that well. He felt his anger rising again. Had she played him? Had she purposely led him on? Amira wasn't who she said she was. She wasn't even fae. She was *cursed.*

Another thought crept into his mind. Maybe she hadn't even been aware of her own abilities. Maybe a distant relative of hers had been a witch and the gene had skipped several generations until Amira. The princess had looked utterly terrified by what was happening in her bedroom. Should he go back and talk to her?

No, he shouldn't make any hasty decisions, those were the kind he always regretted. The memory of Amira rejecting him was only a few minutes old after all. The best thing to do was to stay as far away from her as possible. He had no idea how dangerous she could truly be and he didn't want to find out, to further his entanglement in her mayhem.

No, what he wished now was to be excluded from her life. Rhay wouldn't be dragged into her mess, her darkness. He wouldn't be the one responsible for unleashing a dark fate on Amira, but at the same time, he wouldn't help her any more than that either. Looking away from a problem, that was his preferred way of dealing with things.

With Karwyn he had... No, he didn't want to think about that. The only thing he needed to do now was have another drink. A stronger one that would help him leave this memory behind.

Yet, as he quickened his steps, he couldn't help but think of their kiss. Ever since he'd first seen Amira, he'd wanted to kiss her. Was it because she was his best friend's fiancée? Someone he knew he had no future with? Amira was utterly unavailable to him, yet he had felt an immediate closeness. Maybe it was because he felt like she still had some hope for the Turosian kingdom, because she was blissfully unaware of the darkness that had taken over the palace.

Amira didn't reciprocate his feelings, that much Rhay knew now. Truth be told, he had known what to expect when he'd started flirting with her. She could have never been his and if he was honest with himself, that might have been the reassuring part.

His feet led him to the ground floor after a small detour to his room to grab a bag heavy with silver. As he was walking up to the entrance, he heard a door open on the corridor to his left. His eyes met Karwyn's and he immediately noticed how shifty they were. Karwyn put something in his pocket, his movements too quick for Rhay to discover what it was.

"Karwyn, what are you up to?" Rhay's voice was colder than he had intended.

"I could ask you the same question. You look awful. Are you not happy about my selection?" Karwyn's gaze bored into him, but Rhay refused to drop his stare.

"Of course, I'm glad. Even though it wasn't much of a surprise."

"What, you wanted more of a struggle?" Karwyn said, half teasing, half serious.

"That's not what I meant." Rhay eyed Karwyn's pocket "Anyway, what are you doing now?"

Karwyn avoided the question. "Are you sure you are not hiding something from me? I find myself having trouble trusting you after that little stunt you pulled with Amira." He moved closer to Rhay at a slow, menacing pace.

Should he tell Karwyn what he had found out about Amira? Karwyn was his friend and he deserved to know. But then he thought of the mistreatment witches received, being forced into a life contract in order to survive—if they weren't killed on the spot. Rhay couldn't picture the frail Amira being used, having to obey her rich owner's wishes. And he couldn't bear to be the one responsible for it.

"You have not seen Amira recently, have you? She is not allowed visitors at this time," Karwyn said. His hand was hovering dangerously close to Rhay's as if battling with the decision to invade his thoughts.

"Are you going to break your promise, Karwyn?" Rhay's voice was heavy with mistrust and the soon-to-be high king quickly retreated.

"Are you?" Karwyn asked, clearly offended. "It seems to me Amira has become your priority. How far will you go, Rhay?"

"You know I'm loyal to you. I've proven myself countless times." Rhay had turned a blind eye more than once, never doubting his friend even as a hidden voice in his head screamed he should. "Your jealousy is getting old, Karwyn," Rhay added, knowing he'd strike a nerve.

Karwyn took a step back as his lips parted. "*My jealousy?* What are you trying to imply, Rhay? Have you broken *your* promise?"

Rhay took in his friend's features. The truth was, he didn't need to read Karwyn's emotions to know how the king felt about him. "I wouldn't dare," Rhay said, looking away for a moment. Then he remembered something Amira had said when they'd been in Caligo. "But how about *you?* Did you ask your shadow to impersonate me in front of Amira? After you promised your little spy would never shapeshift into me? Because you know very well that is something I won't forgive."

Something shifted in Karwyn's turquoise eyes. "It seems to me that you have always been very forgiving in the past. Would you end over twenty years of friendship over an assumption?" Karwyn's hand caressed something in his pocket and his eyes darted to the front door, as if he was in a hurry.

Karwyn's suspicious attitude triggered Rhay's curiosity. He tried to gauge where his friend had come from and noticed a door was left slightly ajar. He knew where it led. Rhay shivered, trying to repress a distant memory.

"What were you doing in the underground?" Rhay asked. He couldn't help but think of what Amira had whispered about her maid being dead. "And does it have anything to do with Nalani?"

"Nalani? Why are you asking about a *maid?*" Karwyn replied, not revealing any of his cards. "Are you questioning me, Rhay? After you avoided my own question?"

"You do know that the more you talk, the more suspicious you look?" Rhay countered. "A clear and simple answer would've sufficed, but now I'm fearing the worst."

Karwyn lifted his chin, his wavy golden hair moving with him. "Are you sure you want to know? I thought you avoided all matters that could tie you to being an actual advisor. Did you not make that decision years ago? The inner court is not for the faint-hearted—as you recall."

Usually, Rhay would have retreated, letting Karwyn keep his secrets as he had done countless times before. When he'd first become an advisor, Rhay'd wanted to be involved in everything. He'd felt as if he'd found his purpose, his life blossoming with possibilities. But then the deeper he'd gotten pulled into the on-goings at the palace, especially the underground, the more he'd wanted to turn away. So, he did just that. Turning a blind eye to the king's schemes became his forte.

Yet this time, Rhay wanted to know. After all the things Amira had said, he *needed* to know, to show that he was capable of facing the truth for once in his life.

"Tell me, Karwyn," he said with conviction while fearing the worst.

Karwyn opened his mouth and then closed it immediately. Rhay could see that under his bubbling anger, his friend was hurt by his doubts. Rhay wondered if Nalani was really dead and if so, would his friend tell him the truth? They stayed in a silent staring contest for a few seconds.

Karwyn broke their eye contact. "I do not have time for your mistrust, Rhay. Some of us actually have things to do other than drink themselves to sleep. Time is ticking for the ones in charge." His shoulder brushed against Rhay's as he made his way towards the entrance.

"Who's the one turning away now?" Rhay shouted. His own hypocrisy jumped at him, but he managed to keep a straight face when Karwyn turned back around.

He fished something out of his pocket. "You see this?" Karwyn said as he showed him the vial in his hand. "It is a cure for the human virus. I made Saydren and Cirny work day and night on it. I am going to have an emissary distribute it to the human government. Guess I am not so evil after all, am I?"

Rhay's mouth fell open from the shock of such an uncharacteristic revelation.

"You look like a dying fish, Rhay." Karwyn was clearly enjoying his friend's surprise.

"It's just...you never...I thought you had completely forgotten about the virus on Earth," Rhay replied.

"Well, if you actually cared to be my advisor, you would know I prefer to do my good deeds in secret."

Rhay was completely puzzled by the turn of events. "I guess I don't know everything about you." He didn't like the rift he had created by throwing buried doubts at his friend. Maybe the things he thought he remembered about Karwyn's darkness weren't all true. Was his imagination playing tricks on him?

Rhay opened his arms and stepped forward. Karwyn stared at him for a beat too long, making the gesture awkward. Still, the two men shared a friendly embrace, Rhay showing more enthusiasm than Karwyn.

Under the padding of Karwyn's jacket, Rhay could sense his friend's frail frame. Few fae knew what Karwyn actually looked like without his padded and carefully selected clothes. Rhay had always felt that knowing this secret had strengthened his connection with his friend.

He squeezed his friend tighter to avoid the terrible guilt that was slowly overwhelming him. He'd been wrong to let doubt cloud his judgment. Nalani was probably just visiting her sisters.

"Careful now," Karwyn said. "You do know you are stronger than me."

Rhay knew that Karwyn would have never admitted such a thing in public. He loosened his grip and moved away from the king. "Sorry."

Karwyn patted his friend's shoulder. "Let us forget all about this. You are good at that after all." Rhay thought Karwyn might have meant that as a compliment, but it didn't feel like one. "I will see you at your party tomorrow."

"Wait," Rhay said, grabbing Karwyn's arm. His best friend flinched at the touch. "Can I request something, but you promise to not get mad?" Karwyn nodded. "I think you should stop guarding Amira's room." Karwyn furrowed his brows, obviously annoyed at the mention of his fiancée. "It's unnecessary and it sends the wrong message to the foreign advisors."

Karwyn sighed. "The guards have more crucial tasks anyway. I will ask her brother to keep an eye on her. I am sure she will be delighted." Karwyn didn't wait for a reply before he went outside while Rhay remained rooted in place.

The guilt was starting to eat him up. He sighed, wishing he could return to the easy and carefree life he had been leading up until Amira's arrival.

If he wanted to preserve his friendship with Karwyn, and Amira's life, he needed to make sure that Karwyn would never find out about Amira's powers.

"Great, super easy," he berated himself.

He had apparently been the trigger to the princess's outburst. His kiss had led her to expose her powers, so it was obvious to him that they needed to stop seeing each other. For Amira's sake and Karwyn's.

That decided it. He would cut off all contact with Amira. And if she tried to reach out, he would have to push her away by any means necessary.

CHAPTER 62

AMIRA

Amira's eyes fluttered, trying to adjust to the darkness surrounding her. Everything was so quiet and cold. She moved her hands a bit to try to regain the feeling in them. Pain had taken over her whole body. Flashes of memories were coming back to her, but it was only when she truly opened her eyes that she realised the mess she had created. The room was turned inside out, dresses scattered on the floor, candles broken on her desk. The bed sheets were torn in half and the windows were wide open.

For a second Amira thought that she had broken the glass, but when she stood up to touch it, she noted that it was still intact. The dresses she'd tied together weren't hanging outside her window anymore. Did Rhay pull them back in or did she do it herself?

Shivering, she struggled to light the only candle that hadn't broken. The small flame didn't bring any clarity to her mind. How could she have not remembered that she was a *witch?* Who did she inherit her powers from? Her father had been a high-level fae.

Her mother was a low-level fae and Amira was sure she wasn't a witch. But that didn't mean that someone from her mother's bloodline couldn't have been a witch. They might have not even realised. Amira hadn't unleashed her powers until that unfortunate day when Wryen had provoked her.

And since then, she had repressed a huge part of herself for years to protect herself and now her brother's actions towards her made more sense. He was trying to protect her from the rest of the fae to make sure she wouldn't show her powers. He wouldn't let anyone see them. Was that why he'd removed everyone from her life? Was it the reason he'd banished her mother and rarely let Amira see her? Wryen would assume her witch power came from her mother's side, the side he wasn't related to.

Amira knew what kind of life witches led. They were either hunted down by common fae who feared them or under the orders of a royal. She thought her life couldn't get worse than being married to Karwyn or being controlled by Wryen. Turns out, she was dead wrong. Being a witch was definitely worse.

What if Karwyn found out and forced her into a blood contract? Would she end up like Cirny? Trapped, her mind in shambles, violating the dead on Karwyn's orders?

Maybe she still stood a chance. If she could convince Rhay to not say a word about her true nature and if her half-brother could help her repress her powers like he had done in the past, she might be able to live a somewhat normal life. She could forget about her curse. It wouldn't be a happy life, of course—

she would still have to marry Karwyn. But a life, at least. Would she have to learn to look away as Rhay had?

She needed to find Rhay. Her heart beat faster as she remembered their fight. The usually friendly fae might not be in the best disposition to do her a favour. But it was her last chance and she needed it to work. If he cared about her at all, he had to agree.

A vision stopped her in her tracks. It was Nalani's lifeless body, but with the strange girl's eyes from the bar in Chrysa. The fae was probably already dead too. She couldn't have saved her. She couldn't even save herself. But maybe she could at least prevent an even darker fate for herself if she convinced Rhay to lie.

As she was about to leave the room in a hurry, Amira caught a glimpse of herself in the mirror. The torn-up dress and her sickly pale face made her look completely out of her mind. If she wanted to push Rhay to help her, she should pay a little more attention to her appearance.

On the floor, she found the tight-fitting dress Rhay had gifted her for her first party with him. Going with her instinct, she put it on and tried to make herself look more alive with the few makeup items Nalani had left behind. Just thinking of the maid made her want to cry, but she anchored her sadness deep inside her. She needed to focus. There would be time for mourning later.

When she tried to open the door, she found it locked. Amira felt tears threatening to take over. Anger bubbled up inside her. With force, she pushed the door handle down again. With a cracking noise, the door sprung open. Shocked, Amira stared at her hand as if it was someone else's.

Before her mind could spiral into darkness, she made a fist and focused her eyes on the path in front of her. No breakdowns. Not now.

Thank Caelo, she encountered no guards in her corridor. Yet every time she crossed paths with someone, she feared that they could somehow sense her secret. In her head, her true nature was now clearly visible to everyone else, like a big red light flashing above her head. Yet she reached Rhay's door without anyone stopping her.

Amira was about to knock when she realised that she had no idea how she was going to convince Rhay to lie to his best friend. What could she offer him in exchange for his silence?

Her thoughts ran wild. Should she lie to him about her feelings? Pretend that she cared about him more than friends did? No, that would be terrible. She didn't want to play with the truth. *You do want him to lie for you,* said a little voice in her head.

Wrestling with her thoughts, Amira didn't immediately notice that someone was standing behind her. It was only when a hand touched her shoulder that she registered the presence.

Amira was surprised to see Varsha in a silver jumpsuit. "Rhay's already at the party, I think," the painter said with a smile.

"What party?" Amira replied while trying to remain calm. If Rhay was drinking somewhere, her secret could come out any time. She hadn't realised that she had been out cold for that long.

Varsha looked puzzled by her question. "Rhay's usual afterparty. I thought you were going there too, given your outfit."

Amira looked down at her tight sparkly dress. "Oh yes, I'm going." She had no choice, she had to find him before he revealed her secret.

"Come on, then," Varsha said while offering Amira her arm. She took it with a bit of hesitation. Perched on high heels, the painter was towering over her, yet in a strange way, her presence was reassuring to Amira.

"I've heard that Karwyn has pulled back his guards from your room," Varsha said.

He had? That was a surprising move from her fiancé. What was he planning? She wanted to reply that he had still locked her in, but decided to stay quiet.

"And I'm guessing things are better with Rhay now too," Varsha guessed. Amira looked at her, puzzled. "Since you're going to his party."

"Things are..." *Terrible? Catastrophic? Ruined?* "...fine between us," Amira lied.

Varsha gave her a warm smile. "Good. I told you everything was going to get better."

They reached the party just as Amira was about to break down and confess. She immediately closed her mouth when she witnessed the party room.

"Rhay went all out, I see." Varsha laughed.

Indeed, Rhay had really gone the extra mile. Large pieces of fabric cascaded from the roof and sky dancers wrapped their bodies into the silky veils, letting their heads hang upside down.

Amira had no idea how Rhay had managed to create it, but a river of what looked like iridos flowed through the room, the colours of the rainbow reflecting in the water. A silver barque occupied by a band floated peacefully while other fae bathed in the iridescent liquid.

She had to fight hard to stay focused on her goal, finding Rhay. Amira turned to Varsha, but the painter had already found an occupation and was letting a gorgeous young woman feed her grapes. Amira averted her eyes and went back to her mission. Avoiding a large ice sculpture of Karwyn, she searched the room. Everyone was dancing around her, trying to get her to join their drunken madness.

Pushing away from the crowd, she decided to explore the tiny alcoves hidden around the ballroom. In the third one, she found a clearly intoxicated Rhay laughing with a couple of very attractive fae. A dark-haired girl, lasciviously leaning on Rhay's shoulder, was whispering what Amira imagined to be crude things in his ear. Another guy was stroking Rhay's tinted hair with obvious fascination.

Standing there for what felt like a very long minute, Amira finally cleared her throat to make her presence known. Rhay looked up with a displeased grin.

"Princess," he said like he barely wanted to acknowledge her presence.

"Rhay, can I talk to you in private?" She tried to make her voice sound light.

"Can't you see I'm incredibly busy?"

She wanted to slap his smug face, but instead of acting out her anger, she forced a charming smile on her lips. "Please, Rhay, it will only take a minute."

Rhay made a show of contemplating her request, tapping his finger against the velvet couch. "No," he replied.

The answer felt like a slap to her face. "*No? Why?*"

"You see, I only have time for my true friends. Like Liovy here," he said while pointing at the girl next to him. The brunette playfully bit his finger. "See how well she's treating me? I might even be inclined to share some deep secrets with her."

The veiled threat threw a hard punch at Amira's heart. Gasping for air, she still managed to reply, "You wouldn't dare."

"Maybe I would, maybe I wouldn't," Rhay answered. "Did you think you could just show up here wearing a tight dress and make me your little bitch? Grow up, Amira."

The piercing laughs of Rhay and his two companions made her ears bleed. She wanted to scream, to act out. Hell, she even wanted to use her damned powers just to shut his mouth. But that would just prove what she had tried to forget in her desperate quest—that she was a monster, an *abomination*. That she didn't deserve to walk among fae. That her brother had been right all along.

Rhay's eyes dared her to say something, anything. Instead, Amira backed away and ran out of the alcove. She bumped into a fae as she made her way out and didn't even stop to apologise. Tears flooded her eyes, turning the whole party into a blurry picture.

A waiter carrying a tray of glasses filled with iridos passed by her and Amira grabbed a drink that she immediately downed. The sparkling liquid fogged her mind, but it wasn't enough. She needed something stronger to appease the growing pain in her chest.

On the other side of the river, she saw the fae who had offered her drugs twice. Now she was craving it. Not caring about anyone staring, she walked across the river, the sweet liquid coating her exposed legs.

Thyl smirked as he saw her approach, droplets of iridos running down her skin. "Is it time?" he asked knowingly.

She held out her hand. "Give it to me."

"With pleasure," he said. Instead of handing her the pill, he popped it into Amira's half-open mouth. She swallowed it immediately, repressing the voice of reason that was screaming in her head.

At first, she didn't feel anything. Disappointed, she said, "I think it's not working."

A distorted voice echoed in her ears, "Give it time, princess. You'll feel it soon."

And then, she did. She truly felt it. Amira was weightless, floating high above the room. Her sense of touch had disappeared, but her sight and hearing had been amplified. She could hear everything, even the secret thoughts of the fae around her. On the contrary, everything was dark in herself, like she had turned down the lights and left the room. Her terrifying powers were long forgotten, locked away safely. She was completely empty.

In her foggy state, she saw a strangely familiar face staring at her from across the room. Fiery red hair and witty hazel eyes. A tomboyish attitude and quick reflexes. The mysterious girl disappeared into the crowd.

Amira smiled and went right back into the air, floating on her strange high. She felt detached from all her worries. Free from her ever-present pain, she danced, ignoring everything and everyone around her.

Stumbling out of the party room, Amira shut the door behind her and tried to find her balance by leaning on the wooden panel. She could dimly hear the music from the party, excited voices and so many laughs. Carefree fae celebrating. Rhay was probably having the time of his life. He held all the power now and Amira was left with nothing.

No cards in her favour. No friends. *Nothing.*

The dealer had given her a couple of pills for free before he had taken off. She took another one to erase the knot of sadness growing in her chest again as she shuffled towards her room. "You'll need them tomorrow...and the day after," he had whispered in her ear. She could sense their reassuring presence in her pocket.

Amira hadn't forgotten about the two other pills she had hidden in her bedroom. The one Saydren had tried to force her to take and the one the dealer had gifted her in the corridors only a few days ago. They were her beacons of hope now.

Hope of surviving another day.

At the bottom of the stairs, she stumbled over her own feet and had to use the wall to steady herself, hitting her hand in the process. But the drug was too potent for Amira to feel any pain.

A strange rush of joy filled her heart. For once, she felt in control of her emotions. It was as if she could see the mechanics inside of her that made her feel, that made her *hurt.*

In her heart, she knew that as long as she kept taking the pills, she would not feel pain or fear ever again.

CHAPTER 63

🔥

LORA

Lora felt as if forever and no time at all had passed. There was no window or clock in her cell to tell her the time. She had written the note soon after Karwyn had left. Keeping it short, she gave Marcel only as much information as necessary. Layken had taken the note, and since then she had been alone with her tumbling thoughts.

Lora had spent most of her sleepless night rehearsing what she would tell her family when the time came. How could she explain why she hadn't brought the cure herself? She was interrupted by the sound of the door opening. Lora stood up fast, willing her tired legs to wake up. She faintly felt the stab wound on her stomach straining as she moved.

Karwyn strode in, a rolled-up paper in hand. The sight made her stomach turn. He was planning on having her sign right away. He wasn't wasting any time.

"It is done," he said as he stopped in front of the bars. His free hand moved to his pocket and he pulled out two familiar objects. Her phone and the WiFi cube. "You get five minutes."

Lora grabbed the devices through the bars before he could change his mind. The familiar weight in her hand was a much-needed relief. She looked up at Karwyn. "Some privacy?"

"Are we forgetting I make the rules here? Make your call before I change my mind."

With a withering stare, Lora stepped next to the wall. She didn't know if she would ever get the chance to see her family again. This could very well be her last opportunity. She craved to see their faces one last time, so she decided to start a video call, as risky as it was.

Making sure the bars wouldn't be in the picture, Lora held her phone in front of her as she slipped the cube into her jacket pocket. She needed to make sure her family wouldn't suspect her current dire situation. She tried to ignore Karwyn's presence as she smoothed down her hair and buttoned her jacket all the way, covering the spot where her necklace usually sat. With shaking hands, she pressed call.

She could see herself on the video screen. The exhaustion was etched in her face. Frustrated, Lora forced a smile on her face before her mum accepted the video call.

"Lora," her mother exclaimed through the screen. Seeing her mum's face after the last couple of weeks almost brought tears to her eyes that she quickly shut down.

"Hi, Mum," Lora said, the fake smile still plastered on her face.

Her mum rattled off too many things at once and before she could decipher anything, there was commotion in the background and then her brother and father appeared on screen, squeezing into the frame.

"Oh, my God, Lora, you did it," her brother almost shouted at the same time as her father said, "This stuff is miraculous, honey." Her smile became real as she beheld her family, talking over each other, asking her multiple questions at once.

"Slow down, everyone. First, please tell me you're fine, Mum," Lora said as an attempt to silence the overwhelming chatter.

Her mother squeezed herself to the front of the screen. "I am, honey. The cure you found worked. Within an hour, all my symptoms were gone. I was scared something happened to you when you didn't come back. You look tired. Are you all right?"

"I'm fine. I just had a busy few days getting the cure ready. More will come soon. Who took the second one?"

"I gave it to Marcel. He wouldn't take it at first, he's a stubborn one, but he needed it sooner rather than later." Her father nodded in the background.

"That's what I thought. I'm glad he's okay. Dad, you'll get a cure soon too, I promise. It's taking some time—"

"When are you coming home?" Oscar interrupted, peeking over her mum's shoulder.

This was the feared question she had no good answer for. Lora's gaze drifted up, finding Karwyn. The king. Her cousin in nothing more than blood. He was still standing in the same spot, regarding her with bored interest. How he could be both at the same time was beyond her. Meeting her gaze, he tapped his wrist as his blonde eyebrows drew up.

Her eyes travelled back to the video chat. "I'm not sure yet. I have to help make more of the cure."

"So a few more days?" Oscar asked.

"I...I've met some people. People who helped me and who I promised to help in return."

"People? You mean *fae?*" her mother asked, her forehead wrinkling.

Lora sighed, then caught herself and straightened. "Yes, fae." She could see the concern in her mother's eyes mixing with anger. Her father seemed more confused than anything.

"And they're more important than your family?" her brother commented.

Karwyn tapped the bar once, drawing her attention to him. He was getting more and more impatient.

Lora stared at her brother's hopeful face. He wouldn't stop asking questions, not unless she broke his hope and shattered her promise with it. "I've found...family here. A cousin. I need to stay and find out more about my fae history." She saw the second her brother's face fell. In this moment, she hated herself for speaking the words that broke her brother. But it was better he was mad at her than trying and failing to save her. It was a necessary evil. Let them think the worst of her. She just had to find a way to survive and make it up to them later.

"How did you find this cousin? Did you see your fae...father? You don't even know what he looks like," her mother said, voice carrying an edge of desperation. Her brother disappeared out of view.

Lora forced her words to come out calmly. "No, he's not in Turosian. But my cousin is. I know this is all a lot to take in, but I need to—"

Her mother moved forward, her face covering the whole

screen. "Loraine, you can't even be sure you're related! Don't do this. You don't belong there. Come back. *Please.*"

"I agree. Lora, honey, this isn't right. Come home, think on this. You can always go back another time," her dad added. Her mother cut him an annoyed glance.

"I'm sorry. I know it's hard to accept, but I need to stay for now. I'll explain—" Her words died as the call ended abruptly. Lora quickly tapped on the call button again, but nothing happened. She tried again, putting more pressure on the device. A new sense of panic rode up her body, washing over her like shards of ice. She didn't even get to say goodbye.

Her eyes drifted to the WiFi cube in her pocket. The usually faint green light now flashed red. She'd run out of data. This couldn't be it. Their conversation cut short, ending on the disappointed gaze of her mum.

Karwyn cleared his throat. "Let us get to business."

The tears she had held back ran down her cheeks as she pressed her phone to her chest and closed her eyes. "I need another WiFi cube. I wasn't done talking," Lora said, trying to stop the tears from falling.

"That was not part of the deal and I am in no mood to prolong this."

Opening her eyes, Lora took in the only relative she would see for however long she'd be trapped here. She swiped at her tears, brushing over her faintly bruised skin, before striding forward and taking the roll of paper from him.

As she unrolled the document, she noticed right away it was quite detailed. He promised all the things they'd discussed, but in addition to her agreeing to train and give up her powers, she couldn't kill Karwyn without dying herself. Attacking wasn't out of the question because Karwyn needed her to fight him for the ritual to work. She couldn't talk about their deal to anyone if she wished to live until the ritual would ultimately end her.

The small relief Lora found was the fact that she'd die either way. It sounded bleak even in her own mind, but it gave her solace knowing she could break the contract last minute and take Karwyn down with her. Preferably, she'd find a loophole before it came to that. Karwyn himself had said there was always an exception. Her family would want her to fight for it. Eyden too. She hoped. Maybe.

"Fine, let's get it over with," Lora said, pulling on her courage.

Karwyn pulled out a fountain pen. He pricked his skin, took the contract from her, and signed his name in neat letters.

Lora took the contract back and watched as Karwyn wiped the blood off the pen with a clean handkerchief. The white stained with red felt like a metaphor for her life. It would be stained with the promise of death.

She reached for the pen, but Karwyn pulled back. His hand went to his other pocket and when he revealed the vial of blood Lora was all too familiar with, her heart stopped. "You will sign with this," Karwyn said, dunking the pen in dark red.

The metallic smell of blood filled her senses. "That wasn't part of the deal," Lora said, barely breathing.

"I never specified whose blood we would use. I am not dumb, little cousin. I know you would be tempted to go against the contract once it is only your life on the line. But your mother, on the other hand..."

"Bastard." This changed everything. She couldn't risk her mum's life.

"I have been called worse. Never forget you are nothing more than a pawn to me. You are only useful for so long." His turquoise eyes held the promise of doom.

Lora grasped the paper in both hands, tearing the edge of it. "I'll sign with my own blood. Nothing else."

"Rip it if you like. I will bring you another one in a few days when your father is sicker. Or maybe dead, you never know. And even if the virus somehow does not get them, my people will. I know where they live now." The shocked look on her face gave him the kind of joy only a disturbed person could find. "You think I did not have someone follow Marcel? Right to the Whitner door. One message and they will get a surprise no cure can save them from. Tick tock, cousin." He held the pen out to her, through the bar. When she didn't react, he began to slowly back away.

Lora ripped the pen from his grasp before he was out of reach. A drop of blood fell to the ground. She was about to sign a deal with the devil. There was no way out of it. With this signature, she wasn't just sealing her own fate, but also her mum's. Her mother would either die or lose her daughter. She knew her mum would choose a different path, but Lora didn't want to live in a world where she was responsible for her mother's death.

With trembling hands, she signed her name on the paper with her mother's blood. As soon as the pen lifted from the sheet, both signatures glowed brightly, the magic activating and dooming her forever.

"Smart choice, little cousin. I will keep that for you." Karwyn snatched the phone and the useless WiFi cube from her limp hand. "Now, as long as you behave, you will make the rest of your life quite easy. If you misbehave, you will be right back here. And if you break our contract"—he clicked his tongue—"well, we both know how that would end."

Karwyn didn't wait for a response. Lora was speechless anyway. His words sounded far away to her, nothing more than a rushing in her ears as she found herself on the shiny ground. Her hands touched the icy floor as despair flowed through her frozen veins. She could see her faint reflection on the surface. Her eyes were dull, fearful, hopeless. The weight of the spell settled over her, pulling her underwater and drowning the last shred of hope she'd carried until now.

Through the haze of her mind, one last question emerged. Before Karwyn could disappear through the door, she called out, "How did you make the cure?"

A sinister grin turned his stare diabolic. "Naïve little cousin, you do not let a virus loose without procuring a cure first."

Thank you for reading our debut novel!

If you enjoyed *Through Fire & Ruin*, we would be so immensely grateful if you could leave a review on Amazon, Goodreads, or any other book website. This would make a huge difference to us as it would increase the chances of other readers picking up our novel.

Every review—even if it's just a sentence or two—means so much to us and would make our day.

Acknowledgments - Jennifer Becker

I can't believe I got to this part. Writing the acknowledgments to my debut novel feels unreal, in the best possible way. If you're taking the time to read this, thank you. I'll try to keep it short, but no promises.

Encouragement is so, so important. Without it, I'm not sure we would have made it this far on this crazy (and exciting) ride. That said, thank you to my cousin, Anna, for being the first one to read the full thing and not hate it. Thank you to Kris for asking me again and again what the novel is about until I finally talked about it to someone besides Alice for the first time (I do blame the wine for going into a lot of spoilers). I want to thank Jana for seeing something in our novel and for continuously supporting our publishing journey. It means so, so much. I'm also grateful for my mum, for always believing in me no matter what I decide to do—this novel being no exception. Thank you to my family for always supporting me.

There are many people without whom this novel wouldn't have been possible. Thank you to all our beta readers for taking the time to read our novel and giving it a chance. Charlotte, Jennifer, Madison, Iman, Anakha, Angie, Amanda, Emmy/Ira, Andrea, Zoe, and Jordan—you are all amazing. A big thank you to our amazing Hype Team for all their support. Thank you to our development editor Elise—your feedback and notes helped shape this novel into the version you see here now. I also want to thank our copy editor RaeAnne—thank you for polishing up our novel and being so great to work with. I'm immensely grateful for Rena for creating our stunning cover and Emily for making our title design this amazing. To Melissa Hawkes and her writer group—thank you for always being there to answer any questions we might have. It's truly such a supportive community that I'm so glad to be a part of.

Most of all, I want to thank my co-author Alice without whom I don't think I would have had the courage to seriously pursue publishing a novel and actually finish writing it (we wrote so many words!). I'm so glad to have created this storyworld and characters with you and I can't wait to see where it will lead us. Even with distance between us, I know we'll stay friends forever and mix up more book-character-inspired-drinks when we see each other.

Last but not least, thank you to everyone who picked up our debut novel. I can't properly put into words how much it means. I appreciate you as much as Elyssa loves her throwing stars and Rhay loves his flashy outfits. I hope you enjoyed *Through Fire & Ruin* and found something to relate to.

Jennifer Becker

Acknowledgments - Alice Karpiel

Writing a novel is a journey and my journey would not have been as easy without the following people that I wish to thank.

To my dear friends Jana and Kris, thank you for your constant support and all your encouragement. It was wonderful to see how excited you were to read *Through Fire and Ruin*. Your faith in our project helped us stay sane. I also want to thank Anna, the first to read the book and to give us such positive feedback.

To my parents and my sisters, thank you for your love and your patience with all my writing endeavours, this one being no exception.

This novel wouldn't be as it is now without the help of a few very special people. Thank you to all our beta readers for taking the time to read our baby and give us some much needed feedback. Charlotte, Jennifer, Madison, Iman, Anakha, Angie, Amanda, Emmy/Ira, Andrea, Zoe, and Jordan—we couldn't be more grateful. A huge thank you also to our wonderful Hype Team for their ongoing support. Thank you also to Elise, our development editor, whose notes helped us write the best possible version of our novel. Working with you on our book was such a delight. To our copy editor RaeAnne, thank you for your precious help with our sentences and all your suggestions. But writing is not the only thing needed to create this book. A big thank you to Rena for making our wonderful cover and to Emily for creating our phenomenal title design. For their support and their willingness to answer any question we threw their way, thank you to Melissa Hawkes and her writer group. It felt wonderful to be supported by this strong community of writers.

The biggest thank you has to go to Jenni, my co-author and dear friend. It hasn't been easy but we made it through! I couldn't have done it without you. I am incredibly proud of the work we have accomplished together. Thank you for always seeing the bright side and reminding me of the amazingness of writing a book. I am so excited to continue this journey with you. To many more video calls and wonderful brainstorming sessions in Paris or Vienna!

And lastly, a huge thank you to you, who has decided to read our very first novel. I am extremely grateful for your trust and I hope you enjoy this novel as much as we enjoyed writing it.

Alice Karpiel

About the Authors

Jennifer Becker is one of the debut authors of *Through Fire &
Ruin*, the first book in a New Adult fantasy series. She has been
an avid reader for most of her life and has always craved telling
her own stories.

Jennifer earned her MA degree in film production in the UK
and has since been working in the film industry in her home
country, Austria, while independently working on her own writing projects. The two things she can talk about forever are good
books and TV shows. When she's not obsessing over a great story
or a ship, she's most likely working on her creative endeavours
such as her novel.

Alice Karpiel is one of the authors of the debut New Adult fantasy novel *Through Fire & Ruin*, the first book in a trilogy. She has loved telling stories since childhood, her very first attempt at writing being a short story titled *Murder on Mars* which delighted her friends.

She found a kindred spirit in Jennifer during their MA in the UK. Alice is currently finishing up another Master's degree, Scriptwriting, while working as a script reader in her home country, France. She loves nothing more than to lose herself in a good book, TV show or film.

www.authorsjbandak.com

Lightning Source UK Ltd.
Milton Keynes UK
UKHW010734100522
402764UK00004B/626